Feb 21

DONUT
THE DESTROYER

SARAH GRALEY AND STEF PURENINS

graphix
An Imprint of
SCHOLASTIC

This book is for all the heroes out there,
who always try to do the right thing
and help make the world a better
place for everyone.

Library of Congress Control Number: 2019945255

ISBN 978-1-338-54193-9 (hardcover)
ISBN 978-1-338-54192-2 (paperback)

10 9 8 7 6 5 4 3 2 1   20 21 22 23 24

Printed in China   62
First edition, June 2020
Edited by Cassandra Pelham Fulton
Book design by Shivana Sookdeo
Creative Director: Phil Falco
Publisher: David Saylor

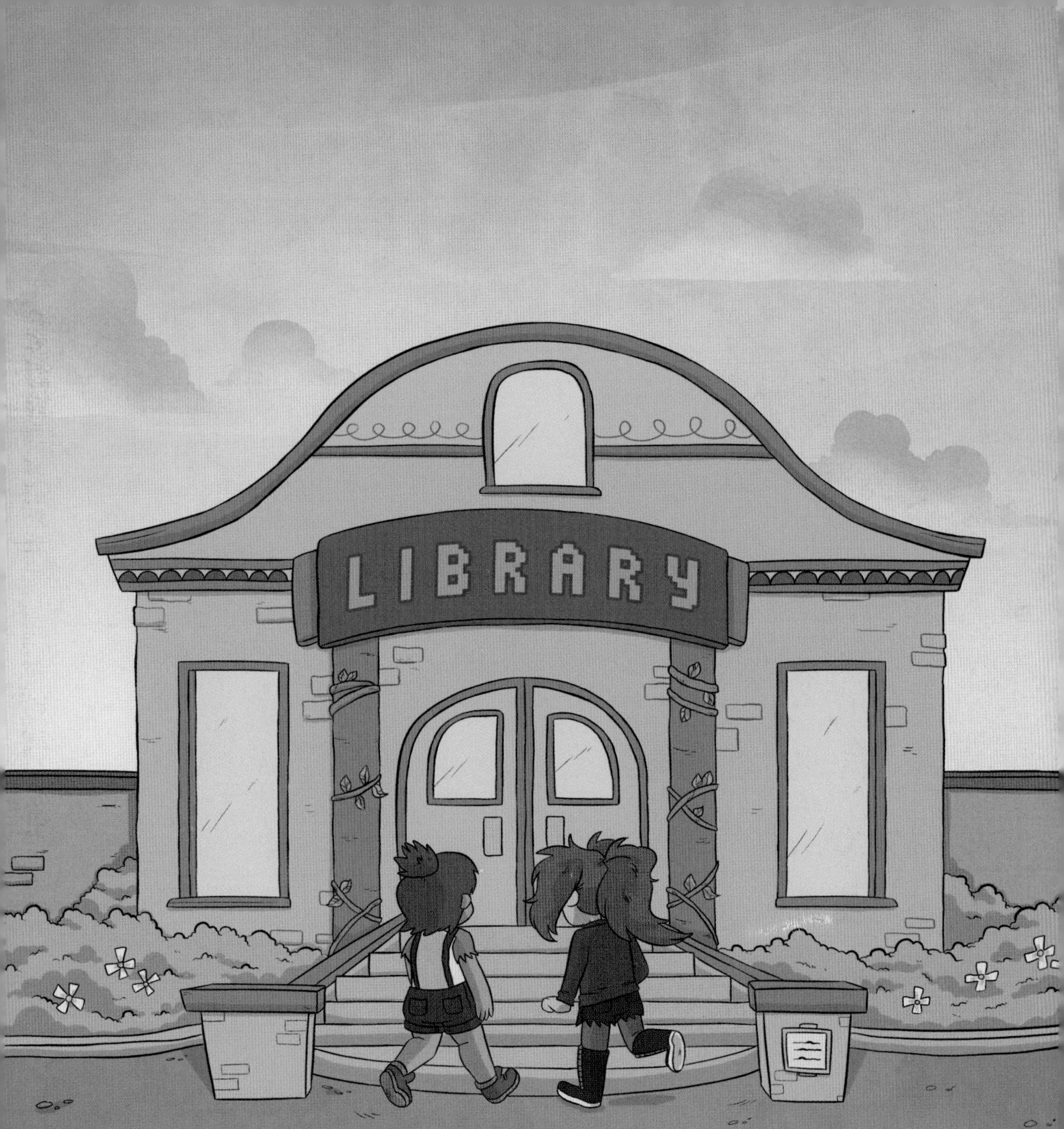
LIBRARY

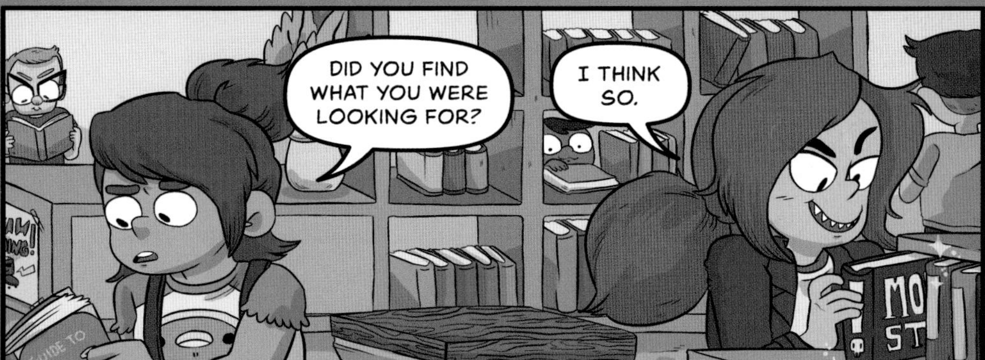
DID YOU FIND WHAT YOU WERE LOOKING FOR?
I THINK SO.

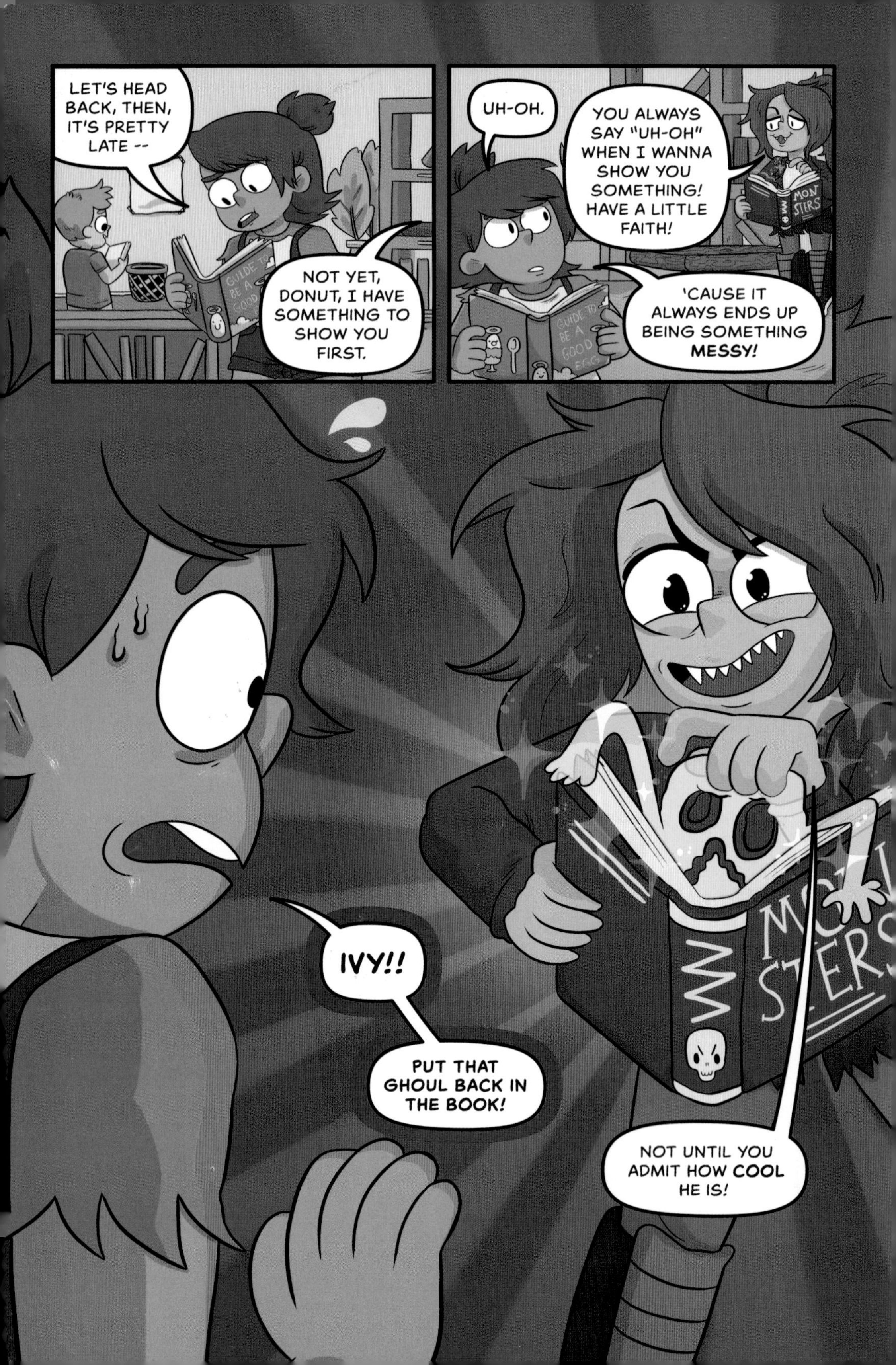
LET'S HEAD BACK, THEN, IT'S PRETTY LATE --
GUIDE TO BE A GOOD EGG
NOT YET, DONUT, I HAVE SOMETHING TO SHOW YOU FIRST.
UH-OH.
YOU ALWAYS SAY "UH-OH" WHEN I WANNA SHOW YOU SOMETHING! HAVE A LITTLE FAITH!
MONSTERS
'CAUSE IT ALWAYS ENDS UP BEING SOMETHING **MESSY!**
IVY!!
PUT THAT GHOUL BACK IN THE BOOK!
NOT UNTIL YOU ADMIT HOW **COOL** HE IS!

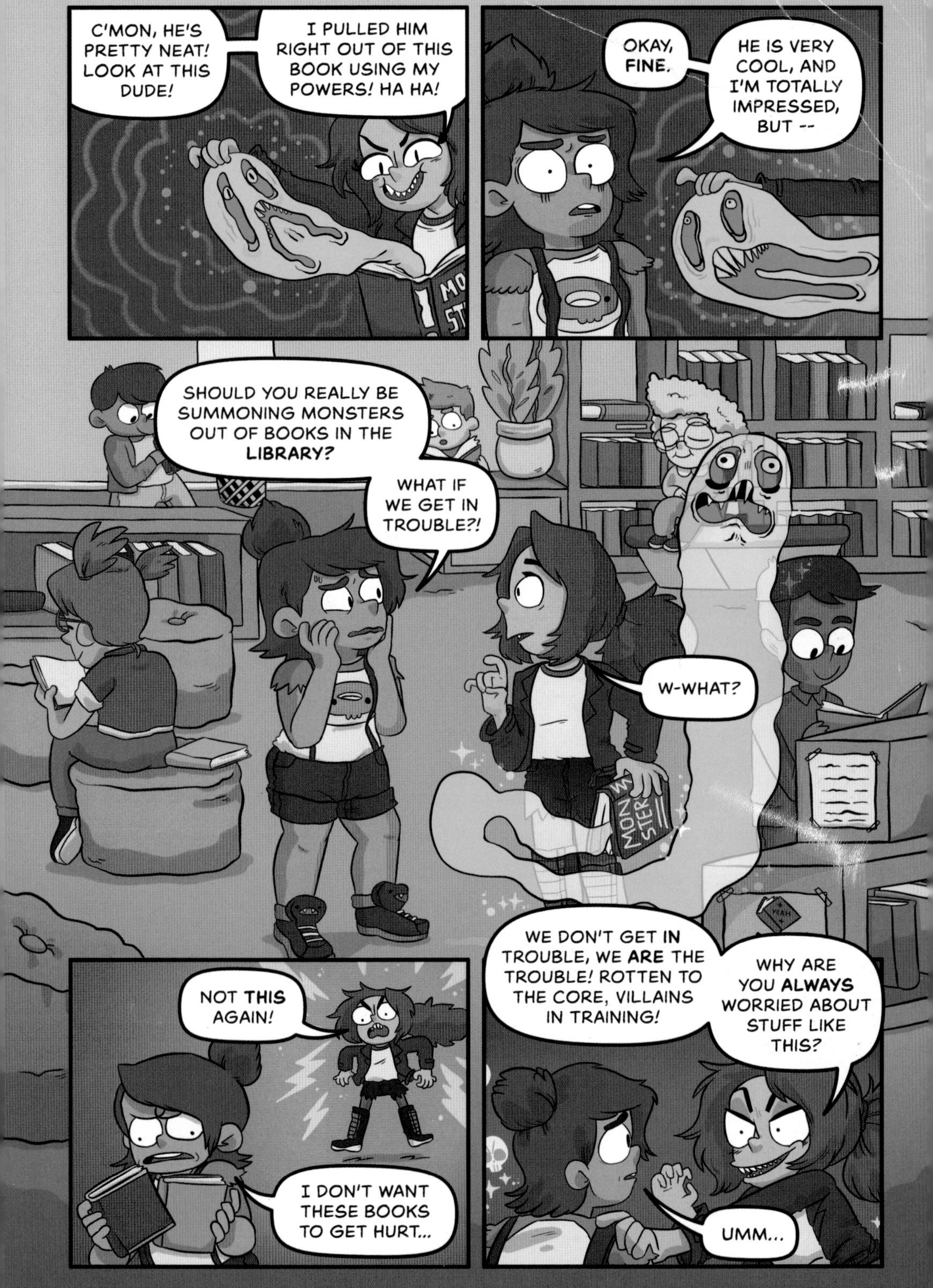
C'MON, HE'S PRETTY NEAT! LOOK AT THIS DUDE!
I PULLED HIM RIGHT OUT OF THIS BOOK USING MY POWERS! HA HA!
MONSTER
OKAY, FINE.
HE IS VERY COOL, AND I'M TOTALLY IMPRESSED, BUT --
SHOULD YOU REALLY BE SUMMONING MONSTERS OUT OF BOOKS IN THE LIBRARY?
WHAT IF WE GET IN TROUBLE?!
W-WHAT?
MONSTER
WE DON'T GET IN TROUBLE, WE ARE THE TROUBLE! ROTTEN TO THE CORE, VILLAINS IN TRAINING!
WHY ARE YOU ALWAYS WORRIED ABOUT STUFF LIKE THIS?
NOT THIS AGAIN!
I DON'T WANT THESE BOOKS TO GET HURT...
UMM...

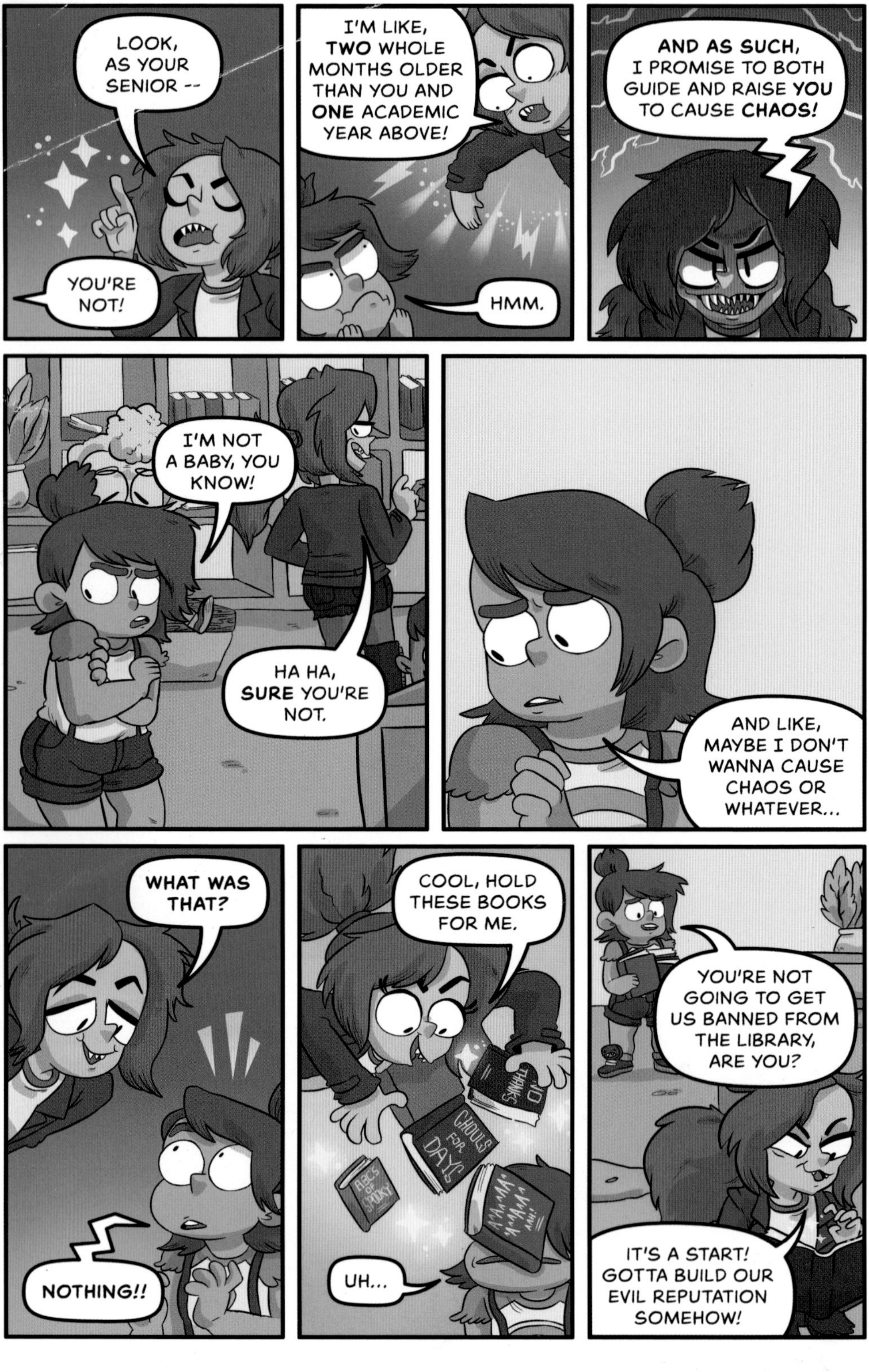
LOOK, AS YOUR SENIOR --
YOU'RE NOT!
I'M LIKE, **TWO** WHOLE MONTHS OLDER THAN YOU AND **ONE** ACADEMIC YEAR ABOVE!
HMM.
AND AS SUCH, I PROMISE TO BOTH GUIDE AND RAISE **YOU** TO CAUSE **CHAOS!**
I'M NOT A BABY, YOU KNOW!
HA HA, **SURE** YOU'RE NOT.
AND LIKE, MAYBE I DON'T WANNA CAUSE CHAOS OR WHATEVER...
WHAT WAS THAT?
NOTHING!!
COOL, HOLD THESE BOOKS FOR ME.
GHOULS FOR DAYS
ABCS OF SPOOKY
UH...
YOU'RE NOT GOING TO GET US BANNED FROM THE LIBRARY, ARE YOU?
IT'S A START! GOTTA BUILD OUR EVIL REPUTATION SOMEHOW!

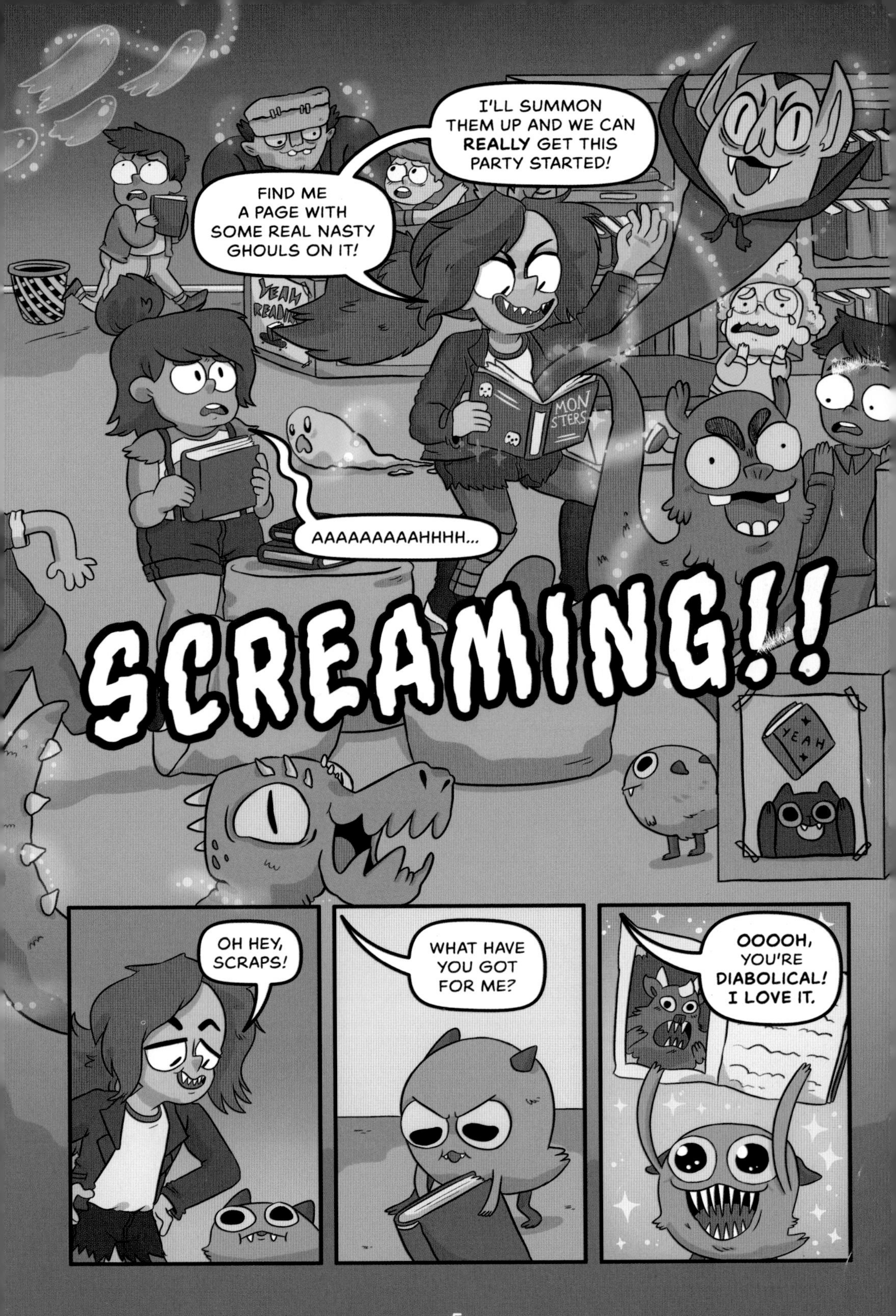
FIND ME A PAGE WITH SOME REAL NASTY GHOULS ON IT!
I'LL SUMMON THEM UP AND WE CAN REALLY GET THIS PARTY STARTED!
YEAH READ
MONSTERS
AAAAAAAAAHHHH...
SCREAMING!!
YEAH
OH HEY, SCRAPS!
WHAT HAVE YOU GOT FOR ME?
OOOOH, YOU'RE DIABOLICAL! I LOVE IT.

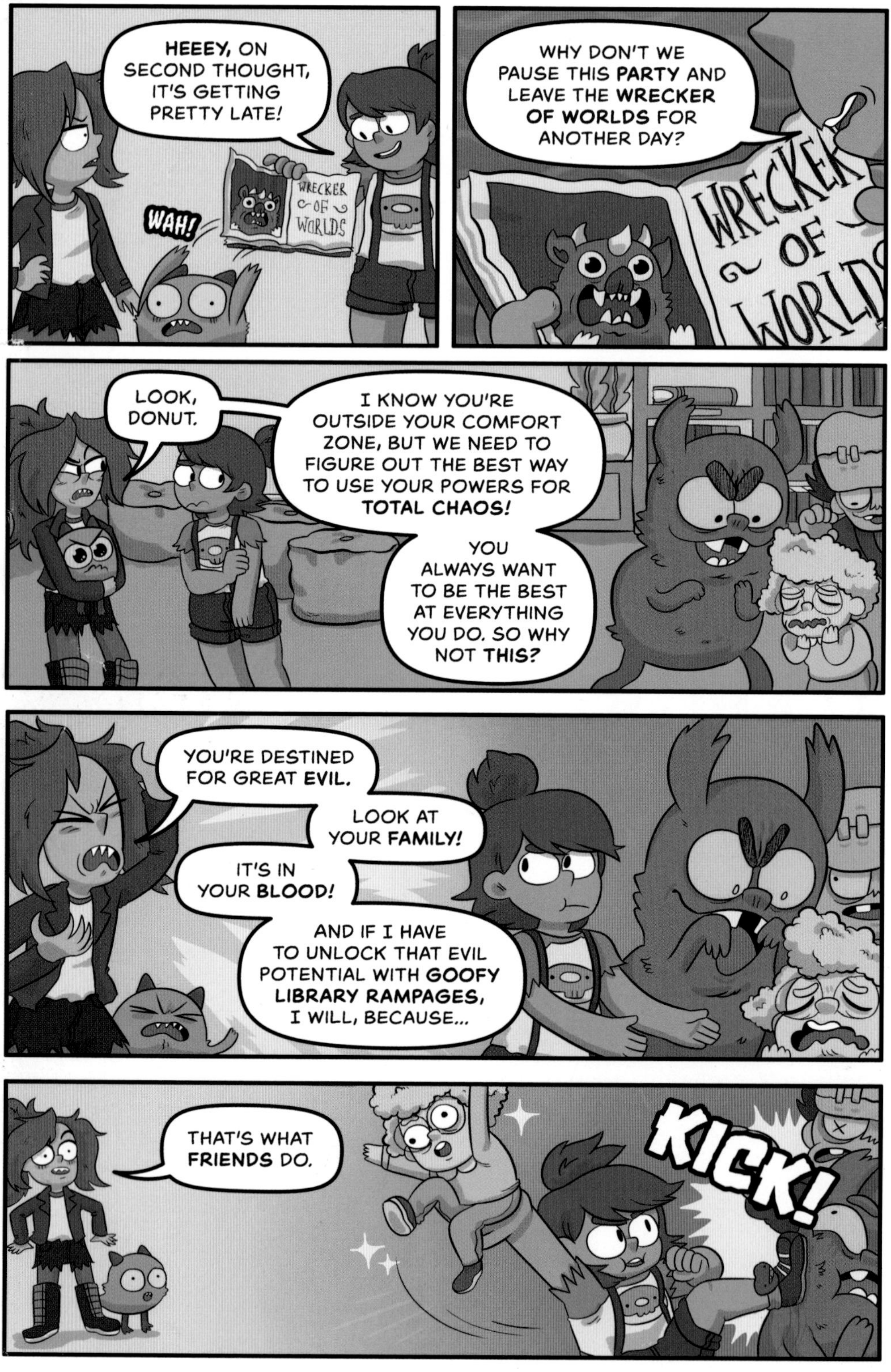

HEEEY, ON SECOND THOUGHT, IT'S GETTING PRETTY LATE!
WRECKER OF WORLDS
WAH!
WHY DON'T WE PAUSE THIS PARTY AND LEAVE THE WRECKER OF WORLDS FOR ANOTHER DAY?
WRECKER OF WORLDS
LOOK, DONUT.
I KNOW YOU'RE OUTSIDE YOUR COMFORT ZONE, BUT WE NEED TO FIGURE OUT THE BEST WAY TO USE YOUR POWERS FOR TOTAL CHAOS!
YOU ALWAYS WANT TO BE THE BEST AT EVERYTHING YOU DO. SO WHY NOT THIS?
YOU'RE DESTINED FOR GREAT EVIL.
LOOK AT YOUR FAMILY!
IT'S IN YOUR BLOOD!
AND IF I HAVE TO UNLOCK THAT EVIL POTENTIAL WITH GOOFY LIBRARY RAMPAGES, I WILL, BECAUSE...
THAT'S WHAT FRIENDS DO.
KICK!

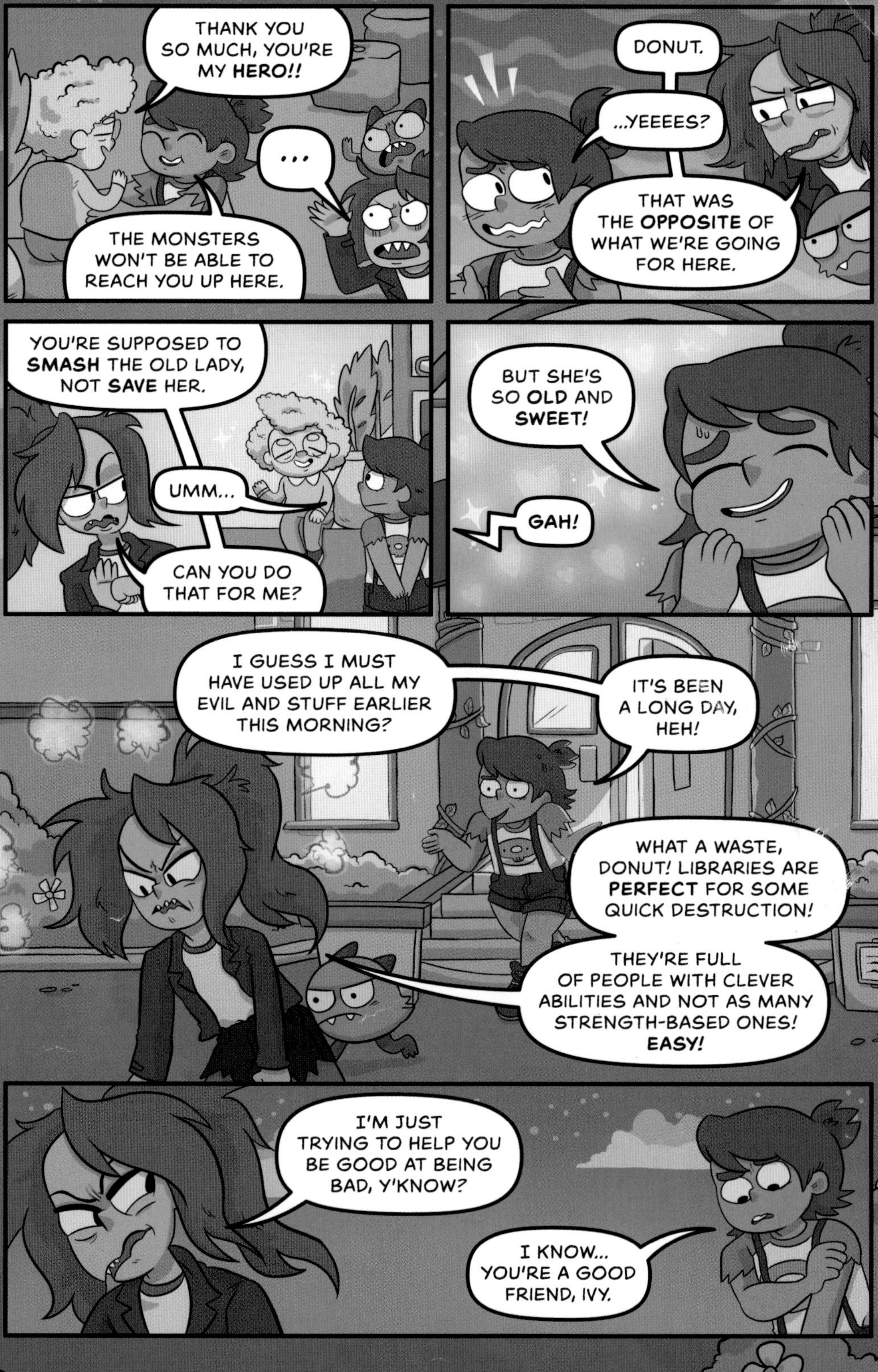
THANK YOU SO MUCH, YOU'RE MY HERO!!
...
THE MONSTERS WON'T BE ABLE TO REACH YOU UP HERE.
DONUT.
...YEEEES?
THAT WAS THE OPPOSITE OF WHAT WE'RE GOING FOR HERE.
YOU'RE SUPPOSED TO SMASH THE OLD LADY, NOT SAVE HER.
UMM...
CAN YOU DO THAT FOR ME?
BUT SHE'S SO OLD AND SWEET!
GAH!
I GUESS I MUST HAVE USED UP ALL MY EVIL AND STUFF EARLIER THIS MORNING?
IT'S BEEN A LONG DAY, HEH!
WHAT A WASTE, DONUT! LIBRARIES ARE PERFECT FOR SOME QUICK DESTRUCTION!
THEY'RE FULL OF PEOPLE WITH CLEVER ABILITIES AND NOT AS MANY STRENGTH-BASED ONES! EASY!
I'M JUST TRYING TO HELP YOU BE GOOD AT BEING BAD, Y'KNOW?
I KNOW... YOU'RE A GOOD FRIEND, IVY.

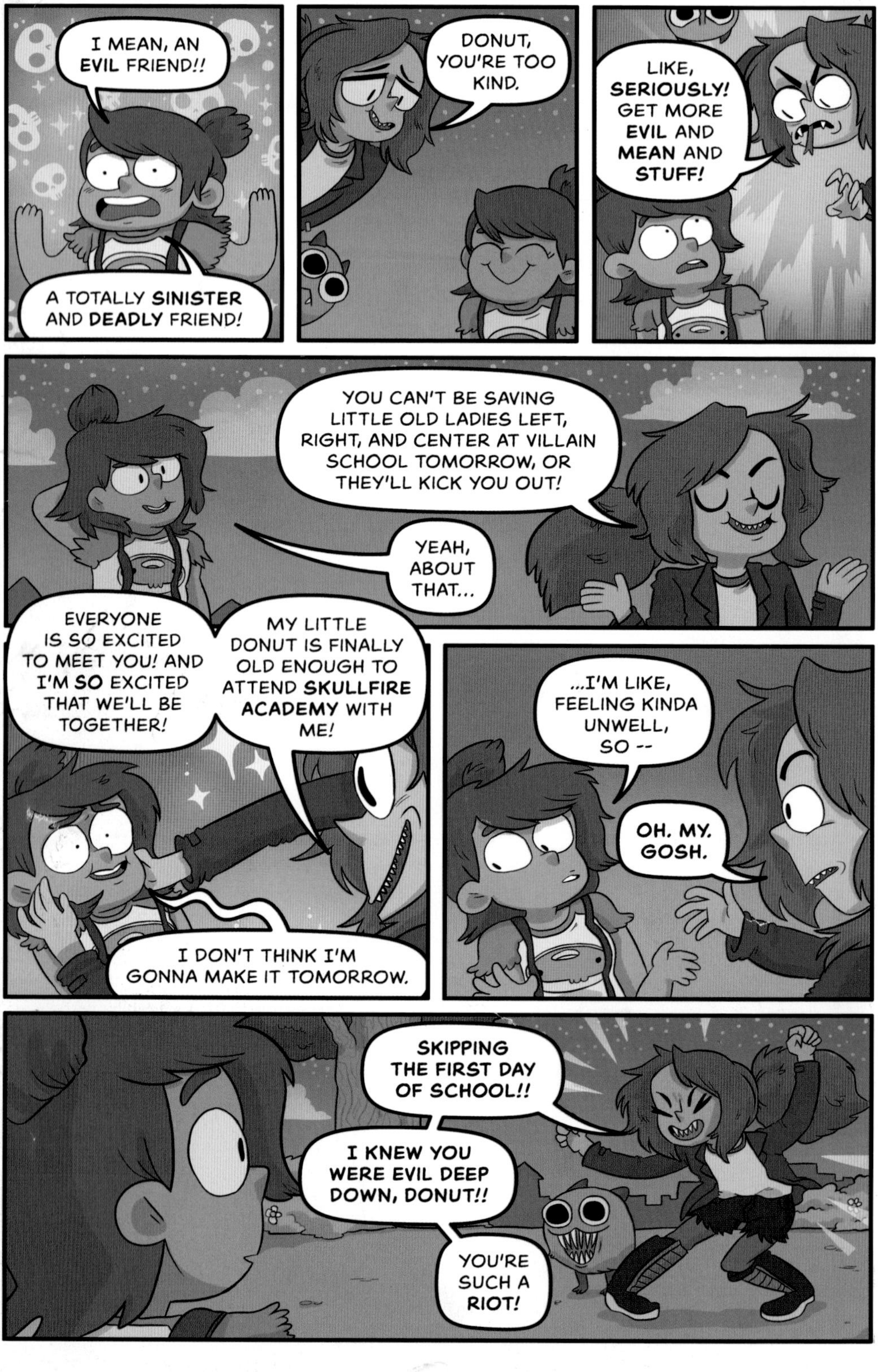
I MEAN, AN EVIL FRIEND!!
A TOTALLY SINISTER AND DEADLY FRIEND!
DONUT, YOU'RE TOO KIND.
LIKE, SERIOUSLY! GET MORE EVIL AND MEAN AND STUFF!
YOU CAN'T BE SAVING LITTLE OLD LADIES LEFT, RIGHT, AND CENTER AT VILLAIN SCHOOL TOMORROW, OR THEY'LL KICK YOU OUT!
YEAH, ABOUT THAT...
EVERYONE IS SO EXCITED TO MEET YOU! AND I'M SO EXCITED THAT WE'LL BE TOGETHER!
MY LITTLE DONUT IS FINALLY OLD ENOUGH TO ATTEND SKULLFIRE ACADEMY WITH ME!
I DON'T THINK I'M GONNA MAKE IT TOMORROW.
...I'M LIKE, FEELING KINDA UNWELL, SO --
OH. MY. GOSH.
SKIPPING THE FIRST DAY OF SCHOOL!!
I KNEW YOU WERE EVIL DEEP DOWN, DONUT!!
YOU'RE SUCH A RIOT!

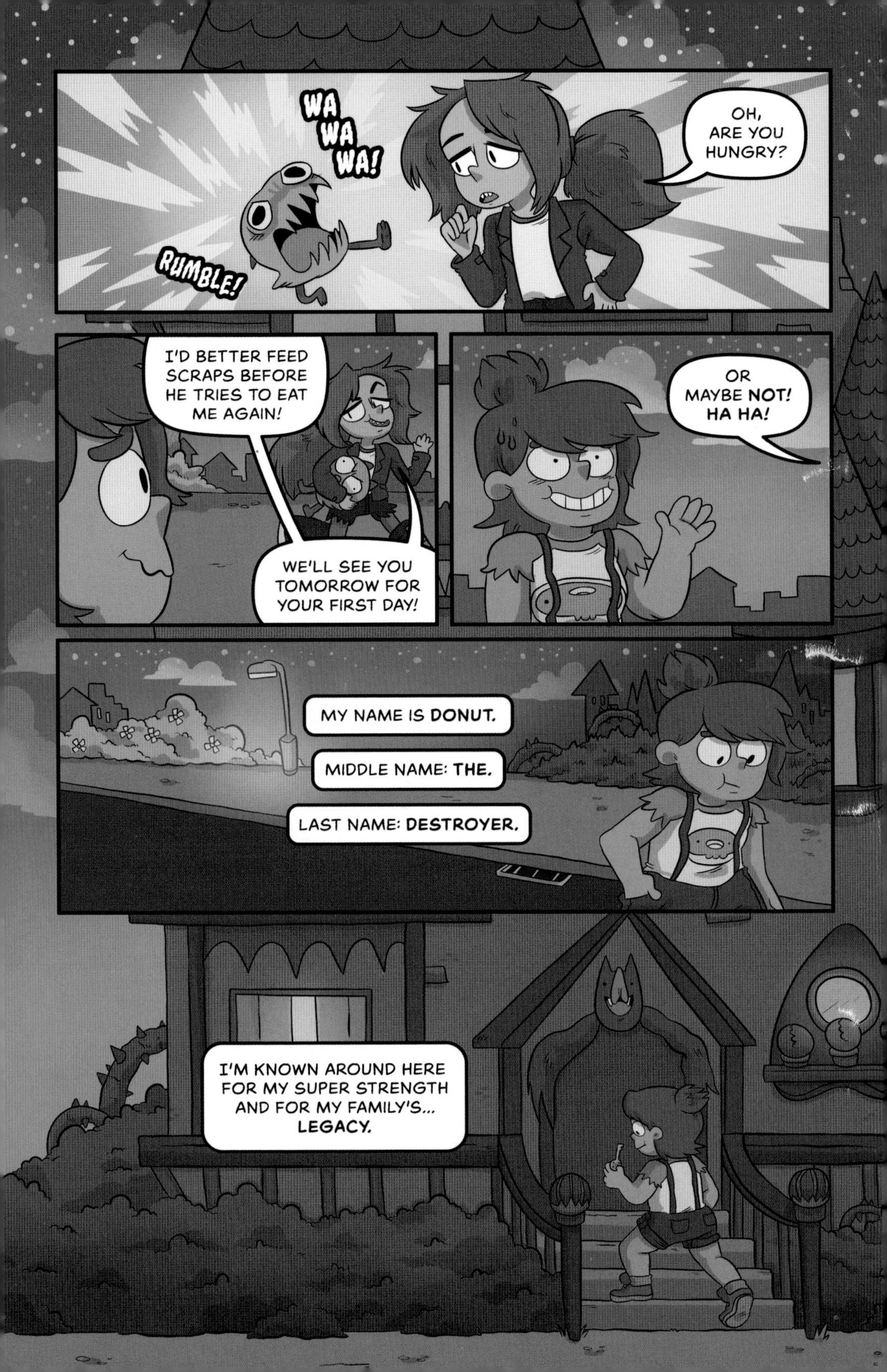
WA WA WA!
RUMBLE!
OH, ARE YOU HUNGRY?
I'D BETTER FEED SCRAPS BEFORE HE TRIES TO EAT ME AGAIN!
WE'LL SEE YOU TOMORROW FOR YOUR FIRST DAY!
OR MAYBE **NOT!** **HA HA!**
MY NAME IS **DONUT.**
MIDDLE NAME: **THE.**
LAST NAME: **DESTROYER.**
I'M KNOWN AROUND HERE FOR MY SUPER STRENGTH AND FOR MY FAMILY'S... **LEGACY.**

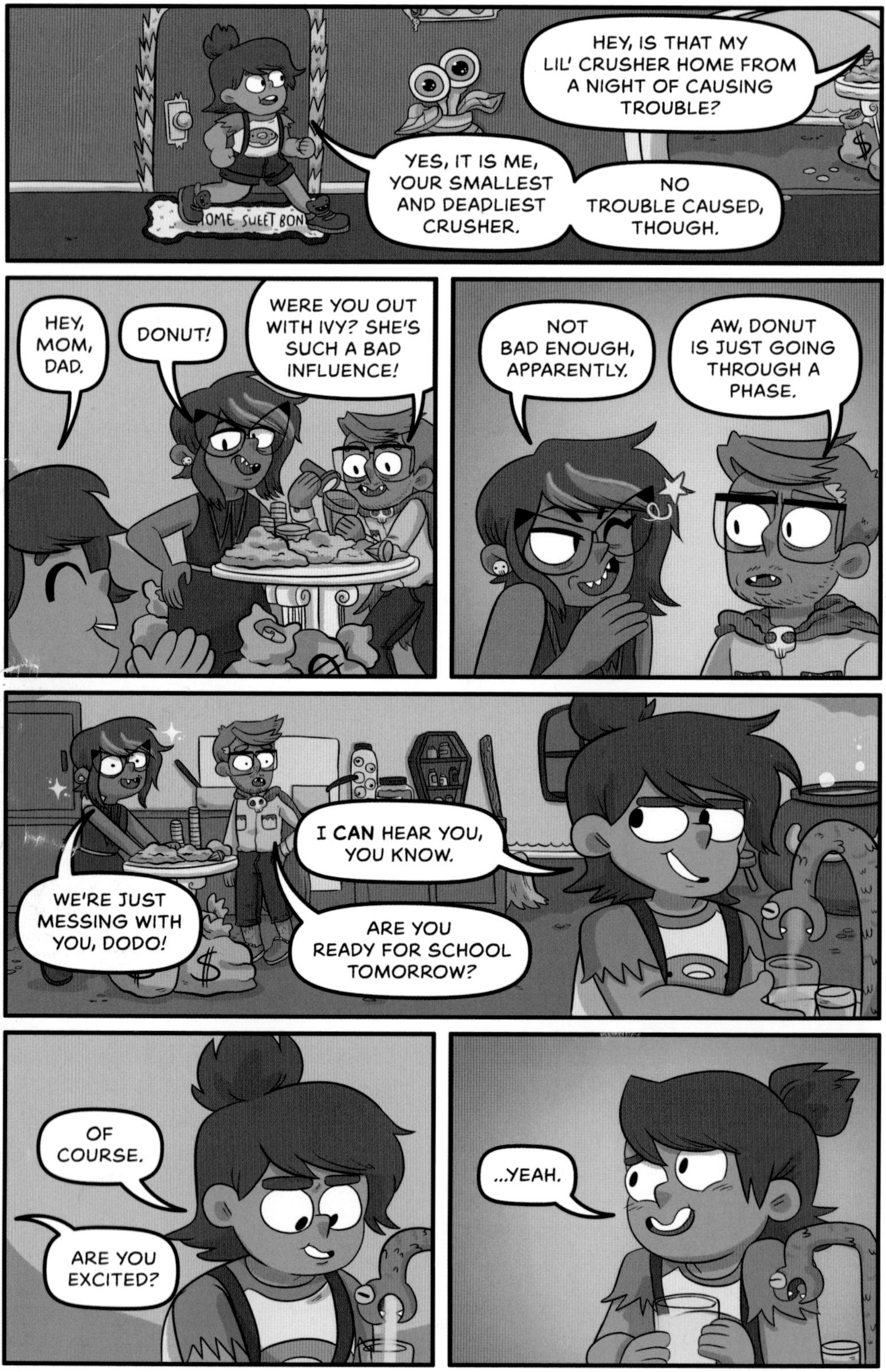
HOME SWEET BON
HEY, IS THAT MY LIL' CRUSHER HOME FROM A NIGHT OF CAUSING TROUBLE?
YES, IT IS ME, YOUR SMALLEST AND DEADLIEST CRUSHER.
NO TROUBLE CAUSED, THOUGH.
HEY, MOM, DAD.
DONUT!
WERE YOU OUT WITH IVY? SHE'S SUCH A BAD INFLUENCE!
NOT BAD ENOUGH, APPARENTLY.
AW, DONUT IS JUST GOING THROUGH A PHASE.
I **CAN** HEAR YOU, YOU KNOW.
WE'RE JUST MESSING WITH YOU, DODO!
ARE YOU READY FOR SCHOOL TOMORROW?
OF COURSE.
ARE YOU EXCITED?
...YEAH.

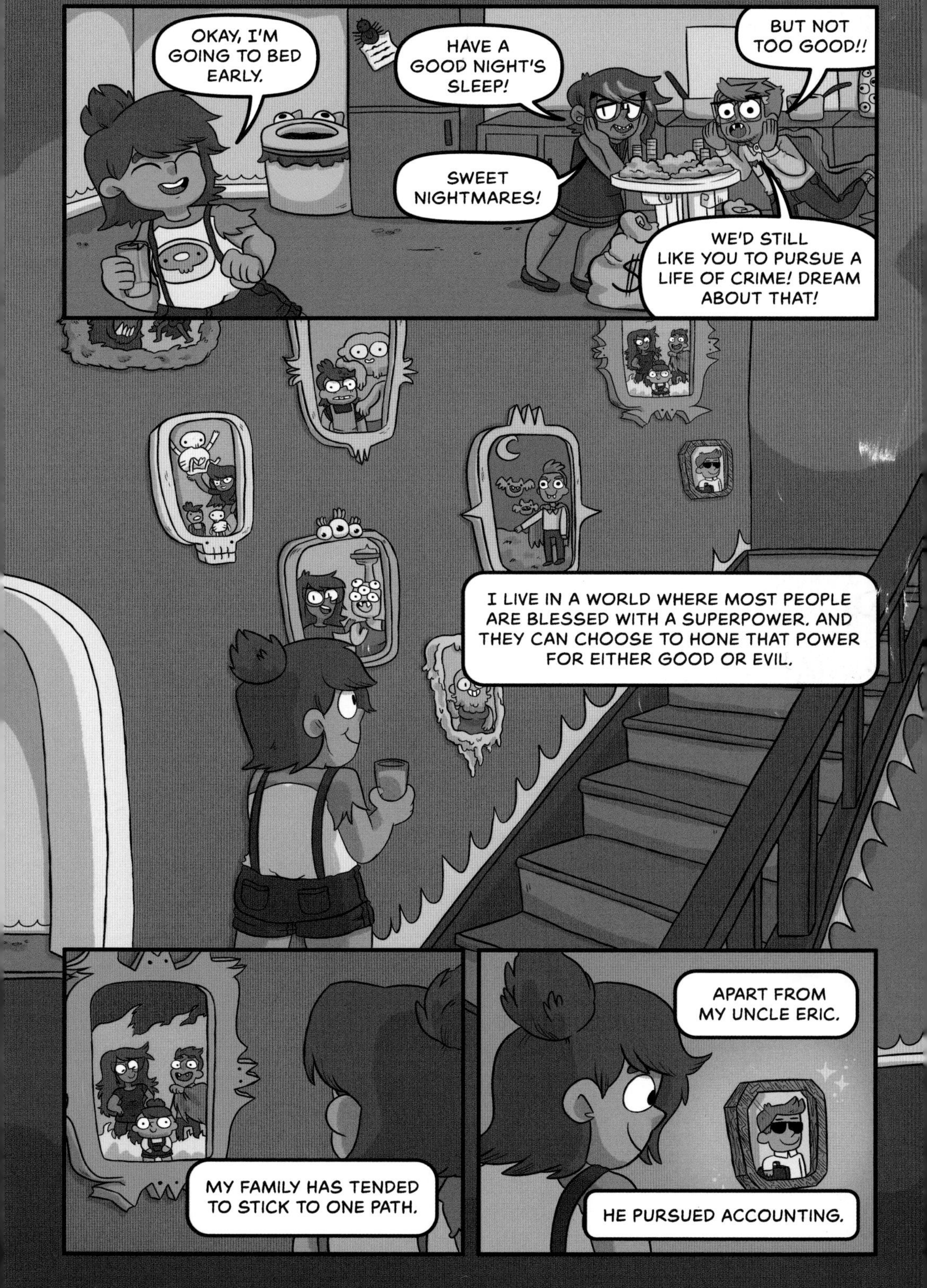
OKAY, I'M GOING TO BED EARLY.
HAVE A GOOD NIGHT'S SLEEP!
BUT NOT TOO GOOD!!
SWEET NIGHTMARES!
WE'D STILL LIKE YOU TO PURSUE A LIFE OF CRIME! DREAM ABOUT THAT!
I LIVE IN A WORLD WHERE MOST PEOPLE ARE BLESSED WITH A SUPERPOWER, AND THEY CAN CHOOSE TO HONE THAT POWER FOR EITHER GOOD OR EVIL.
MY FAMILY HAS TENDED TO STICK TO ONE PATH.
APART FROM MY UNCLE ERIC.
HE PURSUED ACCOUNTING.

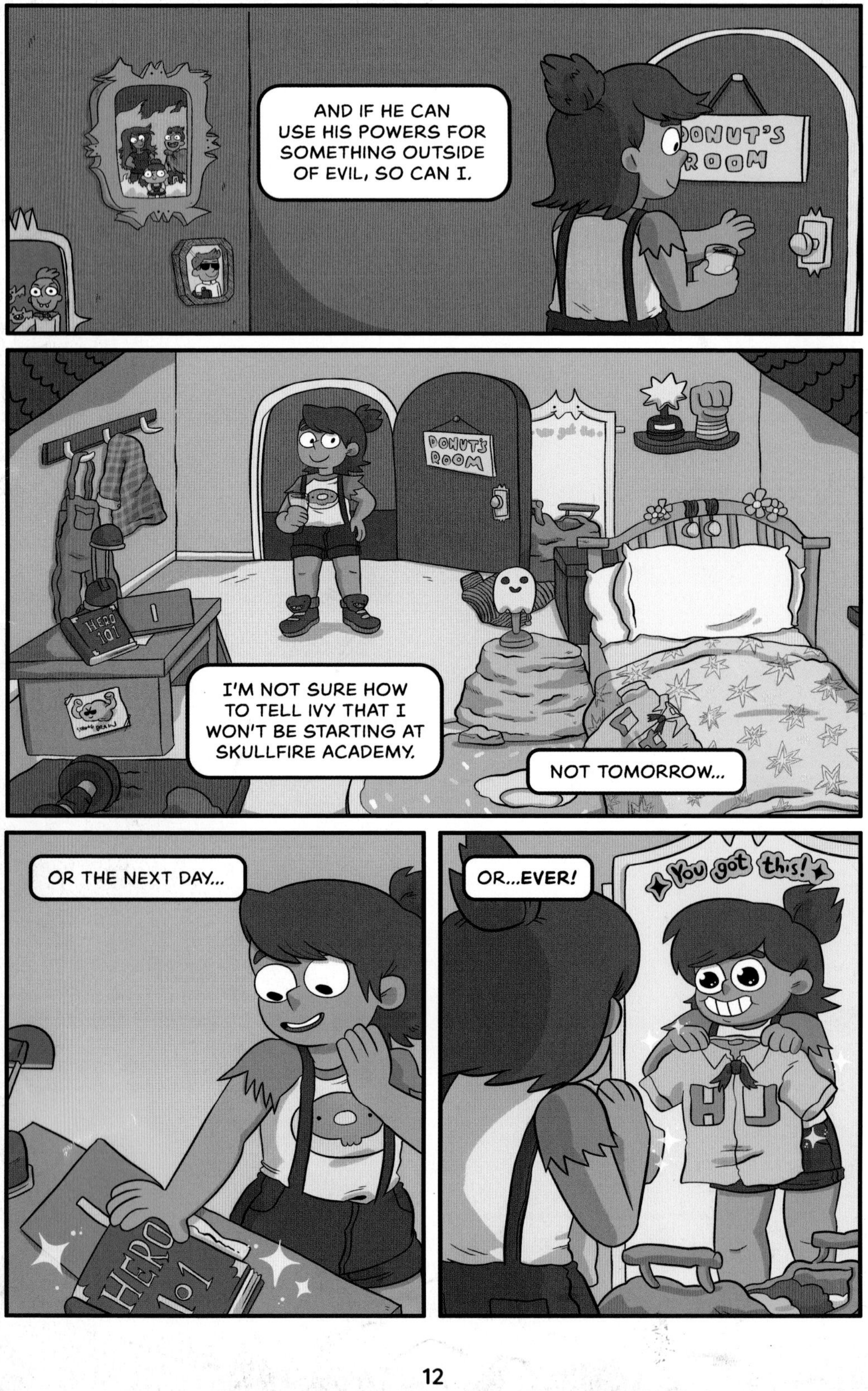
AND IF HE CAN USE HIS POWERS FOR SOMETHING OUTSIDE OF EVIL, SO CAN I.
DONUT'S ROOM
HERO 101
I'M NOT SURE HOW TO TELL IVY THAT I WON'T BE STARTING AT SKULLFIRE ACADEMY.
NOT TOMORROW...
OR THE NEXT DAY...
HERO 101
OR...EVER!
You got this!

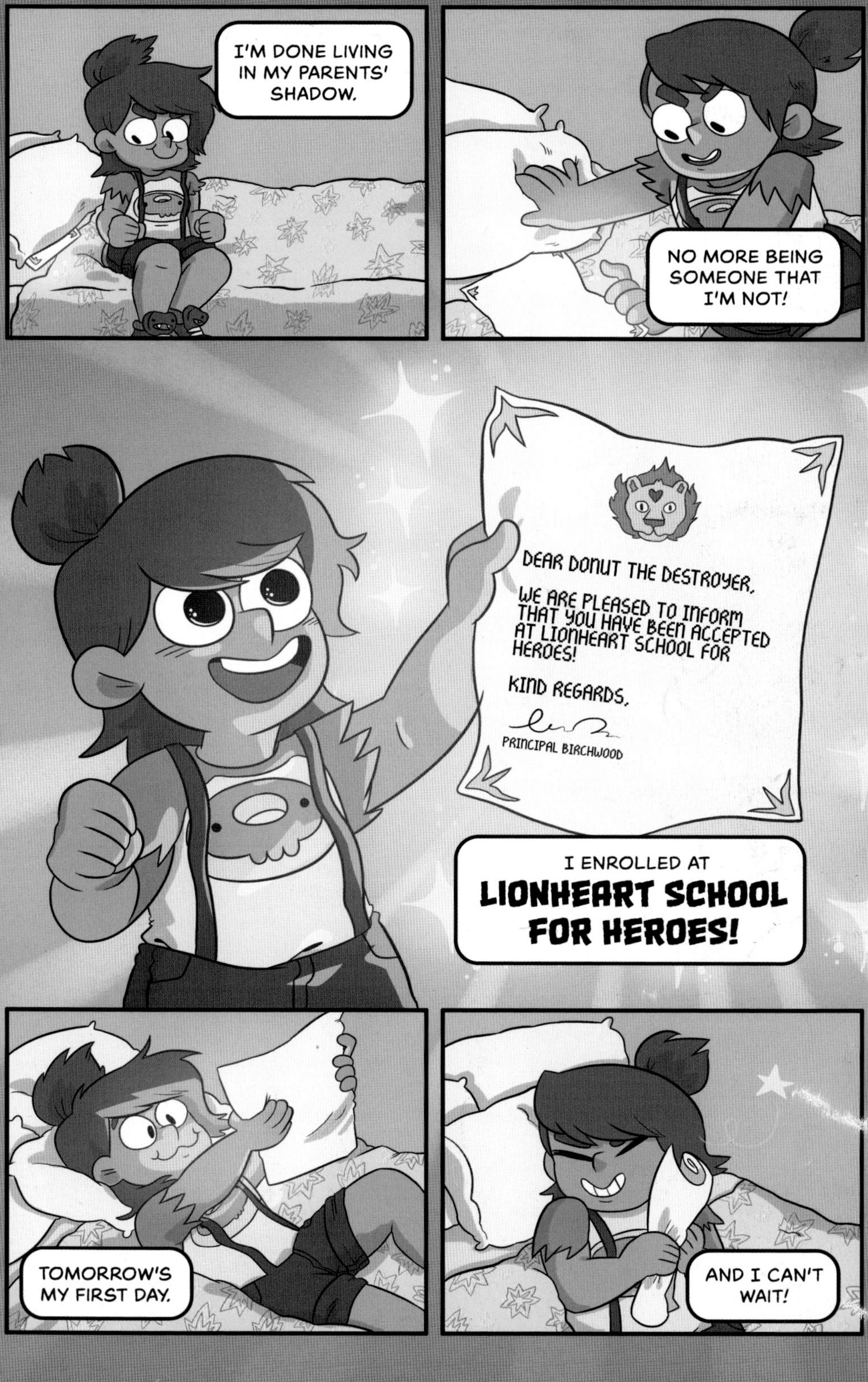
I'M DONE LIVING IN MY PARENTS' SHADOW.
NO MORE BEING SOMEONE THAT I'M NOT!
DEAR DONUT THE DESTROYER,
WE ARE PLEASED TO INFORM THAT YOU HAVE BEEN ACCEPTED AT LIONHEART SCHOOL FOR HEROES!
KIND REGARDS,
PRINCIPAL BIRCHWOOD
I ENROLLED AT
LIONHEART SCHOOL FOR HEROES!
TOMORROW'S MY FIRST DAY.
AND I CAN'T WAIT!

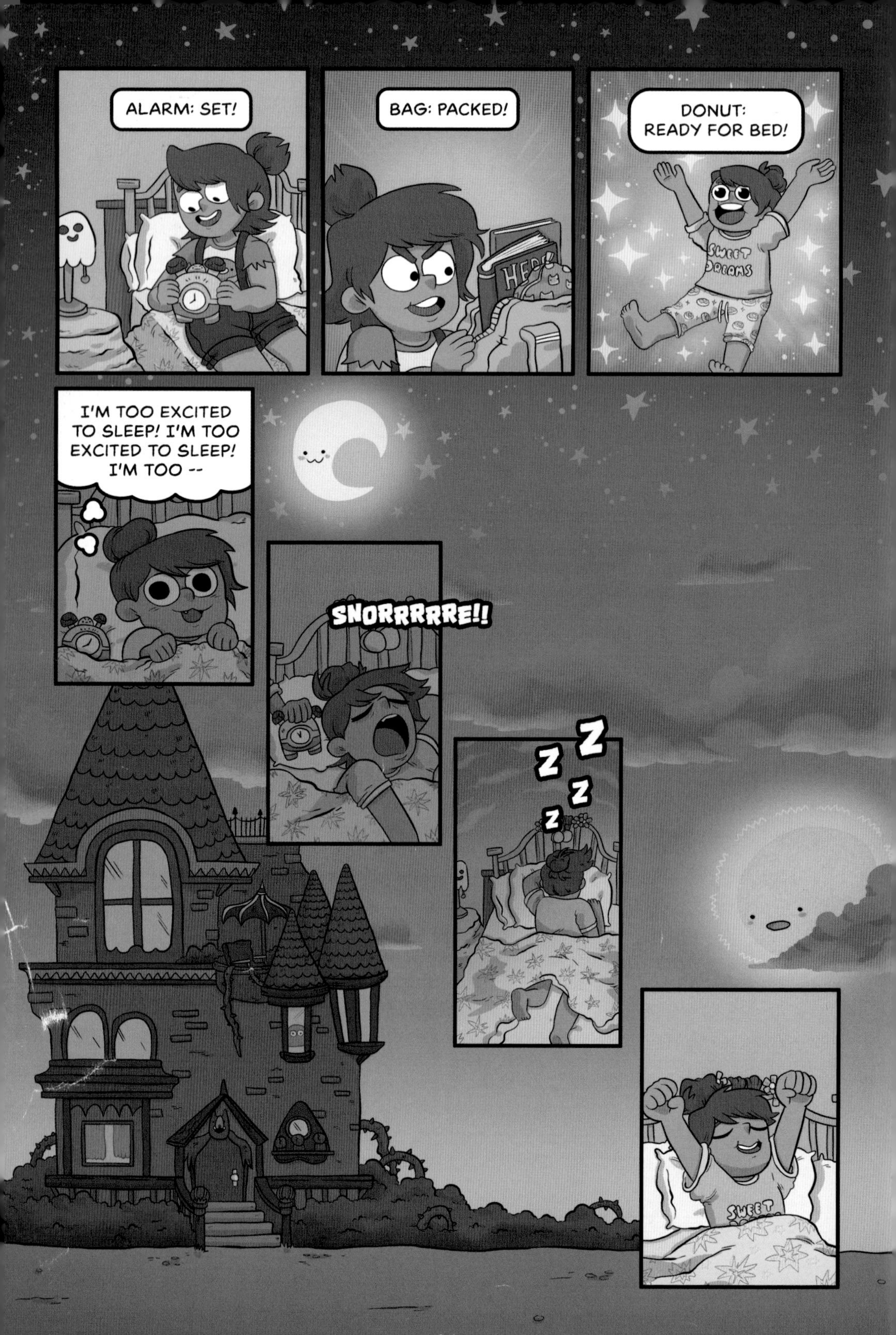

ALARM: SET!
BAG: PACKED!
DONUT: READY FOR BED!
SWEET DREAMS
I'M TOO EXCITED TO SLEEP! I'M TOO EXCITED TO SLEEP! I'M TOO --
SNORRRRRE!!
Z Z Z Z
SWEET

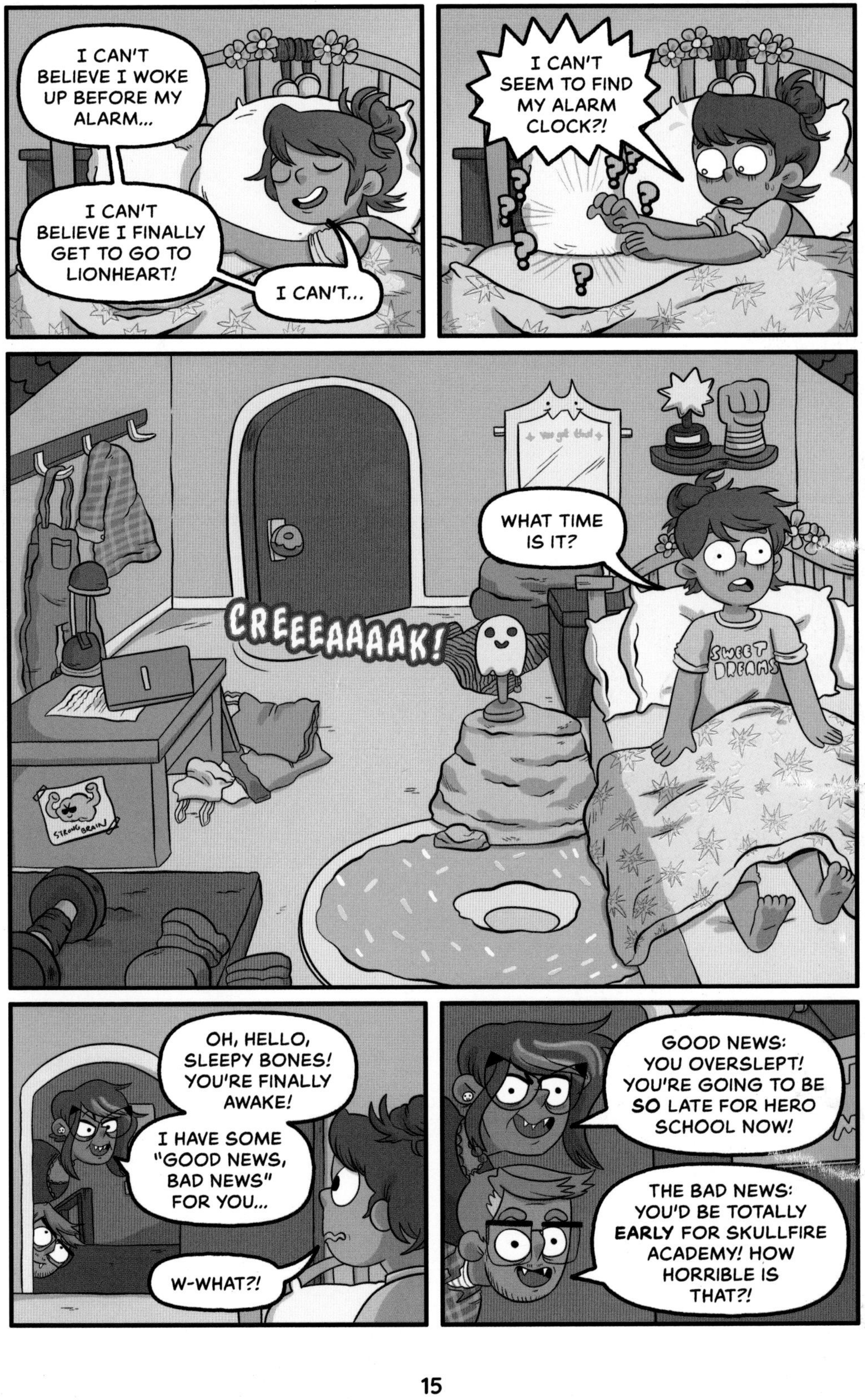
I CAN'T BELIEVE I WOKE UP BEFORE MY ALARM...
I CAN'T BELIEVE I FINALLY GET TO GO TO LIONHEART!
I CAN'T...
I CAN'T SEEM TO FIND MY ALARM CLOCK?!
WHAT TIME IS IT?
CREEEAAAAK!
SWEET DREAMS
STRONG BRAIN
OH, HELLO, SLEEPY BONES! YOU'RE FINALLY AWAKE!
I HAVE SOME "GOOD NEWS, BAD NEWS" FOR YOU...
W-WHAT?!
GOOD NEWS: YOU OVERSLEPT! YOU'RE GOING TO BE SO LATE FOR HERO SCHOOL NOW!
THE BAD NEWS: YOU'D BE TOTALLY EARLY FOR SKULLFIRE ACADEMY! HOW HORRIBLE IS THAT?!

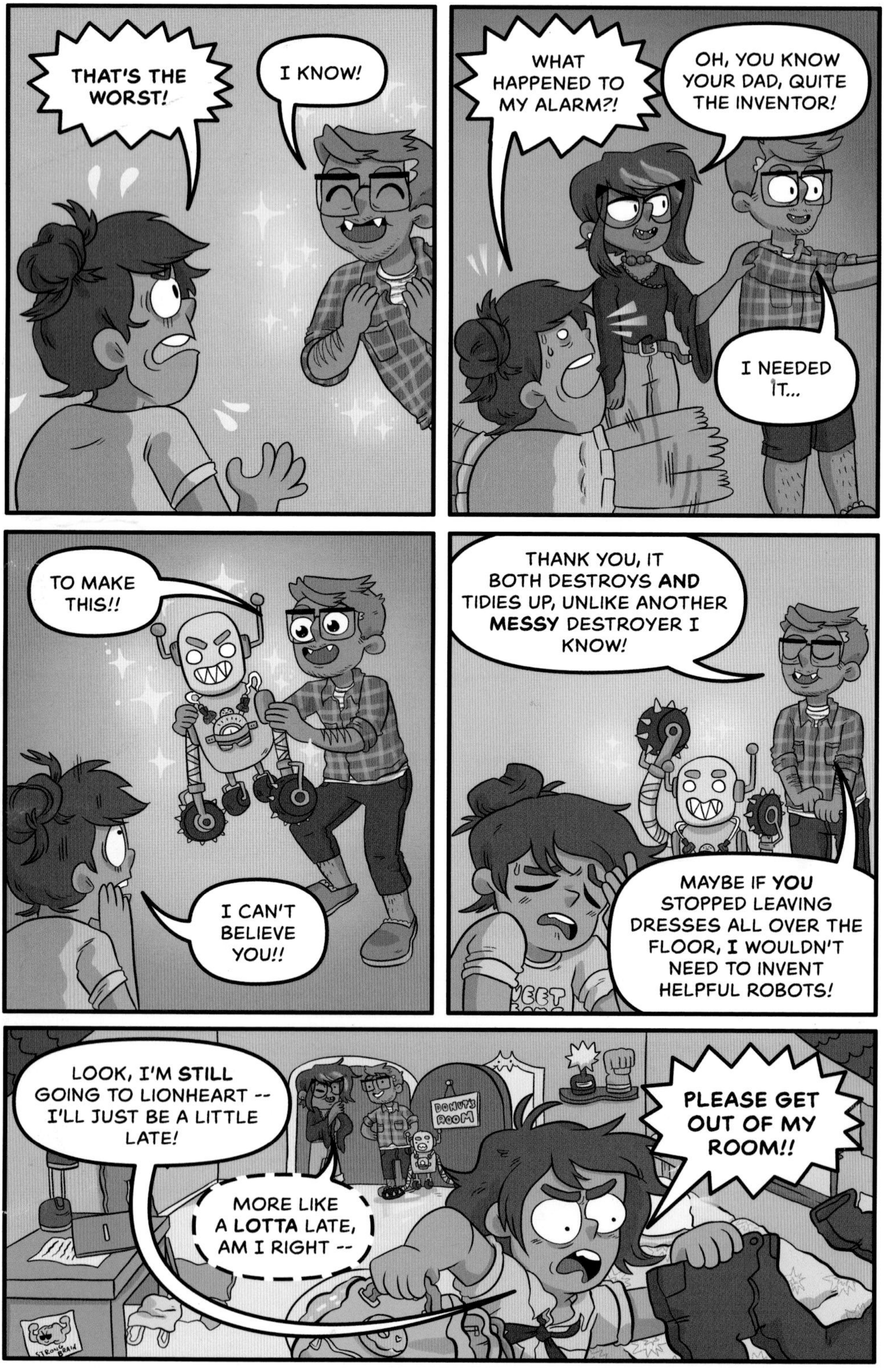

THAT'S THE WORST!
I KNOW!
WHAT HAPPENED TO MY ALARM?!
OH, YOU KNOW YOUR DAD, QUITE THE INVENTOR!
I NEEDED IT...
TO MAKE THIS!!
I CAN'T BELIEVE YOU!!
THANK YOU, IT BOTH DESTROYS **AND** TIDIES UP, UNLIKE ANOTHER **MESSY** DESTROYER I KNOW!
MAYBE IF **YOU** STOPPED LEAVING DRESSES ALL OVER THE FLOOR, **I** WOULDN'T NEED TO INVENT HELPFUL ROBOTS!
LOOK, I'M **STILL** GOING TO LIONHEART -- I'LL JUST BE A LITTLE LATE!
MORE LIKE A **LOTTA** LATE, AM I RIGHT --
DONUT'S ROOM
STRONG BRAIN
PLEASE GET OUT OF MY ROOM!!

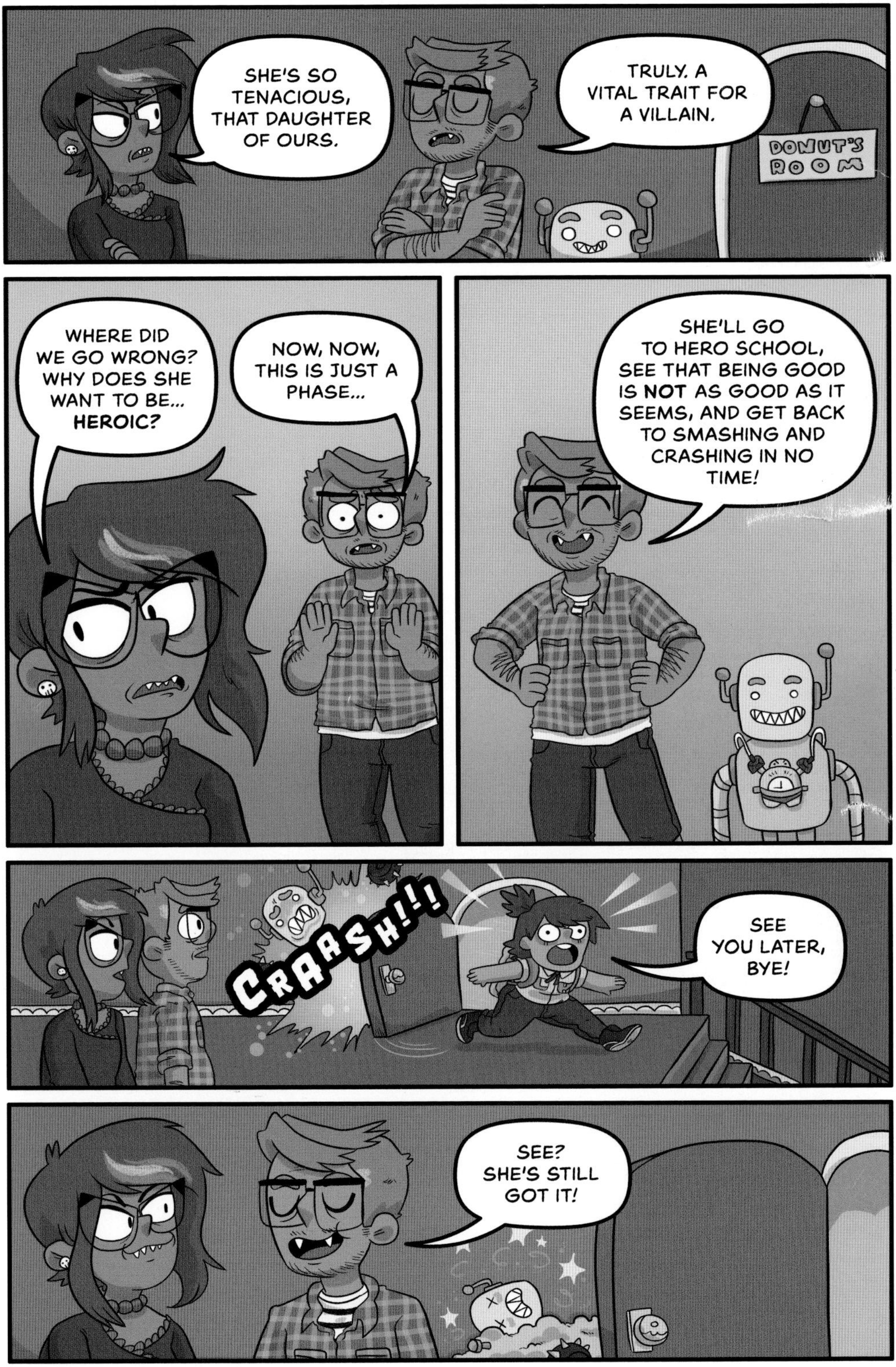
SHE'S SO TENACIOUS, THAT DAUGHTER OF OURS.
TRULY. A VITAL TRAIT FOR A VILLAIN.
DONUT'S ROOM
WHERE DID WE GO WRONG? WHY DOES SHE WANT TO BE... **HEROIC?**
NOW, NOW, THIS IS JUST A PHASE...
SHE'LL GO TO HERO SCHOOL, SEE THAT BEING GOOD IS **NOT** AS GOOD AS IT SEEMS, AND GET BACK TO SMASHING AND CRASHING IN NO TIME!
CRAASH!!!
SEE YOU LATER, BYE!
SEE? SHE'S STILL GOT IT!

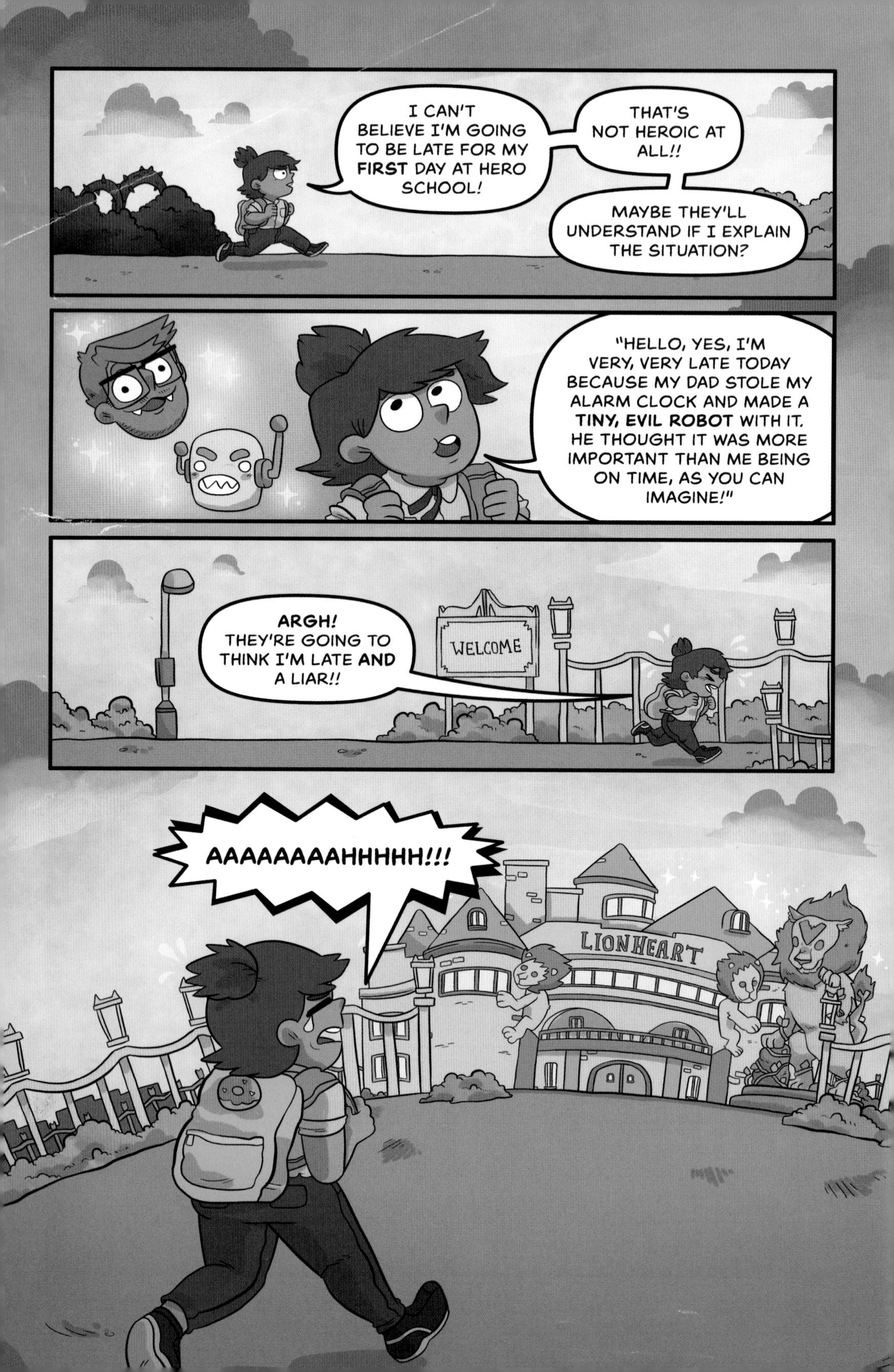

I CAN'T BELIEVE I'M GOING TO BE LATE FOR MY **FIRST** DAY AT HERO SCHOOL!
THAT'S NOT HEROIC AT ALL!!
MAYBE THEY'LL UNDERSTAND IF I EXPLAIN THE SITUATION?
"HELLO, YES, I'M VERY, VERY LATE TODAY BECAUSE MY DAD STOLE MY ALARM CLOCK AND MADE A **TINY, EVIL ROBOT** WITH IT. HE THOUGHT IT WAS MORE IMPORTANT THAN ME BEING ON TIME, AS YOU CAN IMAGINE!"
ARGH! THEY'RE GOING TO THINK I'M LATE **AND** A LIAR!!
WELCOME
AAAAAAAAHHHHH!!!
LIONHEART

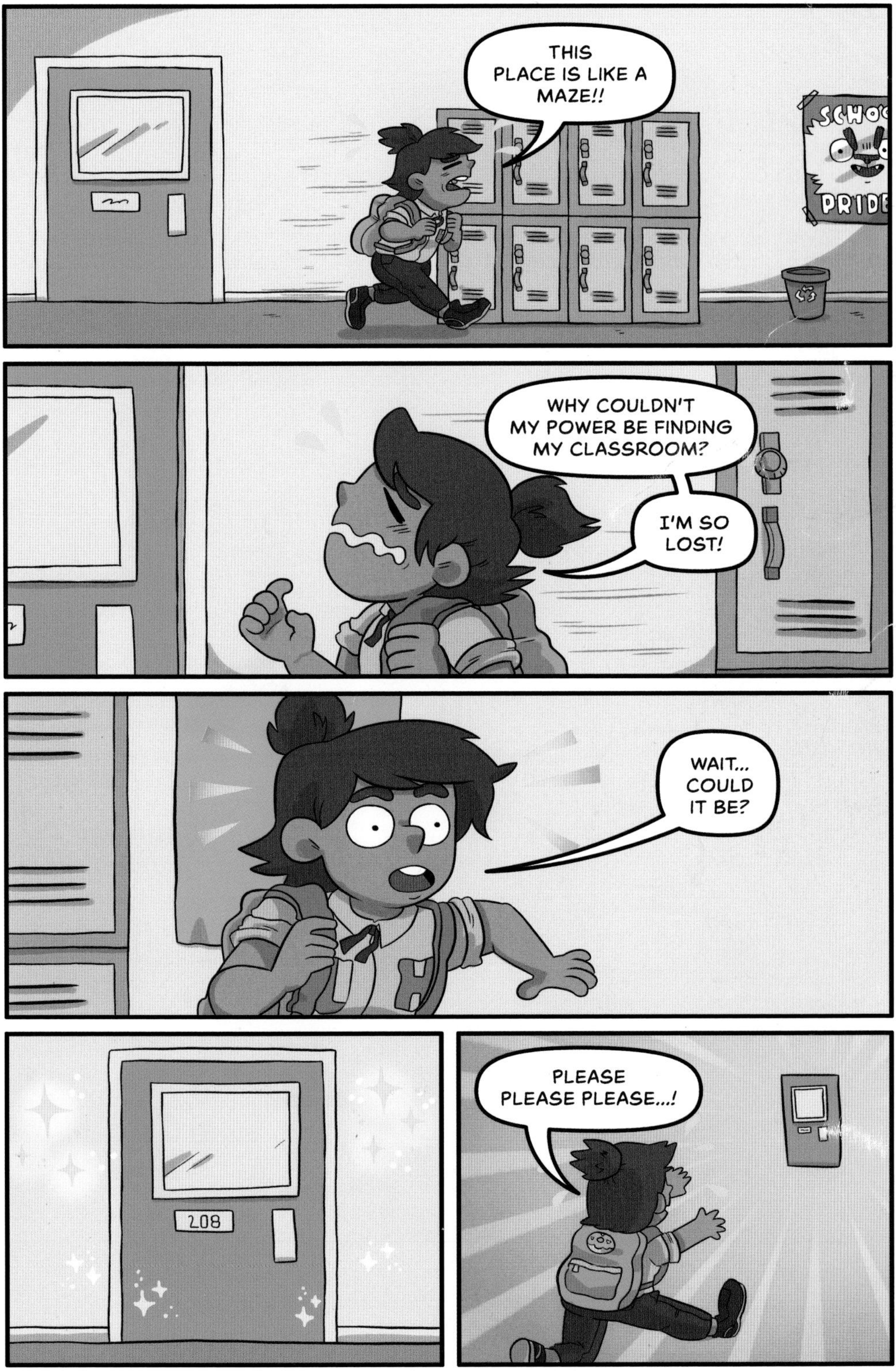
THIS PLACE IS LIKE A MAZE!!
SCHO
PRIDE
WHY COULDN'T MY POWER BE FINDING MY CLASSROOM?
I'M SO LOST!
WAIT... COULD IT BE?
208
PLEASE PLEASE PLEASE...!

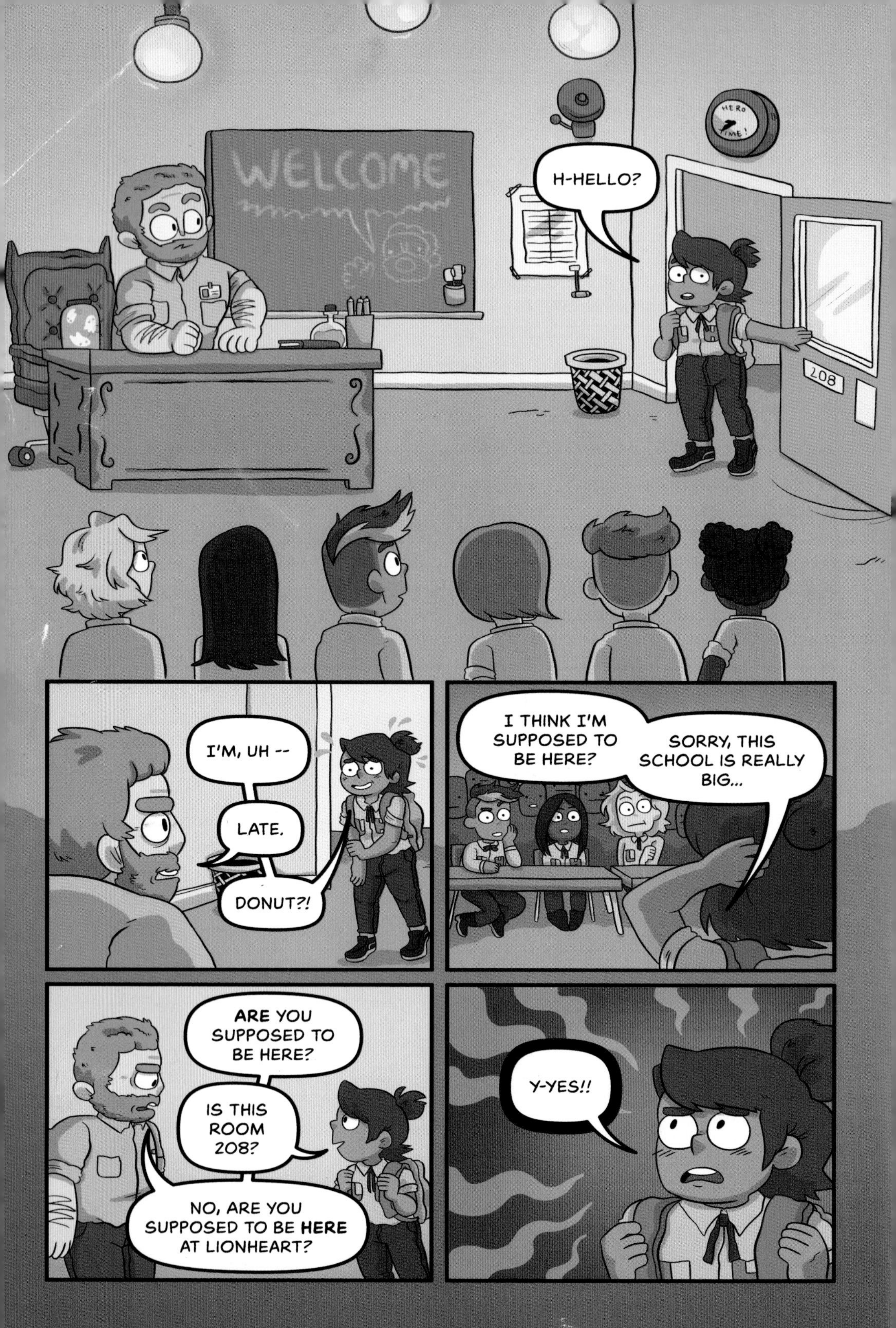
WELCOME
HERO TIME!
H-HELLO?
208
I'M, UH --
LATE.
DONUT?!
I THINK I'M SUPPOSED TO BE HERE?
SORRY, THIS SCHOOL IS REALLY BIG...
ARE YOU SUPPOSED TO BE HERE?
IS THIS ROOM 208?
NO, ARE YOU SUPPOSED TO BE **HERE** AT LIONHEART?
Y-YES!!

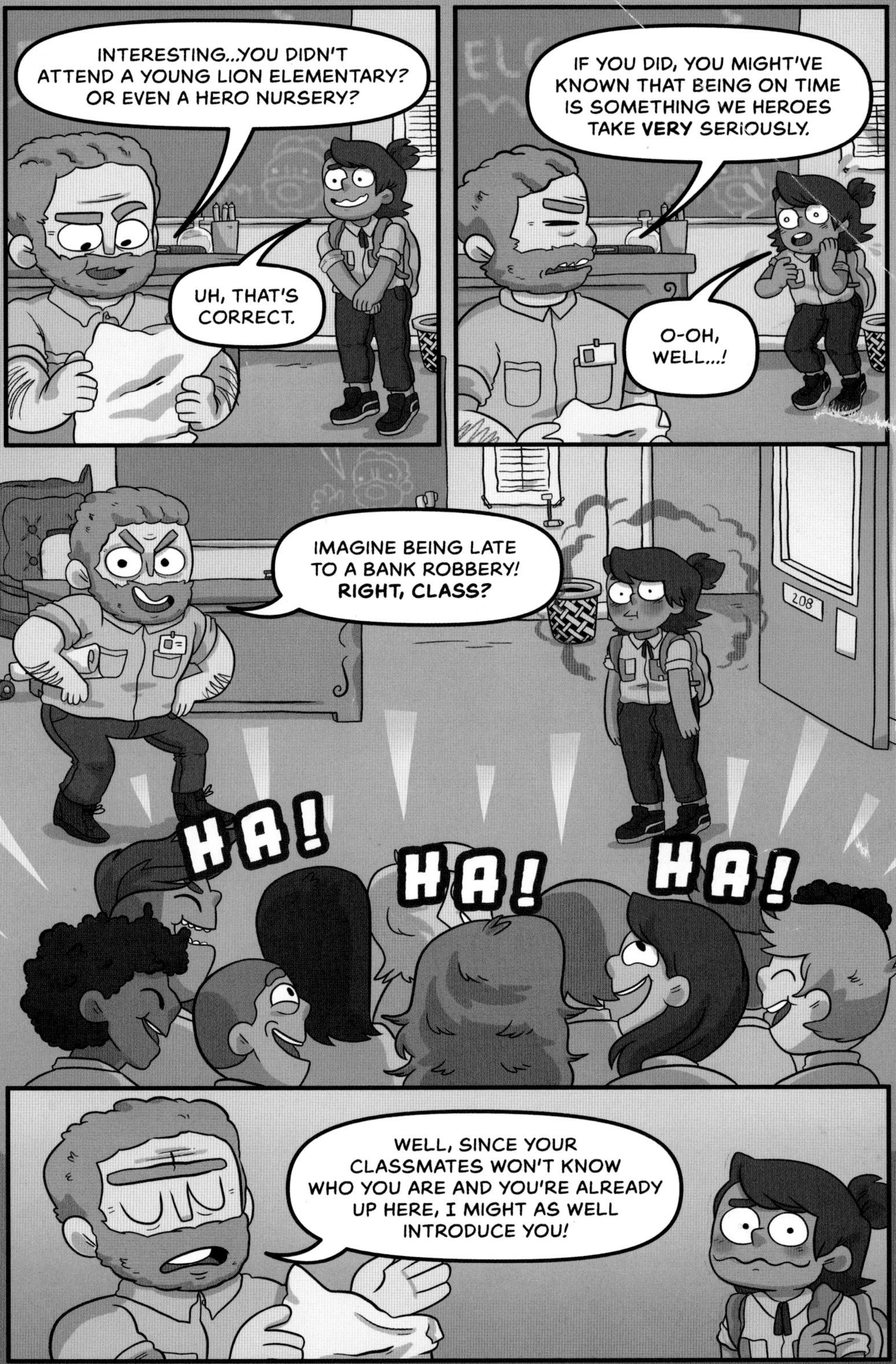
INTERESTING...YOU DIDN'T ATTEND A YOUNG LION ELEMENTARY? OR EVEN A HERO NURSERY?
UH, THAT'S CORRECT.
IF YOU DID, YOU MIGHT'VE KNOWN THAT BEING ON TIME IS SOMETHING WE HEROES TAKE **VERY** SERIOUSLY.
O-OH, WELL...!
IMAGINE BEING LATE TO A BANK ROBBERY! **RIGHT, CLASS?**
208
HA! HA! HA!
WELL, SINCE YOUR CLASSMATES WON'T KNOW WHO YOU ARE AND YOU'RE ALREADY UP HERE, I MIGHT AS WELL INTRODUCE YOU!

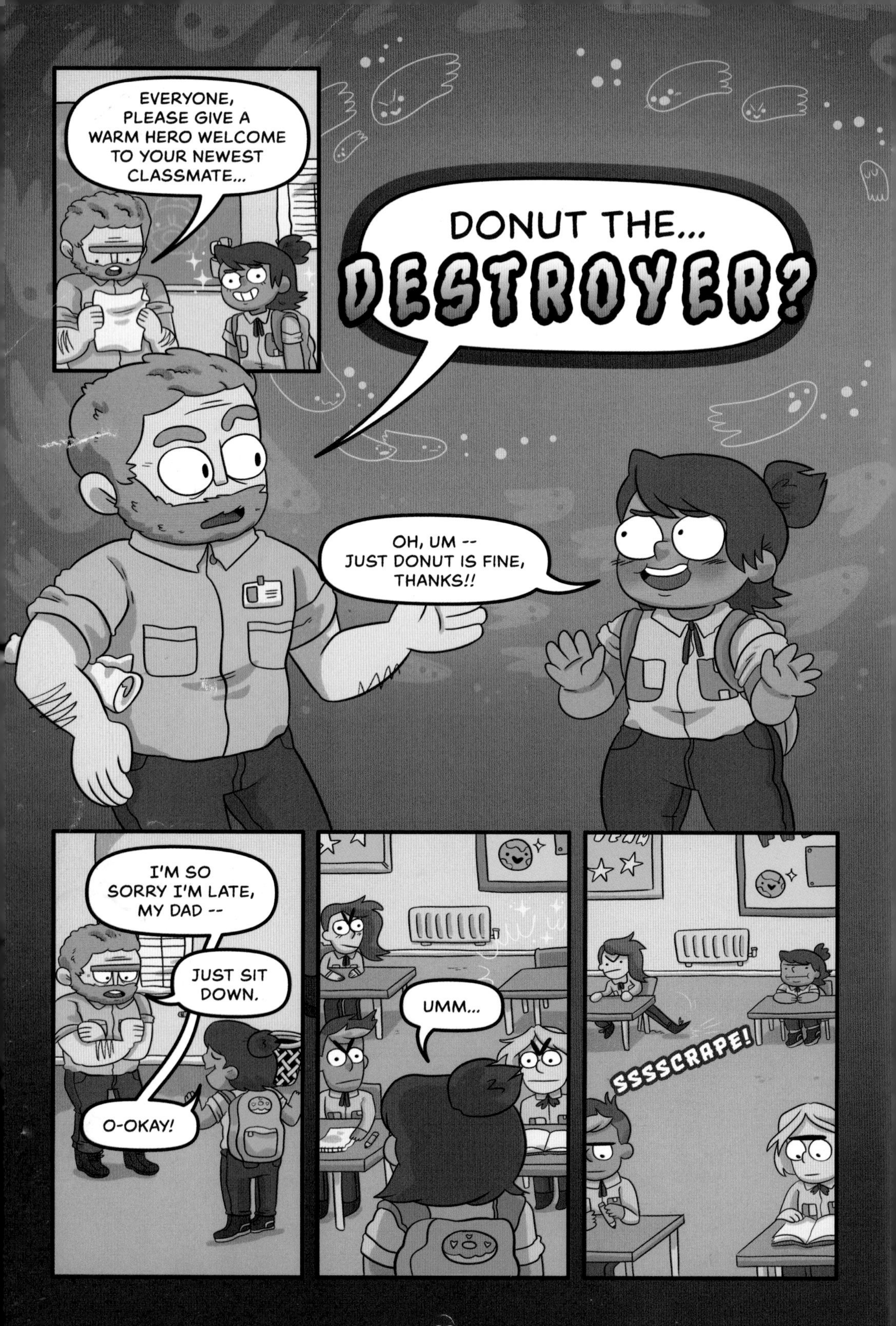
EVERYONE, PLEASE GIVE A WARM HERO WELCOME TO YOUR NEWEST CLASSMATE...
DONUT THE... DESTROYER?
OH, UM -- JUST DONUT IS FINE, THANKS!!
I'M SO SORRY I'M LATE, MY DAD --
JUST SIT DOWN.
O-OKAY!
UMM...
SSSSCRAPE!

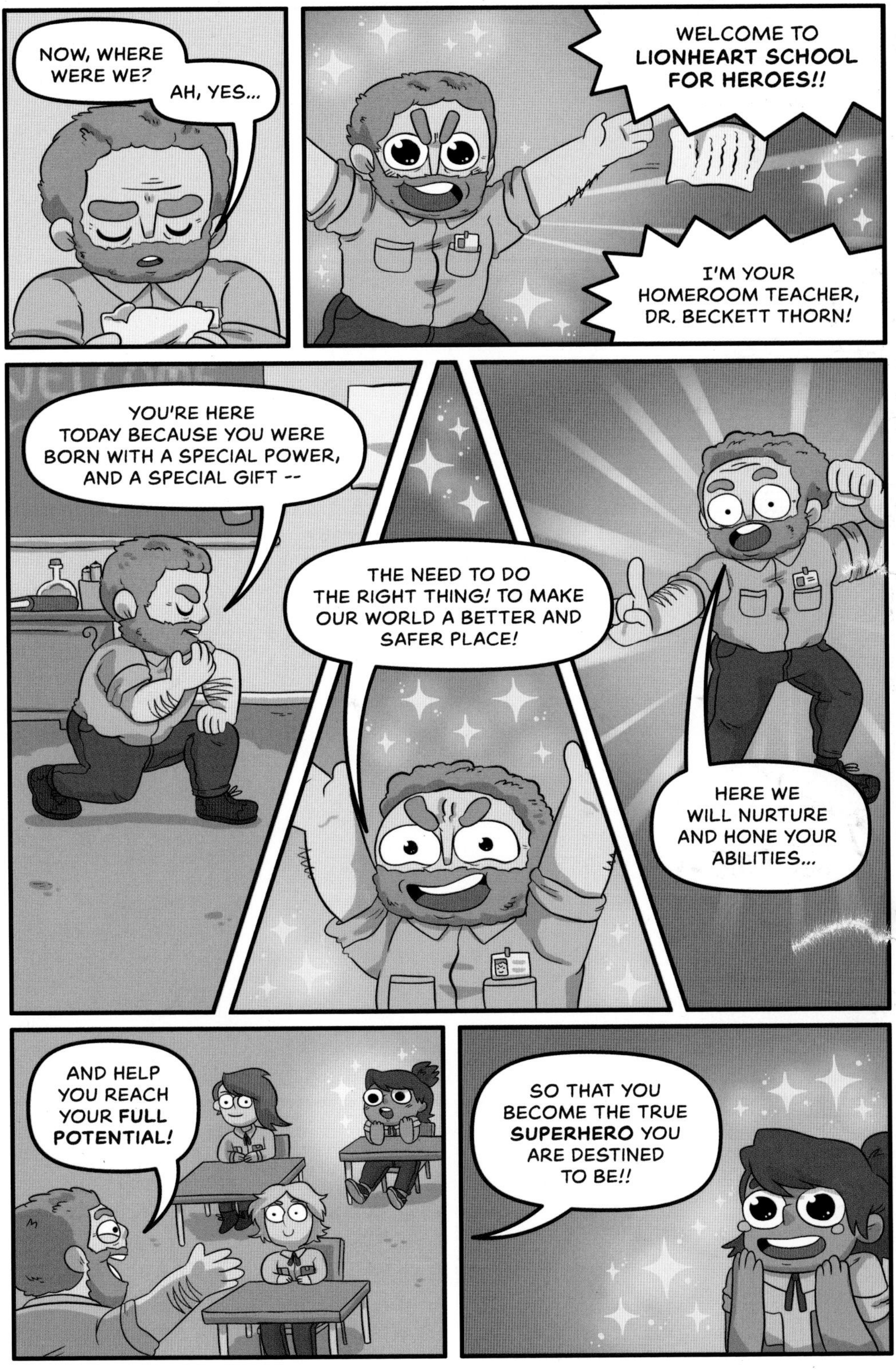
NOW, WHERE WERE WE?
AH, YES...
WELCOME TO **LIONHEART SCHOOL FOR HEROES!!**
I'M YOUR HOMEROOM TEACHER, DR. BECKETT THORN!
YOU'RE HERE TODAY BECAUSE YOU WERE BORN WITH A SPECIAL POWER, AND A SPECIAL GIFT --
THE NEED TO DO THE RIGHT THING! TO MAKE OUR WORLD A BETTER AND SAFER PLACE!
HERE WE WILL NURTURE AND HONE YOUR ABILITIES...
AND HELP YOU REACH YOUR **FULL POTENTIAL!**
SO THAT YOU BECOME THE TRUE **SUPERHERO** YOU ARE DESTINED TO BE!!

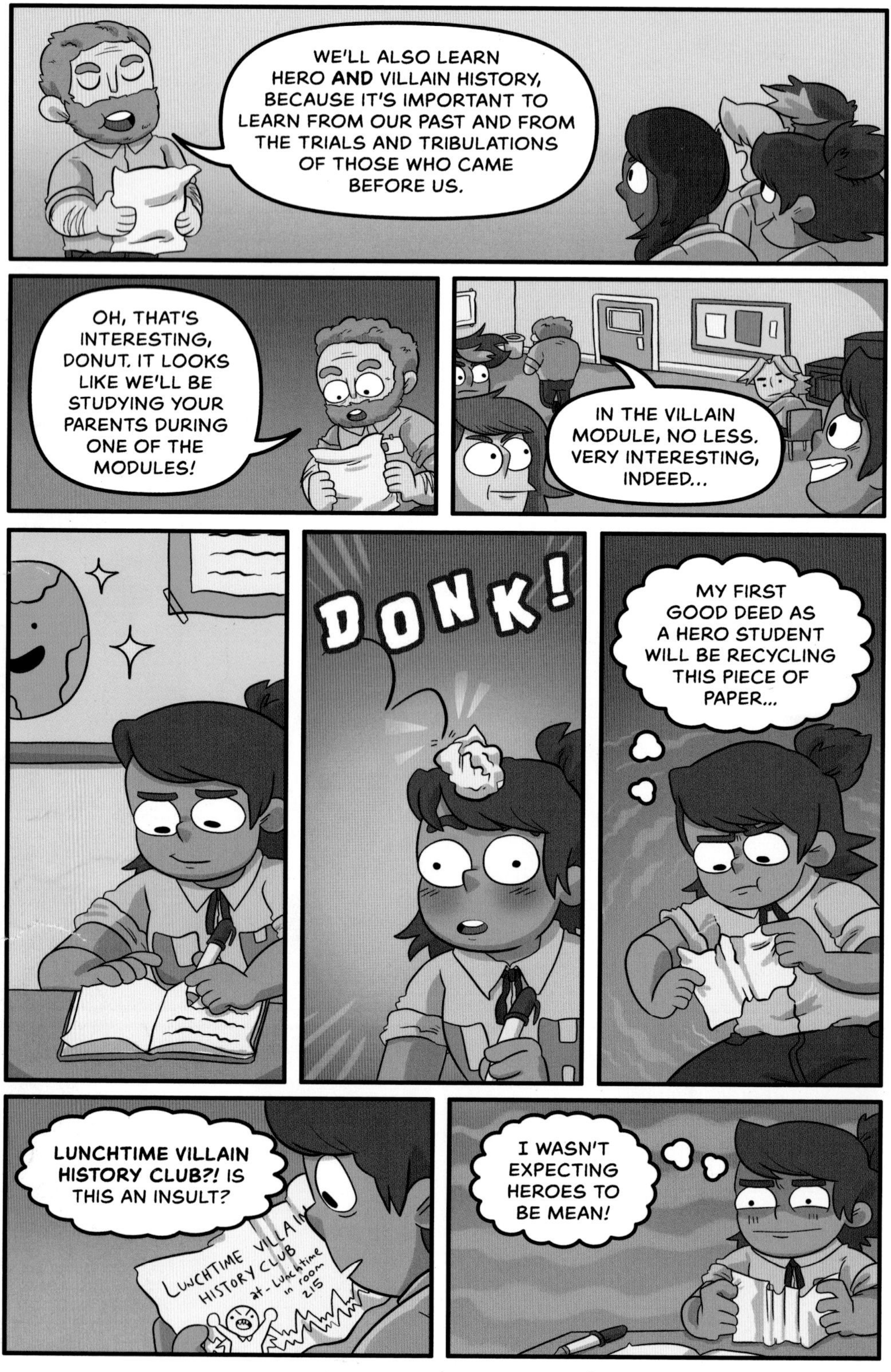
WE'LL ALSO LEARN HERO AND VILLAIN HISTORY, BECAUSE IT'S IMPORTANT TO LEARN FROM OUR PAST AND FROM THE TRIALS AND TRIBULATIONS OF THOSE WHO CAME BEFORE US.
OH, THAT'S INTERESTING, DONUT. IT LOOKS LIKE WE'LL BE STUDYING YOUR PARENTS DURING ONE OF THE MODULES!
IN THE VILLAIN MODULE, NO LESS. VERY INTERESTING, INDEED...
DONK!
MY FIRST GOOD DEED AS A HERO STUDENT WILL BE RECYCLING THIS PIECE OF PAPER...
LUNCHTIME VILLAIN HISTORY CLUB?! IS THIS AN INSULT?
LUNCHTIME VILLAIN HISTORY CLUB
at - Lunchtime in room 215
I WASN'T EXPECTING HEROES TO BE MEAN!

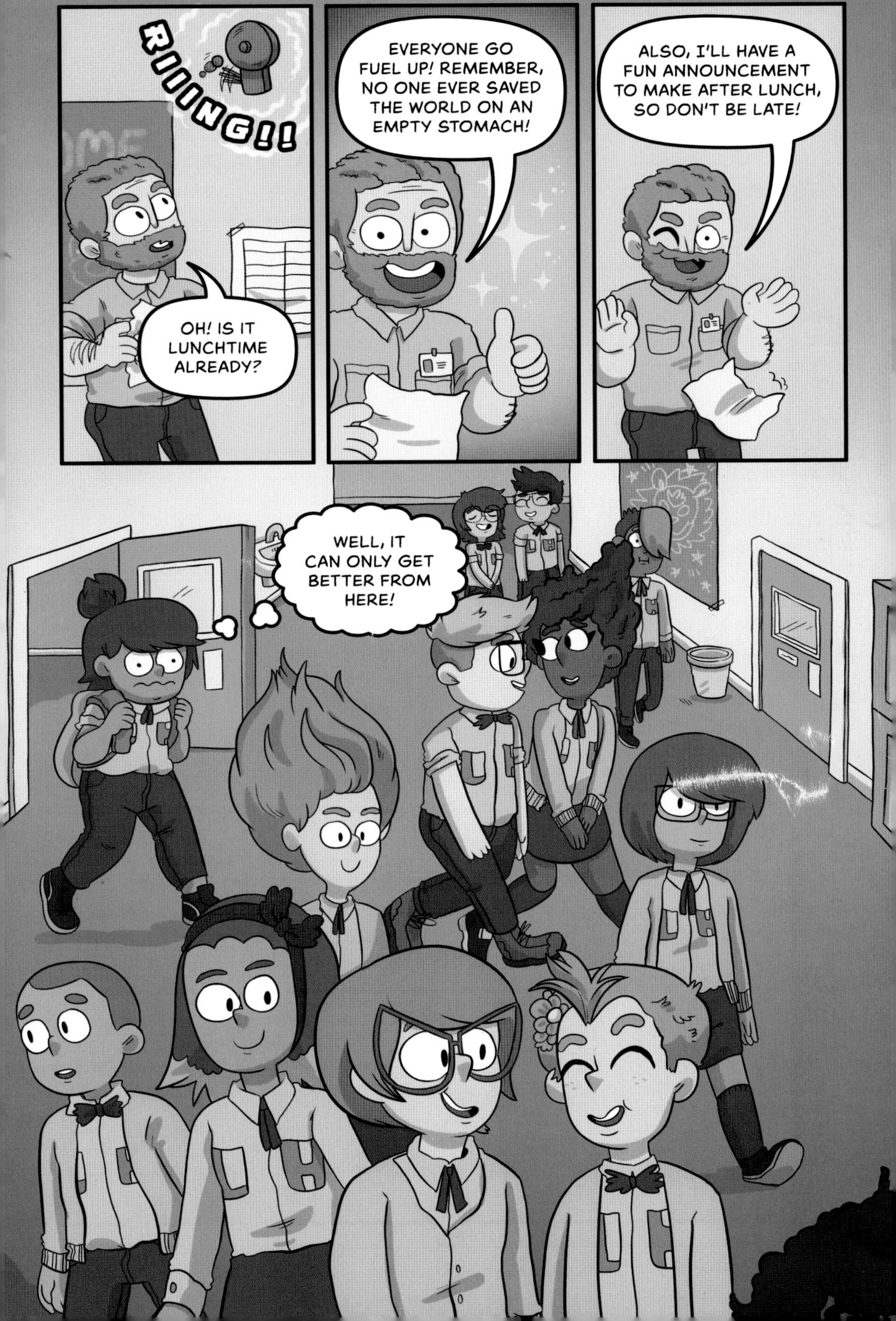
RIIING!!
OH! IS IT LUNCHTIME ALREADY?
EVERYONE GO FUEL UP! REMEMBER, NO ONE EVER SAVED THE WORLD ON AN EMPTY STOMACH!
ALSO, I'LL HAVE A FUN ANNOUNCEMENT TO MAKE AFTER LUNCH, SO DON'T BE LATE!
WELL, IT CAN ONLY GET BETTER FROM HERE!

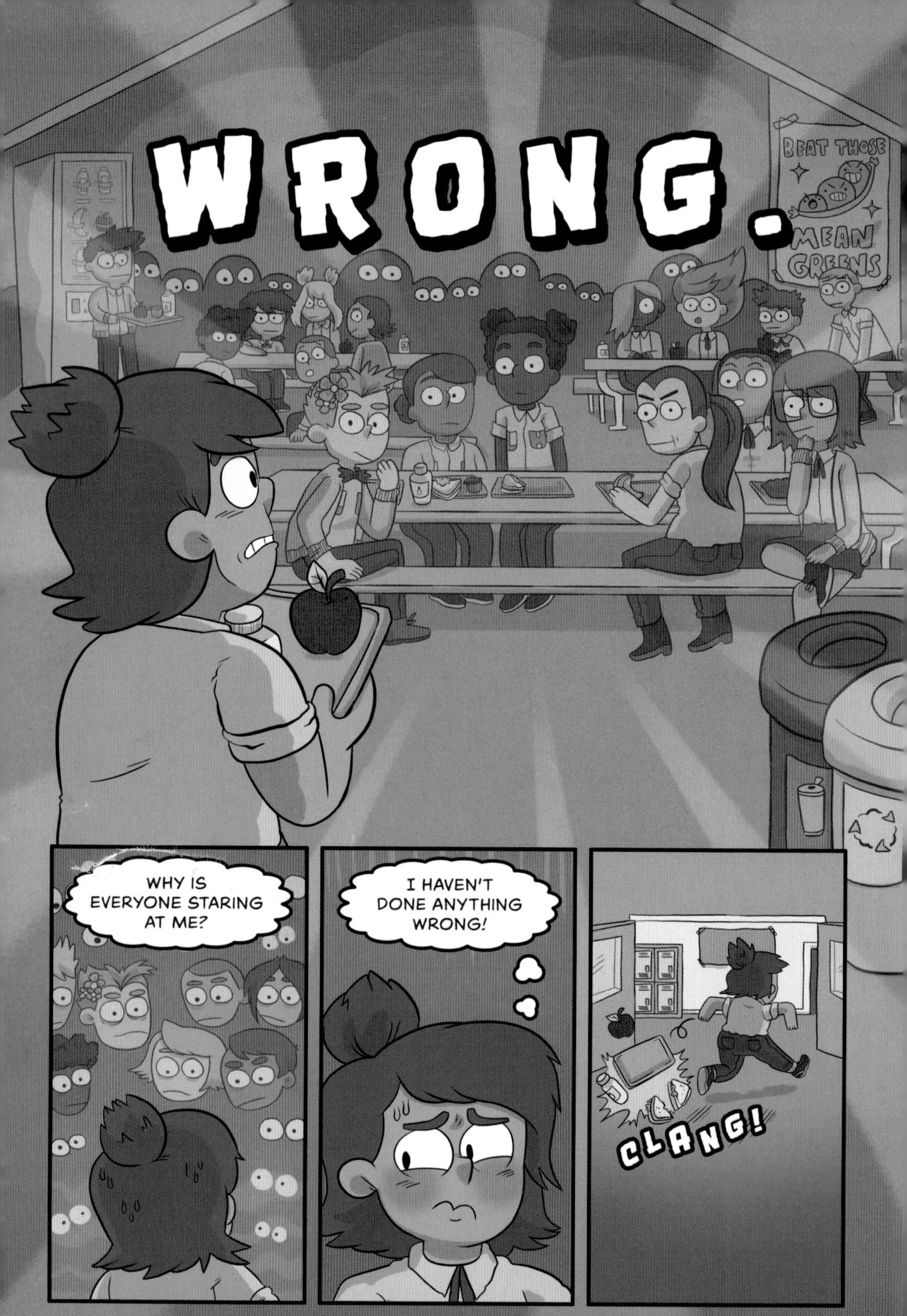
WRONG.
BEAT THOSE
MEAN GREENS
WHY IS EVERYONE STARING AT ME?
I HAVEN'T DONE ANYTHING WRONG!
CLANG!

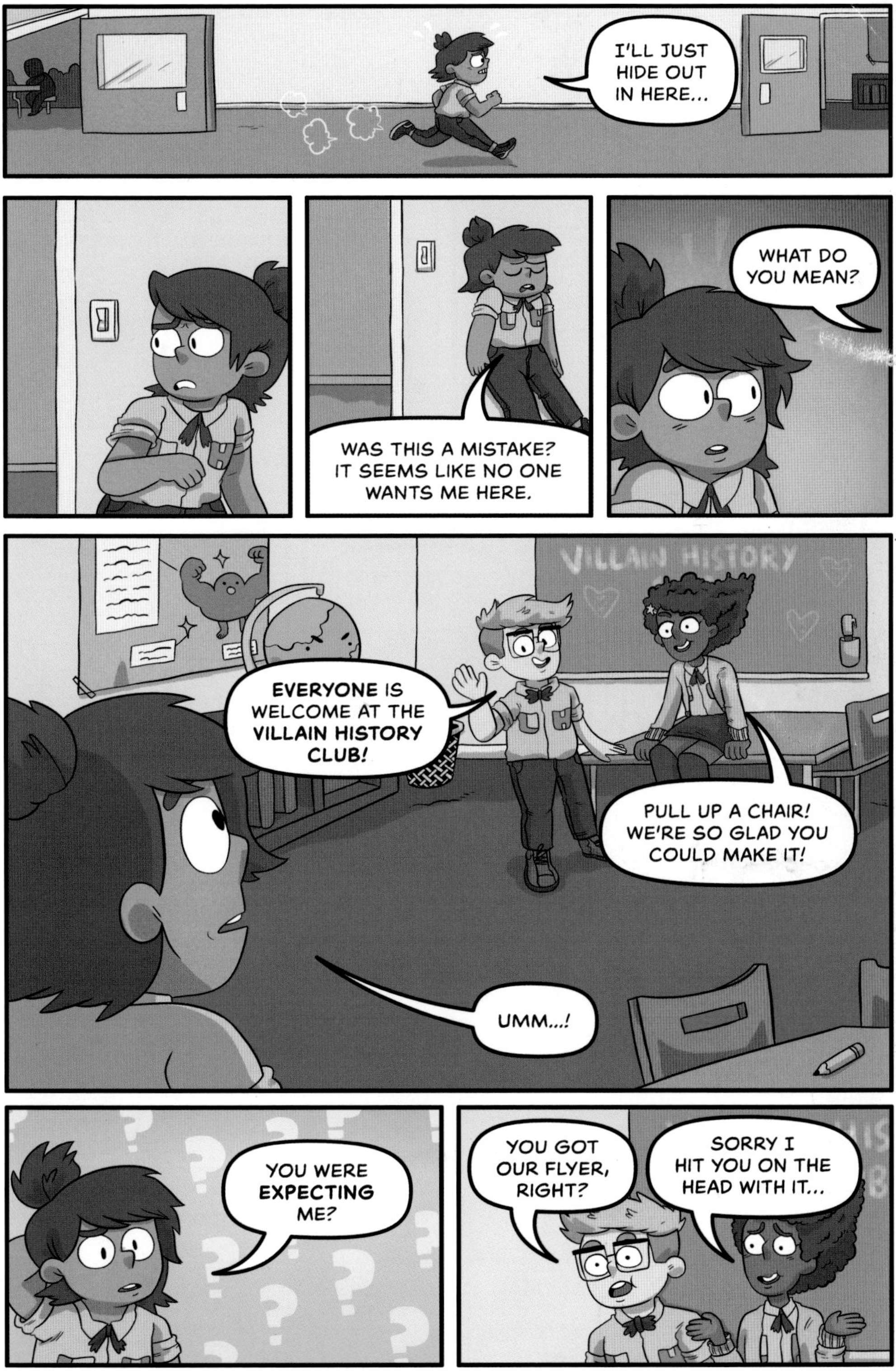
I'LL JUST HIDE OUT IN HERE...
WAS THIS A MISTAKE? IT SEEMS LIKE NO ONE WANTS ME HERE.
WHAT DO YOU MEAN?
VILLAIN HISTORY
EVERYONE IS WELCOME AT THE VILLAIN HISTORY CLUB!
PULL UP A CHAIR! WE'RE SO GLAD YOU COULD MAKE IT!
UMM...!
YOU WERE EXPECTING ME?
YOU GOT OUR FLYER, RIGHT?
SORRY I HIT YOU ON THE HEAD WITH IT...

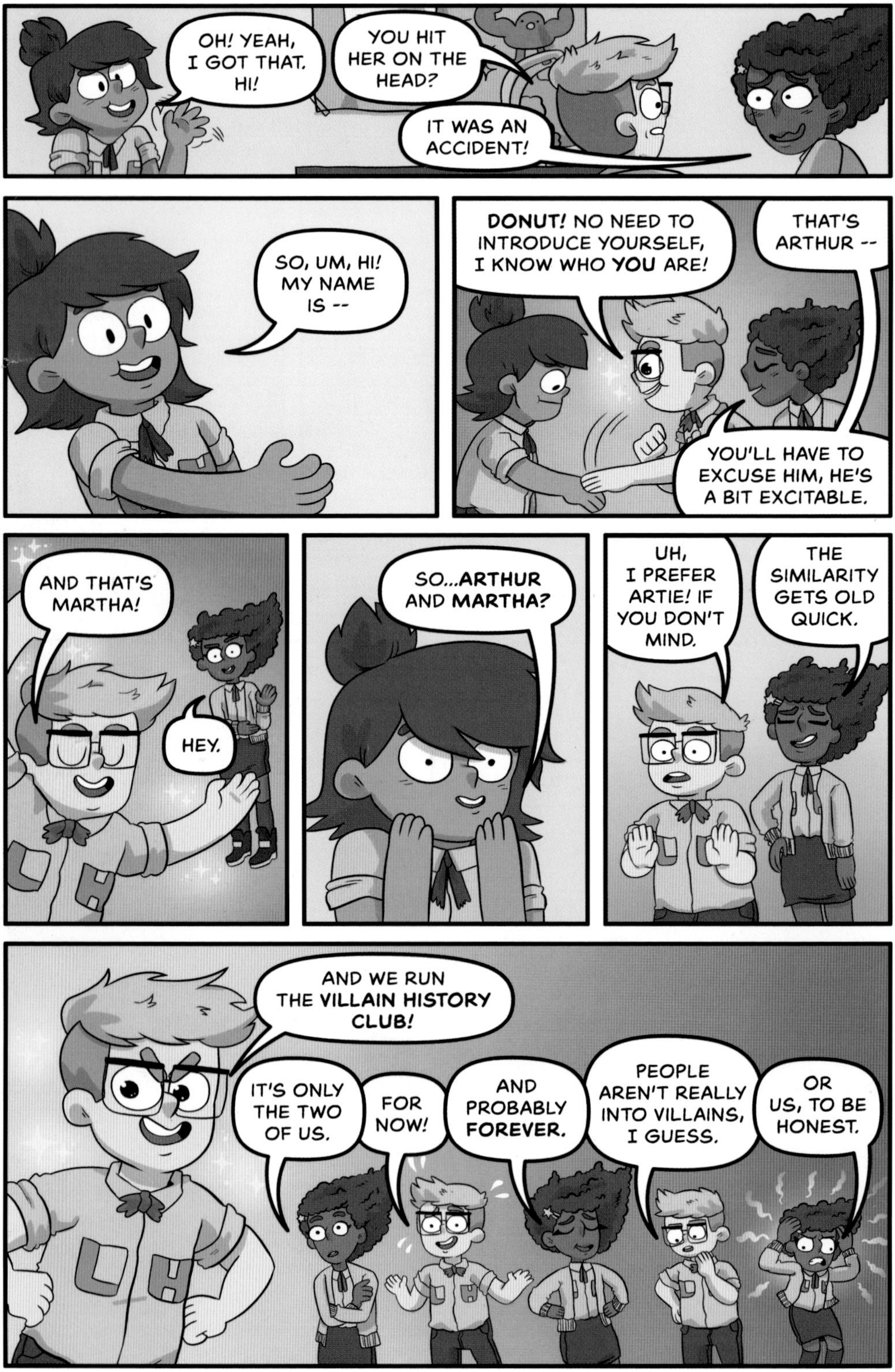

OH! YEAH, I GOT THAT. HI!
YOU HIT HER ON THE HEAD?
IT WAS AN ACCIDENT!
SO, UM, HI! MY NAME IS --
DONUT! NO NEED TO INTRODUCE YOURSELF, I KNOW WHO YOU ARE!
THAT'S ARTHUR --
YOU'LL HAVE TO EXCUSE HIM, HE'S A BIT EXCITABLE.
AND THAT'S MARTHA!
HEY.
SO...ARTHUR AND MARTHA?
UH, I PREFER ARTIE! IF YOU DON'T MIND.
THE SIMILARITY GETS OLD QUICK.
AND WE RUN THE VILLAIN HISTORY CLUB!
IT'S ONLY THE TWO OF US.
FOR NOW!
AND PROBABLY FOREVER.
PEOPLE AREN'T REALLY INTO VILLAINS, I GUESS.
OR US, TO BE HONEST.

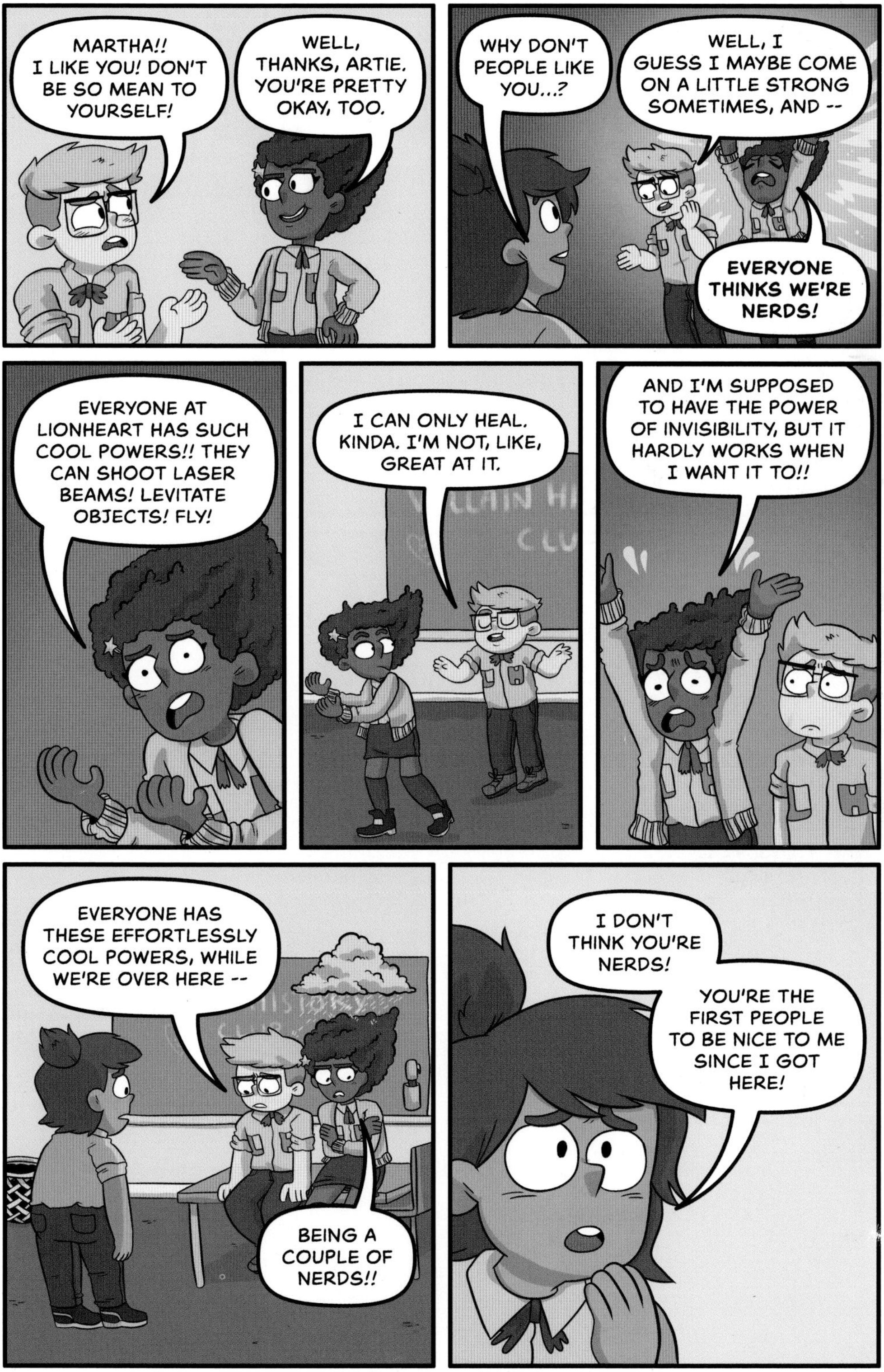

MARTHA!! I LIKE YOU! DON'T BE SO MEAN TO YOURSELF!
WELL, THANKS, ARTIE. YOU'RE PRETTY OKAY, TOO.
WHY DON'T PEOPLE LIKE YOU...?
WELL, I GUESS I MAYBE COME ON A LITTLE STRONG SOMETIMES, AND --
EVERYONE THINKS WE'RE NERDS!
EVERYONE AT LIONHEART HAS SUCH COOL POWERS!! THEY CAN SHOOT LASER BEAMS! LEVITATE OBJECTS! FLY!
I CAN ONLY HEAL. KINDA. I'M NOT, LIKE, GREAT AT IT.
AND I'M SUPPOSED TO HAVE THE POWER OF INVISIBILITY, BUT IT HARDLY WORKS WHEN I WANT IT TO!!
EVERYONE HAS THESE EFFORTLESSLY COOL POWERS, WHILE WE'RE OVER HERE --
BEING A COUPLE OF NERDS!!
I DON'T THINK YOU'RE NERDS!
YOU'RE THE FIRST PEOPLE TO BE NICE TO ME SINCE I GOT HERE!

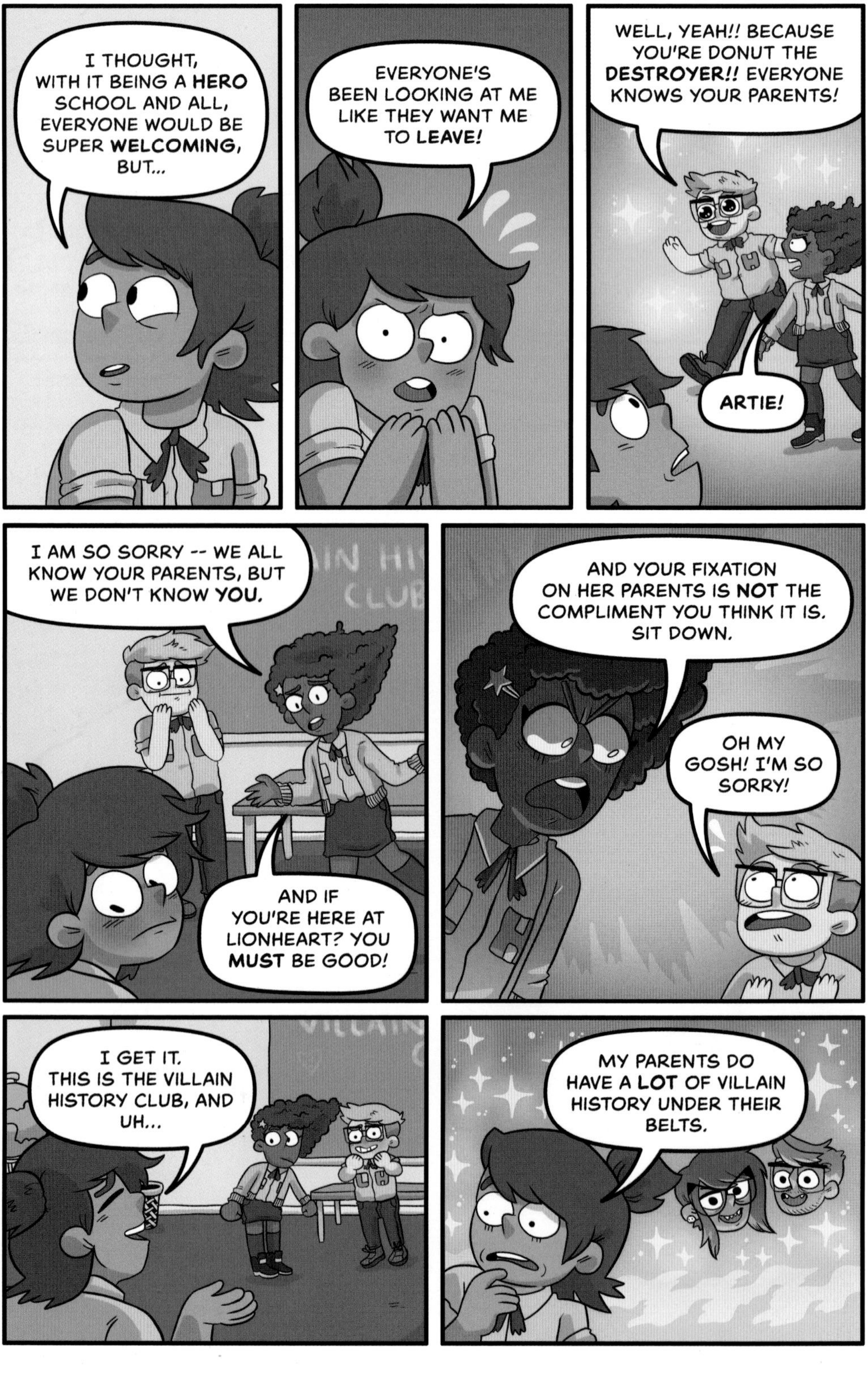
I THOUGHT, WITH IT BEING A HERO SCHOOL AND ALL, EVERYONE WOULD BE SUPER WELCOMING, BUT...
EVERYONE'S BEEN LOOKING AT ME LIKE THEY WANT ME TO LEAVE!
WELL, YEAH!! BECAUSE YOU'RE DONUT THE DESTROYER!! EVERYONE KNOWS YOUR PARENTS!
ARTIE!
I AM SO SORRY -- WE ALL KNOW YOUR PARENTS, BUT WE DON'T KNOW YOU.
AND IF YOU'RE HERE AT LIONHEART? YOU MUST BE GOOD!
AND YOUR FIXATION ON HER PARENTS IS NOT THE COMPLIMENT YOU THINK IT IS. SIT DOWN.
OH MY GOSH! I'M SO SORRY!
I GET IT. THIS IS THE VILLAIN HISTORY CLUB, AND UH...
MY PARENTS DO HAVE A LOT OF VILLAIN HISTORY UNDER THEIR BELTS.

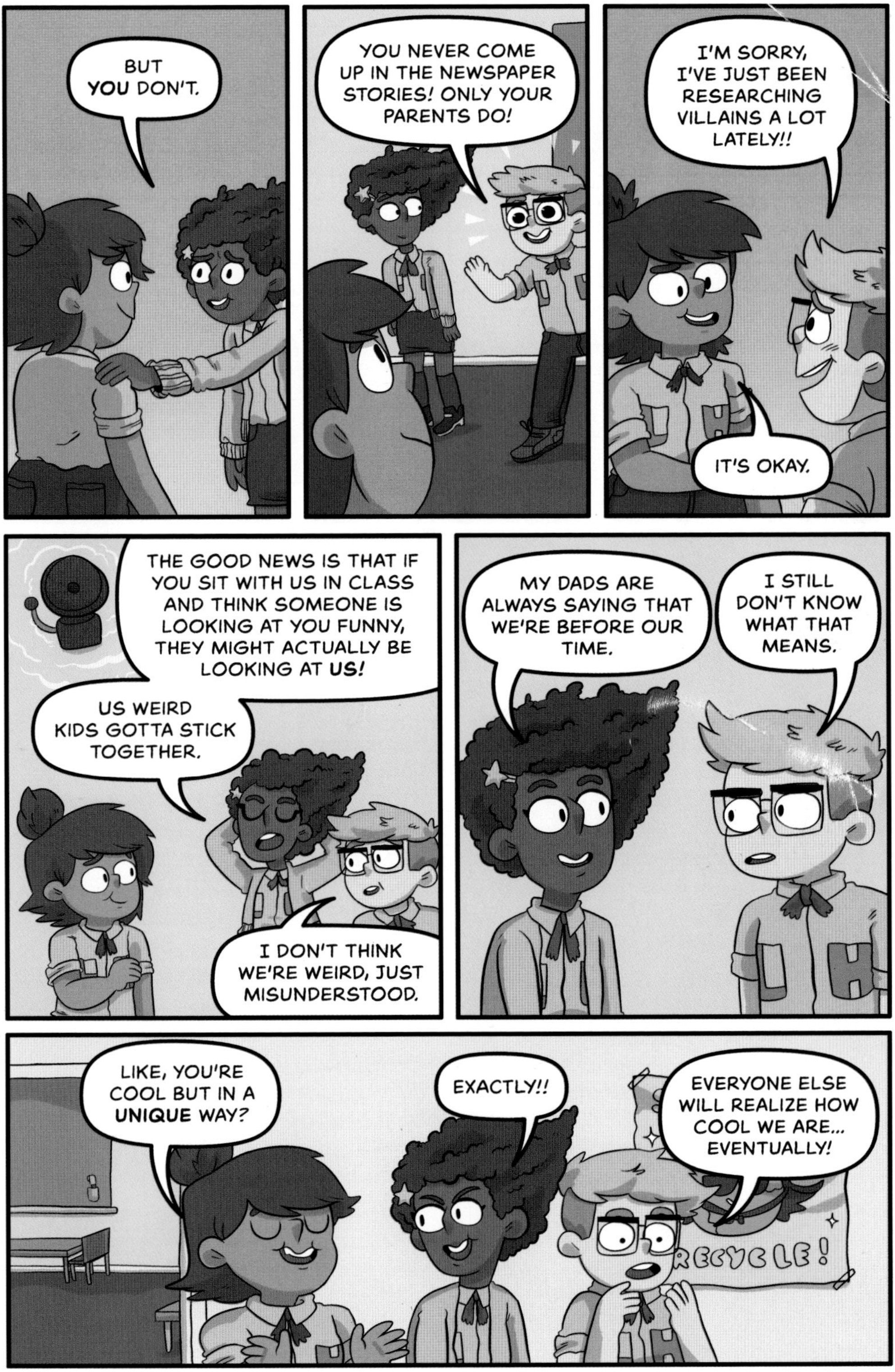
BUT YOU DON'T.
YOU NEVER COME UP IN THE NEWSPAPER STORIES! ONLY YOUR PARENTS DO!
I'M SORRY, I'VE JUST BEEN RESEARCHING VILLAINS A LOT LATELY!!
IT'S OKAY.
THE GOOD NEWS IS THAT IF YOU SIT WITH US IN CLASS AND THINK SOMEONE IS LOOKING AT YOU FUNNY, THEY MIGHT ACTUALLY BE LOOKING AT US!
US WEIRD KIDS GOTTA STICK TOGETHER.
I DON'T THINK WE'RE WEIRD, JUST MISUNDERSTOOD.
MY DADS ARE ALWAYS SAYING THAT WE'RE BEFORE OUR TIME.
I STILL DON'T KNOW WHAT THAT MEANS.
LIKE, YOU'RE COOL BUT IN A UNIQUE WAY?
EXACTLY!!
EVERYONE ELSE WILL REALIZE HOW COOL WE ARE... EVENTUALLY!
RECYCLE!

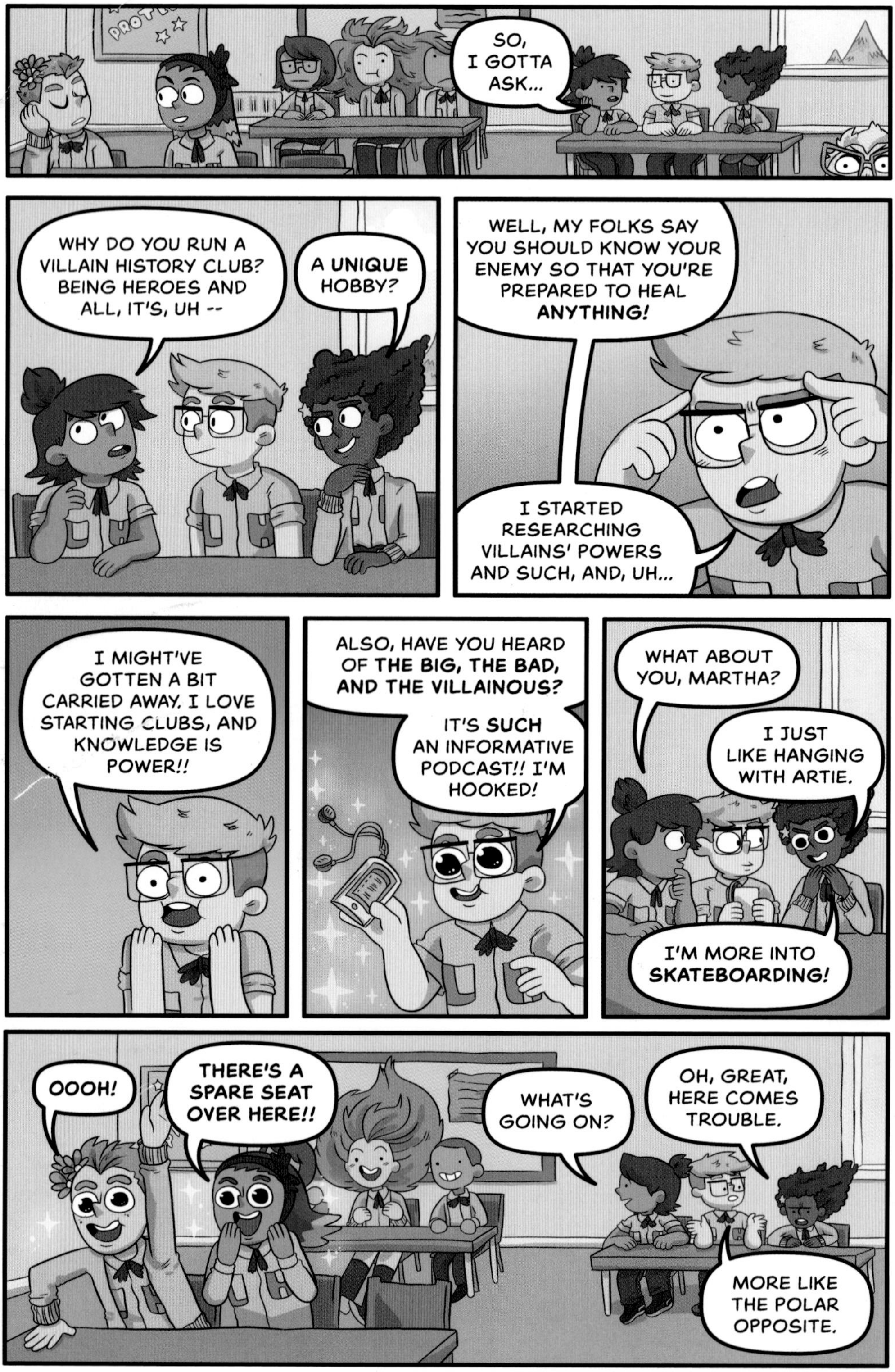

PROTE
SO, I GOTTA ASK...
WHY DO YOU RUN A VILLAIN HISTORY CLUB? BEING HEROES AND ALL, IT'S, UH --
A **UNIQUE** HOBBY?
WELL, MY FOLKS SAY YOU SHOULD KNOW YOUR ENEMY SO THAT YOU'RE PREPARED TO HEAL **ANYTHING!**
I STARTED RESEARCHING VILLAINS' POWERS AND SUCH, AND, UH...
I MIGHT'VE GOTTEN A BIT CARRIED AWAY. I LOVE STARTING CLUBS, AND KNOWLEDGE IS POWER!!
ALSO, HAVE YOU HEARD OF **THE BIG, THE BAD, AND THE VILLAINOUS?**
IT'S **SUCH** AN INFORMATIVE PODCAST!! I'M HOOKED!
WHAT ABOUT YOU, MARTHA?
I JUST LIKE HANGING WITH ARTIE.
I'M MORE INTO **SKATEBOARDING!**
OOOH!
THERE'S A SPARE SEAT OVER HERE!!
WHAT'S GOING ON?
OH, GREAT, HERE COMES TROUBLE.
MORE LIKE THE POLAR OPPOSITE.

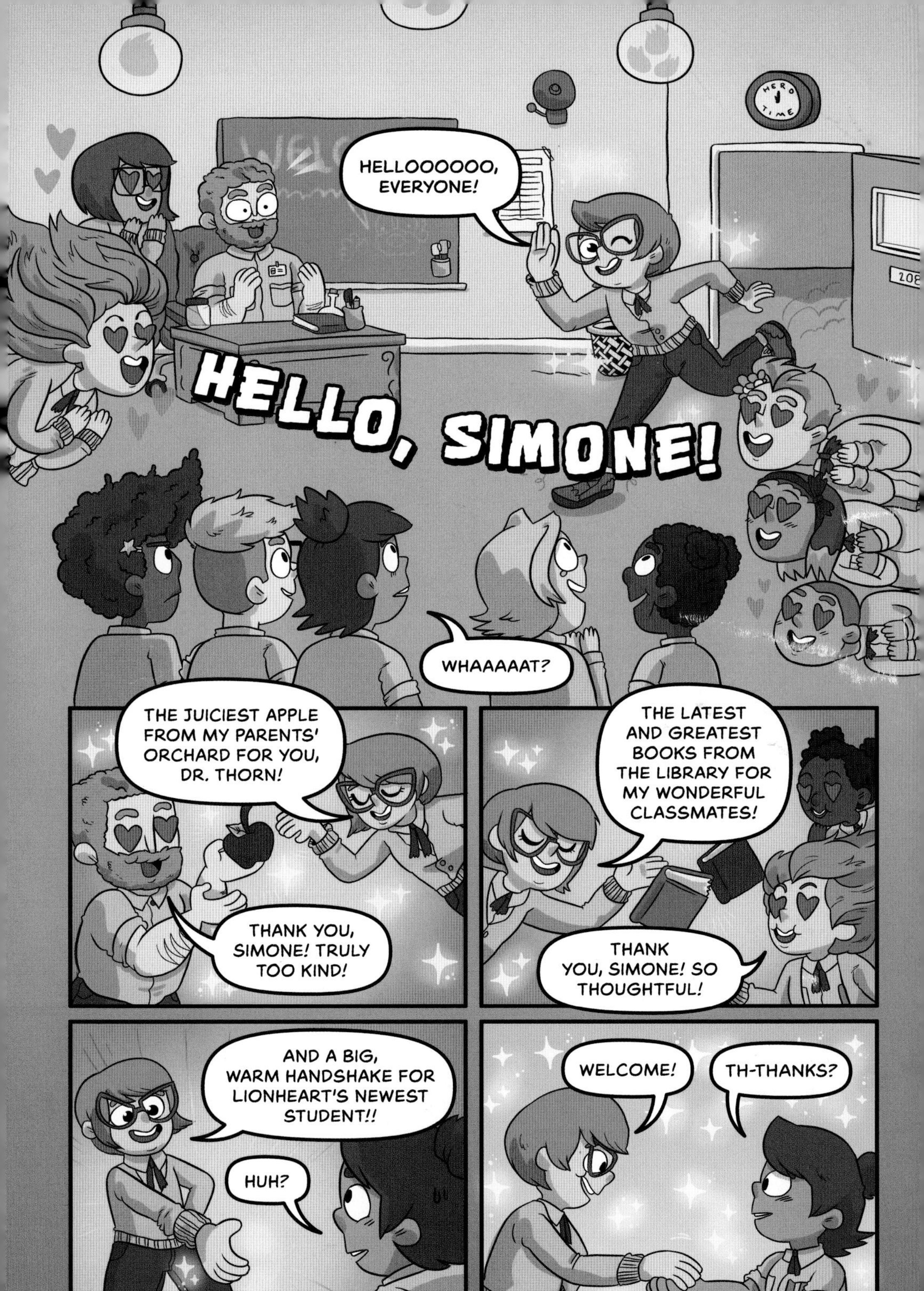
HELLOOOOOO, EVERYONE!
HELLO, SIMONE!
WHAAAAAT?
THE JUICIEST APPLE FROM MY PARENTS' ORCHARD FOR YOU, DR. THORN!
THANK YOU, SIMONE! TRULY TOO KIND!
THE LATEST AND GREATEST BOOKS FROM THE LIBRARY FOR MY WONDERFUL CLASSMATES!
THANK YOU, SIMONE! SO THOUGHTFUL!
AND A BIG, WARM HANDSHAKE FOR LIONHEART'S NEWEST STUDENT!!
HUH?
WELCOME!
TH-THANKS?

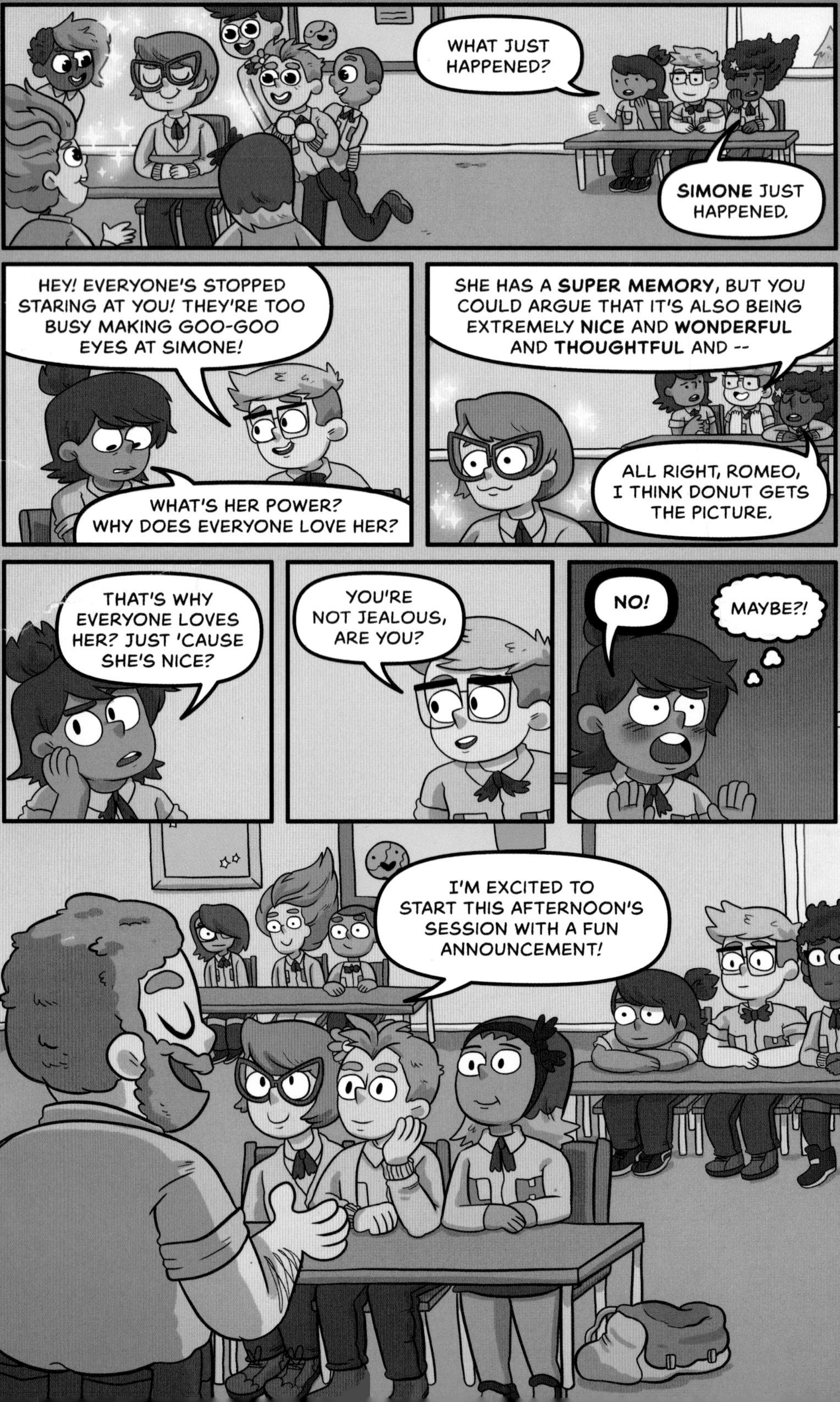
WHAT JUST HAPPENED?
SIMONE JUST HAPPENED.
HEY! EVERYONE'S STOPPED STARING AT YOU! THEY'RE TOO BUSY MAKING GOO-GOO EYES AT SIMONE!
WHAT'S HER POWER? WHY DOES EVERYONE LOVE HER?
SHE HAS A SUPER MEMORY, BUT YOU COULD ARGUE THAT IT'S ALSO BEING EXTREMELY NICE AND WONDERFUL AND THOUGHTFUL AND --
ALL RIGHT, ROMEO, I THINK DONUT GETS THE PICTURE.
THAT'S WHY EVERYONE LOVES HER? JUST 'CAUSE SHE'S NICE?
YOU'RE NOT JEALOUS, ARE YOU?
NO!
MAYBE?!
I'M EXCITED TO START THIS AFTERNOON'S SESSION WITH A FUN ANNOUNCEMENT!

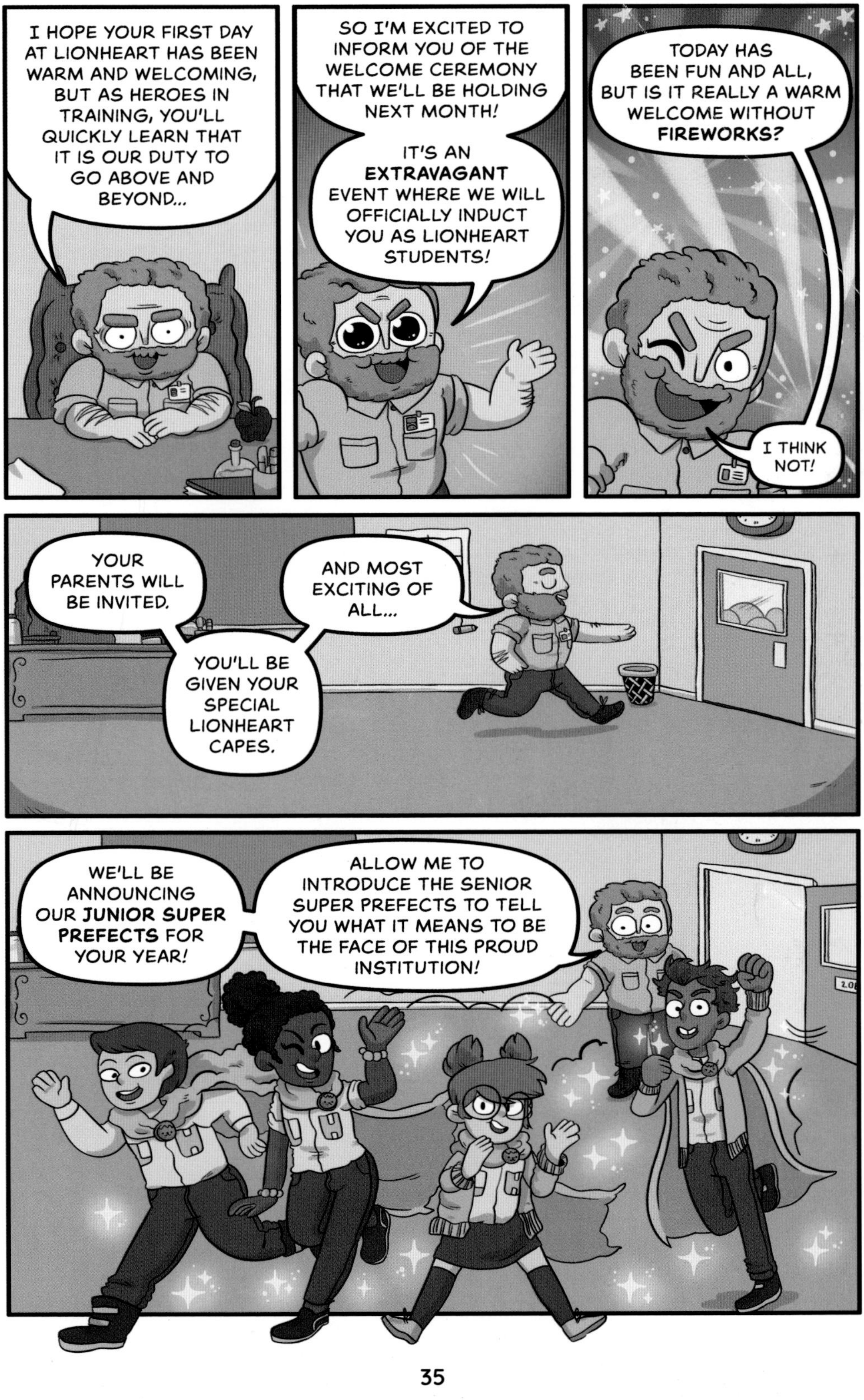
I HOPE YOUR FIRST DAY AT LIONHEART HAS BEEN WARM AND WELCOMING, BUT AS HEROES IN TRAINING, YOU'LL QUICKLY LEARN THAT IT IS OUR DUTY TO GO ABOVE AND BEYOND...
SO I'M EXCITED TO INFORM YOU OF THE WELCOME CEREMONY THAT WE'LL BE HOLDING NEXT MONTH!
IT'S AN **EXTRAVAGANT** EVENT WHERE WE WILL OFFICIALLY INDUCT YOU AS LIONHEART STUDENTS!
TODAY HAS BEEN FUN AND ALL, BUT IS IT REALLY A WARM WELCOME WITHOUT **FIREWORKS?**
I THINK NOT!
YOUR PARENTS WILL BE INVITED.
AND MOST EXCITING OF ALL...
YOU'LL BE GIVEN YOUR SPECIAL LIONHEART CAPES.
WE'LL BE ANNOUNCING OUR **JUNIOR SUPER PREFECTS** FOR YOUR YEAR!
ALLOW ME TO INTRODUCE THE SENIOR SUPER PREFECTS TO TELL YOU WHAT IT MEANS TO BE THE FACE OF THIS PROUD INSTITUTION!

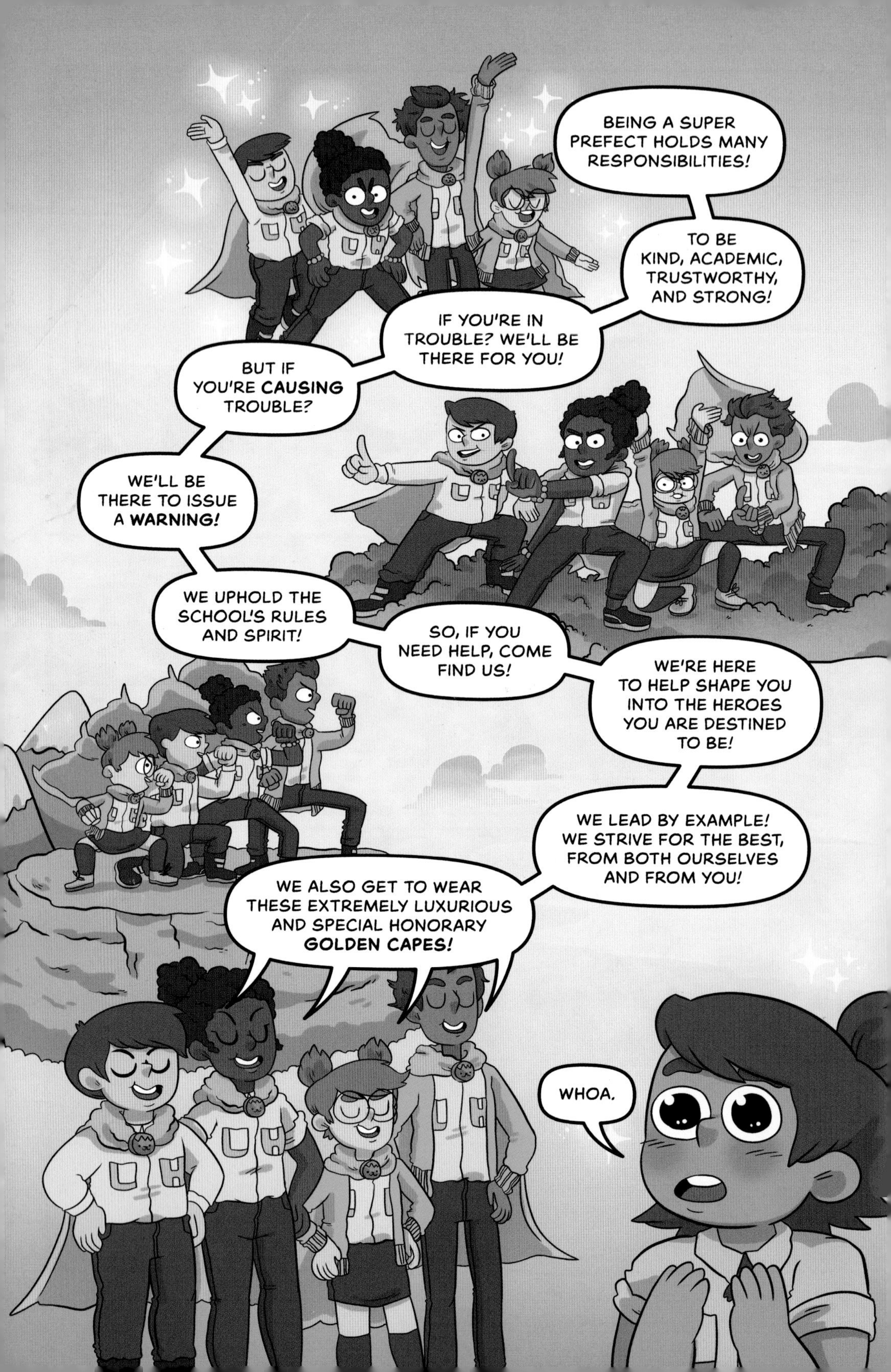
BEING A SUPER PREFECT HOLDS MANY RESPONSIBILITIES!
TO BE KIND, ACADEMIC, TRUSTWORTHY, AND STRONG!
IF YOU'RE IN TROUBLE? WE'LL BE THERE FOR YOU!
BUT IF YOU'RE **CAUSING** TROUBLE?
WE'LL BE THERE TO ISSUE A **WARNING!**
WE UPHOLD THE SCHOOL'S RULES AND SPIRIT!
SO, IF YOU NEED HELP, COME FIND US!
WE'RE HERE TO HELP SHAPE YOU INTO THE HEROES YOU ARE DESTINED TO BE!
WE LEAD BY EXAMPLE! WE STRIVE FOR THE BEST, FROM BOTH OURSELVES AND FROM YOU!
WE ALSO GET TO WEAR THESE EXTREMELY LUXURIOUS AND SPECIAL HONORARY **GOLDEN CAPES!**
WHOA.

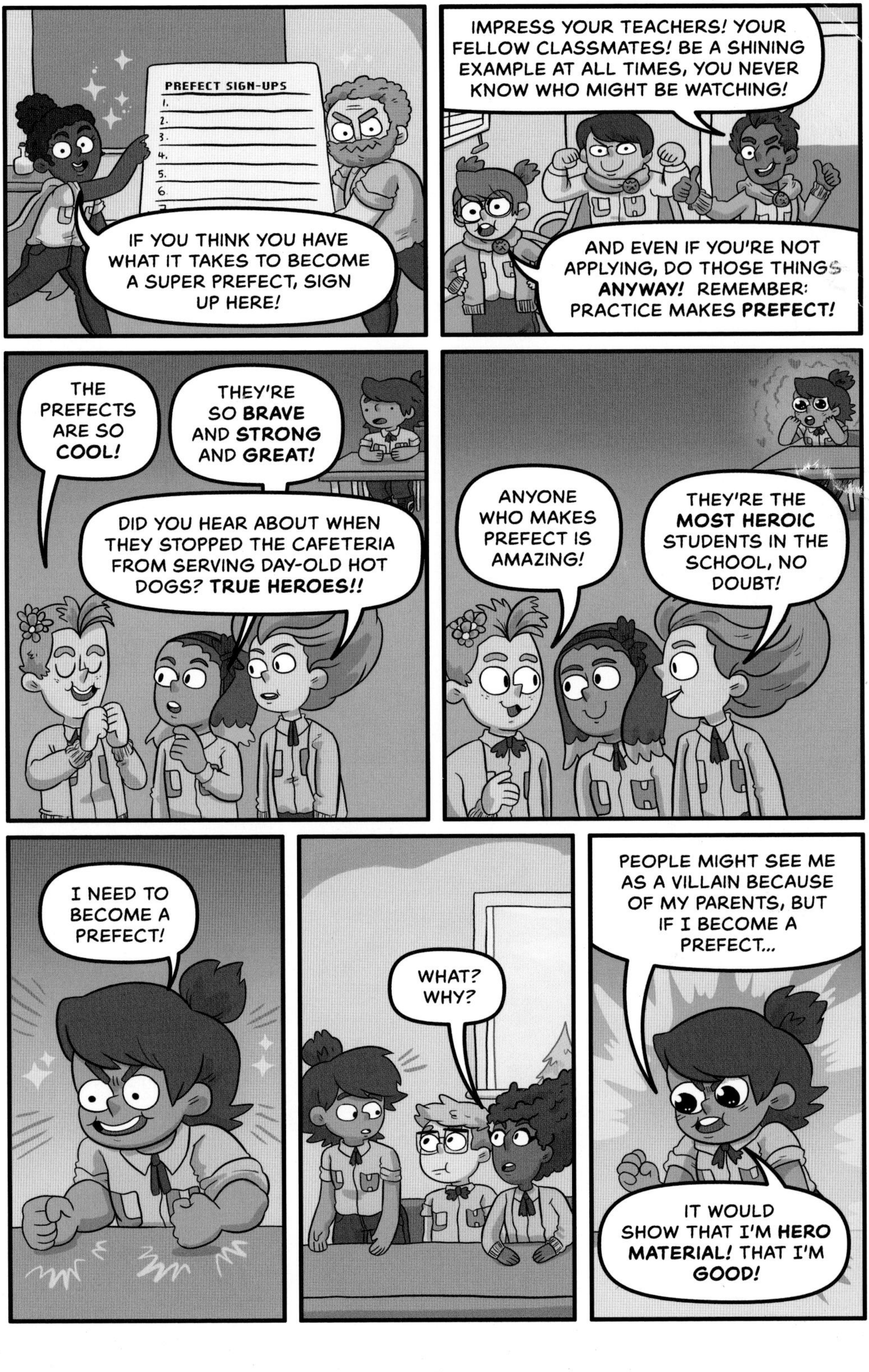
PREFECT SIGN-UPS
1.
2.
3.
4.
5.
6.
IF YOU THINK YOU HAVE WHAT IT TAKES TO BECOME A SUPER PREFECT, SIGN UP HERE!
IMPRESS YOUR TEACHERS! YOUR FELLOW CLASSMATES! BE A SHINING EXAMPLE AT ALL TIMES, YOU NEVER KNOW WHO MIGHT BE WATCHING!
AND EVEN IF YOU'RE NOT APPLYING, DO THOSE THINGS ANYWAY! REMEMBER: PRACTICE MAKES PREFECT!
THE PREFECTS ARE SO COOL!
THEY'RE SO BRAVE AND STRONG AND GREAT!
DID YOU HEAR ABOUT WHEN THEY STOPPED THE CAFETERIA FROM SERVING DAY-OLD HOT DOGS? TRUE HEROES!!
ANYONE WHO MAKES PREFECT IS AMAZING!
THEY'RE THE MOST HEROIC STUDENTS IN THE SCHOOL, NO DOUBT!
I NEED TO BECOME A PREFECT!
WHAT? WHY?
PEOPLE MIGHT SEE ME AS A VILLAIN BECAUSE OF MY PARENTS, BUT IF I BECOME A PREFECT...
IT WOULD SHOW THAT I'M HERO MATERIAL! THAT I'M GOOD!

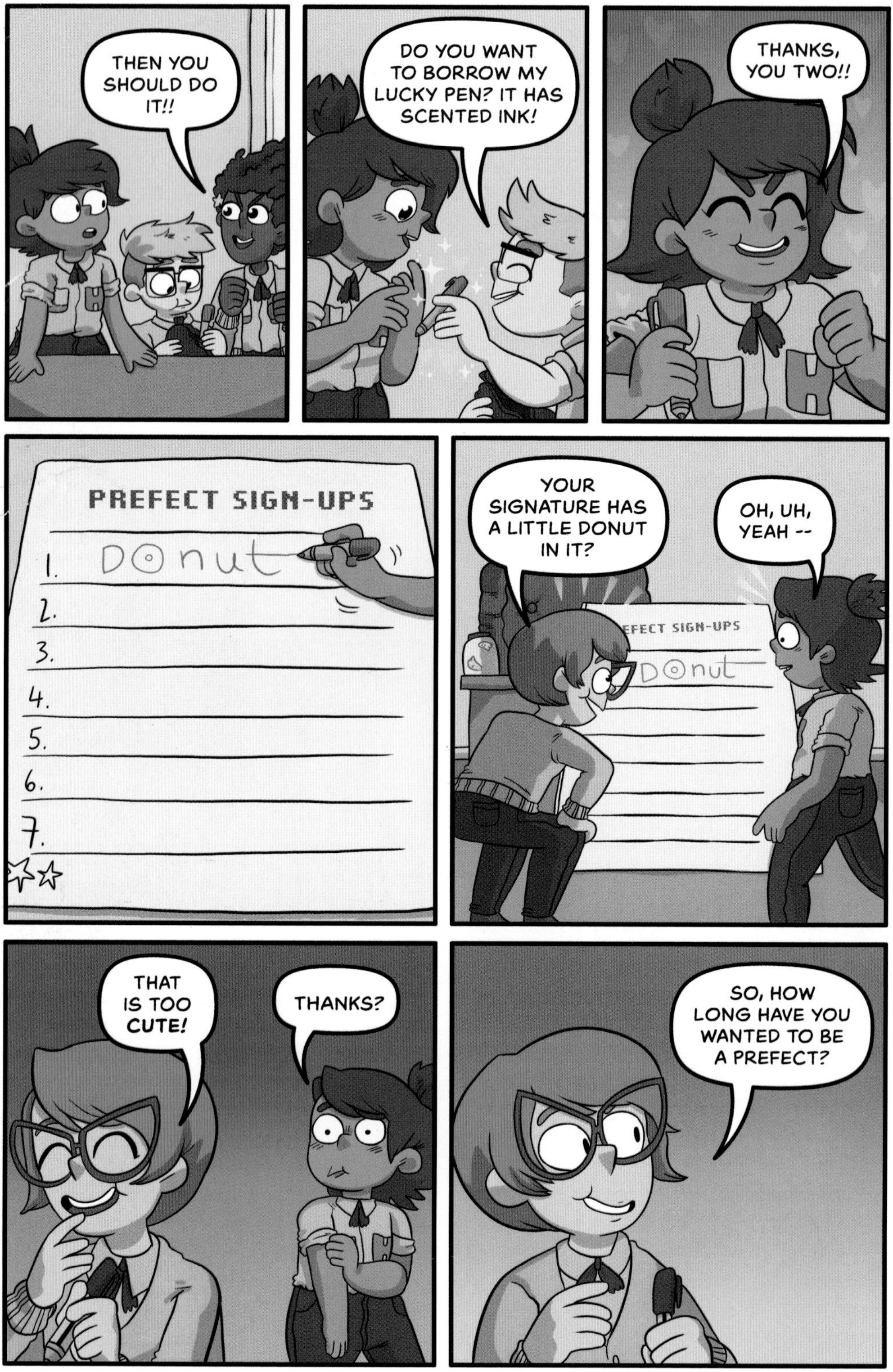
THEN YOU SHOULD DO IT!!
DO YOU WANT TO BORROW MY LUCKY PEN? IT HAS SCENTED INK!
THANKS, YOU TWO!!
PREFECT SIGN-UPS
1. DOnut
2.
3.
4.
5.
6.
7.
YOUR SIGNATURE HAS A LITTLE DONUT IN IT?
OH, UH, YEAH --
THAT IS TOO CUTE!
THANKS?
SO, HOW LONG HAVE YOU WANTED TO BE A PREFECT?

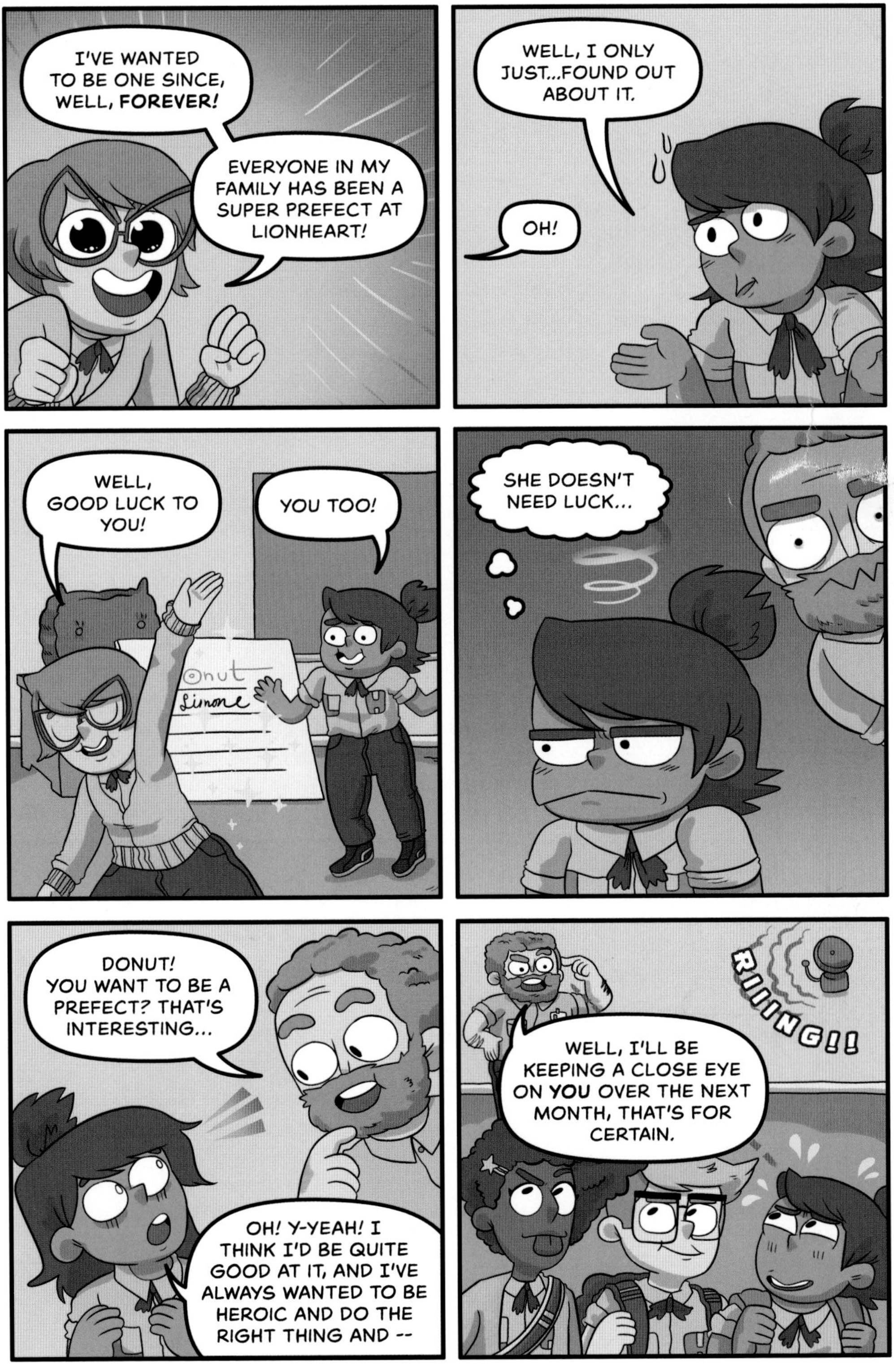
I'VE WANTED TO BE ONE SINCE, WELL, **FOREVER!**
EVERYONE IN MY FAMILY HAS BEEN A SUPER PREFECT AT LIONHEART!
WELL, I ONLY JUST...FOUND OUT ABOUT IT.
OH!
WELL, GOOD LUCK TO YOU!
YOU TOO!
Donut
Limone
SHE DOESN'T NEED LUCK...
DONUT! YOU WANT TO BE A PREFECT? THAT'S INTERESTING...
OH! Y-YEAH! I THINK I'D BE QUITE GOOD AT IT, AND I'VE ALWAYS WANTED TO BE HEROIC AND DO THE RIGHT THING AND --
RIIIING!!
WELL, I'LL BE KEEPING A CLOSE EYE ON **YOU** OVER THE NEXT MONTH, THAT'S FOR CERTAIN.

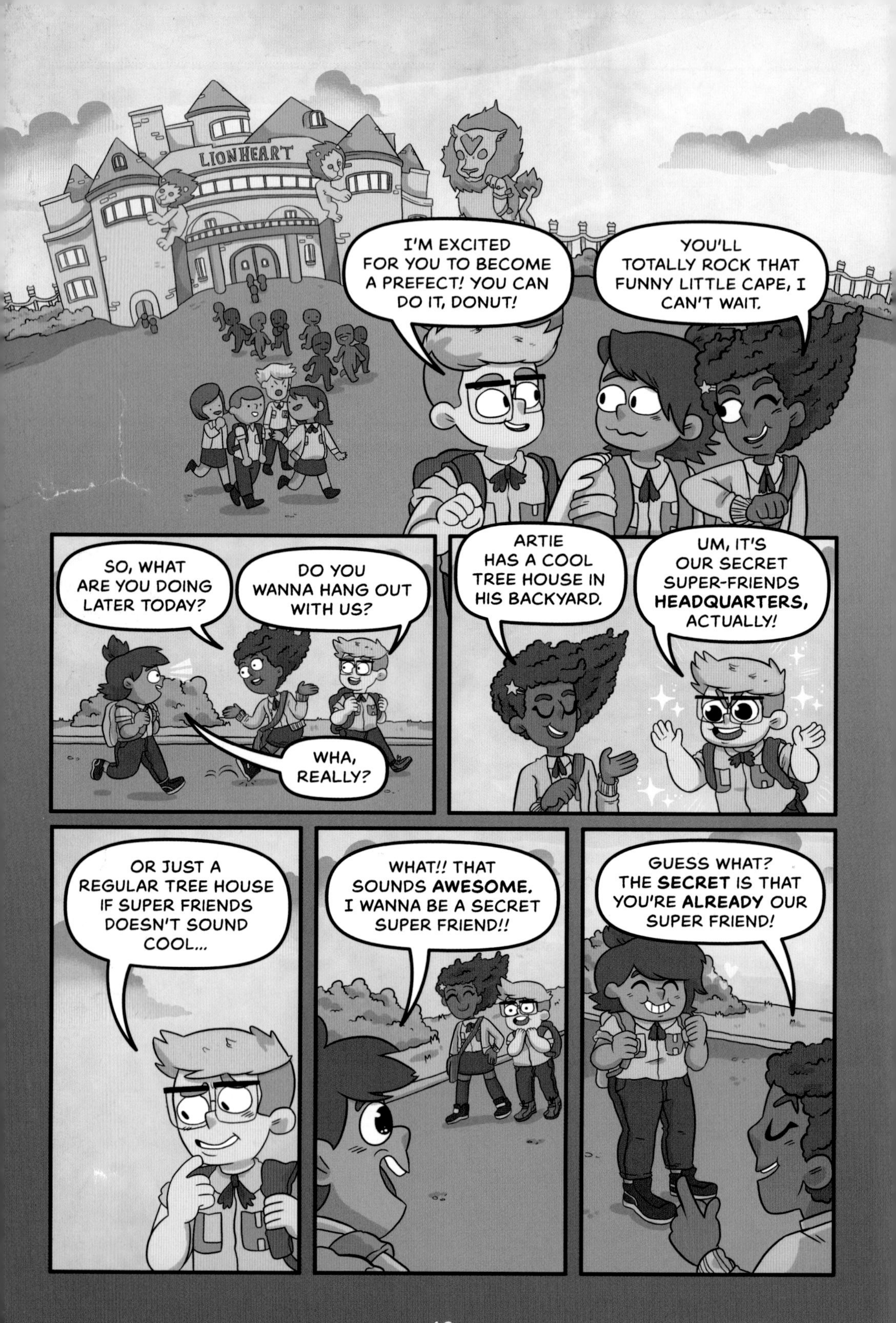
LIONHEART
I'M EXCITED FOR YOU TO BECOME A PREFECT! YOU CAN DO IT, DONUT!
YOU'LL TOTALLY ROCK THAT FUNNY LITTLE CAPE, I CAN'T WAIT.
SO, WHAT ARE YOU DOING LATER TODAY?
DO YOU WANNA HANG OUT WITH US?
WHA, REALLY?
ARTIE HAS A COOL TREE HOUSE IN HIS BACKYARD.
UM, IT'S OUR SECRET SUPER-FRIENDS **HEADQUARTERS,** ACTUALLY!
OR JUST A REGULAR TREE HOUSE IF SUPER FRIENDS DOESN'T SOUND COOL...
WHAT!! THAT SOUNDS **AWESOME.** I WANNA BE A SECRET SUPER FRIEND!!
GUESS WHAT? THE **SECRET** IS THAT YOU'RE **ALREADY** OUR SUPER FRIEND!

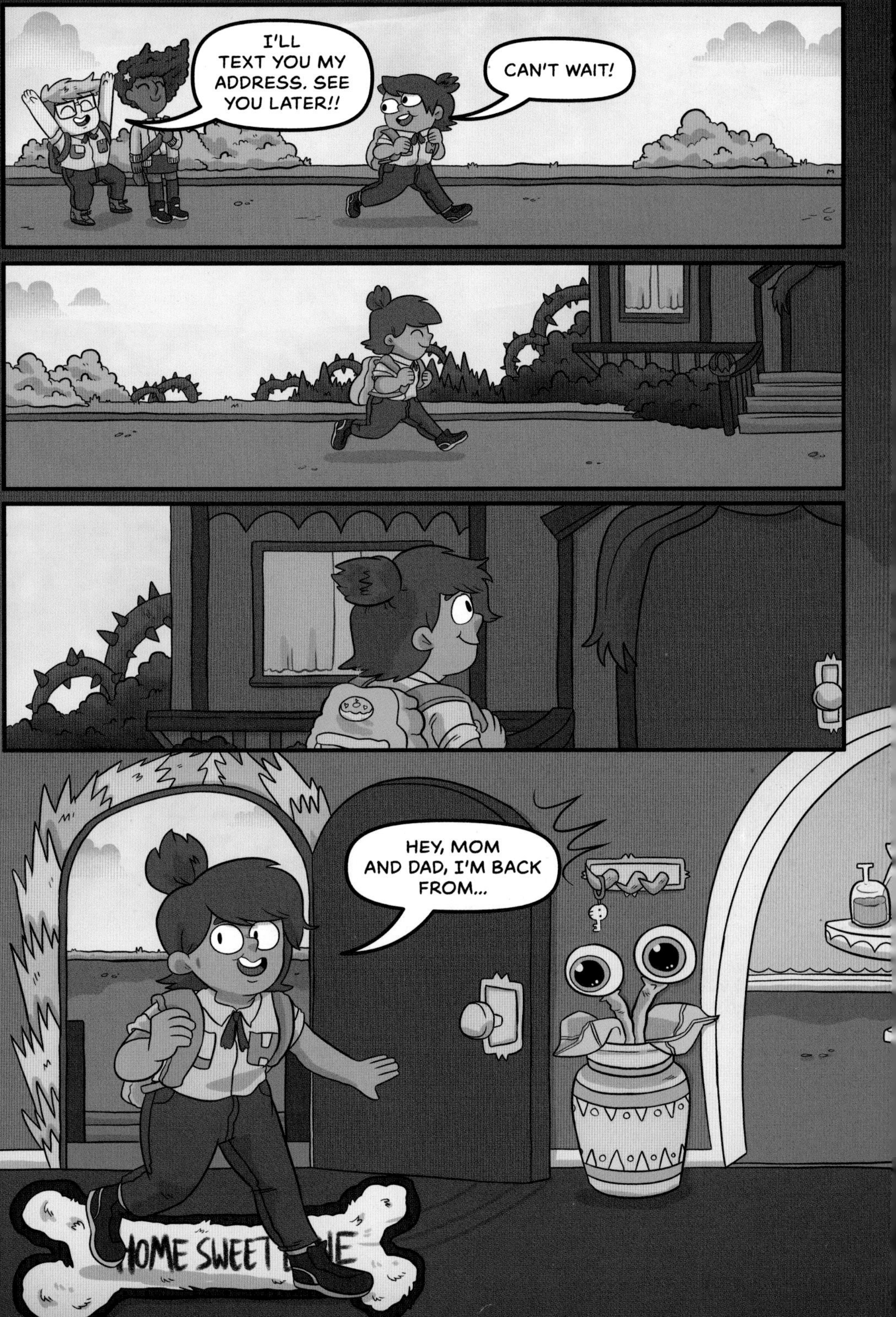
I'LL TEXT YOU MY ADDRESS. SEE YOU LATER!!
CAN'T WAIT!
HEY, MOM AND DAD, I'M BACK FROM...
HOME SWEET

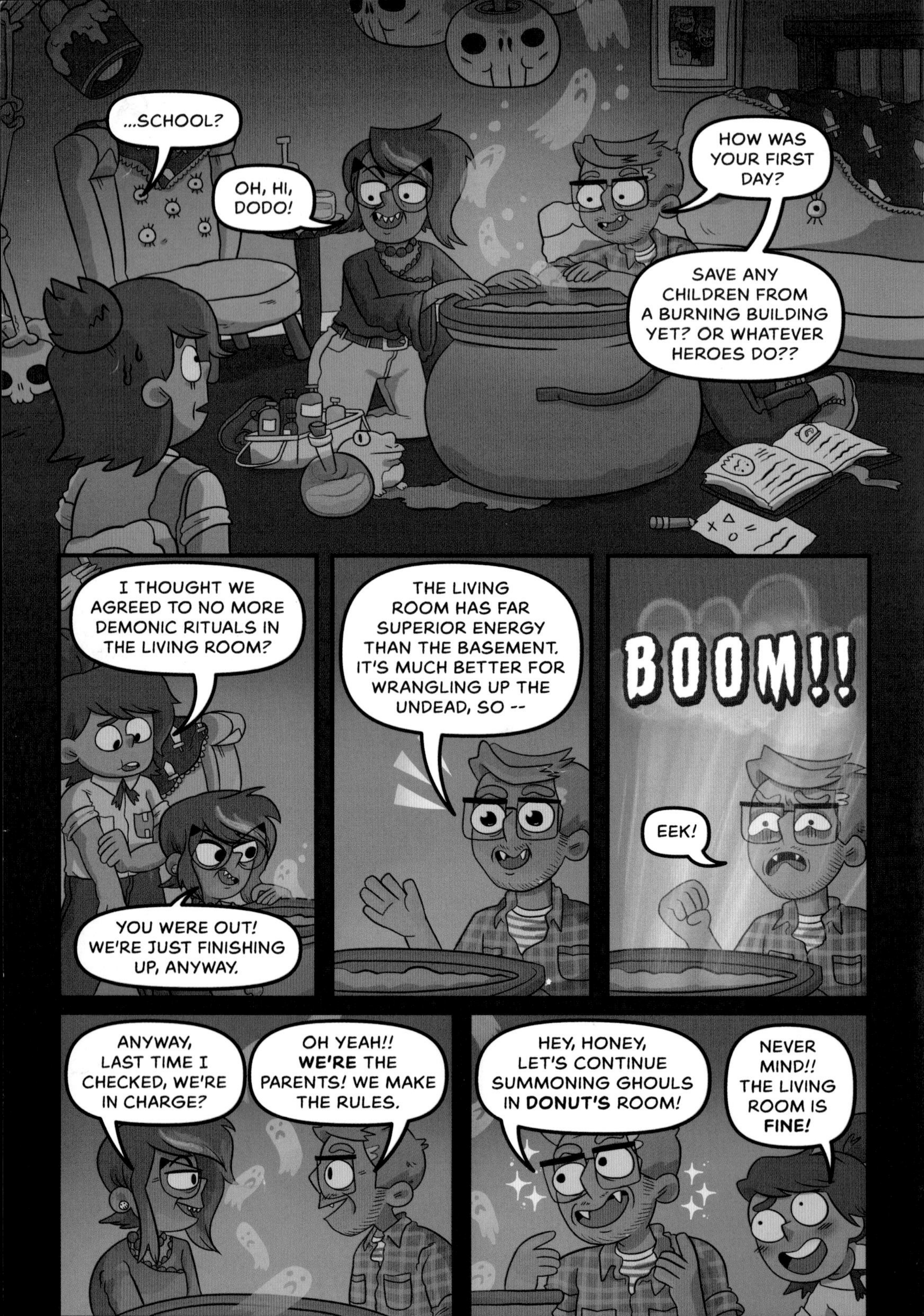
...SCHOOL?
OH, HI, DODO!
HOW WAS YOUR FIRST DAY?
SAVE ANY CHILDREN FROM A BURNING BUILDING YET? OR WHATEVER HEROES DO??
I THOUGHT WE AGREED TO NO MORE DEMONIC RITUALS IN THE LIVING ROOM?
YOU WERE OUT! WE'RE JUST FINISHING UP, ANYWAY.
THE LIVING ROOM HAS FAR SUPERIOR ENERGY THAN THE BASEMENT. IT'S MUCH BETTER FOR WRANGLING UP THE UNDEAD, SO --
BOOM!!
EEK!
ANYWAY, LAST TIME I CHECKED, WE'RE IN CHARGE?
OH YEAH!! **WE'RE** THE PARENTS! WE MAKE THE RULES.
HEY, HONEY, LET'S CONTINUE SUMMONING GHOULS IN **DONUT'S** ROOM!
NEVER MIND!! THE LIVING ROOM IS **FINE!**

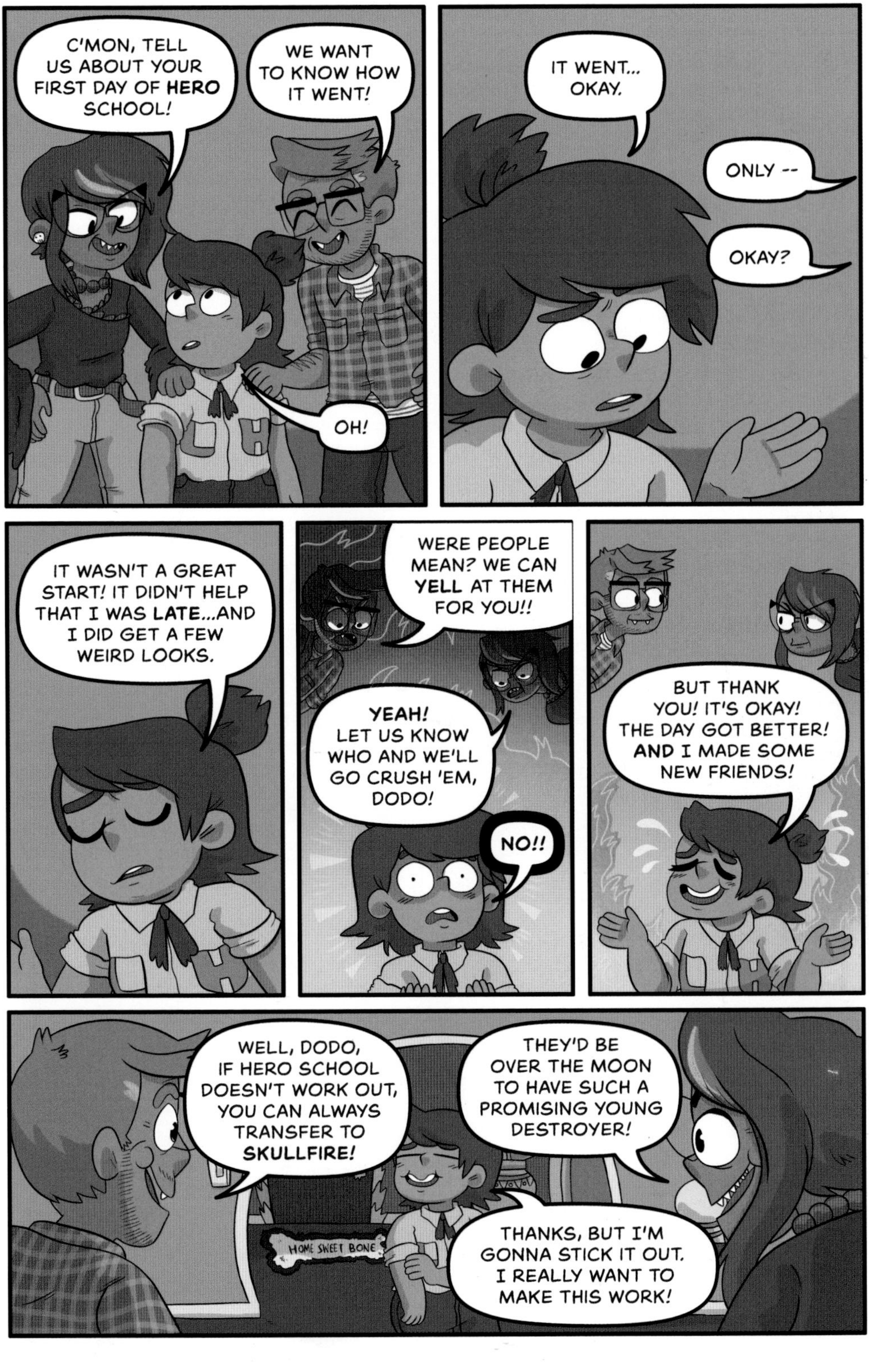
C'MON, TELL US ABOUT YOUR FIRST DAY OF **HERO** SCHOOL!
WE WANT TO KNOW HOW IT WENT!
OH!
IT WENT... OKAY.
ONLY --
OKAY?
IT WASN'T A GREAT START! IT DIDN'T HELP THAT I WAS **LATE**...AND I DID GET A FEW WEIRD LOOKS.
WERE PEOPLE MEAN? WE CAN **YELL** AT THEM FOR YOU!!
YEAH! LET US KNOW WHO AND WE'LL GO CRUSH 'EM, DODO!
NO!!
BUT THANK YOU! IT'S OKAY! THE DAY GOT BETTER! **AND** I MADE SOME NEW FRIENDS!
WELL, DODO, IF HERO SCHOOL DOESN'T WORK OUT, YOU CAN ALWAYS TRANSFER TO **SKULLFIRE!**
THEY'D BE OVER THE MOON TO HAVE SUCH A PROMISING YOUNG DESTROYER!
HOME SWEET BONE
THANKS, BUT I'M GONNA STICK IT OUT. I REALLY WANT TO MAKE THIS WORK!

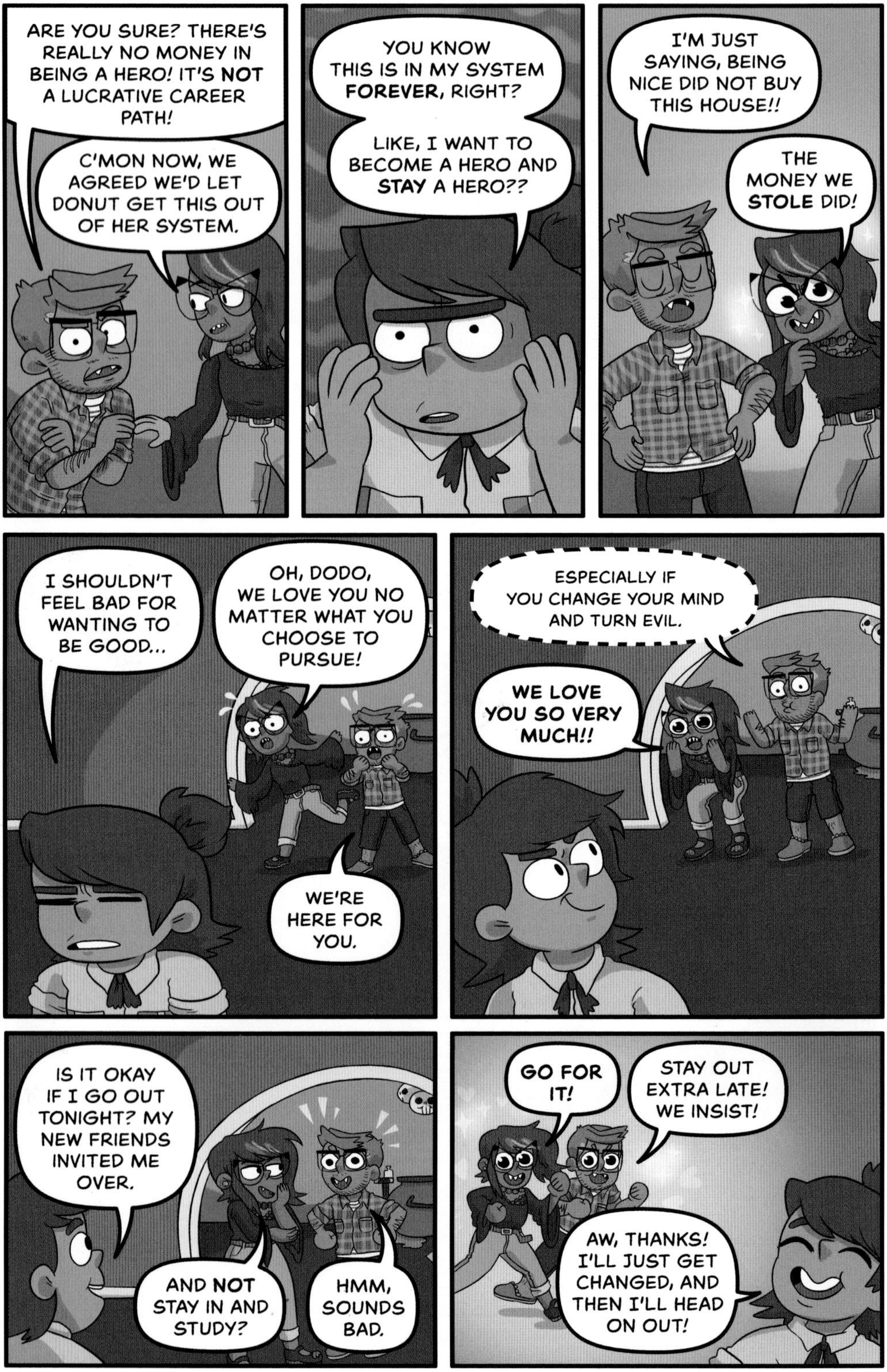
ARE YOU SURE? THERE'S REALLY NO MONEY IN BEING A HERO! IT'S **NOT** A LUCRATIVE CAREER PATH!
C'MON NOW, WE AGREED WE'D LET DONUT GET THIS OUT OF HER SYSTEM.
YOU KNOW THIS IS IN MY SYSTEM **FOREVER**, RIGHT?
LIKE, I WANT TO BECOME A HERO AND **STAY** A HERO??
I'M JUST SAYING, BEING NICE DID NOT BUY THIS HOUSE!!
THE MONEY WE **STOLE** DID!
I SHOULDN'T FEEL BAD FOR WANTING TO BE GOOD...
OH, DODO, WE LOVE YOU NO MATTER WHAT YOU CHOOSE TO PURSUE!
WE'RE HERE FOR YOU.
ESPECIALLY IF YOU CHANGE YOUR MIND AND TURN EVIL.
WE LOVE YOU SO VERY MUCH!!
IS IT OKAY IF I GO OUT TONIGHT? MY NEW FRIENDS INVITED ME OVER.
AND **NOT** STAY IN AND STUDY?
HMM, SOUNDS BAD.
GO FOR IT!
STAY OUT EXTRA LATE! WE INSIST!
AW, THANKS! I'LL JUST GET CHANGED, AND THEN I'LL HEAD ON OUT!

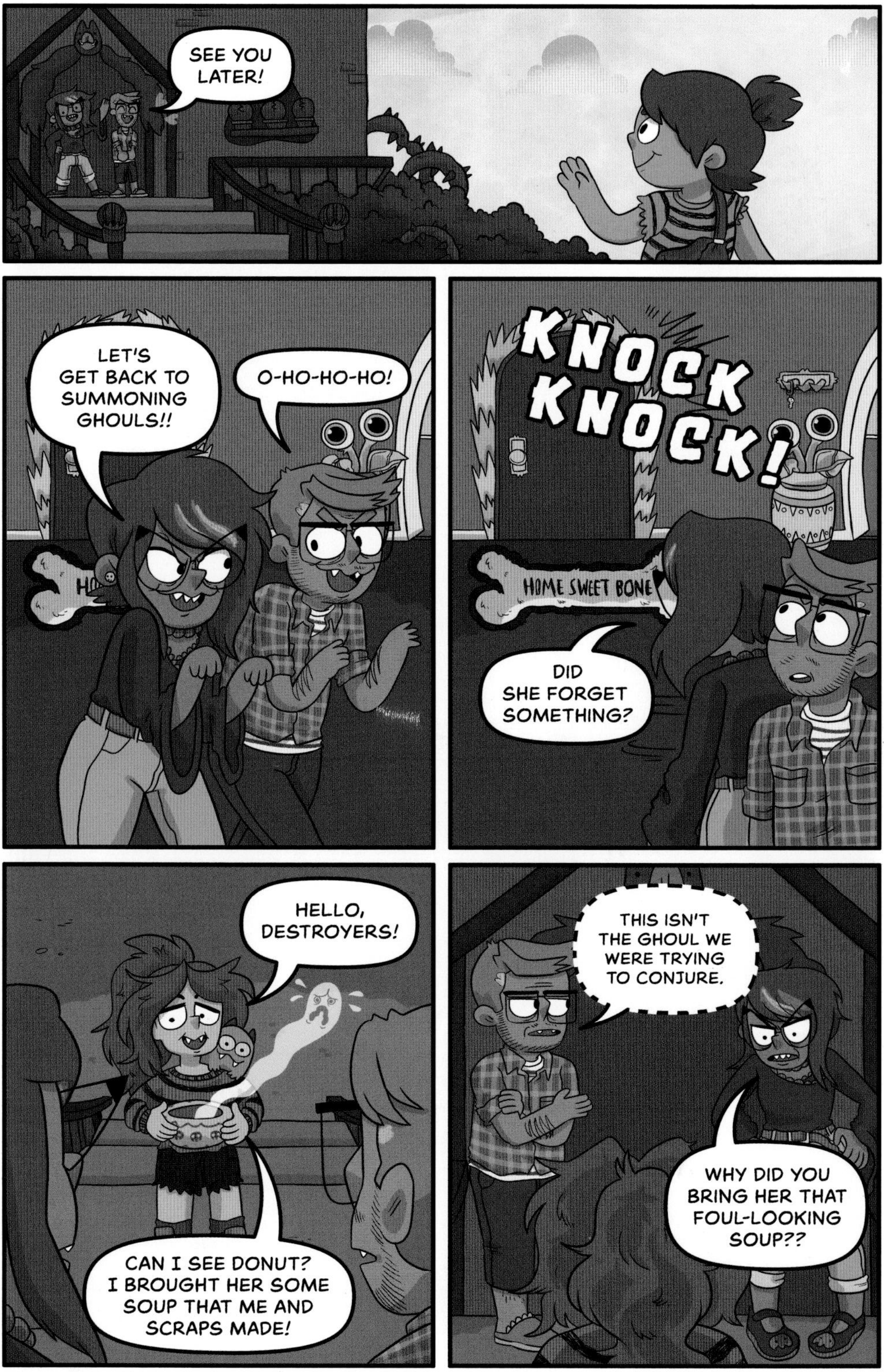
SEE YOU LATER!
LET'S GET BACK TO SUMMONING GHOULS!!
O-HO-HO-HO!
KNOCK KNOCK!
HOME SWEET BONE
DID SHE FORGET SOMETHING?
HELLO, DESTROYERS!
CAN I SEE DONUT? I BROUGHT HER SOME SOUP THAT ME AND SCRAPS MADE!
THIS ISN'T THE GHOUL WE WERE TRYING TO CONJURE.
WHY DID YOU BRING HER THAT FOUL-LOOKING SOUP??

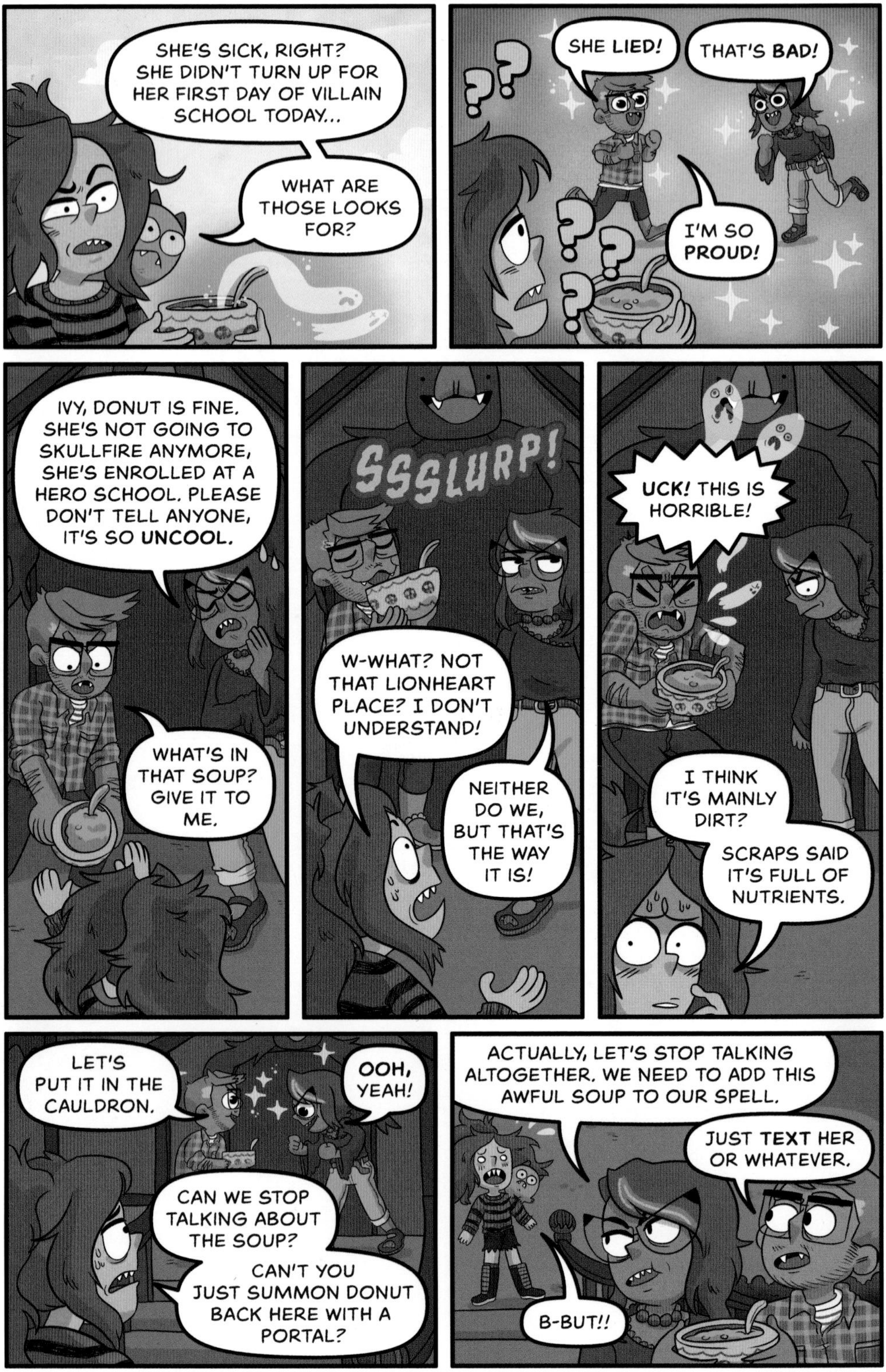
SHE'S SICK, RIGHT? SHE DIDN'T TURN UP FOR HER FIRST DAY OF VILLAIN SCHOOL TODAY...
WHAT ARE THOSE LOOKS FOR?
SHE LIED!
THAT'S BAD!
I'M SO PROUD!
IVY, DONUT IS FINE. SHE'S NOT GOING TO SKULLFIRE ANYMORE, SHE'S ENROLLED AT A HERO SCHOOL. PLEASE DON'T TELL ANYONE, IT'S SO UNCOOL.
WHAT'S IN THAT SOUP? GIVE IT TO ME.
SSSLURP!
W-WHAT? NOT THAT LIONHEART PLACE? I DON'T UNDERSTAND!
NEITHER DO WE, BUT THAT'S THE WAY IT IS!
UCK! THIS IS HORRIBLE!
I THINK IT'S MAINLY DIRT?
SCRAPS SAID IT'S FULL OF NUTRIENTS.
LET'S PUT IT IN THE CAULDRON.
OOH, YEAH!
CAN WE STOP TALKING ABOUT THE SOUP?
CAN'T YOU JUST SUMMON DONUT BACK HERE WITH A PORTAL?
ACTUALLY, LET'S STOP TALKING ALTOGETHER. WE NEED TO ADD THIS AWFUL SOUP TO OUR SPELL.
JUST TEXT HER OR WHATEVER.
B-BUT!!

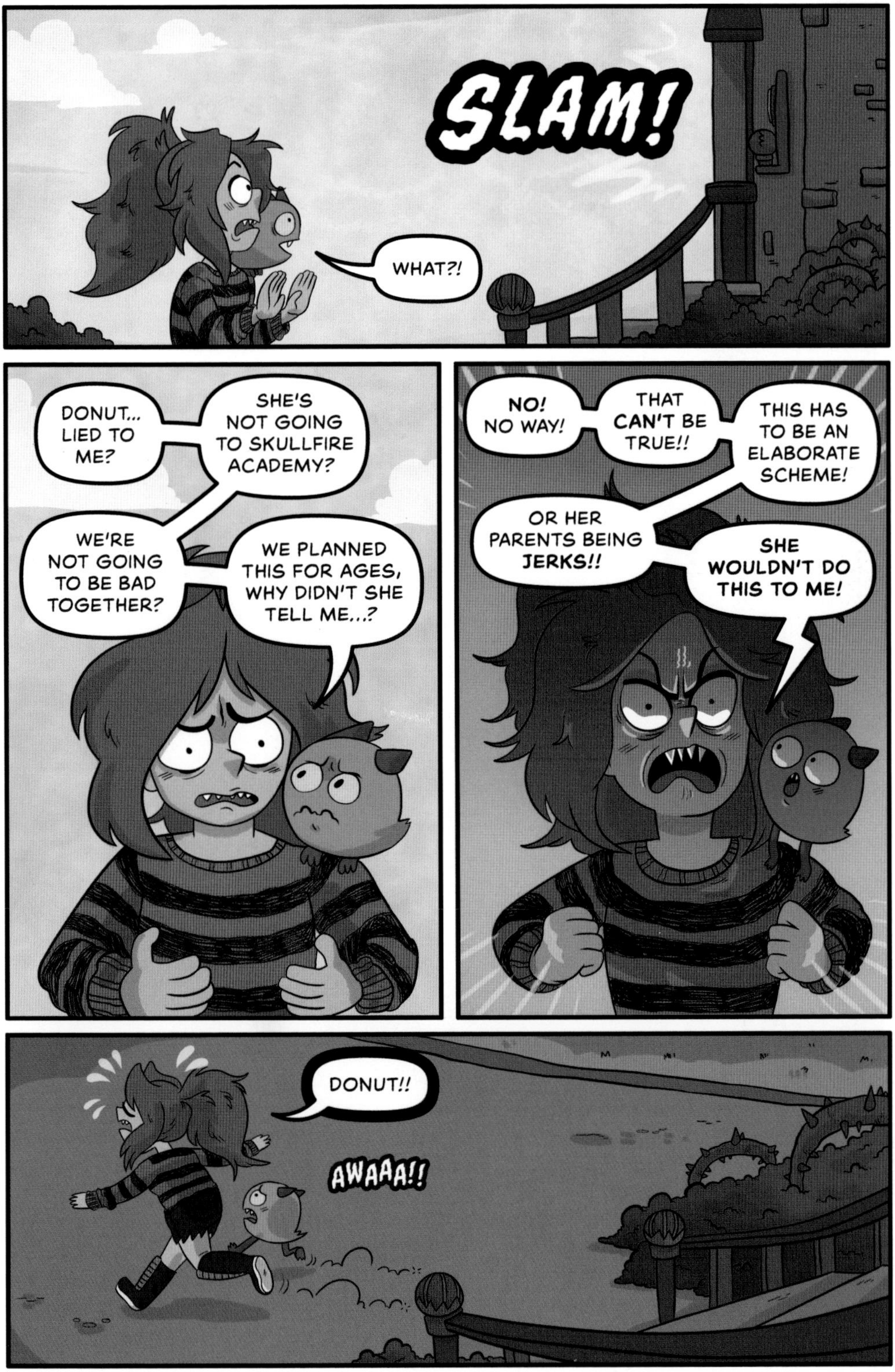
SLAM!
WHAT?!
DONUT... LIED TO ME?
SHE'S NOT GOING TO SKULLFIRE ACADEMY?
WE'RE NOT GOING TO BE BAD TOGETHER?
WE PLANNED THIS FOR AGES, WHY DIDN'T SHE TELL ME...?
NO! NO WAY!
THAT **CAN'T** BE TRUE!!
THIS HAS TO BE AN ELABORATE SCHEME!
OR HER PARENTS BEING **JERKS!!**
SHE WOULDN'T DO THIS TO ME!
DONUT!!
AWAAA!!

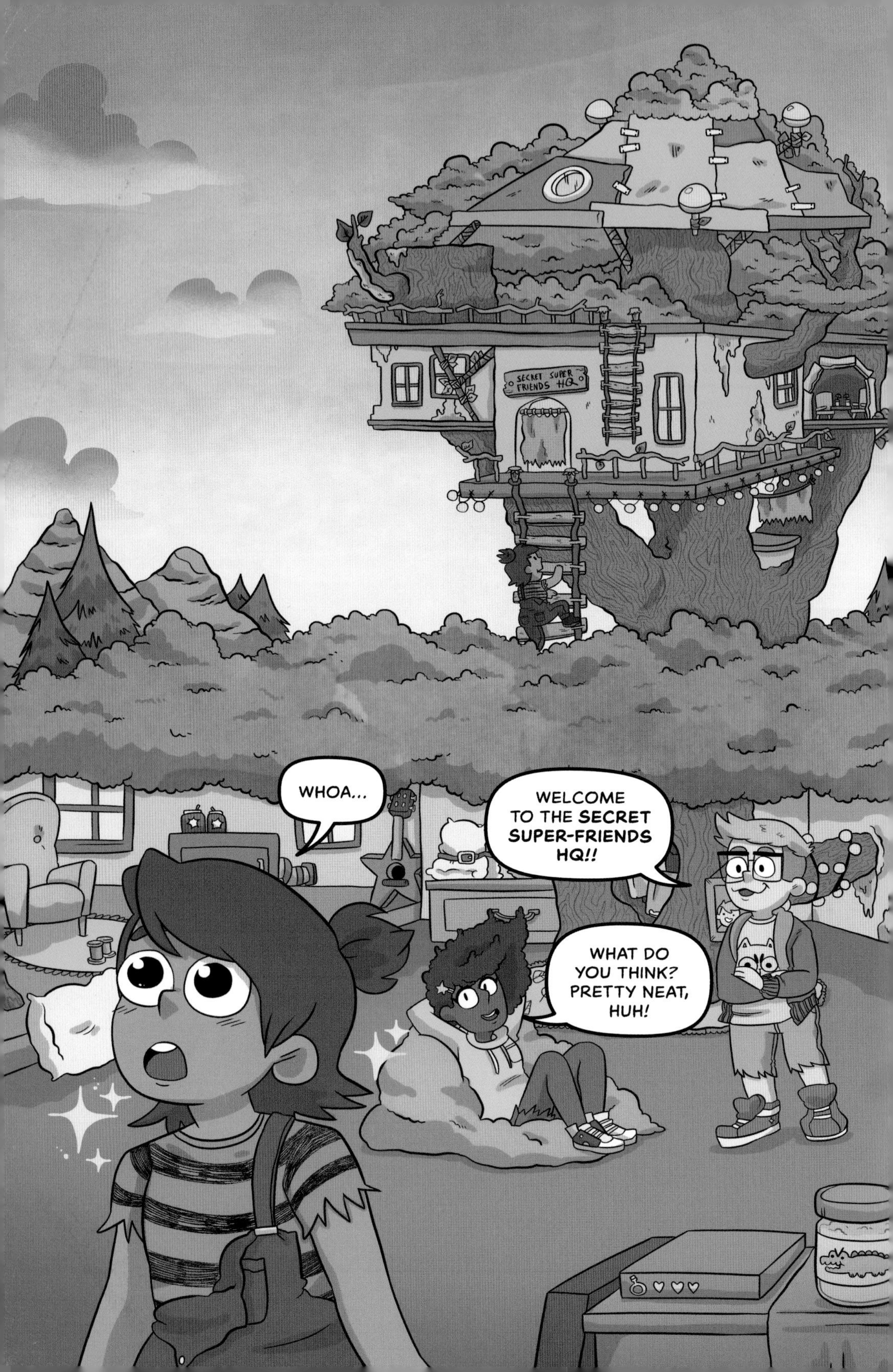
SECRET SUPER FRIENDS HQ
WHOA...
WELCOME TO THE SECRET SUPER-FRIENDS HQ!!
WHAT DO YOU THINK? PRETTY NEAT, HUH!

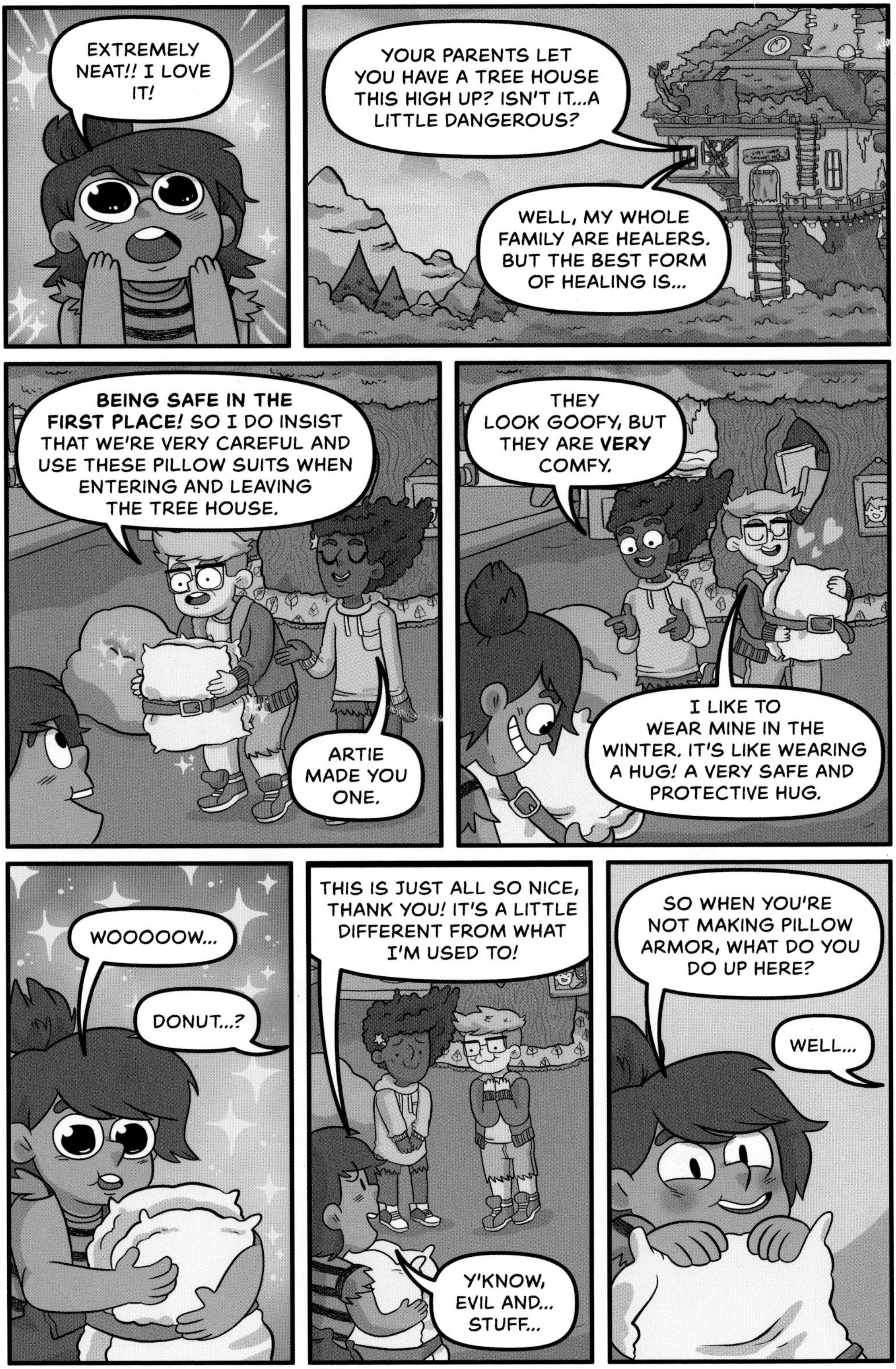
EXTREMELY NEAT!! I LOVE IT!
YOUR PARENTS LET YOU HAVE A TREE HOUSE THIS HIGH UP? ISN'T IT...A LITTLE DANGEROUS?
WELL, MY WHOLE FAMILY ARE HEALERS. BUT THE BEST FORM OF HEALING IS...
BEING SAFE IN THE FIRST PLACE! SO I DO INSIST THAT WE'RE VERY CAREFUL AND USE THESE PILLOW SUITS WHEN ENTERING AND LEAVING THE TREE HOUSE.
ARTIE MADE YOU ONE.
THEY LOOK GOOFY, BUT THEY ARE VERY COMFY.
I LIKE TO WEAR MINE IN THE WINTER. IT'S LIKE WEARING A HUG! A VERY SAFE AND PROTECTIVE HUG.
WOOOOOW...
DONUT...?
THIS IS JUST ALL SO NICE, THANK YOU! IT'S A LITTLE DIFFERENT FROM WHAT I'M USED TO!
Y'KNOW, EVIL AND... STUFF...
SO WHEN YOU'RE NOT MAKING PILLOW ARMOR, WHAT DO YOU DO UP HERE?
WELL...

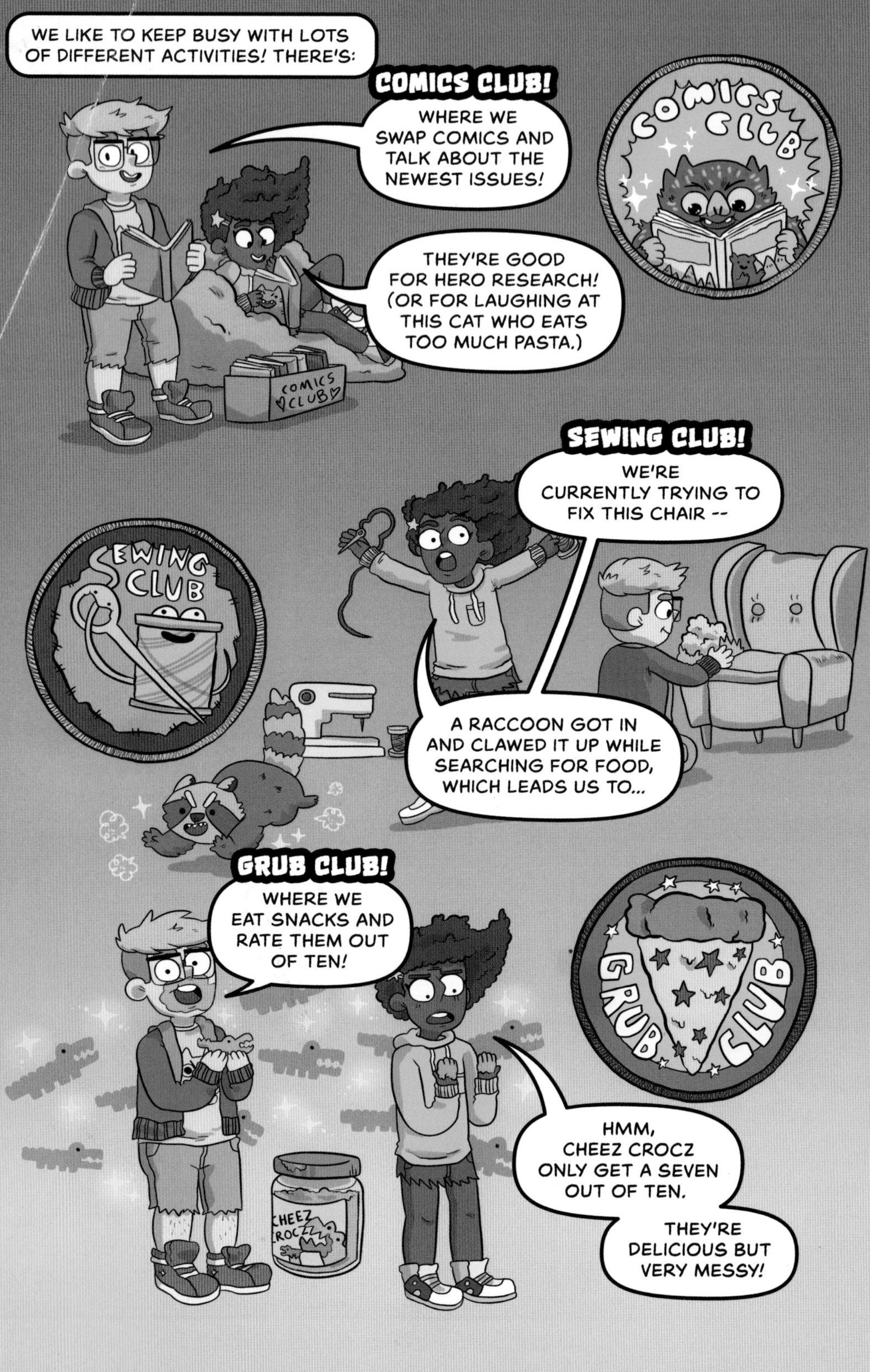
WE LIKE TO KEEP BUSY WITH LOTS OF DIFFERENT ACTIVITIES! THERE'S:
COMICS CLUB!
WHERE WE SWAP COMICS AND TALK ABOUT THE NEWEST ISSUES!
COMICS CLUB
THEY'RE GOOD FOR HERO RESEARCH! (OR FOR LAUGHING AT THIS CAT WHO EATS TOO MUCH PASTA.)
COMICS CLUB
SEWING CLUB!
WE'RE CURRENTLY TRYING TO FIX THIS CHAIR --
SEWING CLUB
A RACCOON GOT IN AND CLAWED IT UP WHILE SEARCHING FOR FOOD, WHICH LEADS US TO...
GRUB CLUB!
WHERE WE EAT SNACKS AND RATE THEM OUT OF TEN!
GRUB CLUB
HMM, CHEEZ CROCZ ONLY GET A SEVEN OUT OF TEN.
THEY'RE DELICIOUS BUT VERY MESSY!
CHEEZ CROCZ

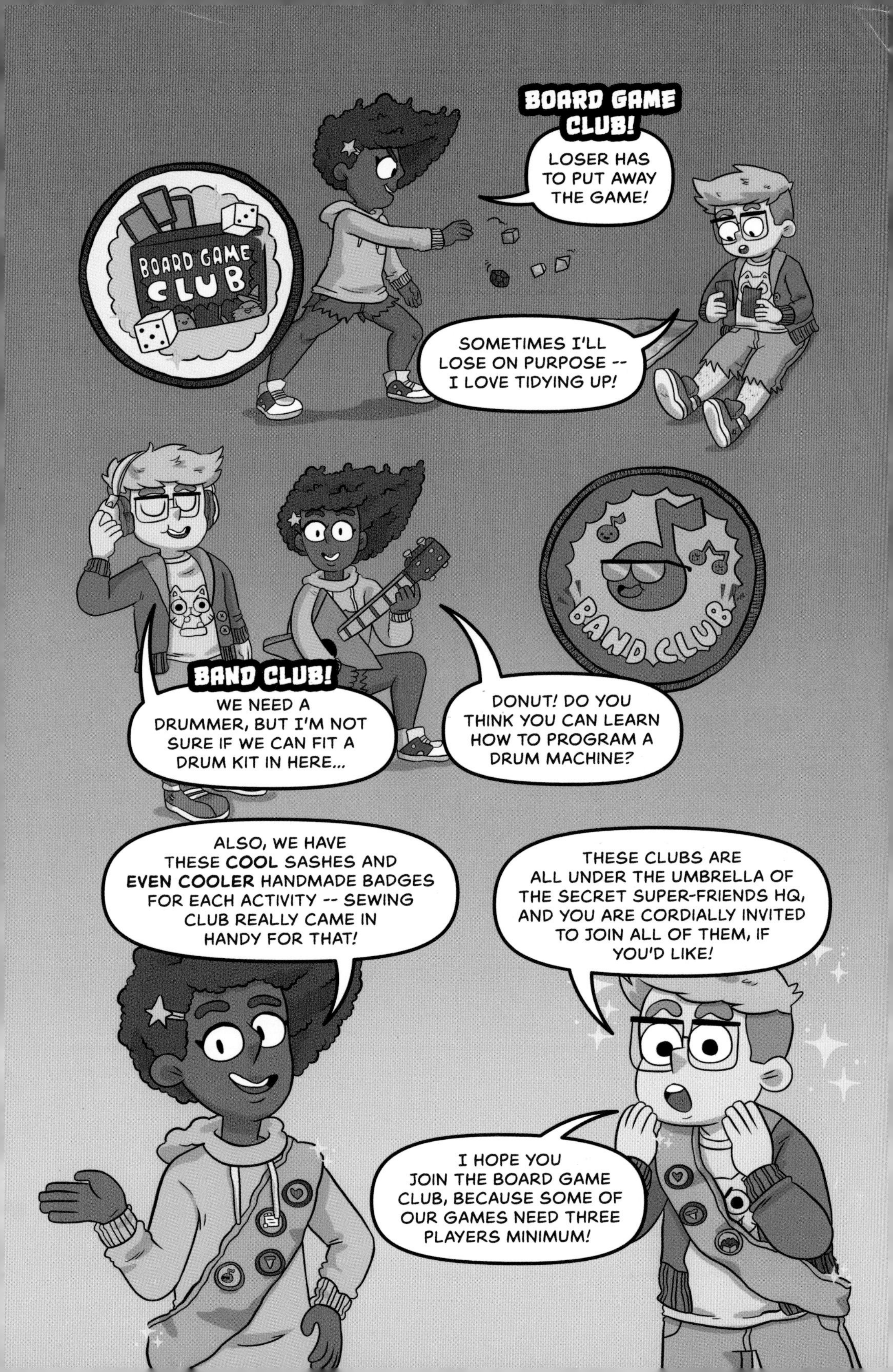
BOARD GAME CLUB!
LOSER HAS TO PUT AWAY THE GAME!
BOARD GAME CLUB
SOMETIMES I'LL LOSE ON PURPOSE -- I LOVE TIDYING UP!
BAND CLUB
BAND CLUB!
WE NEED A DRUMMER, BUT I'M NOT SURE IF WE CAN FIT A DRUM KIT IN HERE...
DONUT! DO YOU THINK YOU CAN LEARN HOW TO PROGRAM A DRUM MACHINE?
ALSO, WE HAVE THESE **COOL** SASHES AND **EVEN COOLER** HANDMADE BADGES FOR EACH ACTIVITY -- SEWING CLUB REALLY CAME IN HANDY FOR THAT!
THESE CLUBS ARE ALL UNDER THE UMBRELLA OF THE SECRET SUPER-FRIENDS HQ, AND YOU ARE CORDIALLY INVITED TO JOIN ALL OF THEM, IF YOU'D LIKE!
I HOPE YOU JOIN THE BOARD GAME CLUB, BECAUSE SOME OF OUR GAMES NEED THREE PLAYERS MINIMUM!

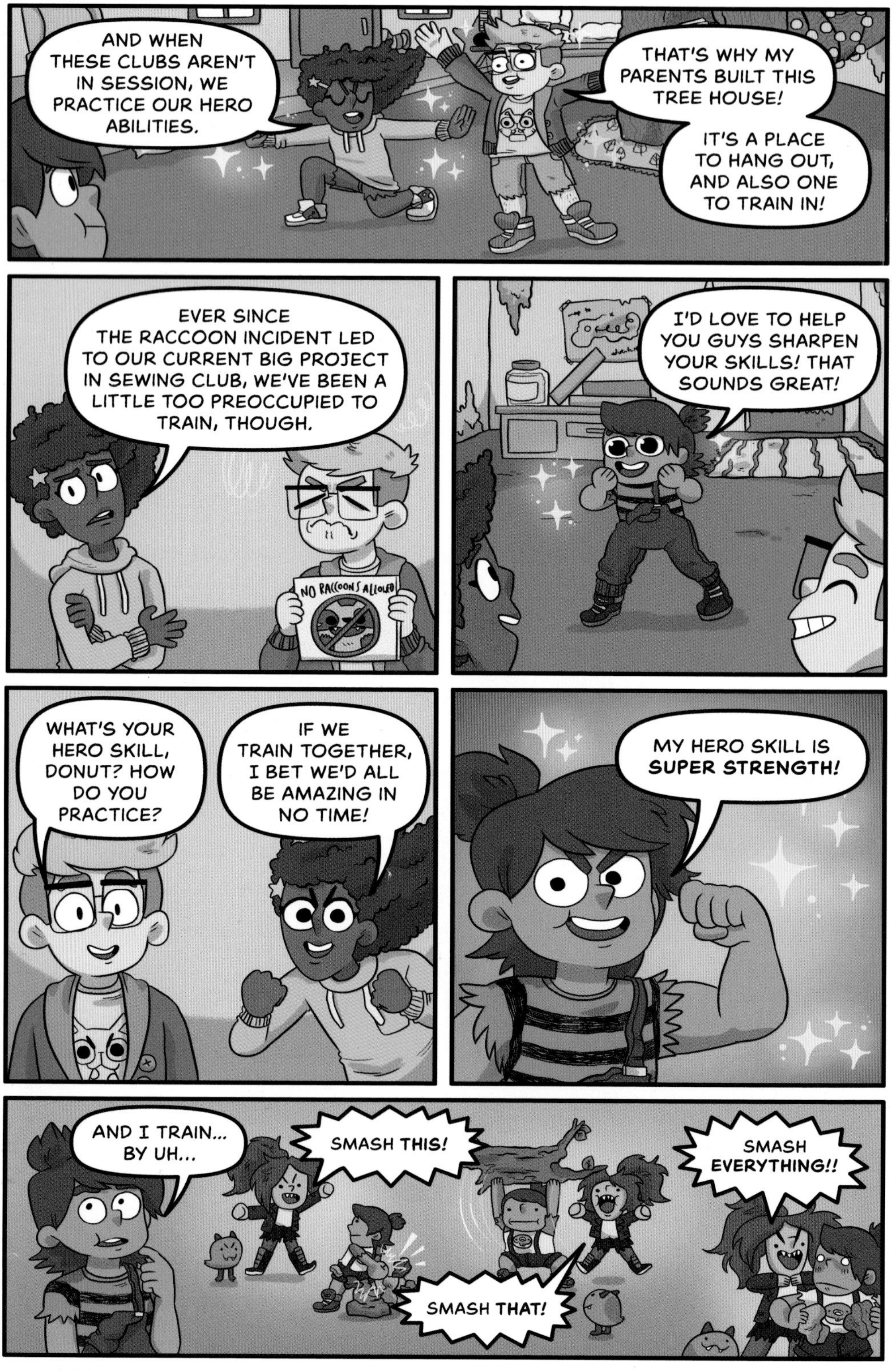
AND WHEN THESE CLUBS AREN'T IN SESSION, WE PRACTICE OUR HERO ABILITIES.
THAT'S WHY MY PARENTS BUILT THIS TREE HOUSE!
IT'S A PLACE TO HANG OUT, AND ALSO ONE TO TRAIN IN!
EVER SINCE THE RACCOON INCIDENT LED TO OUR CURRENT BIG PROJECT IN SEWING CLUB, WE'VE BEEN A LITTLE TOO PREOCCUPIED TO TRAIN, THOUGH.
NO RACCOONS ALLOWED
I'D LOVE TO HELP YOU GUYS SHARPEN YOUR SKILLS! THAT SOUNDS GREAT!
WHAT'S YOUR HERO SKILL, DONUT? HOW DO YOU PRACTICE?
IF WE TRAIN TOGETHER, I BET WE'D ALL BE AMAZING IN NO TIME!
MY HERO SKILL IS **SUPER STRENGTH!**
AND I TRAIN... BY UH...
SMASH THIS!
SMASH EVERYTHING!!
SMASH THAT!

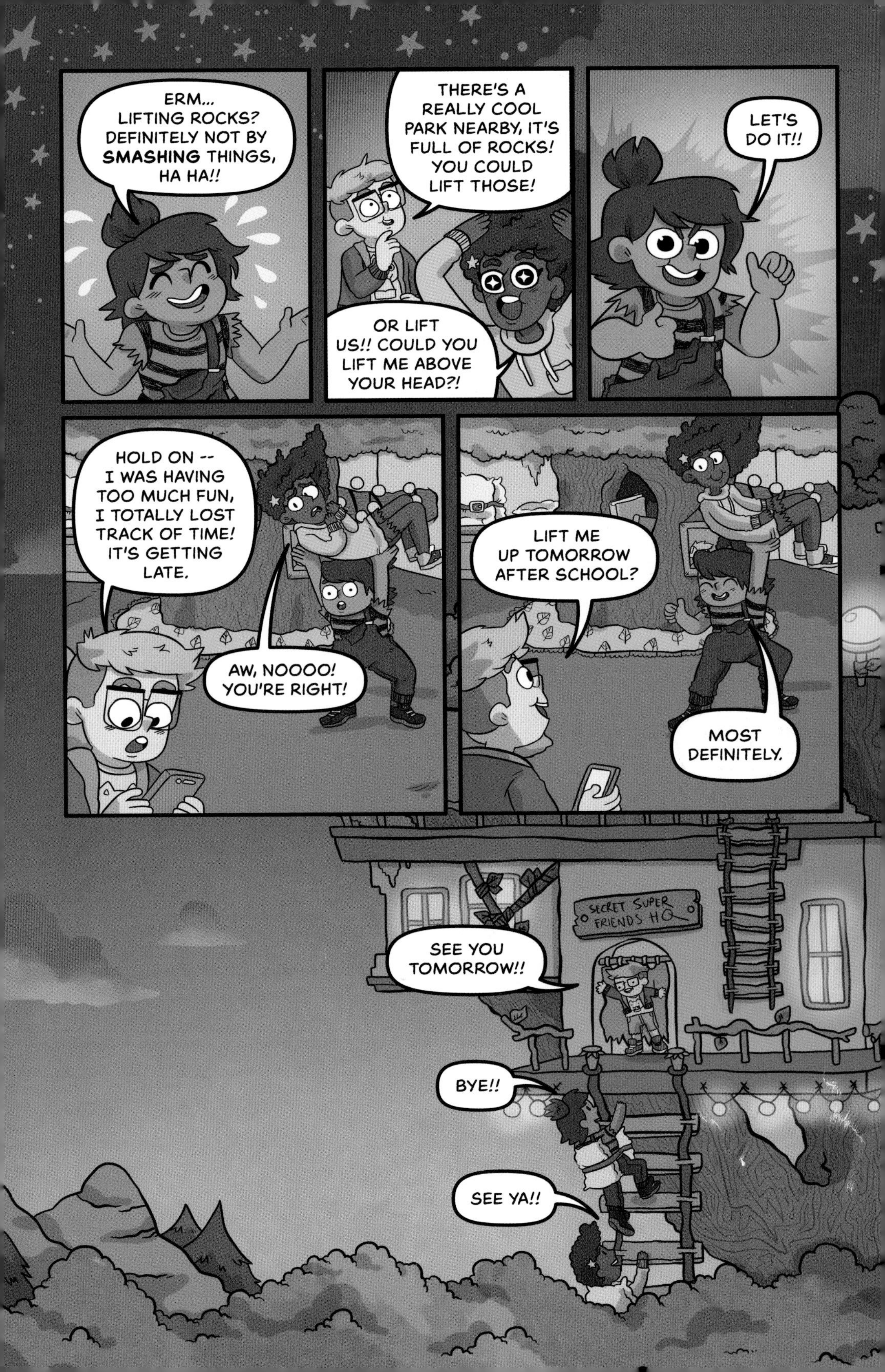
ERM... LIFTING ROCKS? DEFINITELY NOT BY **SMASHING** THINGS, HA HA!!
THERE'S A REALLY COOL PARK NEARBY, IT'S FULL OF ROCKS! YOU COULD LIFT THOSE!
OR LIFT US!! COULD YOU LIFT ME ABOVE YOUR HEAD?!
LET'S DO IT!!
HOLD ON -- I WAS HAVING TOO MUCH FUN, I TOTALLY LOST TRACK OF TIME! IT'S GETTING LATE.
AW, NOOOO! YOU'RE RIGHT!
LIFT ME UP TOMORROW AFTER SCHOOL?
MOST DEFINITELY.
SECRET SUPER FRIENDS HQ
SEE YOU TOMORROW!!
BYE!!
SEE YA!!

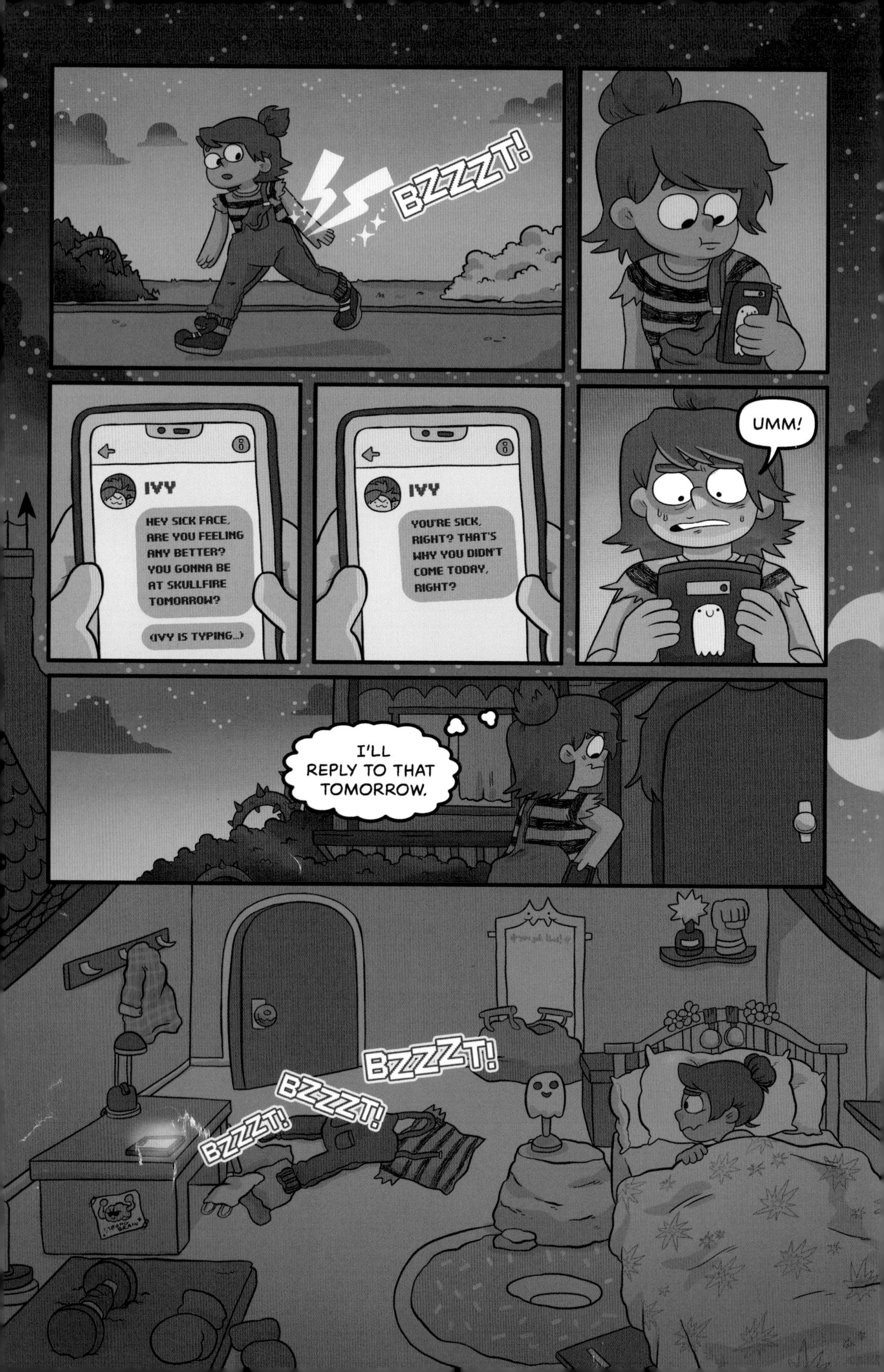
BZZZZT!
IVY
HEY SICK FACE, ARE YOU FEELING ANY BETTER? YOU GONNA BE AT SKULLFIRE TOMORROW?
(IVY IS TYPING...)
IVY
YOU'RE SICK, RIGHT? THAT'S WHY YOU DIDN'T COME TODAY, RIGHT?
UMM!
I'LL REPLY TO THAT TOMORROW.
BZZZT!
BZZZZT!
BZZZT!

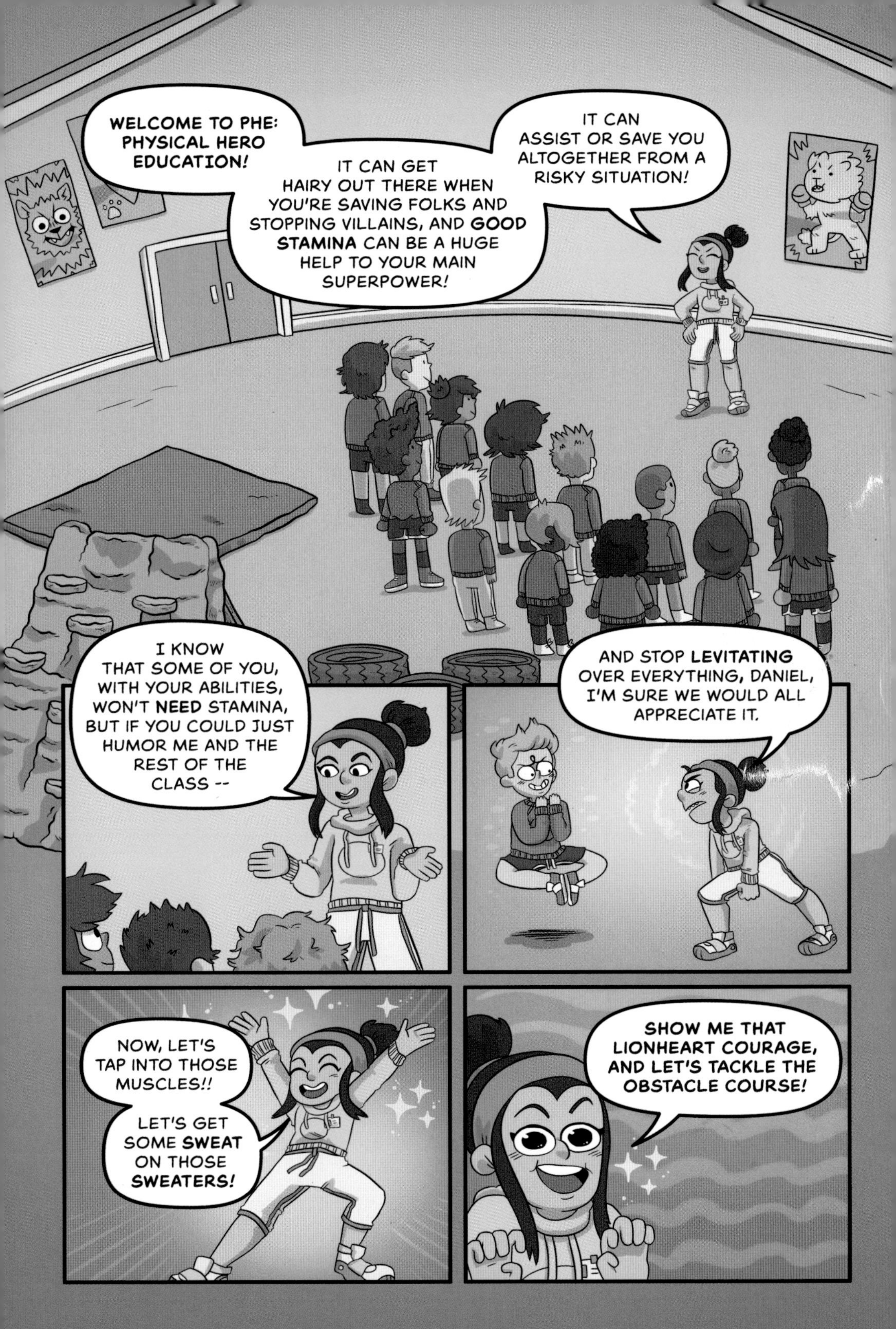

WELCOME TO PHE: PHYSICAL HERO EDUCATION!
IT CAN GET HAIRY OUT THERE WHEN YOU'RE SAVING FOLKS AND STOPPING VILLAINS, AND GOOD STAMINA CAN BE A HUGE HELP TO YOUR MAIN SUPERPOWER!
IT CAN ASSIST OR SAVE YOU ALTOGETHER FROM A RISKY SITUATION!
I KNOW THAT SOME OF YOU, WITH YOUR ABILITIES, WON'T NEED STAMINA, BUT IF YOU COULD JUST HUMOR ME AND THE REST OF THE CLASS --
AND STOP LEVITATING OVER EVERYTHING, DANIEL, I'M SURE WE WOULD ALL APPRECIATE IT.
NOW, LET'S TAP INTO THOSE MUSCLES!!
LET'S GET SOME SWEAT ON THOSE SWEATERS!
SHOW ME THAT LIONHEART COURAGE, AND LET'S TACKLE THE OBSTACLE COURSE!

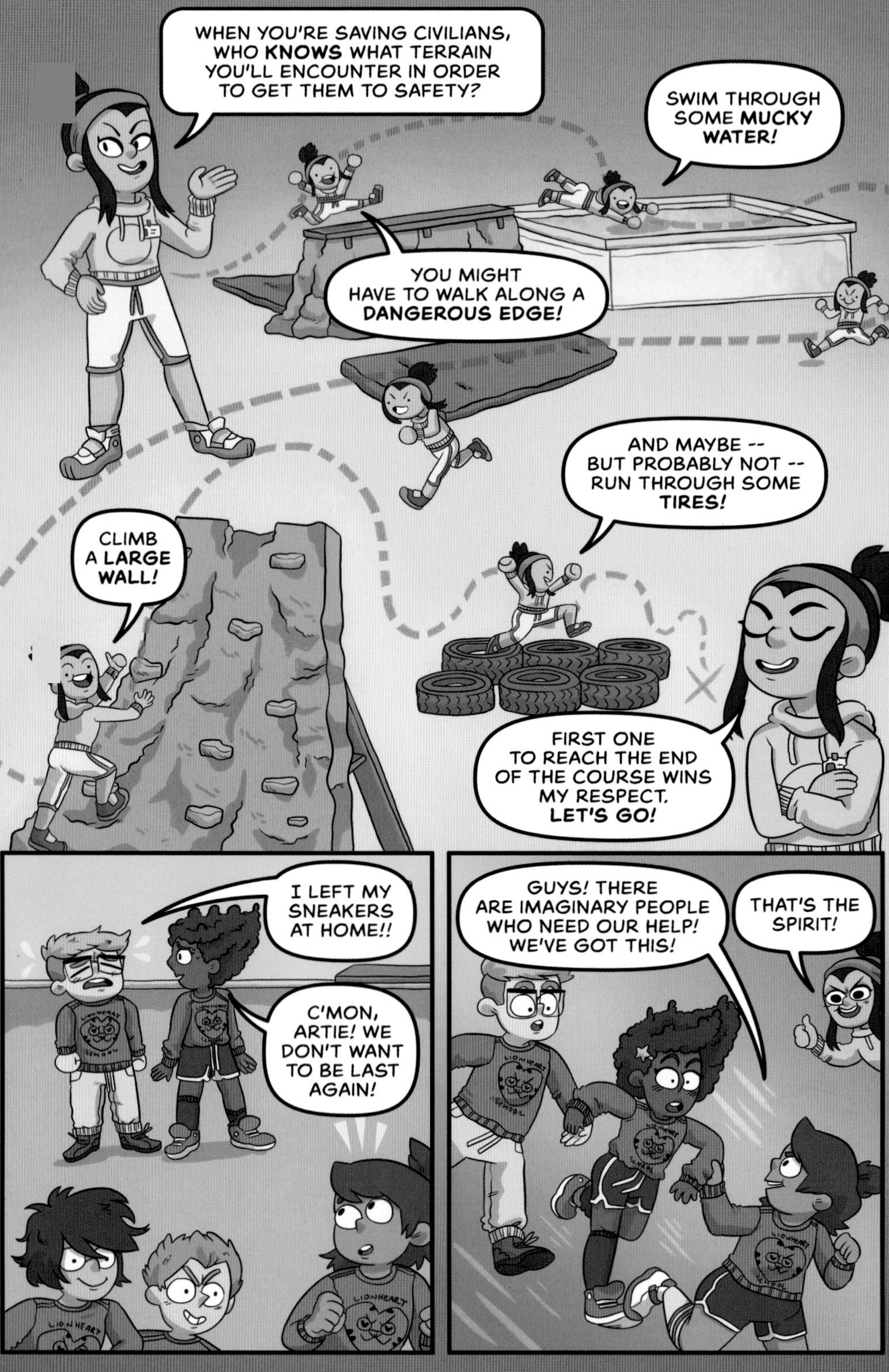
WHEN YOU'RE SAVING CIVILIANS, WHO KNOWS WHAT TERRAIN YOU'LL ENCOUNTER IN ORDER TO GET THEM TO SAFETY?
SWIM THROUGH SOME MUCKY WATER!
YOU MIGHT HAVE TO WALK ALONG A DANGEROUS EDGE!
AND MAYBE -- BUT PROBABLY NOT -- RUN THROUGH SOME TIRES!
CLIMB A LARGE WALL!
FIRST ONE TO REACH THE END OF THE COURSE WINS MY RESPECT. LET'S GO!
I LEFT MY SNEAKERS AT HOME!!
C'MON, ARTIE! WE DON'T WANT TO BE LAST AGAIN!
GUYS! THERE ARE IMAGINARY PEOPLE WHO NEED OUR HELP! WE'VE GOT THIS!
THAT'S THE SPIRIT!

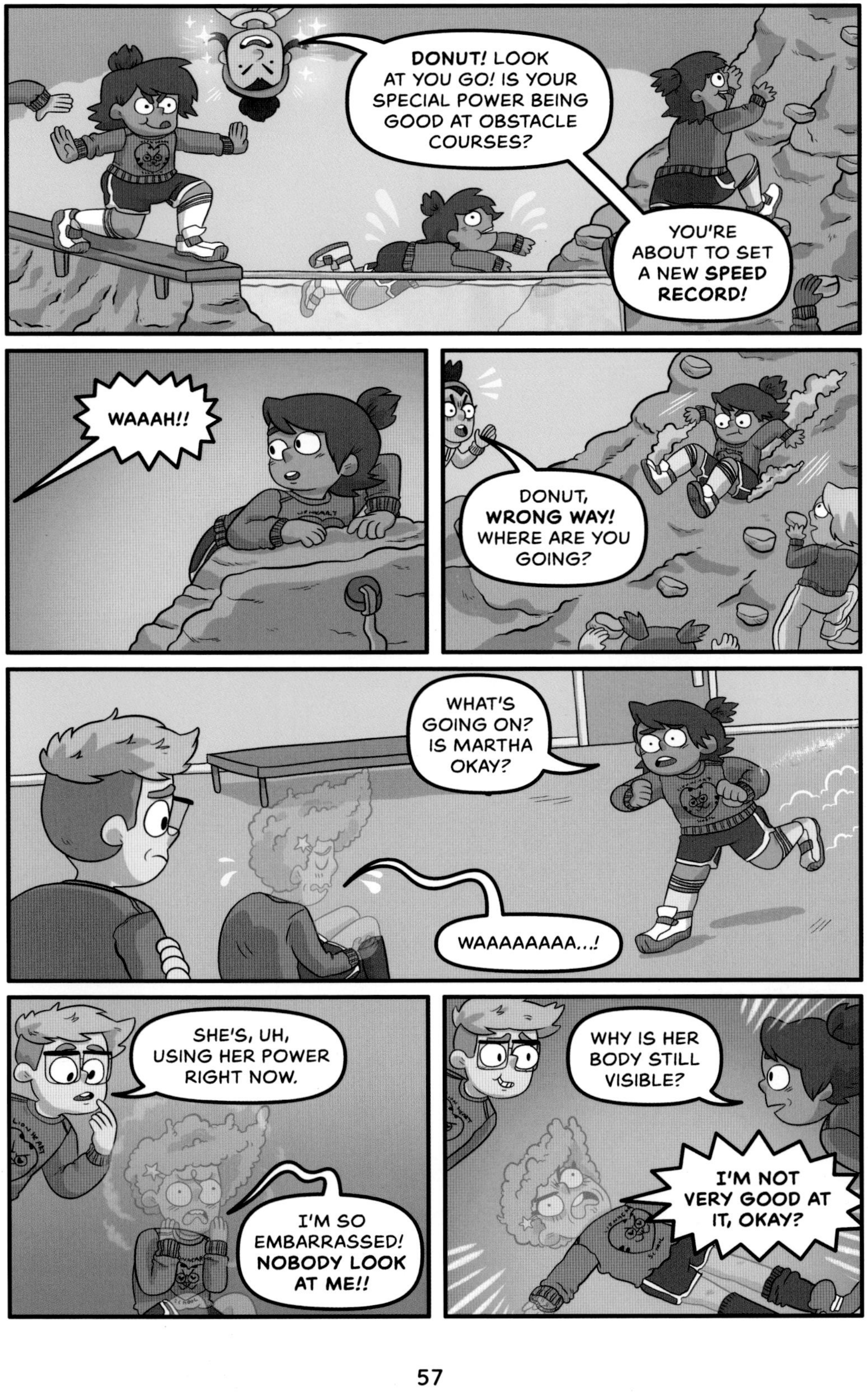
DONUT! LOOK AT YOU GO! IS YOUR SPECIAL POWER BEING GOOD AT OBSTACLE COURSES?
YOU'RE ABOUT TO SET A NEW SPEED RECORD!
WAAAH!!
DONUT, WRONG WAY! WHERE ARE YOU GOING?
WHAT'S GOING ON? IS MARTHA OKAY?
WAAAAAAAA...!
SHE'S, UH, USING HER POWER RIGHT NOW.
I'M SO EMBARRASSED! NOBODY LOOK AT ME!!
WHY IS HER BODY STILL VISIBLE?
I'M NOT VERY GOOD AT IT, OKAY?

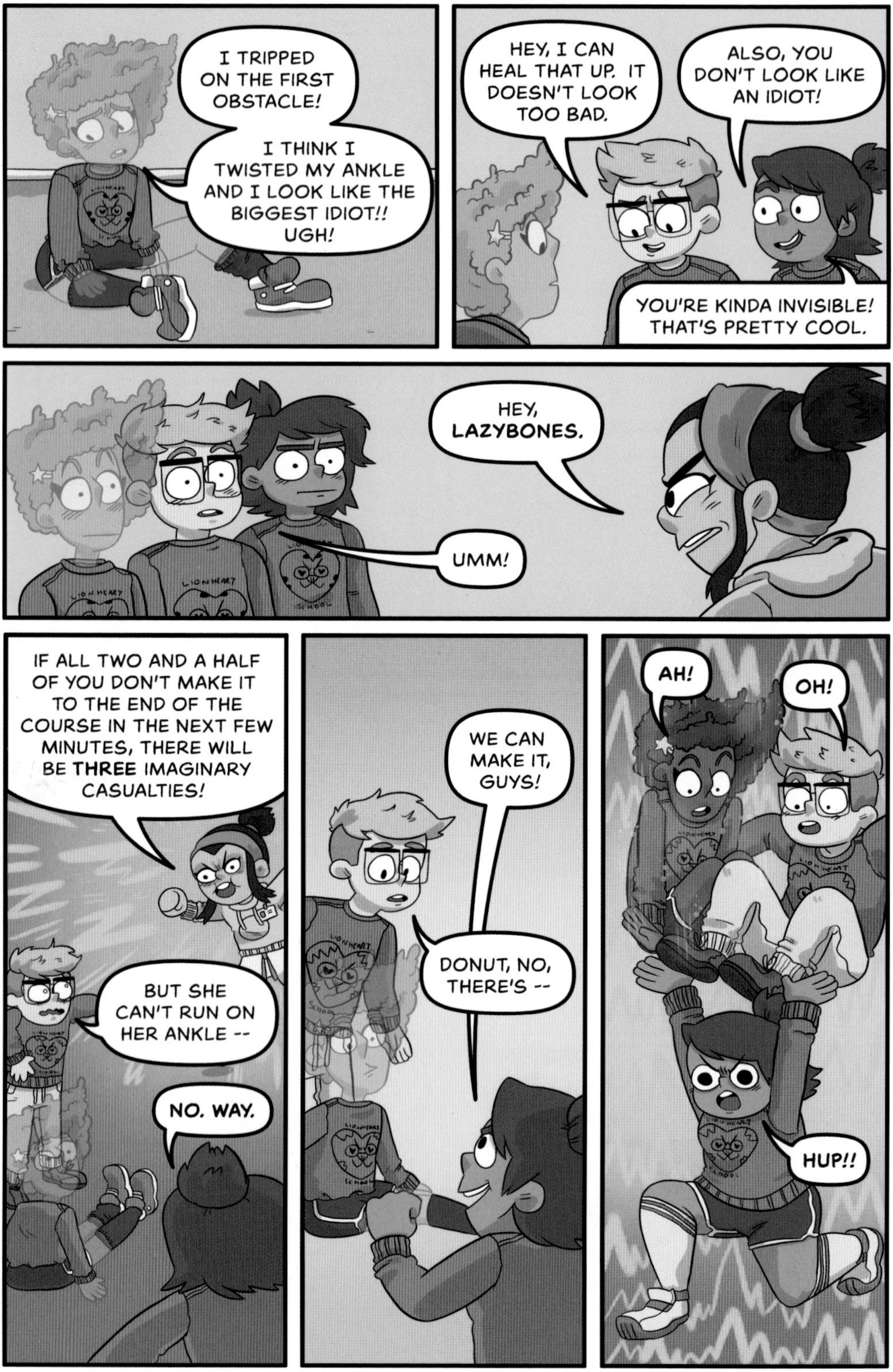
I TRIPPED ON THE FIRST OBSTACLE!
I THINK I TWISTED MY ANKLE AND I LOOK LIKE THE BIGGEST IDIOT!! UGH!
HEY, I CAN HEAL THAT UP. IT DOESN'T LOOK TOO BAD.
ALSO, YOU DON'T LOOK LIKE AN IDIOT!
YOU'RE KINDA INVISIBLE! THAT'S PRETTY COOL.
HEY, **LAZYBONES.**
UMM!
IF ALL TWO AND A HALF OF YOU DON'T MAKE IT TO THE END OF THE COURSE IN THE NEXT FEW MINUTES, THERE WILL BE **THREE** IMAGINARY CASUALTIES!
BUT SHE CAN'T RUN ON HER ANKLE --
NO. WAY.
WE CAN MAKE IT, GUYS!
DONUT, NO, THERE'S --
AH!
OH!
HUP!!

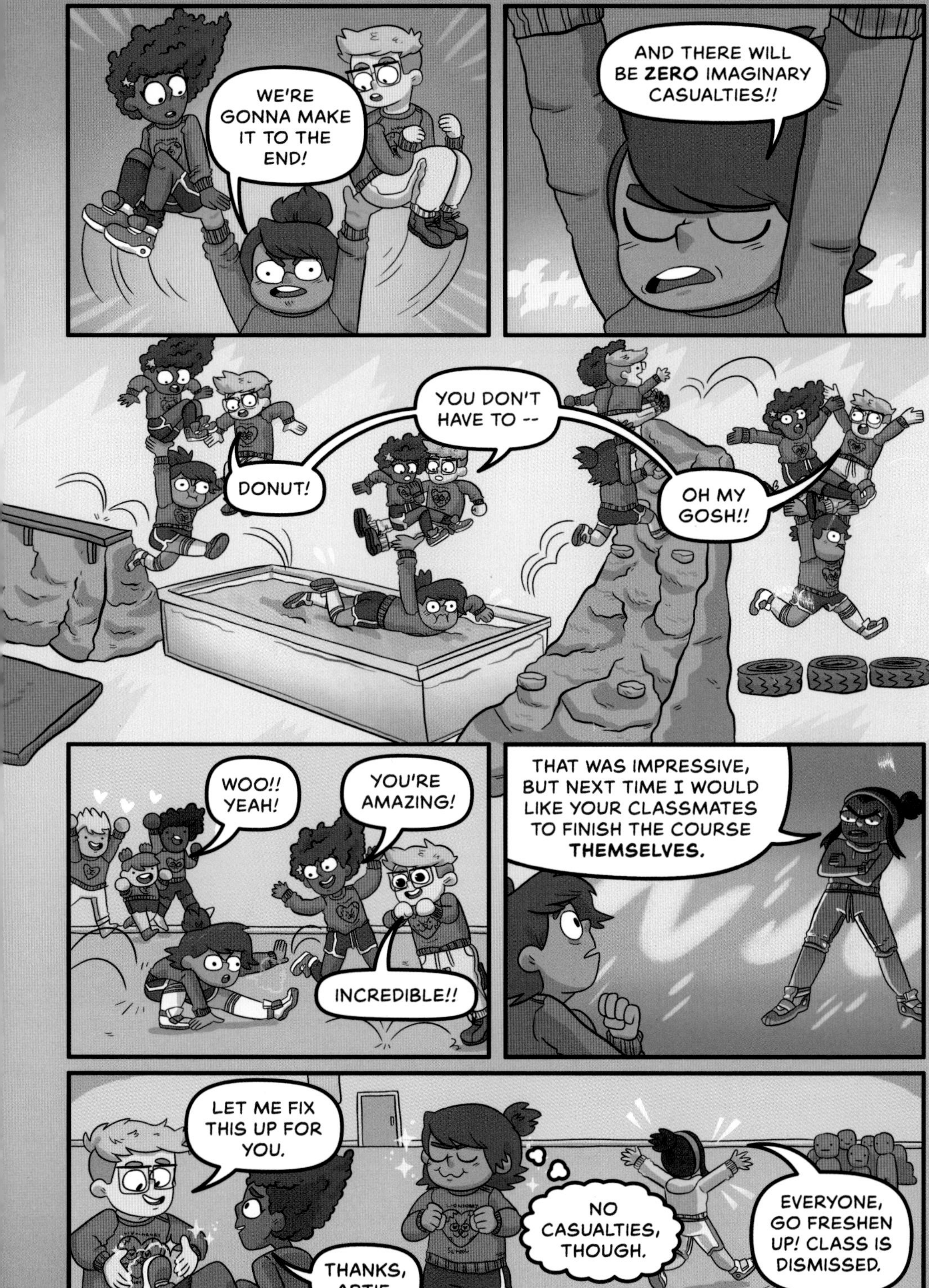
WE'RE GONNA MAKE IT TO THE END!
AND THERE WILL BE ZERO IMAGINARY CASUALTIES!!
DONUT!
YOU DON'T HAVE TO --
OH MY GOSH!!
WOO!! YEAH!
YOU'RE AMAZING!
INCREDIBLE!!
THAT WAS IMPRESSIVE, BUT NEXT TIME I WOULD LIKE YOUR CLASSMATES TO FINISH THE COURSE THEMSELVES.
LET ME FIX THIS UP FOR YOU.
THANKS, ARTIE.
NO CASUALTIES, THOUGH.
EVERYONE, GO FRESHEN UP! CLASS IS DISMISSED.

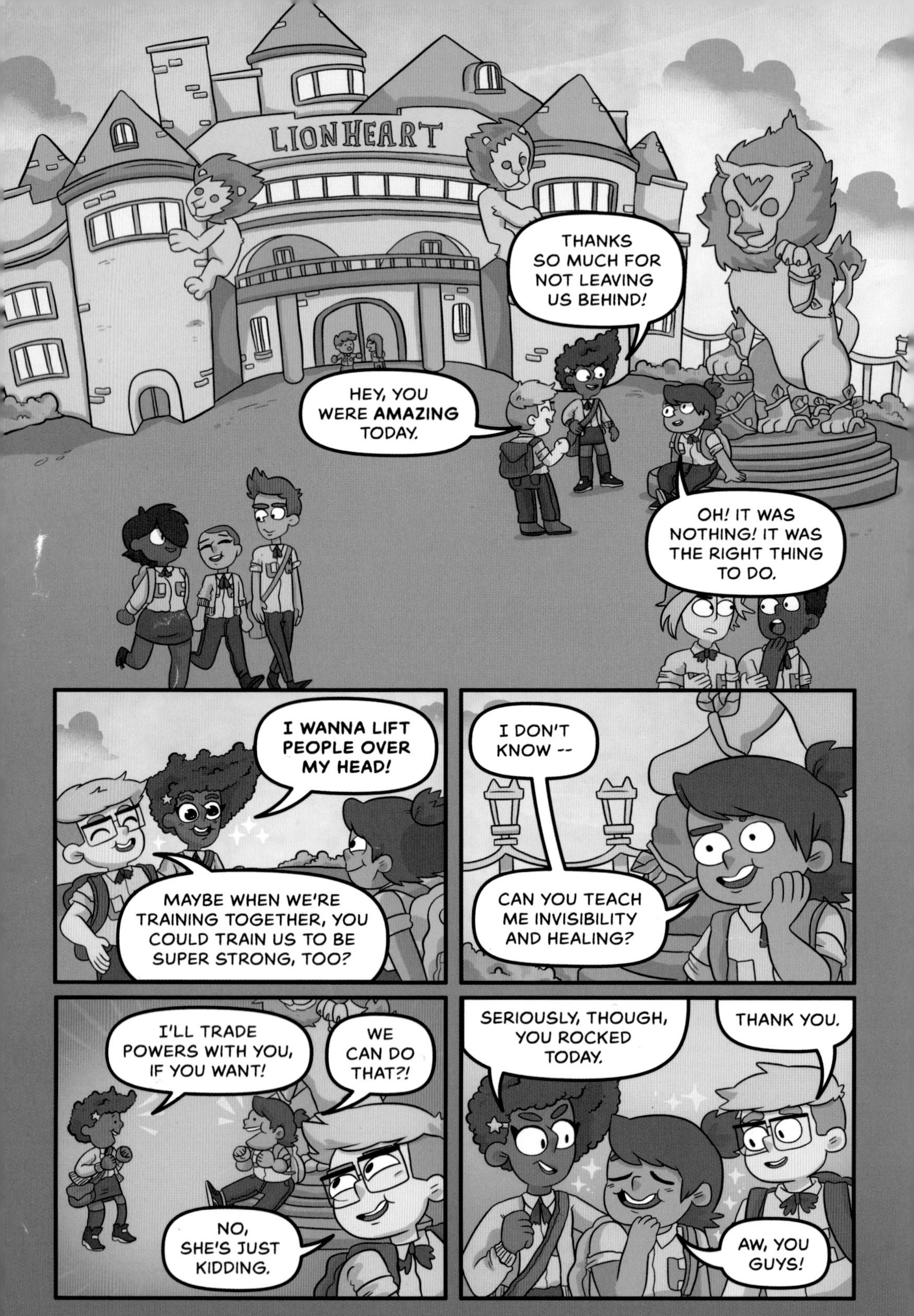
LIONHEART
THANKS SO MUCH FOR NOT LEAVING US BEHIND!
HEY, YOU WERE AMAZING TODAY.
OH! IT WAS NOTHING! IT WAS THE RIGHT THING TO DO.
I WANNA LIFT PEOPLE OVER MY HEAD!
MAYBE WHEN WE'RE TRAINING TOGETHER, YOU COULD TRAIN US TO BE SUPER STRONG, TOO?
I DON'T KNOW --
CAN YOU TEACH ME INVISIBILITY AND HEALING?
I'LL TRADE POWERS WITH YOU, IF YOU WANT!
WE CAN DO THAT?!
NO, SHE'S JUST KIDDING.
SERIOUSLY, THOUGH, YOU ROCKED TODAY.
THANK YOU.
AW, YOU GUYS!

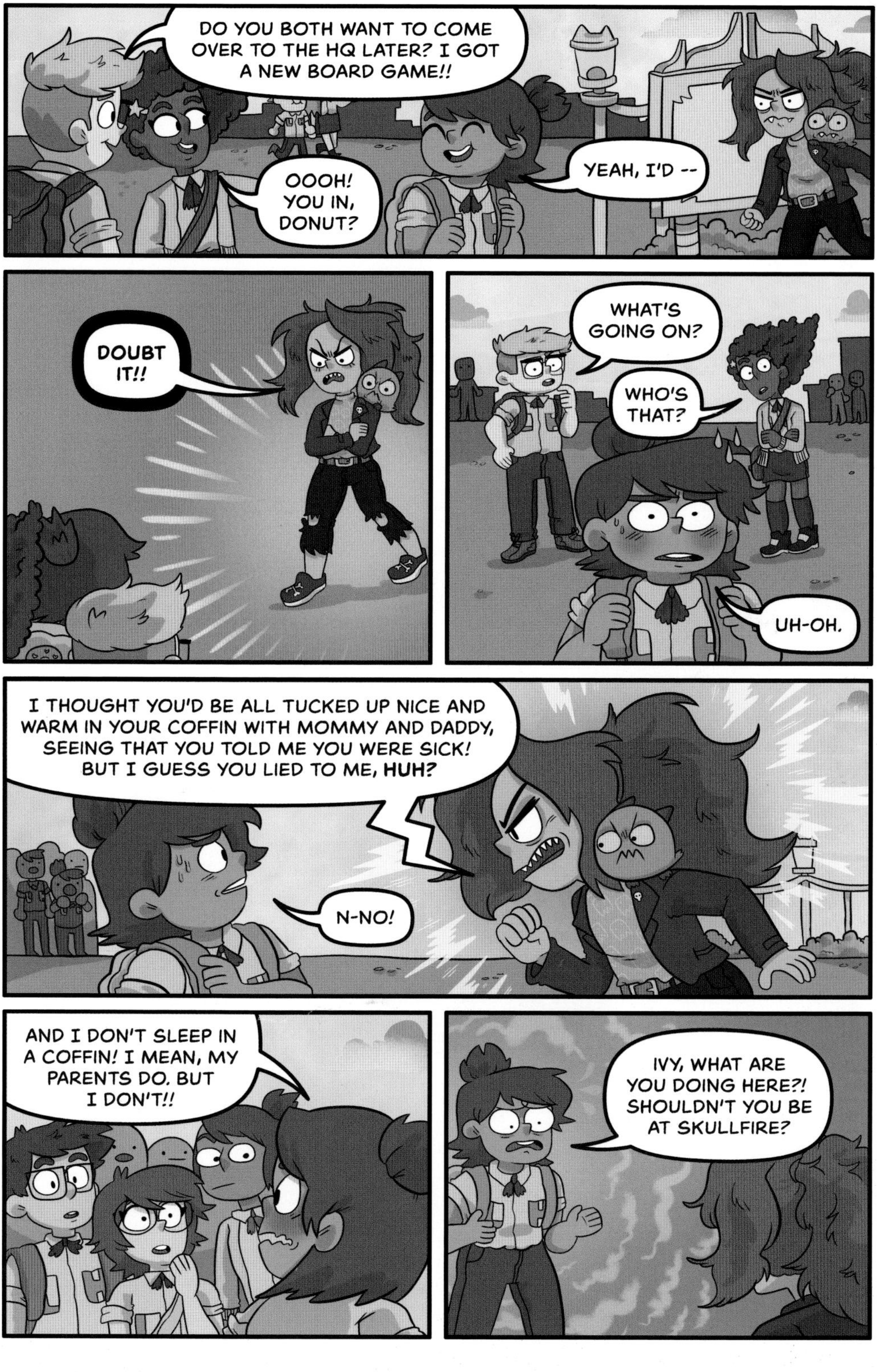
DO YOU BOTH WANT TO COME OVER TO THE HQ LATER? I GOT A NEW BOARD GAME!!
OOOH! YOU IN, DONUT?
YEAH, I'D --
DOUBT IT!!
WHAT'S GOING ON?
WHO'S THAT?
UH-OH.
I THOUGHT YOU'D BE ALL TUCKED UP NICE AND WARM IN YOUR COFFIN WITH MOMMY AND DADDY, SEEING THAT YOU TOLD ME YOU WERE SICK! BUT I GUESS YOU LIED TO ME, HUH?
N-NO!
AND I DON'T SLEEP IN A COFFIN! I MEAN, MY PARENTS DO, BUT I DON'T!!
IVY, WHAT ARE YOU DOING HERE?! SHOULDN'T YOU BE AT SKULLFIRE?

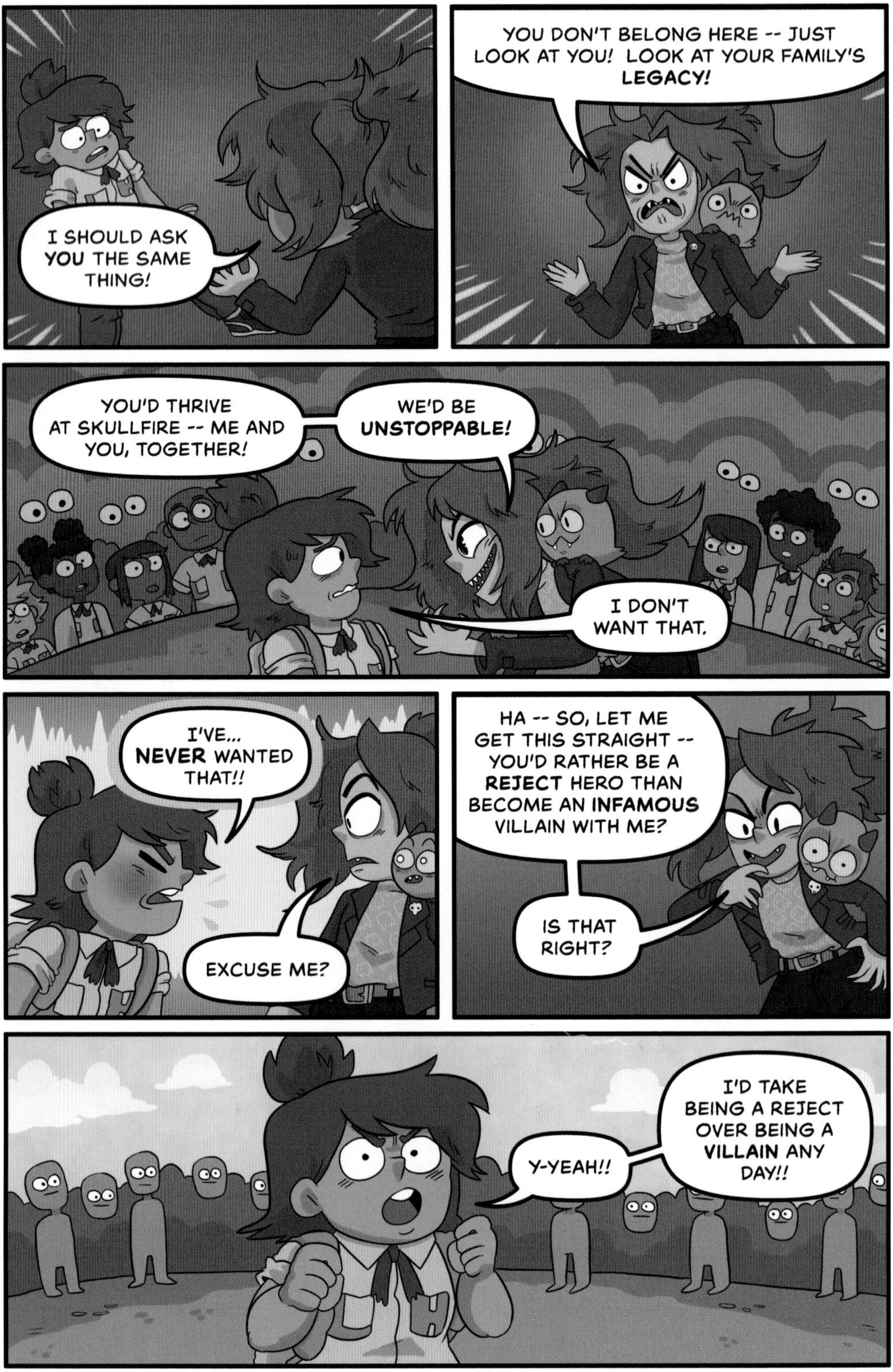
I SHOULD ASK YOU THE SAME THING!
YOU DON'T BELONG HERE -- JUST LOOK AT YOU! LOOK AT YOUR FAMILY'S LEGACY!
YOU'D THRIVE AT SKULLFIRE -- ME AND YOU, TOGETHER!
WE'D BE UNSTOPPABLE!
I DON'T WANT THAT.
I'VE... NEVER WANTED THAT!!
EXCUSE ME?
HA -- SO, LET ME GET THIS STRAIGHT -- YOU'D RATHER BE A REJECT HERO THAN BECOME AN INFAMOUS VILLAIN WITH ME?
IS THAT RIGHT?
Y-YEAH!!
I'D TAKE BEING A REJECT OVER BEING A VILLAIN ANY DAY!!

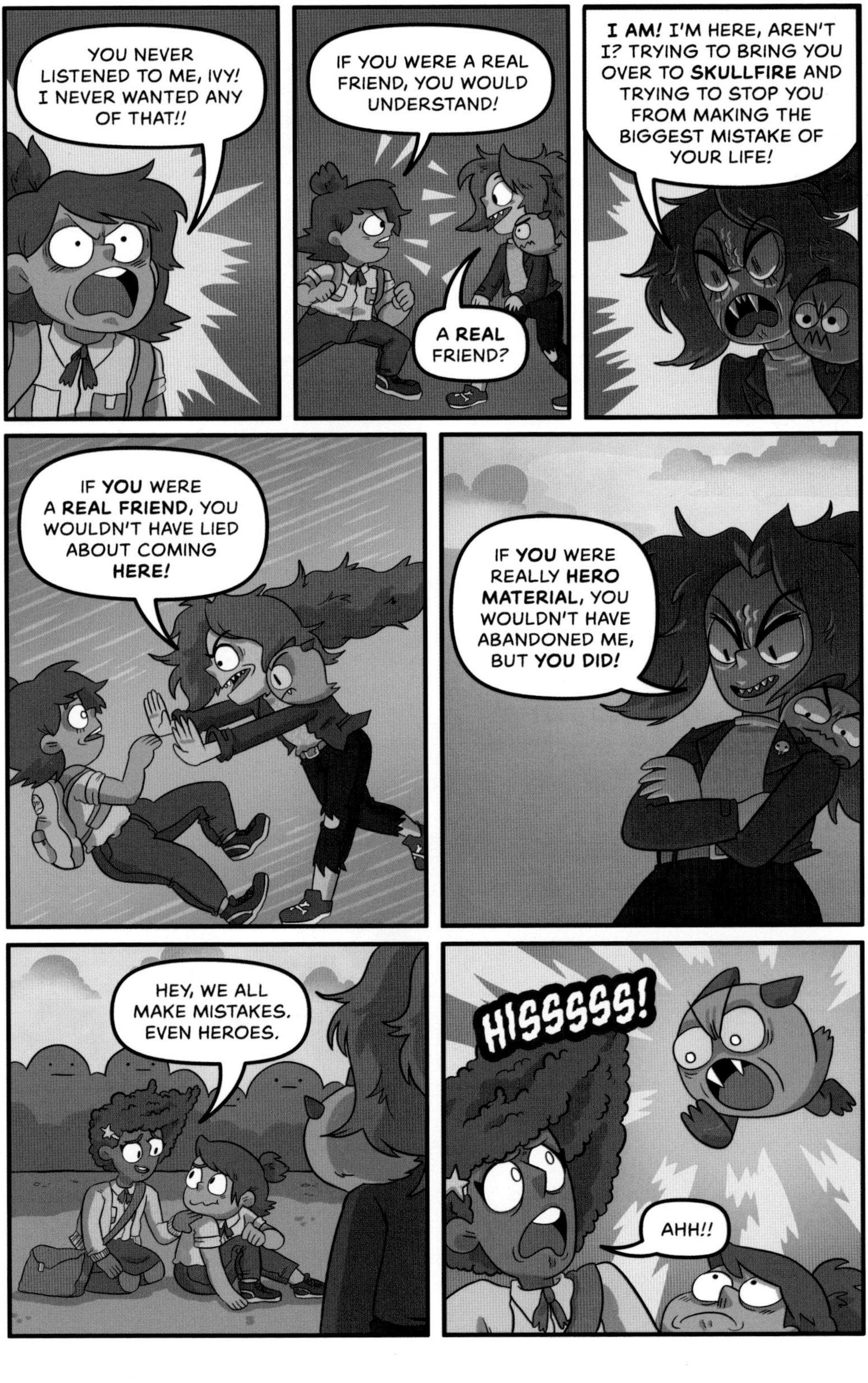
YOU NEVER LISTENED TO ME, IVY! I NEVER WANTED ANY OF THAT!!
IF YOU WERE A REAL FRIEND, YOU WOULD UNDERSTAND!
A REAL FRIEND?
I AM! I'M HERE, AREN'T I? TRYING TO BRING YOU OVER TO SKULLFIRE AND TRYING TO STOP YOU FROM MAKING THE BIGGEST MISTAKE OF YOUR LIFE!
IF YOU WERE A REAL FRIEND, YOU WOULDN'T HAVE LIED ABOUT COMING HERE!
IF YOU WERE REALLY HERO MATERIAL, YOU WOULDN'T HAVE ABANDONED ME, BUT YOU DID!
HEY, WE ALL MAKE MISTAKES. EVEN HEROES.
HISSSSS!
AHH!!

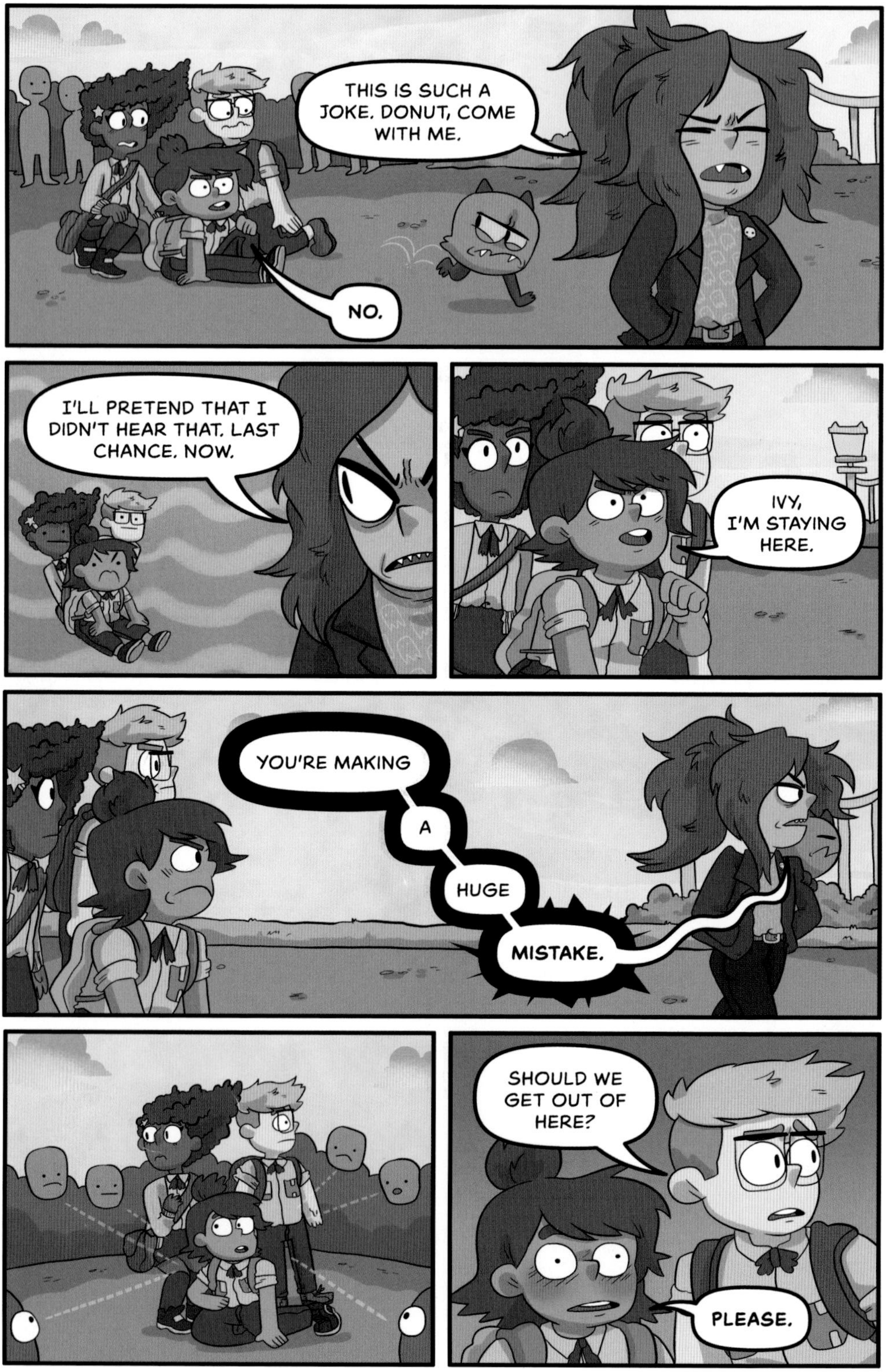
THIS IS SUCH A JOKE. DONUT, COME WITH ME.
NO.
I'LL PRETEND THAT I DIDN'T HEAR THAT. LAST CHANCE. NOW.
IVY, I'M STAYING HERE.
YOU'RE MAKING A HUGE MISTAKE.
SHOULD WE GET OUT OF HERE?
PLEASE.

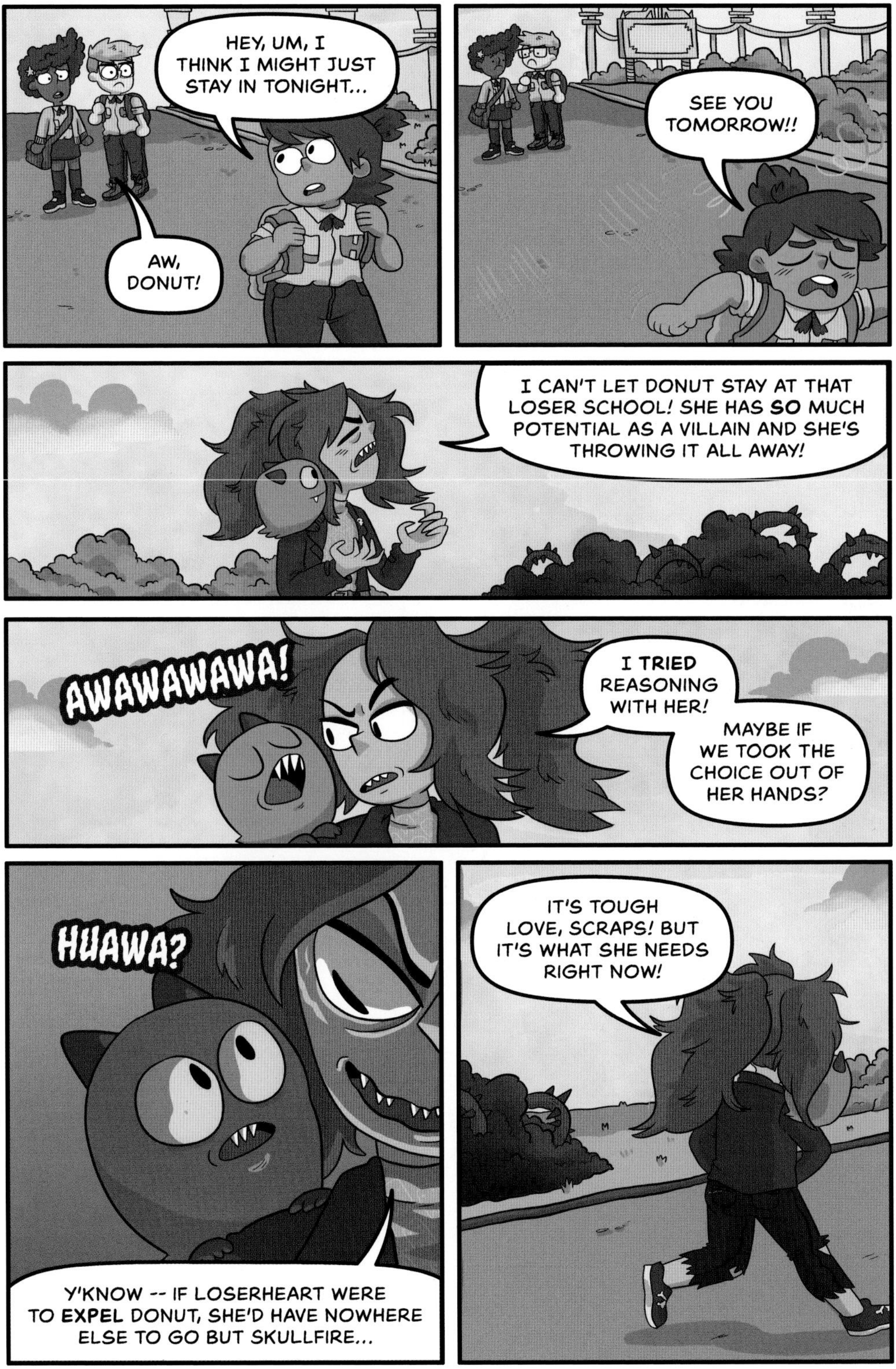
HEY, UM, I THINK I MIGHT JUST STAY IN TONIGHT...
AW, DONUT!
SEE YOU TOMORROW!!
I CAN'T LET DONUT STAY AT THAT LOSER SCHOOL! SHE HAS SO MUCH POTENTIAL AS A VILLAIN AND SHE'S THROWING IT ALL AWAY!
AWAWAWAWA!
I TRIED REASONING WITH HER!
MAYBE IF WE TOOK THE CHOICE OUT OF HER HANDS?
HUAWA?
Y'KNOW -- IF LOSERHEART WERE TO EXPEL DONUT, SHE'D HAVE NOWHERE ELSE TO GO BUT SKULLFIRE...
IT'S TOUGH LOVE, SCRAPS! BUT IT'S WHAT SHE NEEDS RIGHT NOW!

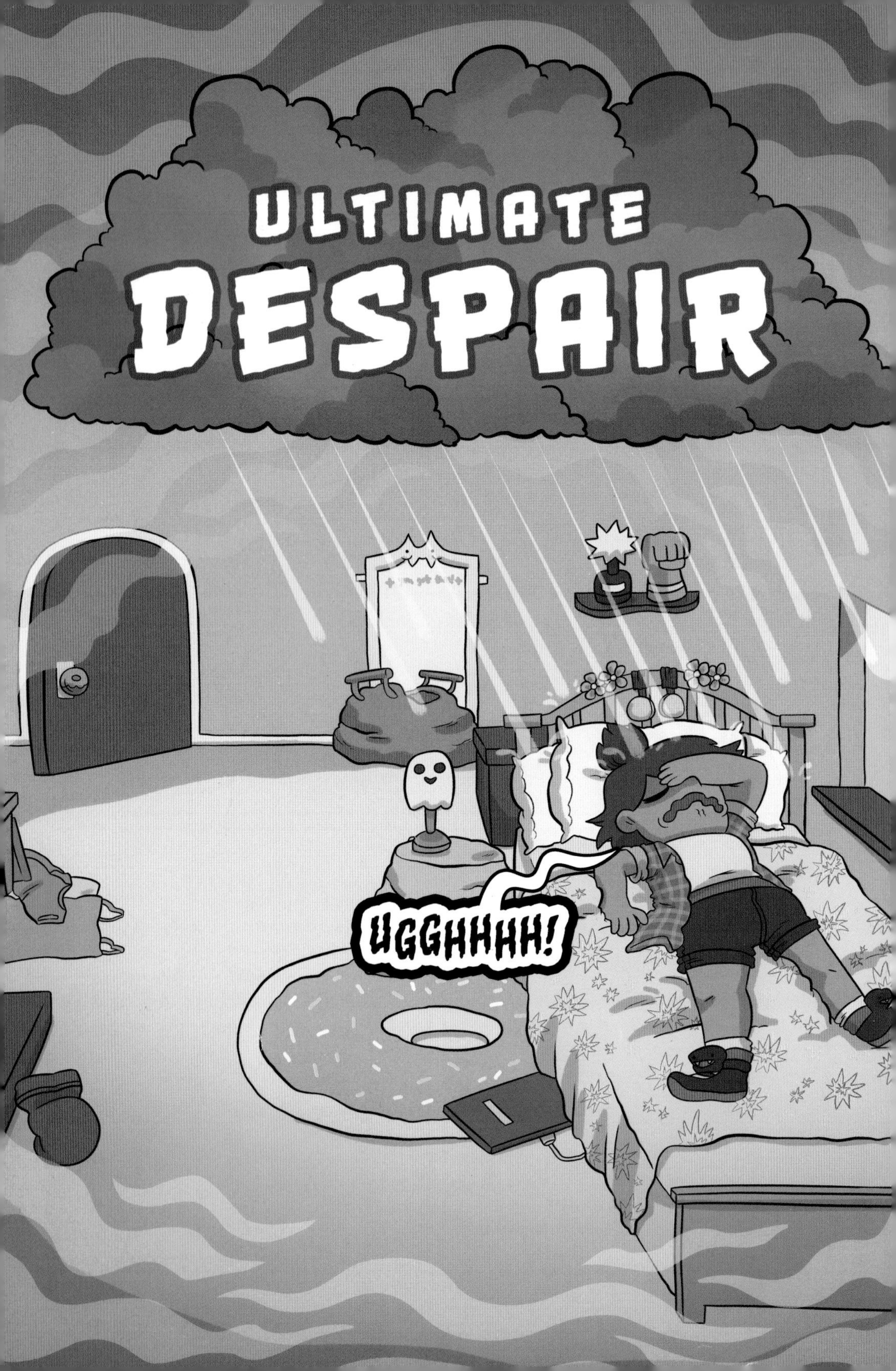
ULTIMATE
DESPAIR
UGGHHHH!

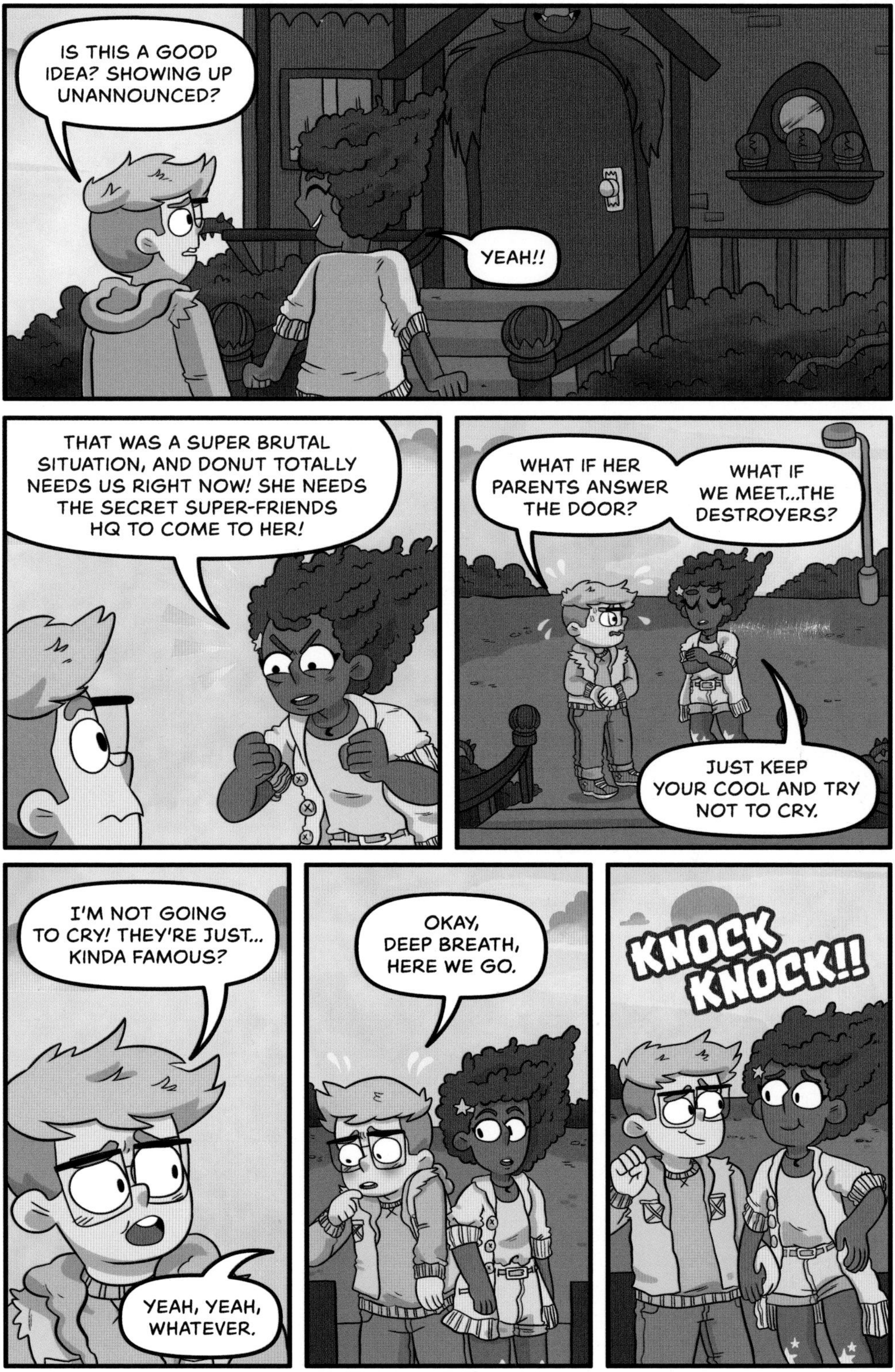
IS THIS A GOOD IDEA? SHOWING UP UNANNOUNCED?
YEAH!!
THAT WAS A SUPER BRUTAL SITUATION, AND DONUT TOTALLY NEEDS US RIGHT NOW! SHE NEEDS THE SECRET SUPER-FRIENDS HQ TO COME TO HER!
WHAT IF HER PARENTS ANSWER THE DOOR?
WHAT IF WE MEET...THE DESTROYERS?
JUST KEEP YOUR COOL AND TRY NOT TO CRY.
I'M NOT GOING TO CRY! THEY'RE JUST... KINDA FAMOUS?
YEAH, YEAH, WHATEVER.
OKAY, DEEP BREATH, HERE WE GO.
KNOCK KNOCK!!

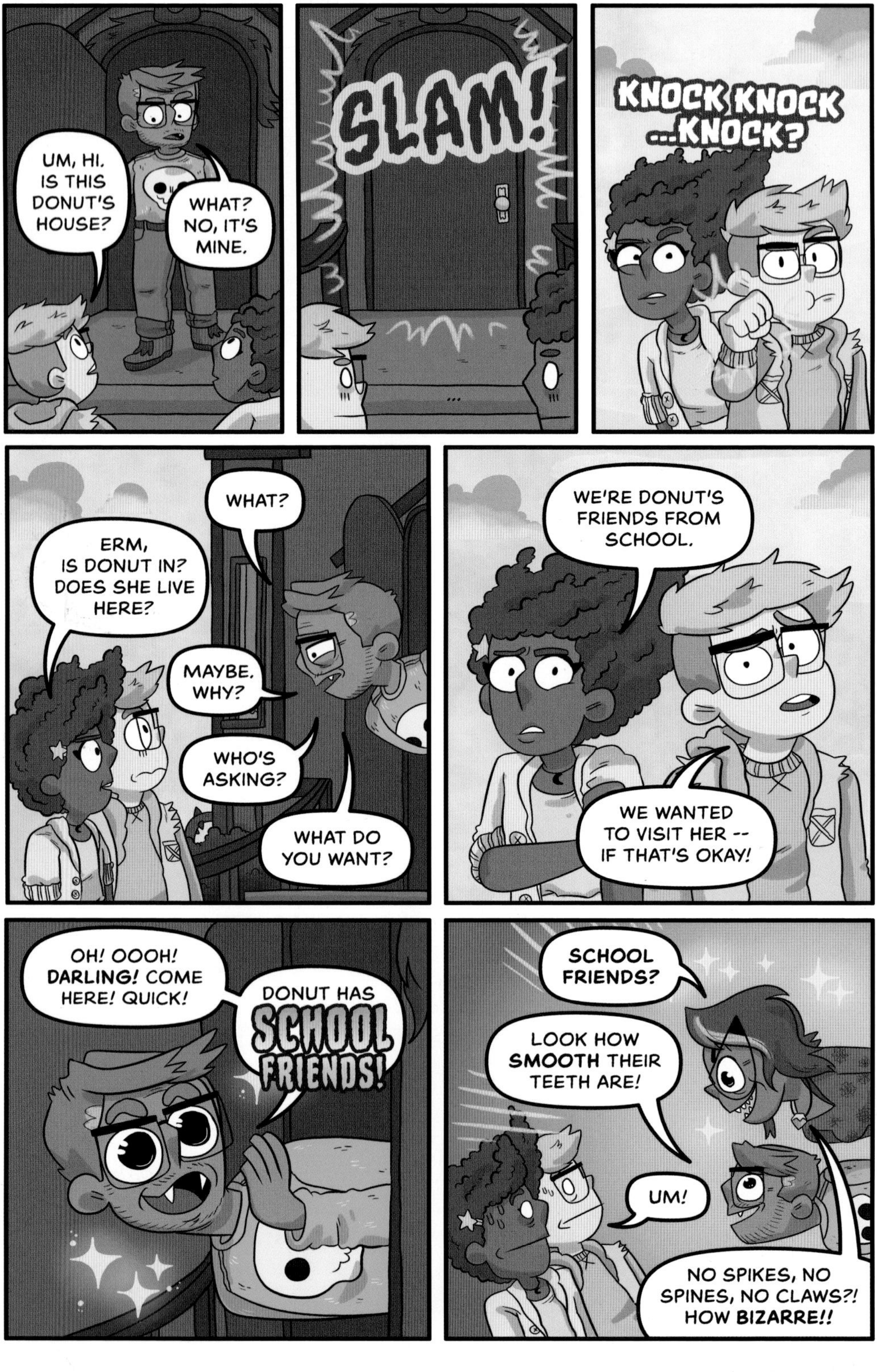
UM, HI. IS THIS DONUT'S HOUSE?
WHAT? NO, IT'S MINE.
SLAM!
KNOCK KNOCK ...KNOCK?
ERM, IS DONUT IN? DOES SHE LIVE HERE?
WHAT?
MAYBE. WHY?
WHO'S ASKING?
WHAT DO YOU WANT?
WE'RE DONUT'S FRIENDS FROM SCHOOL.
WE WANTED TO VISIT HER -- IF THAT'S OKAY!
OH! OOOH! DARLING! COME HERE! QUICK!
DONUT HAS SCHOOL FRIENDS!
SCHOOL FRIENDS?
LOOK HOW SMOOTH THEIR TEETH ARE!
UM!
NO SPIKES, NO SPINES, NO CLAWS?! HOW BIZARRE!!

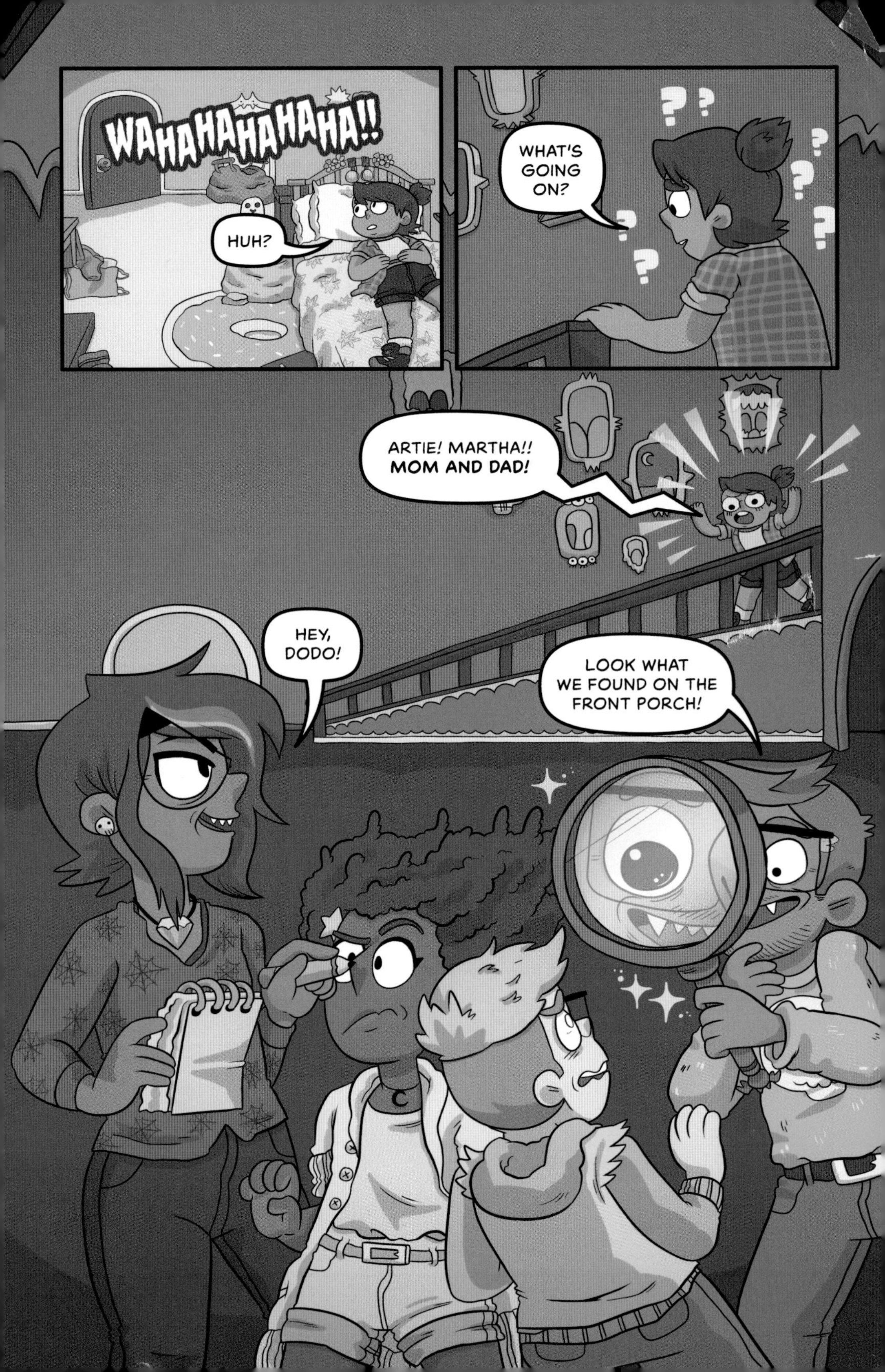
WAHAHAHAHAHAHA!!
HUH?
WHAT'S GOING ON?
ARTIE! MARTHA!! **MOM AND DAD!**
HEY, DODO!
LOOK WHAT WE FOUND ON THE FRONT PORCH!

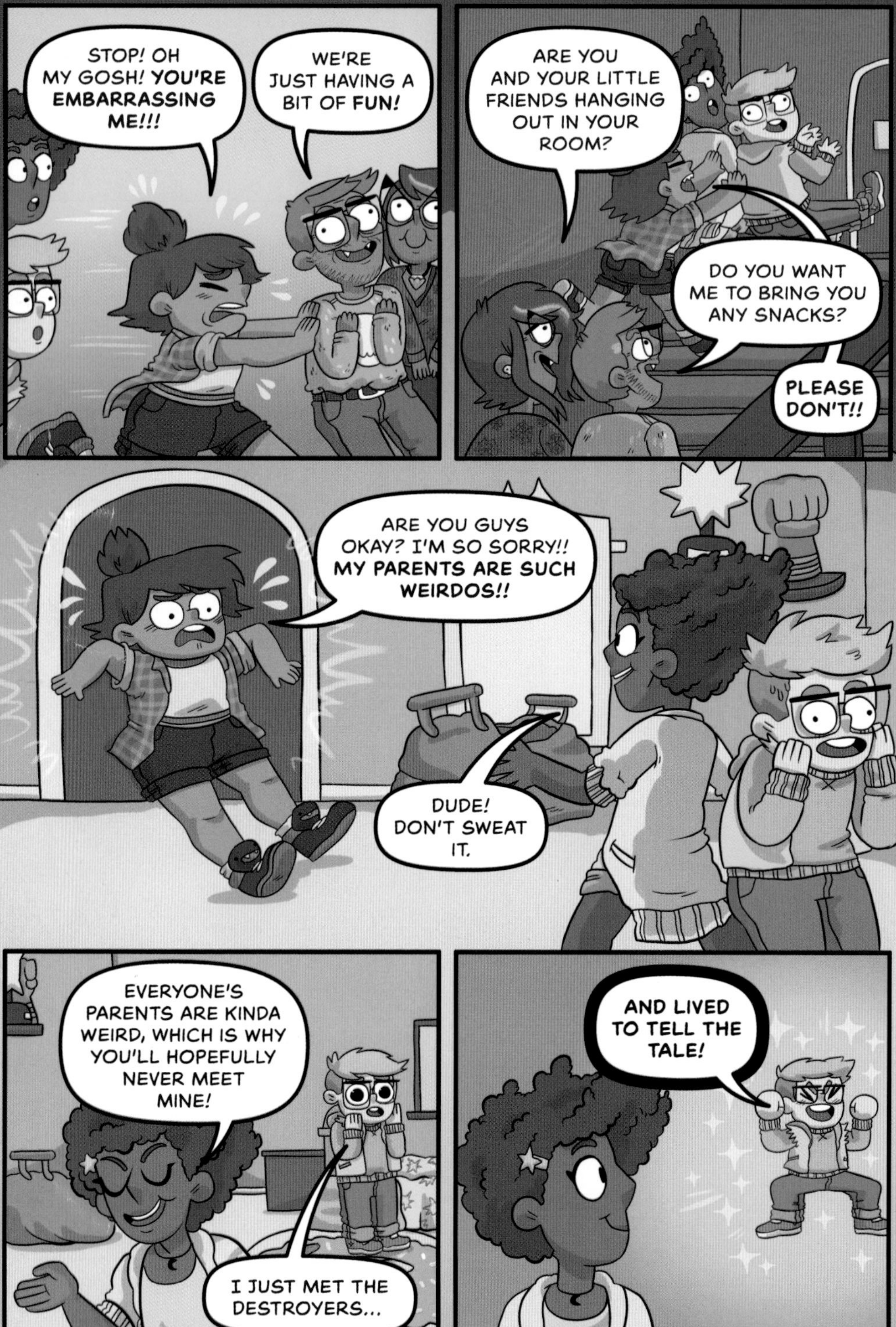
STOP! OH MY GOSH! YOU'RE EMBARRASSING ME!!!
WE'RE JUST HAVING A BIT OF FUN!
ARE YOU AND YOUR LITTLE FRIENDS HANGING OUT IN YOUR ROOM?
DO YOU WANT ME TO BRING YOU ANY SNACKS?
PLEASE DON'T!!
ARE YOU GUYS OKAY? I'M SO SORRY!! MY PARENTS ARE SUCH WEIRDOS!!
DUDE! DON'T SWEAT IT.
EVERYONE'S PARENTS ARE KINDA WEIRD, WHICH IS WHY YOU'LL HOPEFULLY NEVER MEET MINE!
I JUST MET THE DESTROYERS...
AND LIVED TO TELL THE TALE!

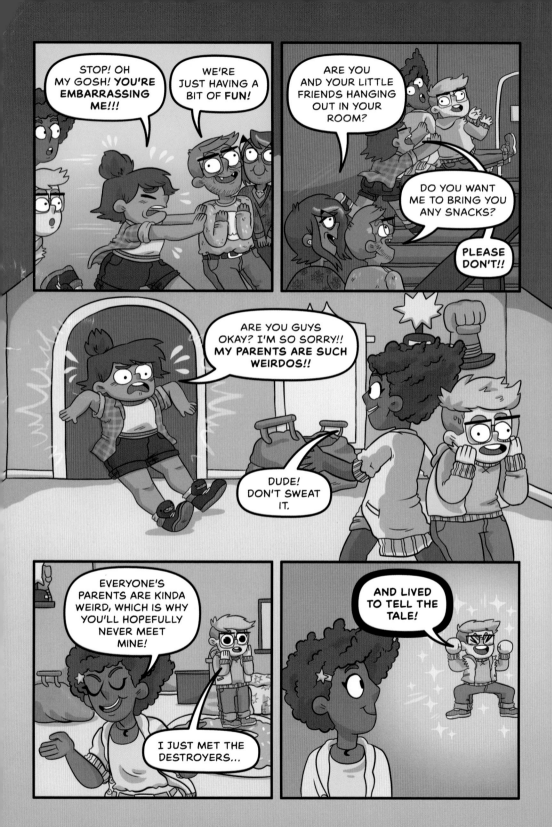

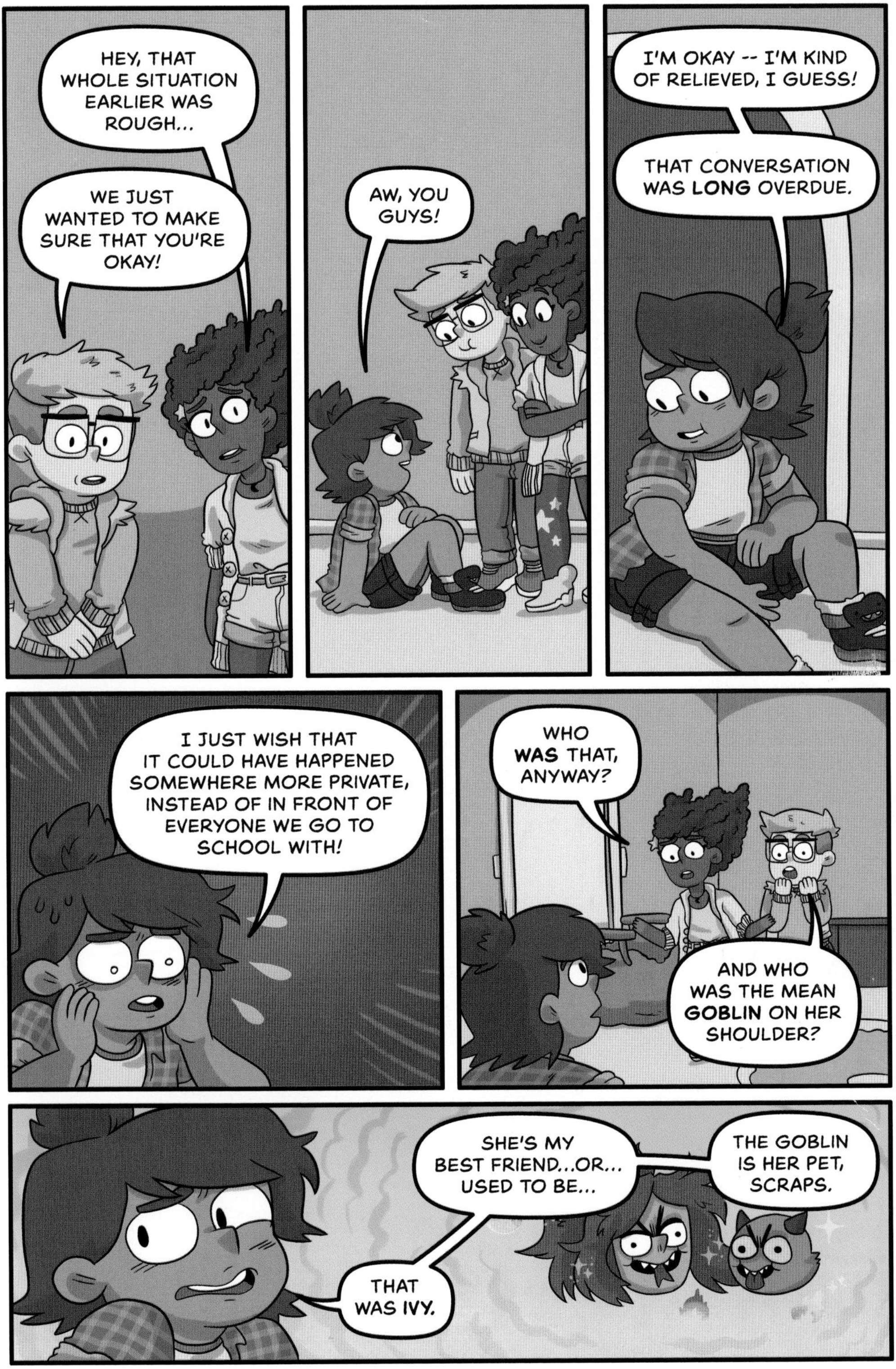
HEY, THAT WHOLE SITUATION EARLIER WAS ROUGH...
WE JUST WANTED TO MAKE SURE THAT YOU'RE OKAY!
AW, YOU GUYS!
I'M OKAY -- I'M KIND OF RELIEVED, I GUESS!
THAT CONVERSATION WAS **LONG** OVERDUE.
I JUST WISH THAT IT COULD HAVE HAPPENED SOMEWHERE MORE PRIVATE, INSTEAD OF IN FRONT OF EVERYONE WE GO TO SCHOOL WITH!
WHO **WAS** THAT, ANYWAY?
AND WHO WAS THE MEAN **GOBLIN** ON HER SHOULDER?
THAT WAS IVY.
SHE'S MY BEST FRIEND...OR... USED TO BE...
THE GOBLIN IS HER PET, SCRAPS.

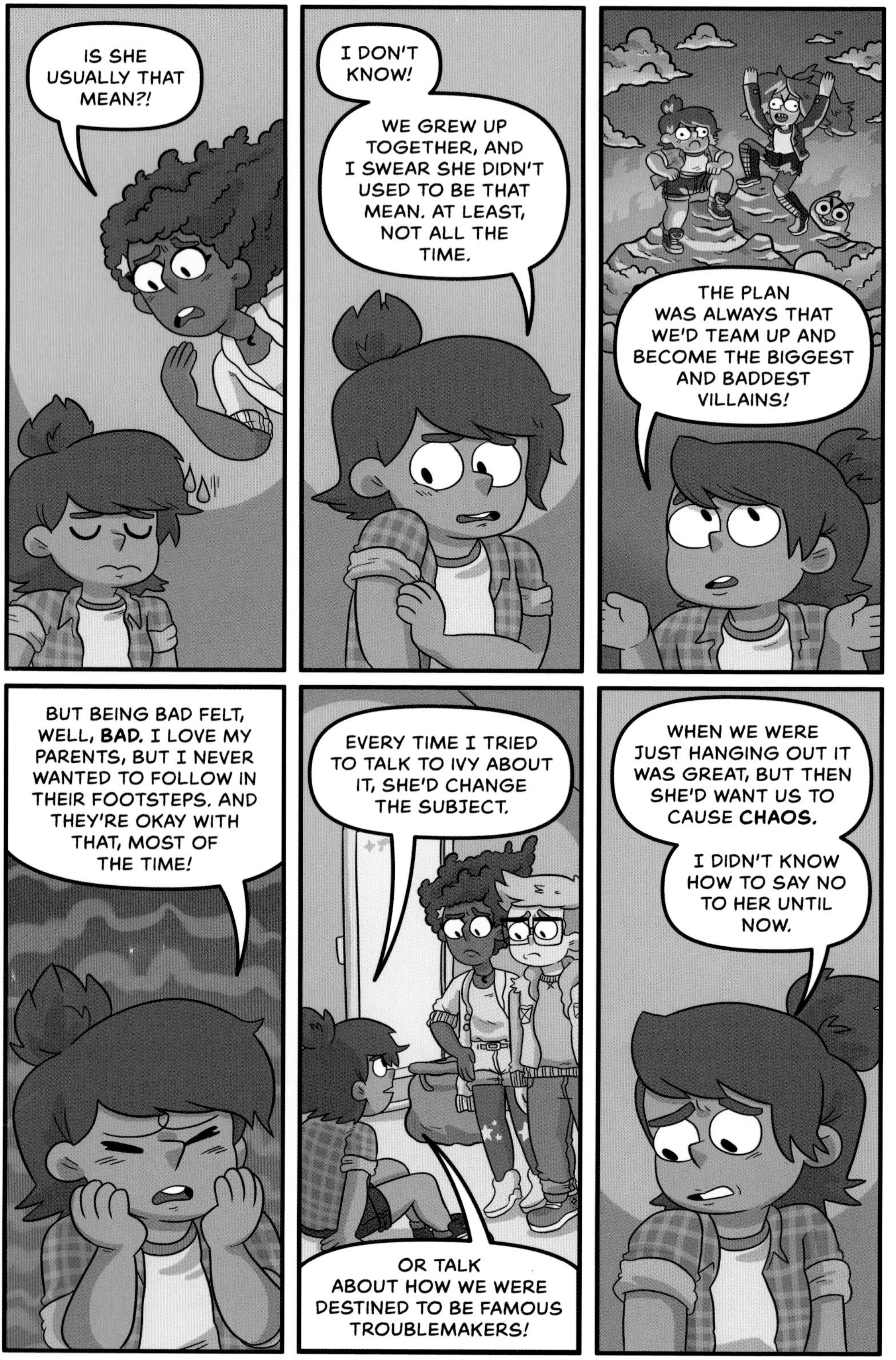
IS SHE USUALLY THAT MEAN?!
I DON'T KNOW!
WE GREW UP TOGETHER, AND I SWEAR SHE DIDN'T USED TO BE THAT MEAN. AT LEAST, NOT ALL THE TIME.
THE PLAN WAS ALWAYS THAT WE'D TEAM UP AND BECOME THE BIGGEST AND BADDEST VILLAINS!
BUT BEING BAD FELT, WELL, **BAD.** I LOVE MY PARENTS, BUT I NEVER WANTED TO FOLLOW IN THEIR FOOTSTEPS. AND THEY'RE OKAY WITH THAT, MOST OF THE TIME!
EVERY TIME I TRIED TO TALK TO IVY ABOUT IT, SHE'D CHANGE THE SUBJECT.
OR TALK ABOUT HOW WE WERE DESTINED TO BE FAMOUS TROUBLEMAKERS!
WHEN WE WERE JUST HANGING OUT IT WAS GREAT, BUT THEN SHE'D WANT US TO CAUSE **CHAOS.**
I DIDN'T KNOW HOW TO SAY NO TO HER UNTIL NOW.

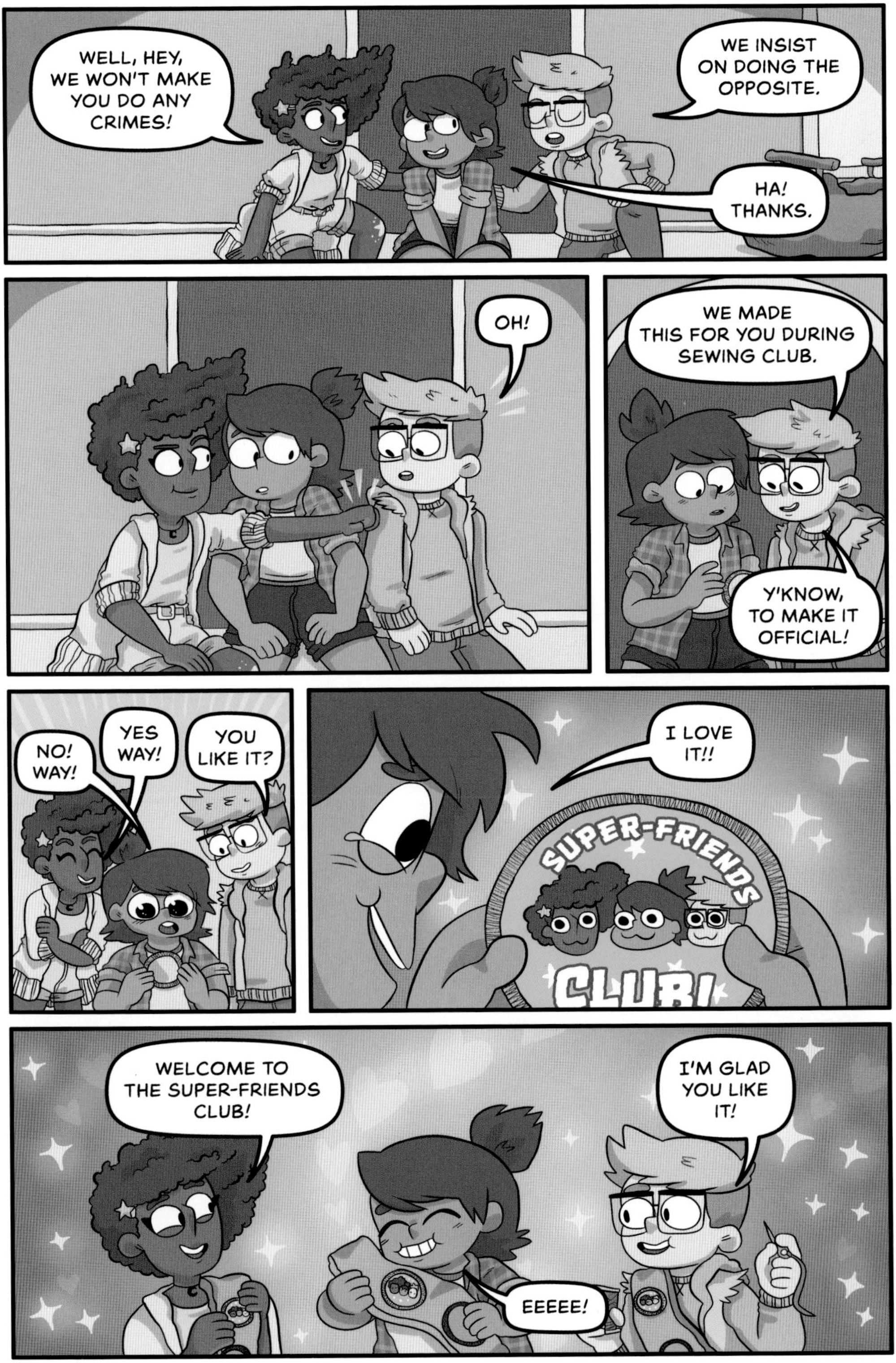
WELL, HEY, WE WON'T MAKE YOU DO ANY CRIMES!
WE INSIST ON DOING THE OPPOSITE.
HA! THANKS.
OH!
WE MADE THIS FOR YOU DURING SEWING CLUB.
Y'KNOW, TO MAKE IT OFFICIAL!
NO! WAY!
YES WAY!
YOU LIKE IT?
I LOVE IT!!
SUPER-FRIENDS
CLUB
WELCOME TO THE SUPER-FRIENDS CLUB!
I'M GLAD YOU LIKE IT!
EEEEE!

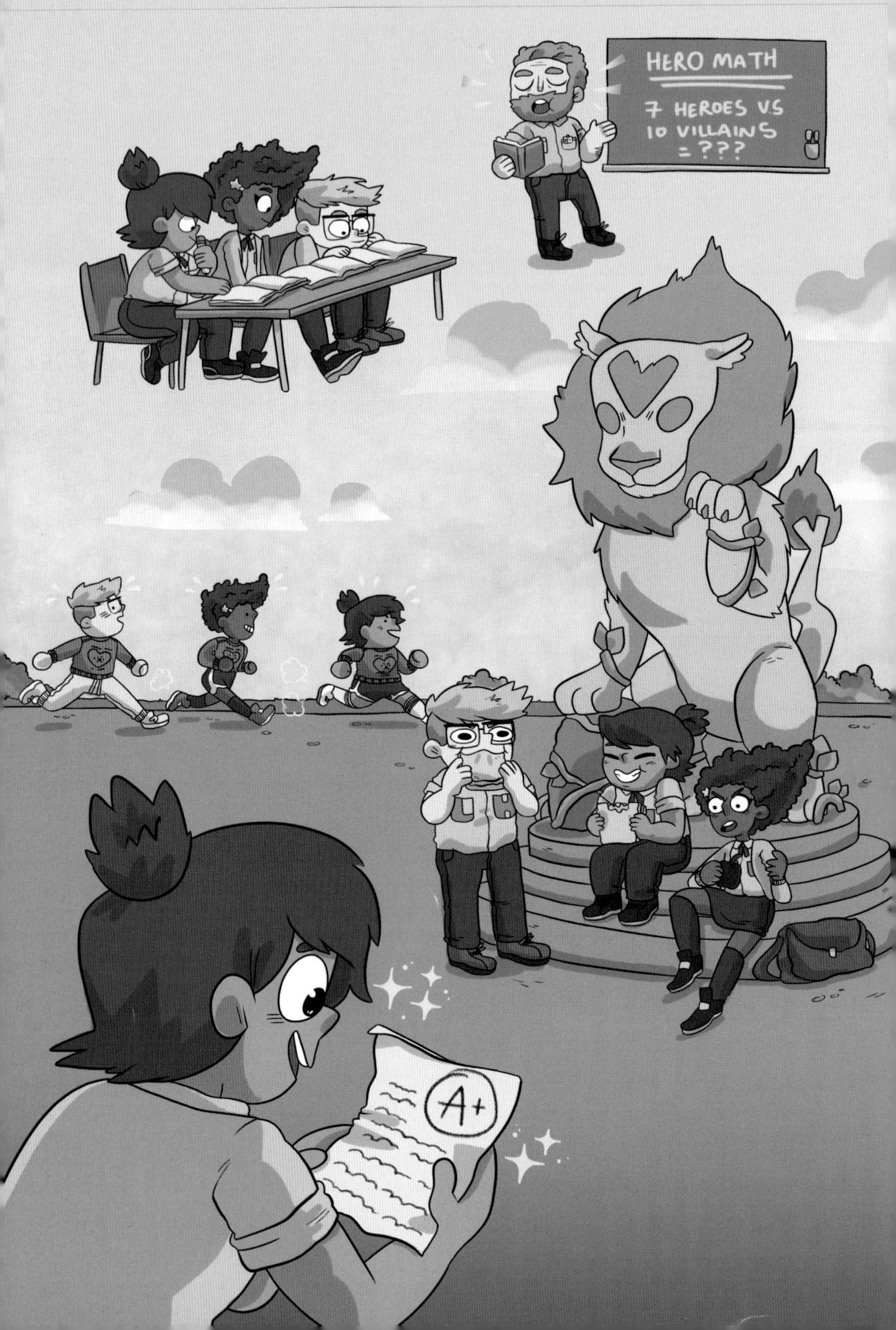
HERO MATH
7 HEROES V.S
10 VILLAINS
= ???
A+

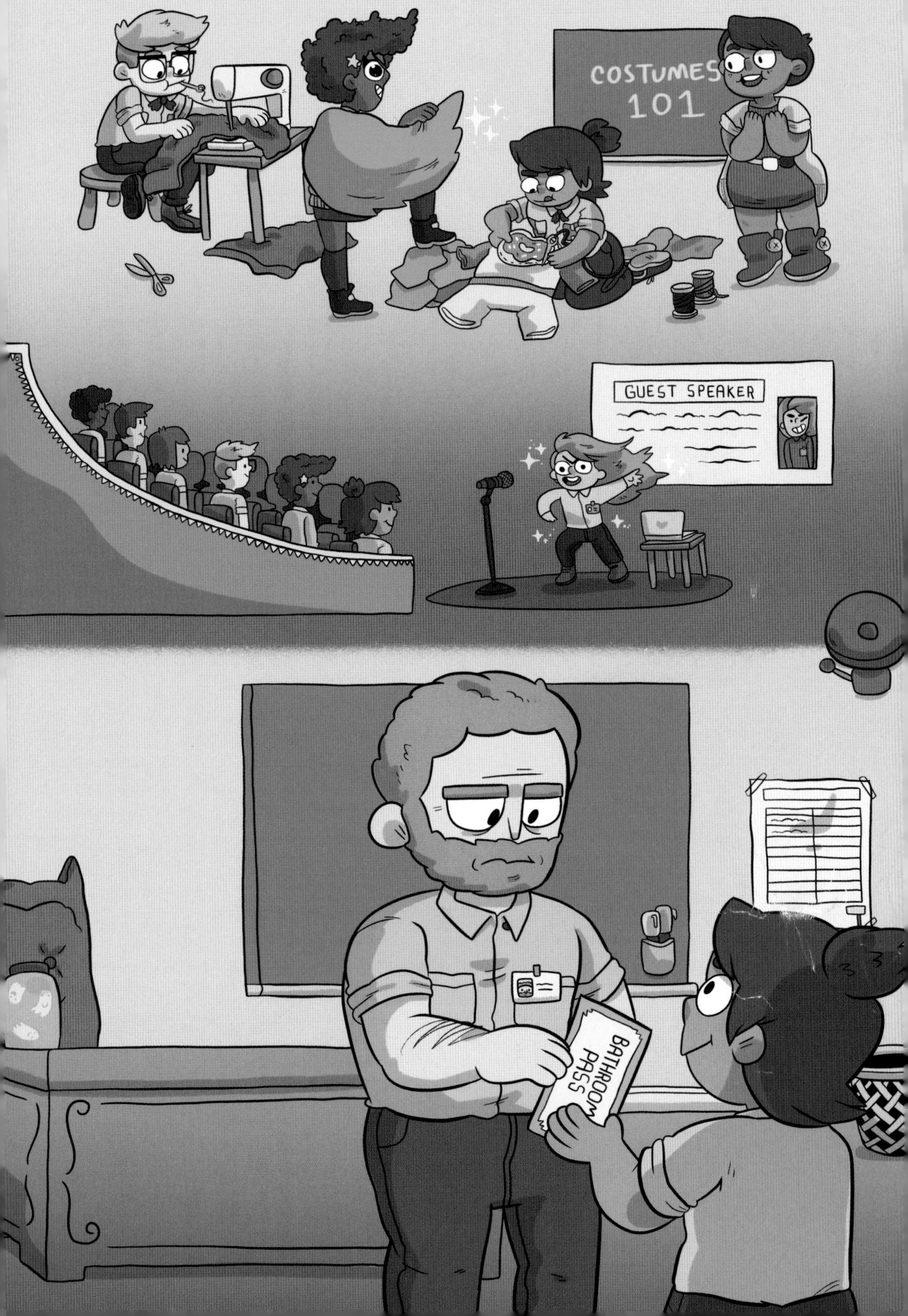
COSTUMES 101
GUEST SPEAKER
BATHROOM PASS

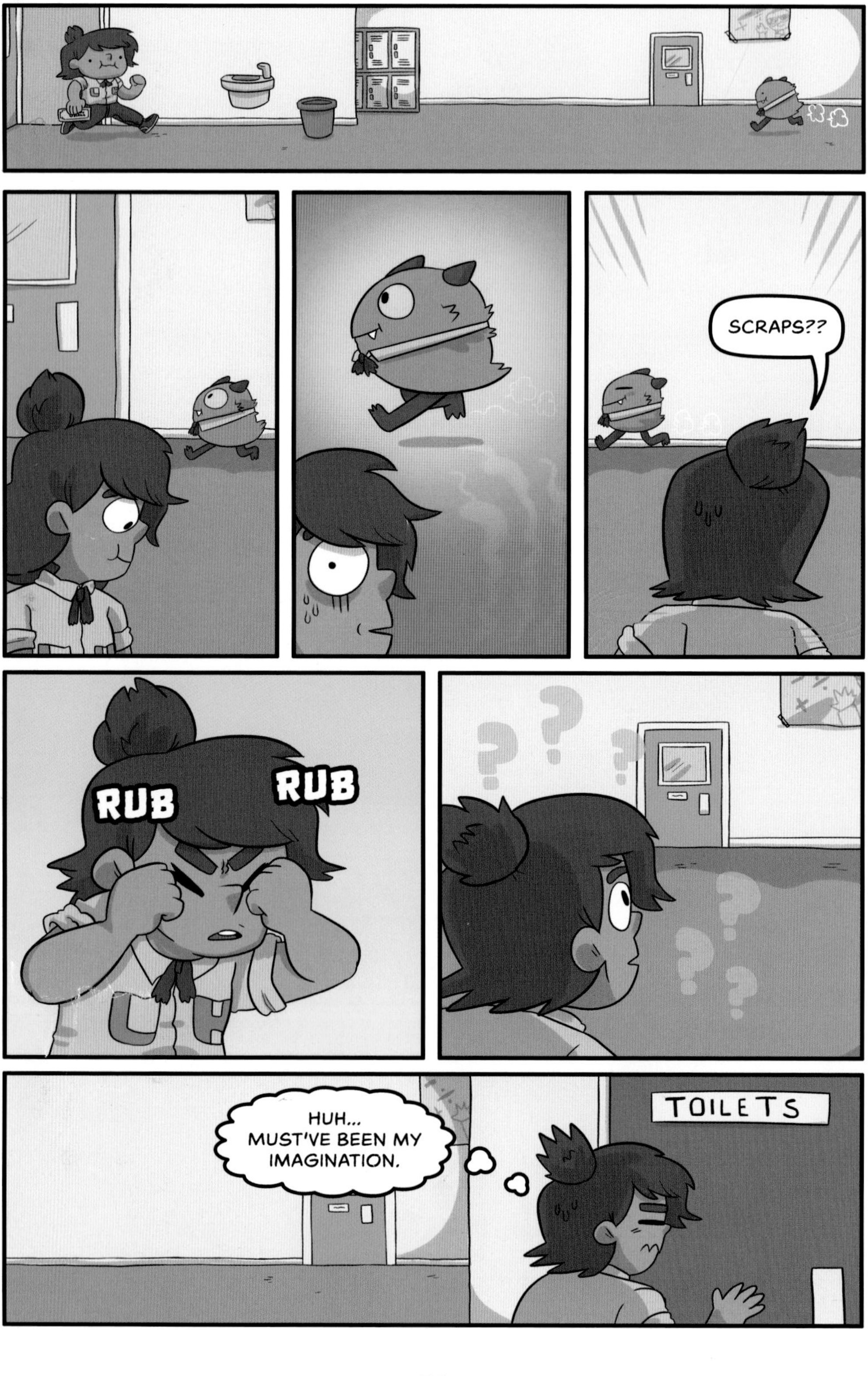
SCRAPS??
RUB
RUB
HUH...
MUST'VE BEEN MY
IMAGINATION.
TOILETS

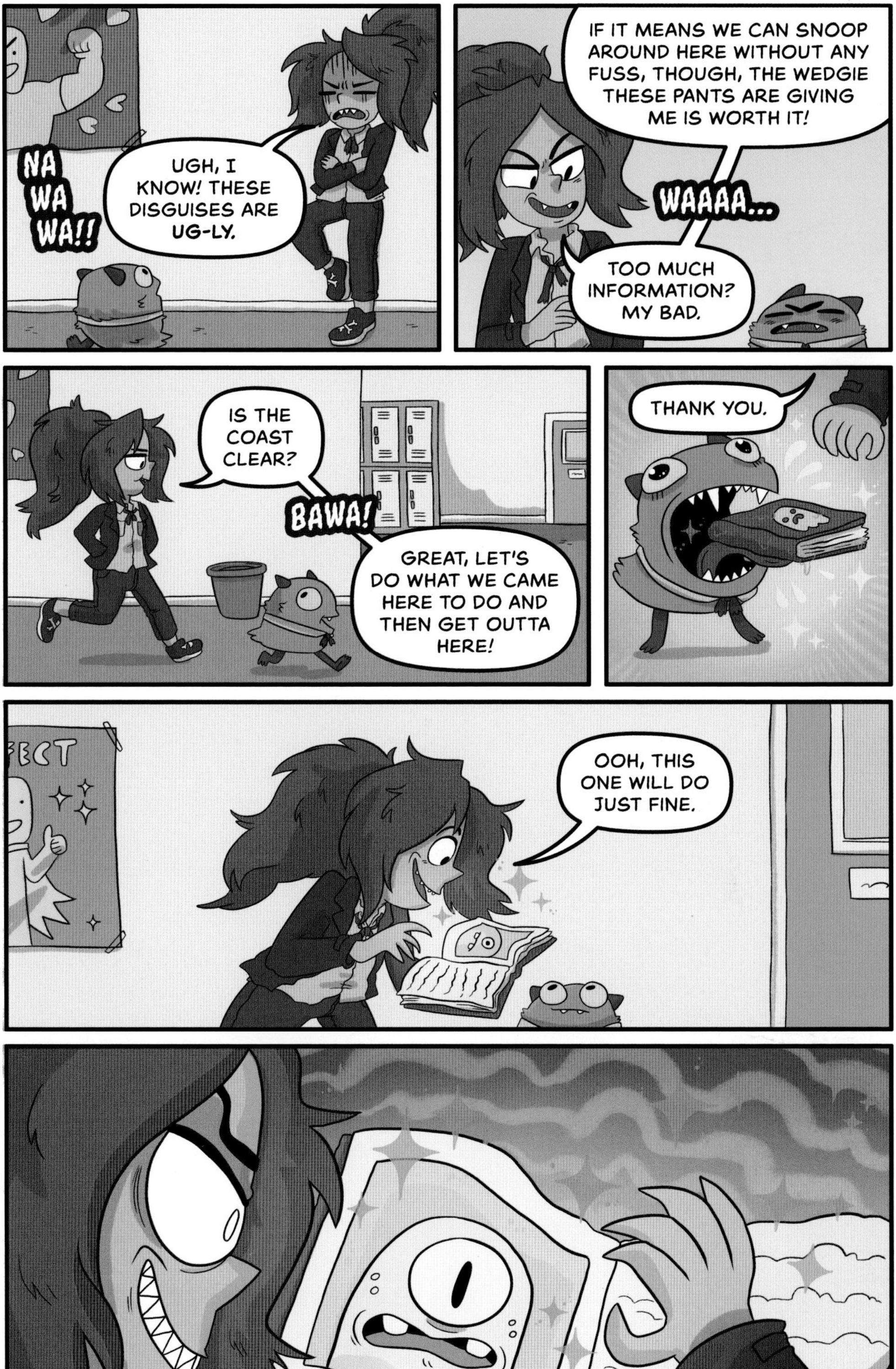
NA WA WA!!
UGH, I KNOW! THESE DISGUISES ARE UG-LY.
IF IT MEANS WE CAN SNOOP AROUND HERE WITHOUT ANY FUSS, THOUGH, THE WEDGIE THESE PANTS ARE GIVING ME IS WORTH IT!
WAAAA...
TOO MUCH INFORMATION? MY BAD.
IS THE COAST CLEAR?
BAWA!
GREAT, LET'S DO WHAT WE CAME HERE TO DO AND THEN GET OUTTA HERE!
THANK YOU.
OOH, THIS ONE WILL DO JUST FINE.

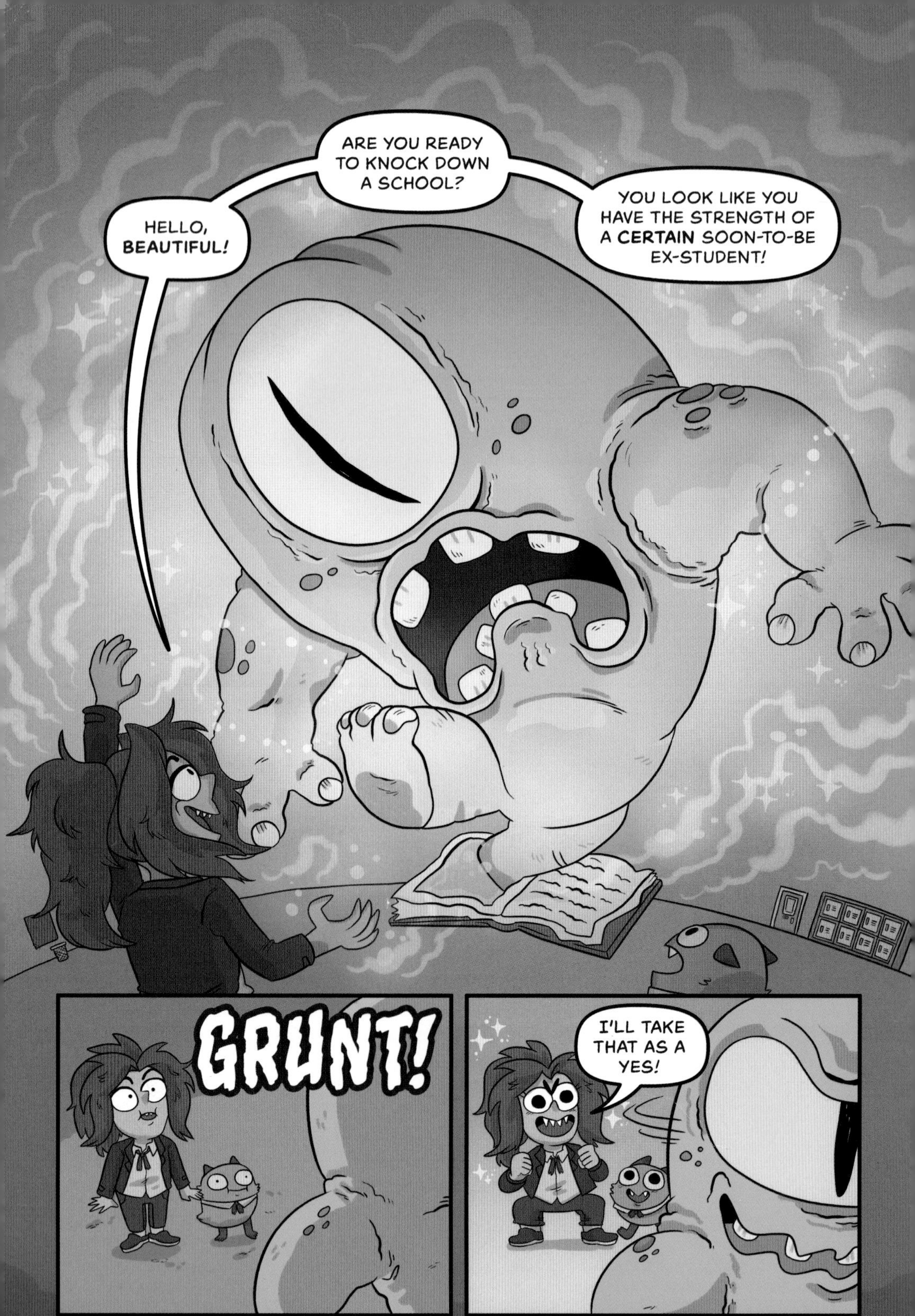
HELLO, BEAUTIFUL!
ARE YOU READY TO KNOCK DOWN A SCHOOL?
YOU LOOK LIKE YOU HAVE THE STRENGTH OF A **CERTAIN** SOON-TO-BE EX-STUDENT!
GRUNT!
I'LL TAKE THAT AS A YES!

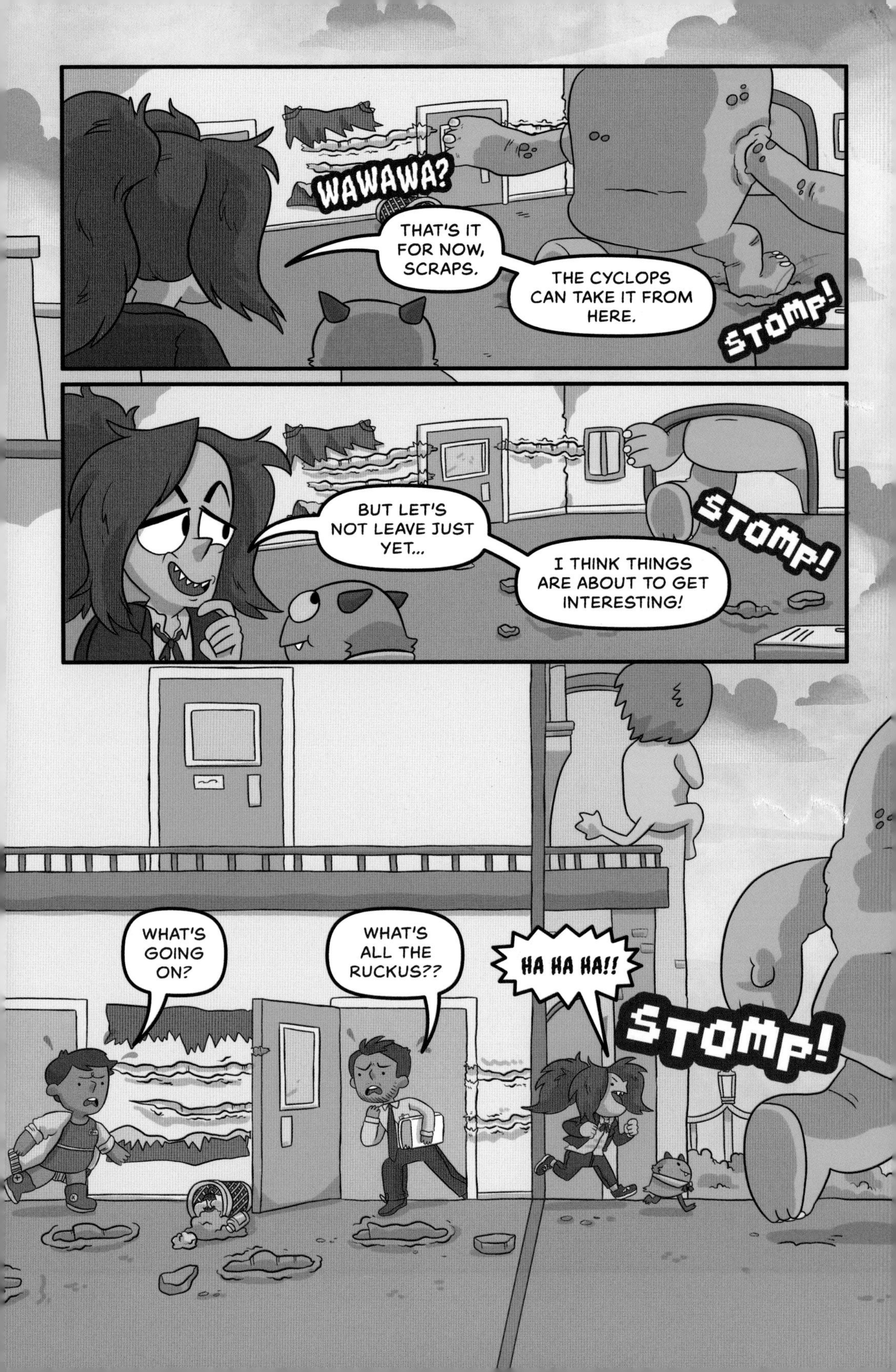
WAWAWA?
THAT'S IT FOR NOW, SCRAPS.
THE CYCLOPS CAN TAKE IT FROM HERE.
STOMP!
BUT LET'S NOT LEAVE JUST YET...
I THINK THINGS ARE ABOUT TO GET INTERESTING!
STOMP!
WHAT'S GOING ON?
WHAT'S ALL THE RUCKUS??
HA HA HA!!
STOMP!

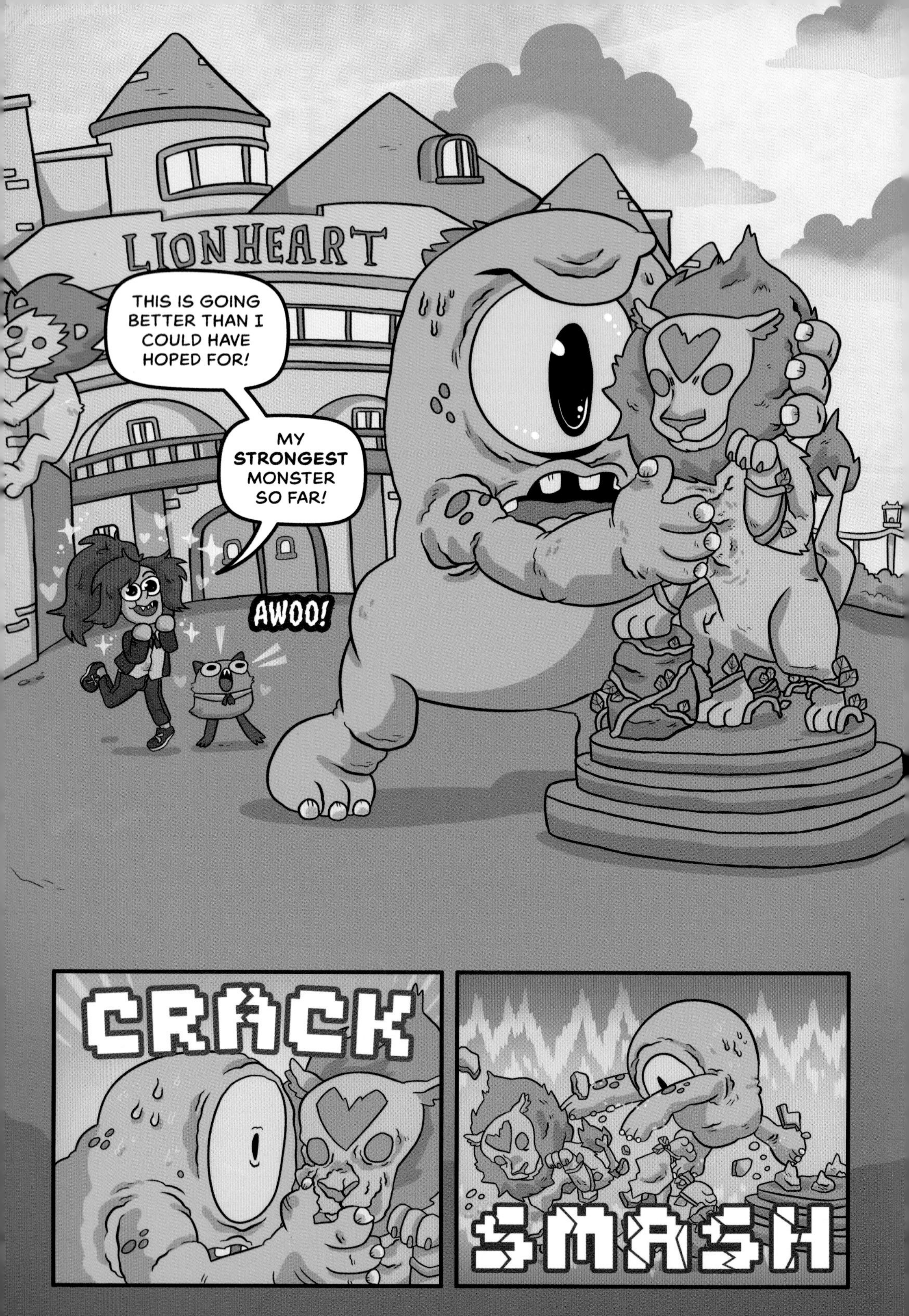
LIONHEART
THIS IS GOING BETTER THAN I COULD HAVE HOPED FOR!
MY **STRONGEST** MONSTER SO FAR!
AWOO!
CRACK
SMASH

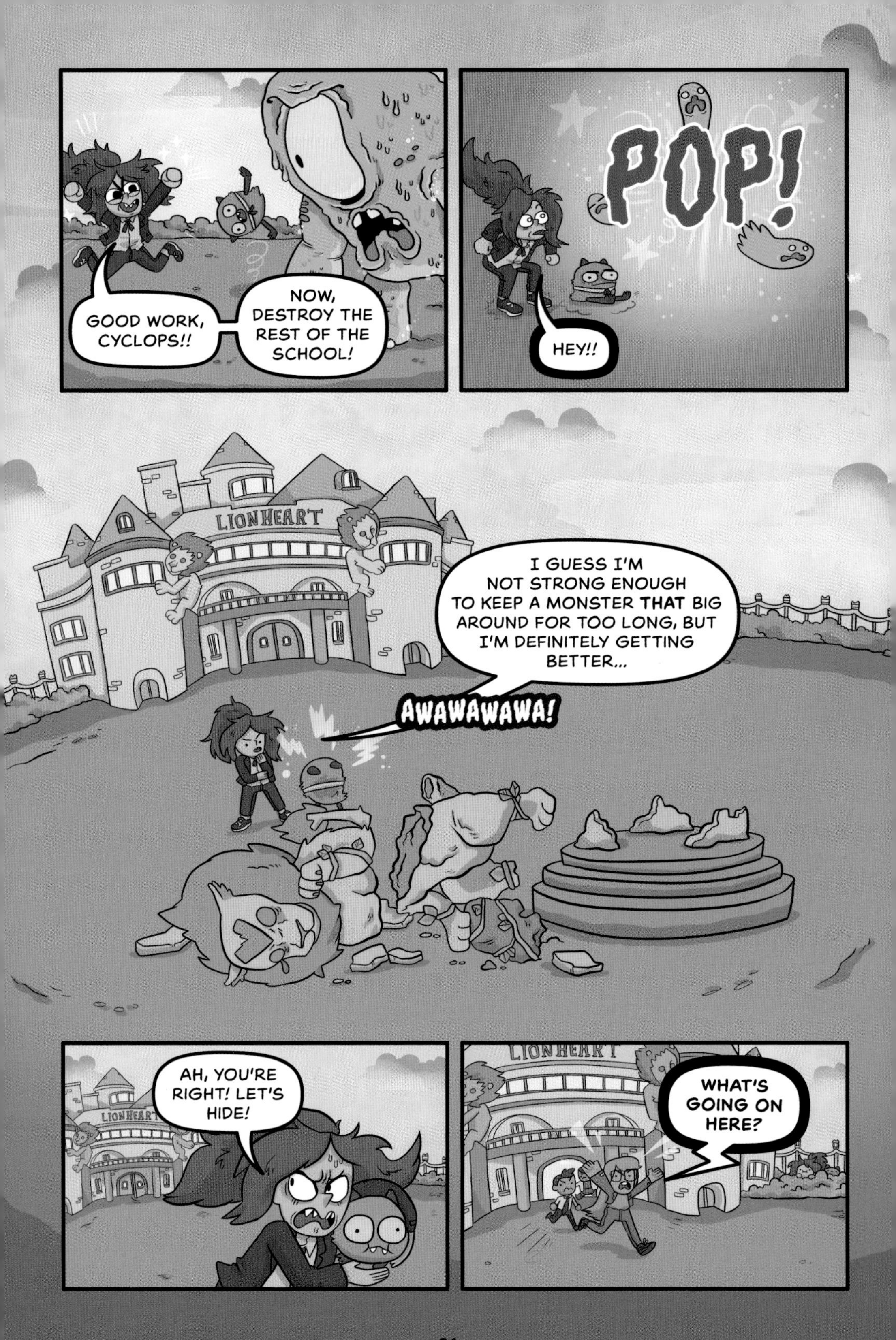
GOOD WORK, CYCLOPS!!
NOW, DESTROY THE REST OF THE SCHOOL!
POP!
HEY!!
LIONHEART
I GUESS I'M NOT STRONG ENOUGH TO KEEP A MONSTER THAT BIG AROUND FOR TOO LONG, BUT I'M DEFINITELY GETTING BETTER...
AWAWAWAWA!
LIONHEART
AH, YOU'RE RIGHT! LET'S HIDE!
LIONHEART
WHAT'S GOING ON HERE?

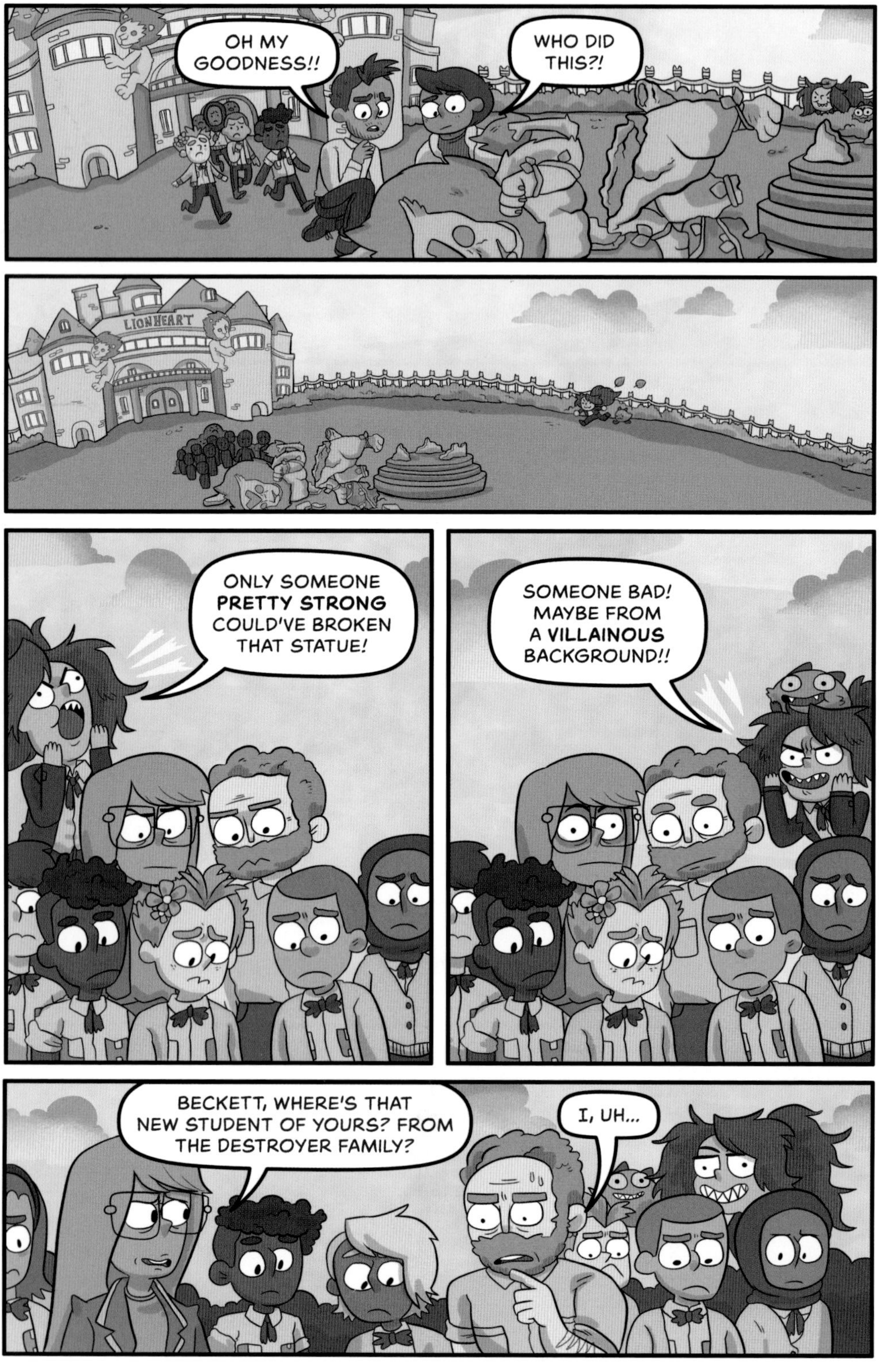

OH MY GOODNESS!!
WHO DID THIS?!
LIONHEART
ONLY SOMEONE **PRETTY STRONG** COULD'VE BROKEN THAT STATUE!
SOMEONE BAD! MAYBE FROM A **VILLAINOUS** BACKGROUND!!
BECKETT, WHERE'S THAT NEW STUDENT OF YOURS? FROM THE DESTROYER FAMILY?
I, UH...

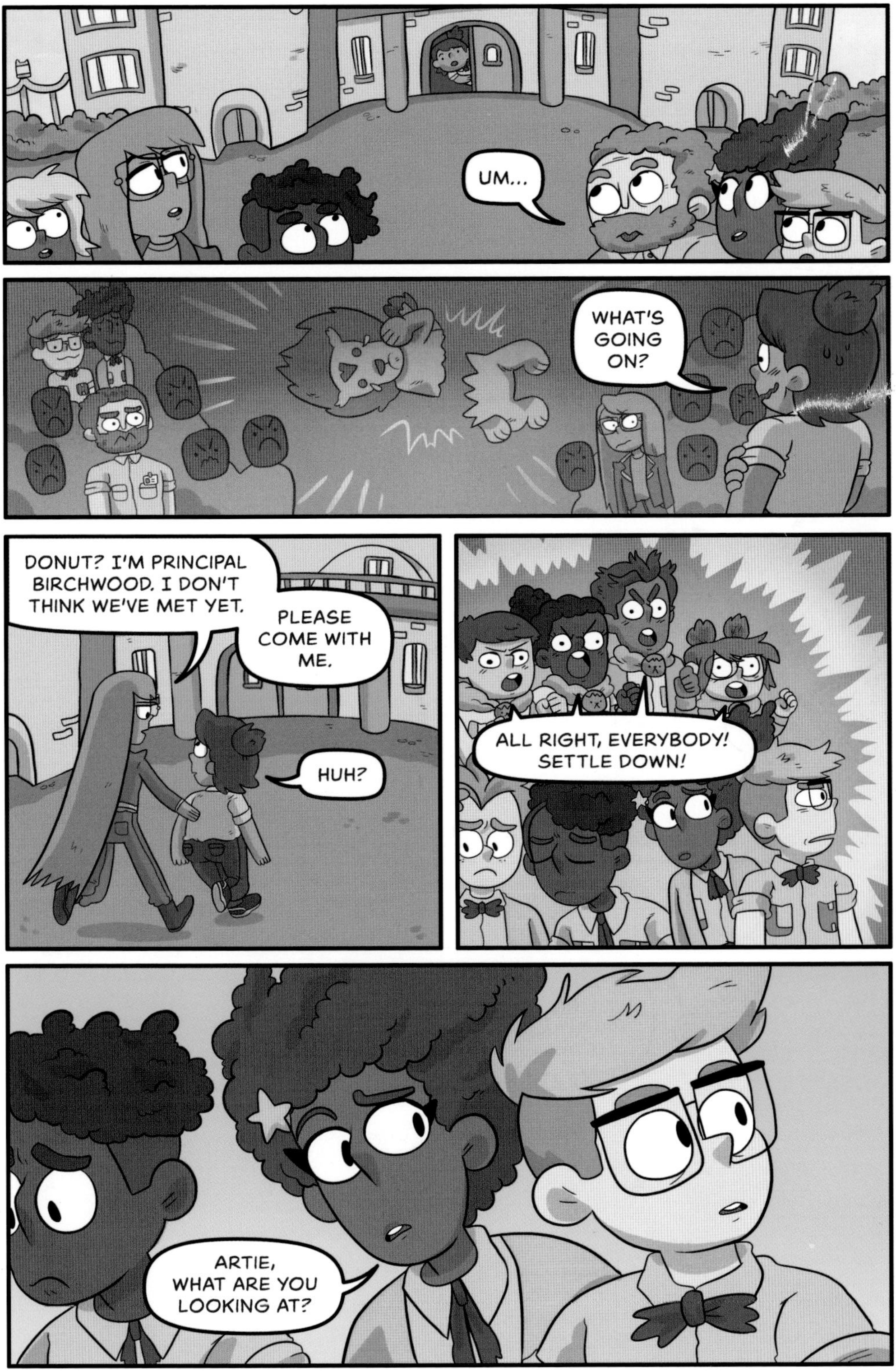
UM...
WHAT'S GOING ON?
DONUT? I'M PRINCIPAL BIRCHWOOD. I DON'T THINK WE'VE MET YET.
PLEASE COME WITH ME.
HUH?
ALL RIGHT, EVERYBODY! SETTLE DOWN!
ARTIE, WHAT ARE YOU LOOKING AT?

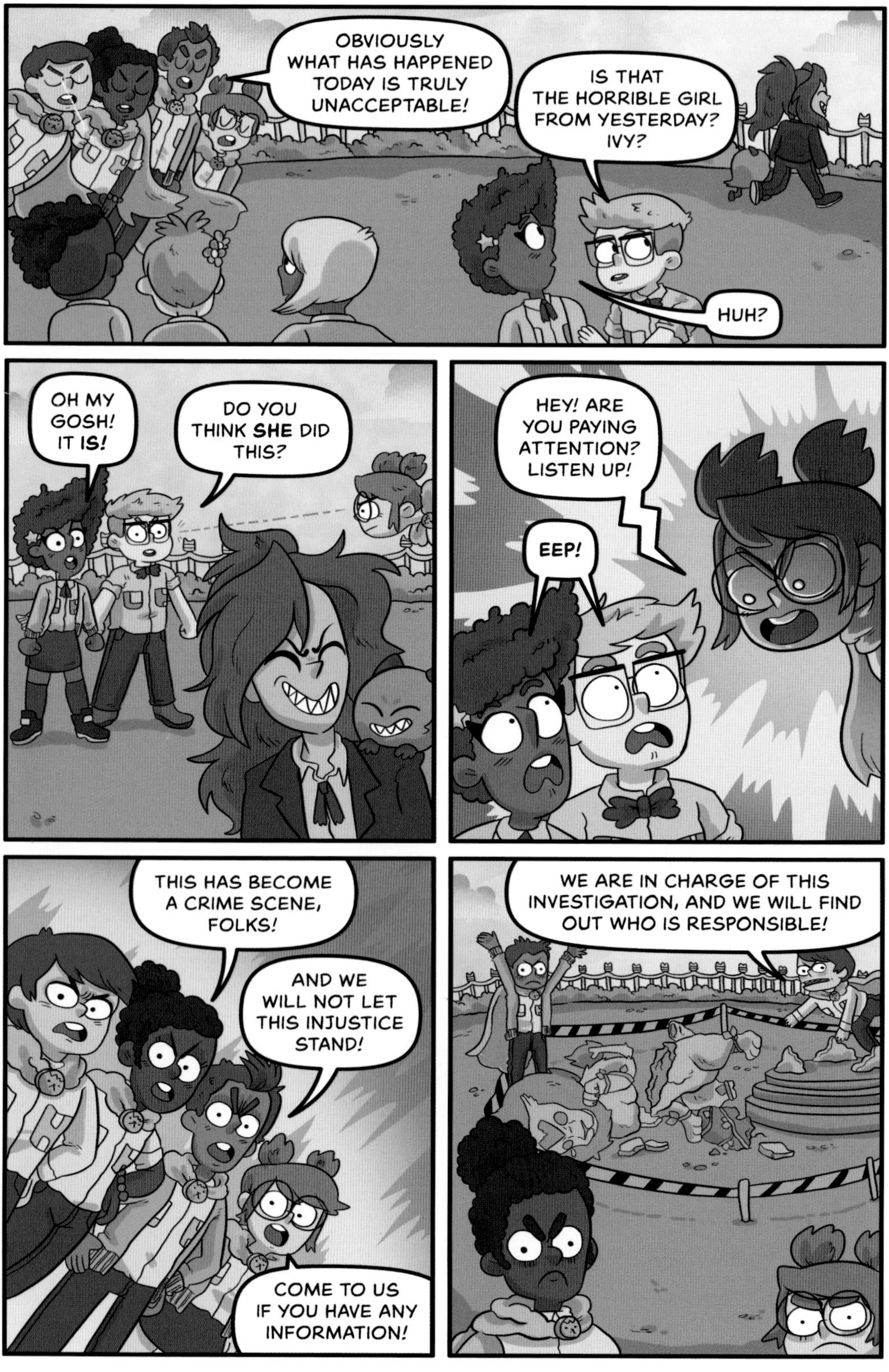

OBVIOUSLY WHAT HAS HAPPENED TODAY IS TRULY UNACCEPTABLE!
IS THAT THE HORRIBLE GIRL FROM YESTERDAY? IVY?
HUH?
OH MY GOSH! IT IS!
DO YOU THINK SHE DID THIS?
HEY! ARE YOU PAYING ATTENTION? LISTEN UP!
EEP!
THIS HAS BECOME A CRIME SCENE, FOLKS!
AND WE WILL NOT LET THIS INJUSTICE STAND!
COME TO US IF YOU HAVE ANY INFORMATION!
WE ARE IN CHARGE OF THIS INVESTIGATION, AND WE WILL FIND OUT WHO IS RESPONSIBLE!

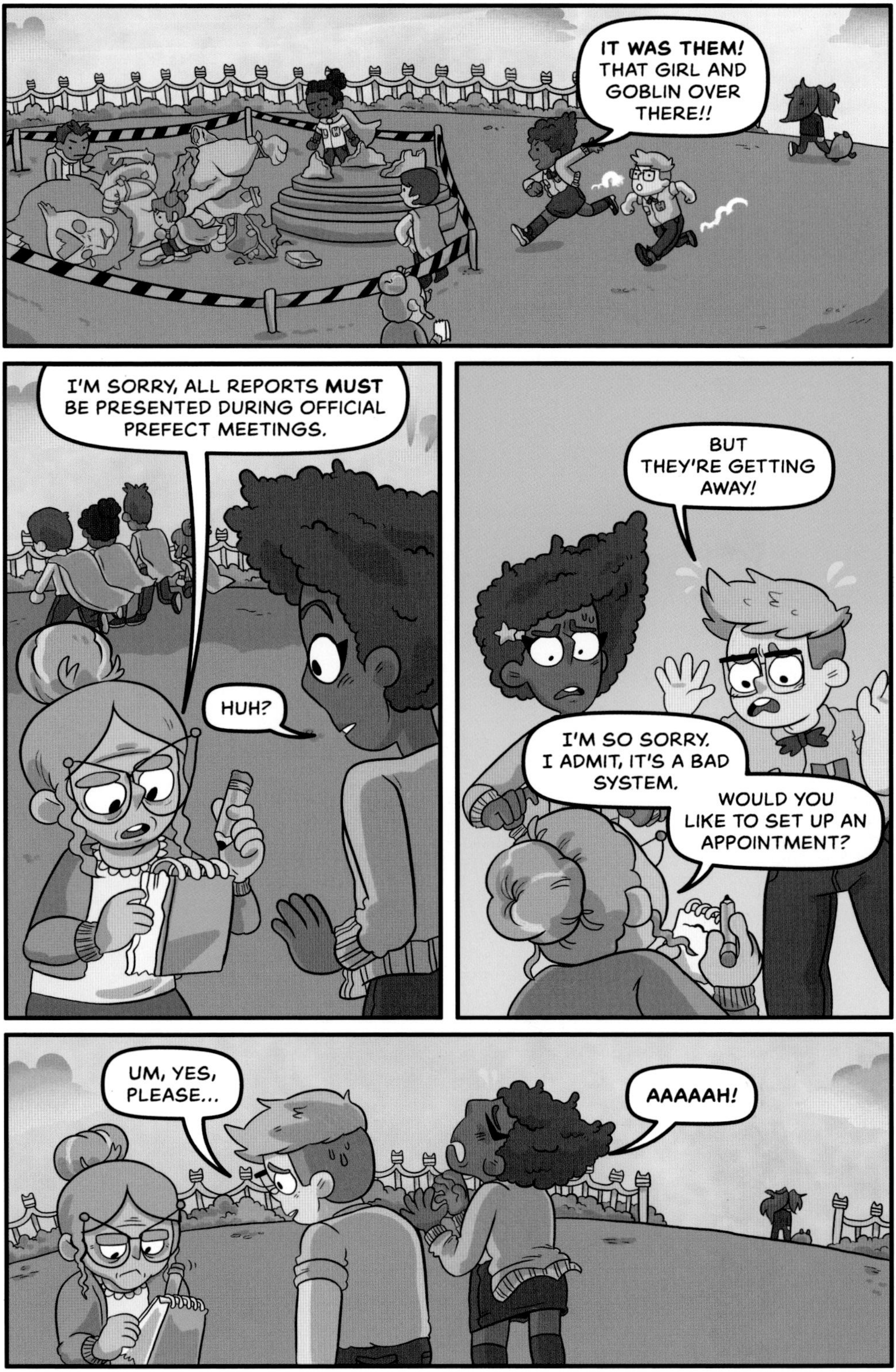
IT WAS THEM! THAT GIRL AND GOBLIN OVER THERE!!
I'M SORRY, ALL REPORTS MUST BE PRESENTED DURING OFFICIAL PREFECT MEETINGS.
HUH?
BUT THEY'RE GETTING AWAY!
I'M SO SORRY. I ADMIT, IT'S A BAD SYSTEM.
WOULD YOU LIKE TO SET UP AN APPOINTMENT?
UM, YES, PLEASE...
AAAAAH!

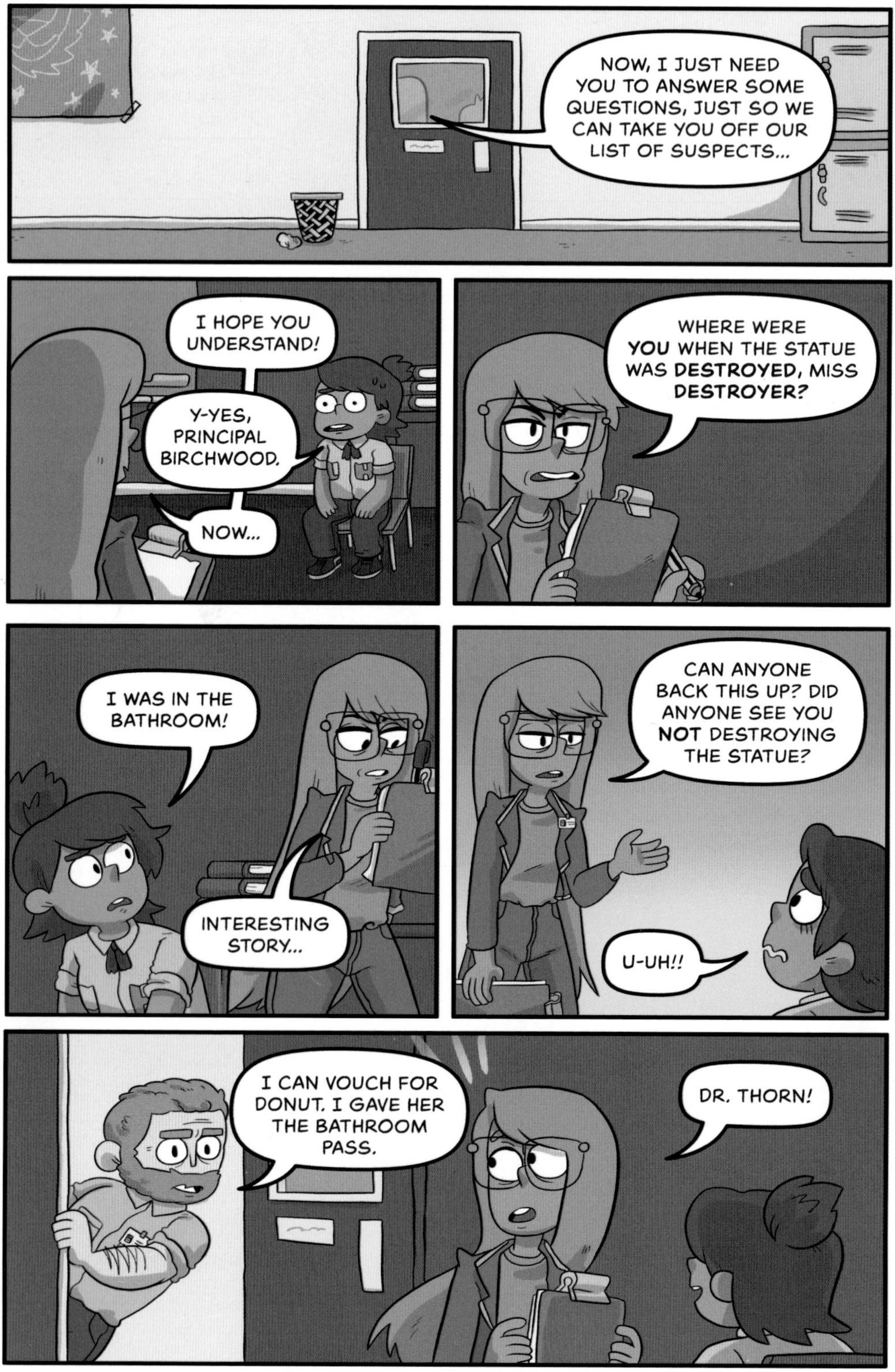
NOW, I JUST NEED YOU TO ANSWER SOME QUESTIONS, JUST SO WE CAN TAKE YOU OFF OUR LIST OF SUSPECTS...
I HOPE YOU UNDERSTAND!
Y-YES, PRINCIPAL BIRCHWOOD.
NOW...
WHERE WERE YOU WHEN THE STATUE WAS DESTROYED, MISS DESTROYER?
I WAS IN THE BATHROOM!
INTERESTING STORY...
CAN ANYONE BACK THIS UP? DID ANYONE SEE YOU NOT DESTROYING THE STATUE?
U-UH!!
I CAN VOUCH FOR DONUT. I GAVE HER THE BATHROOM PASS.
DR. THORN!

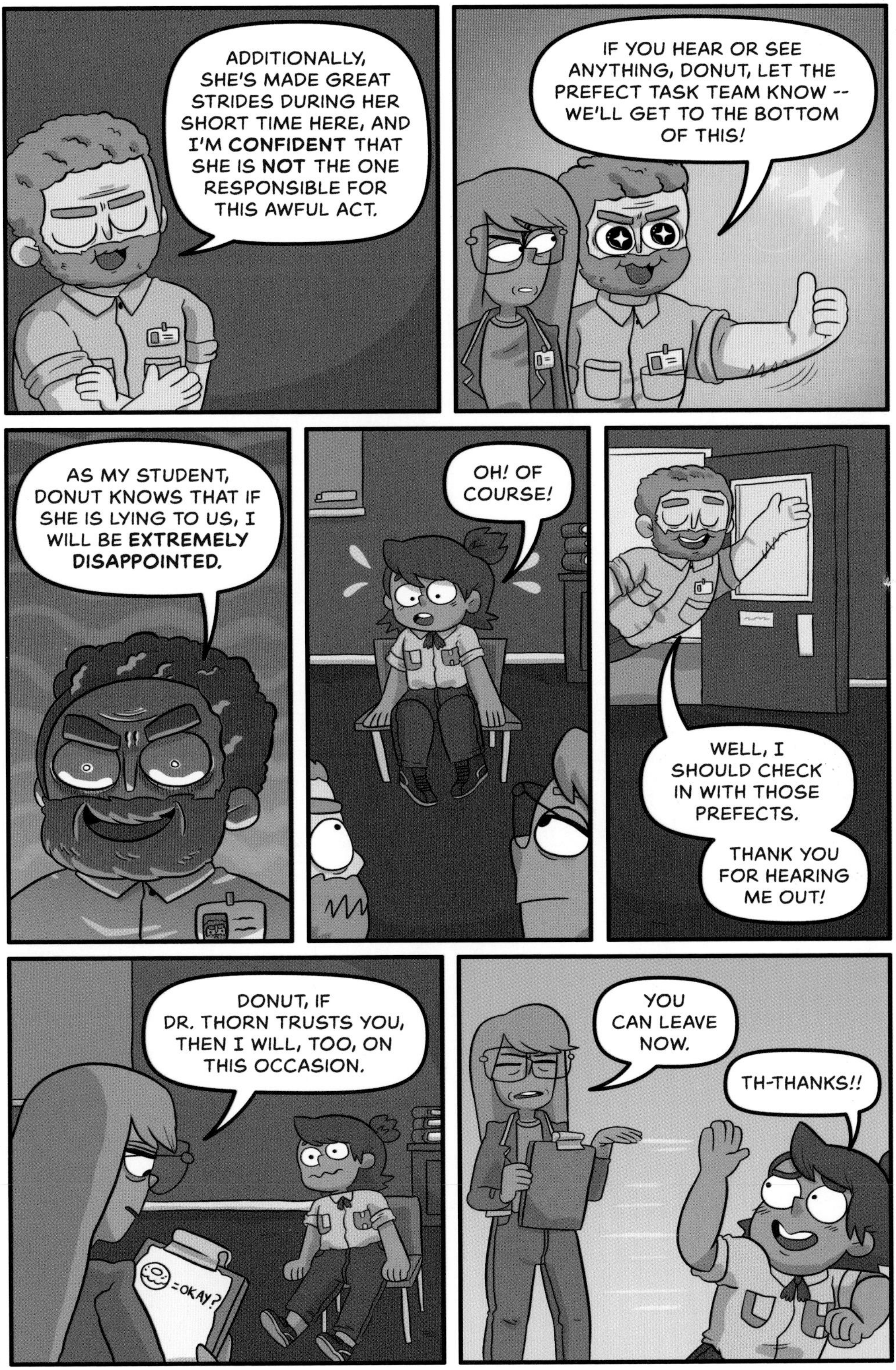
ADDITIONALLY, SHE'S MADE GREAT STRIDES DURING HER SHORT TIME HERE, AND I'M **CONFIDENT** THAT SHE IS **NOT** THE ONE RESPONSIBLE FOR THIS AWFUL ACT.
IF YOU HEAR OR SEE ANYTHING, DONUT, LET THE PREFECT TASK TEAM KNOW -- WE'LL GET TO THE BOTTOM OF THIS!
AS MY STUDENT, DONUT KNOWS THAT IF SHE IS LYING TO US, I WILL BE **EXTREMELY DISAPPOINTED.**
OH! OF COURSE!
WELL, I SHOULD CHECK IN WITH THOSE PREFECTS.
THANK YOU FOR HEARING ME OUT!
DONUT, IF DR. THORN TRUSTS YOU, THEN I WILL, TOO, ON THIS OCCASION.
=OKAY?
YOU CAN LEAVE NOW.
TH-THANKS!!

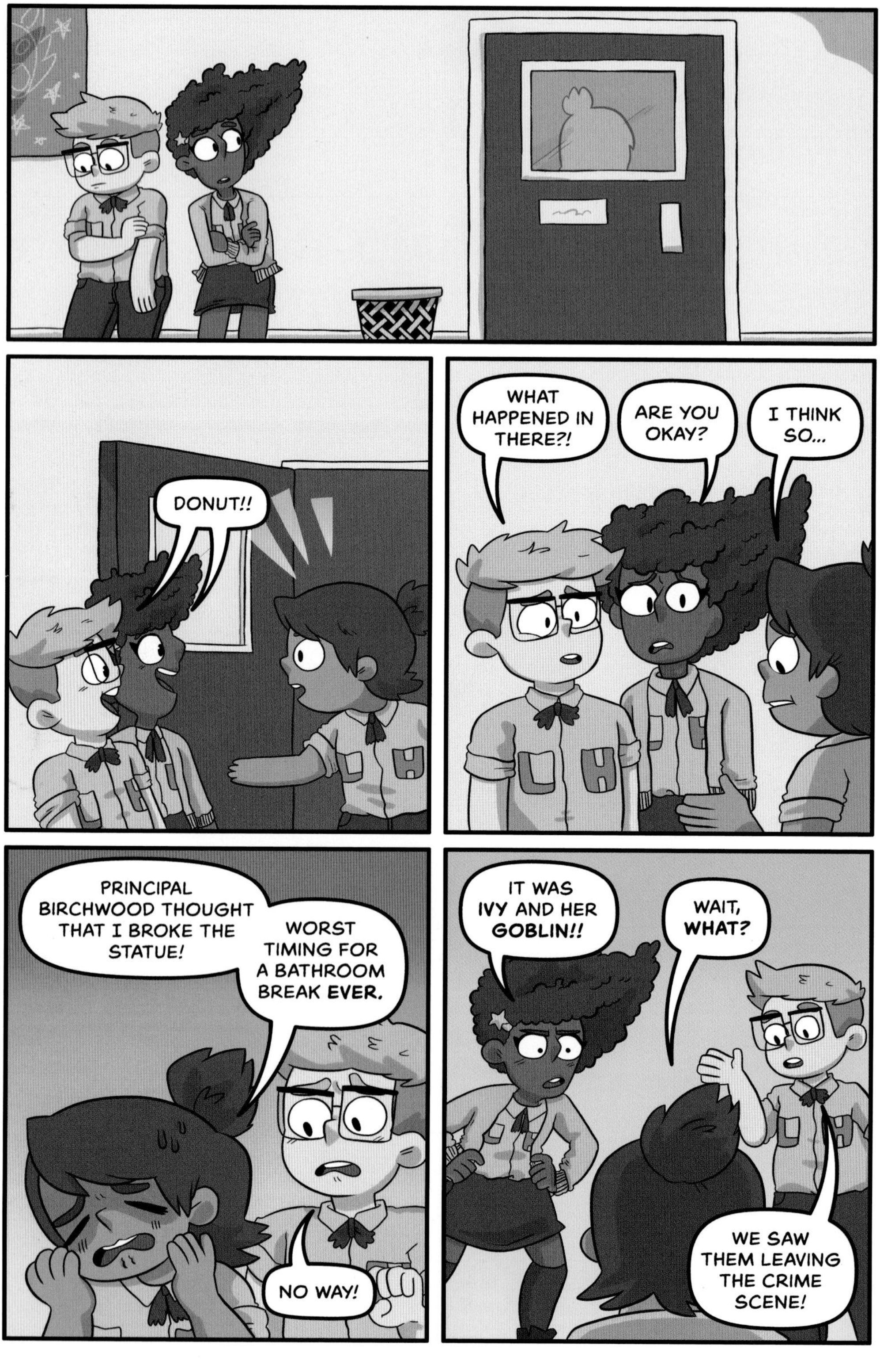
DONUT!!
WHAT HAPPENED IN THERE?!
ARE YOU OKAY?
I THINK SO...
PRINCIPAL BIRCHWOOD THOUGHT THAT I BROKE THE STATUE!
WORST TIMING FOR A BATHROOM BREAK EVER.
NO WAY!
IT WAS IVY AND HER GOBLIN!!
WAIT, WHAT?
WE SAW THEM LEAVING THE CRIME SCENE!

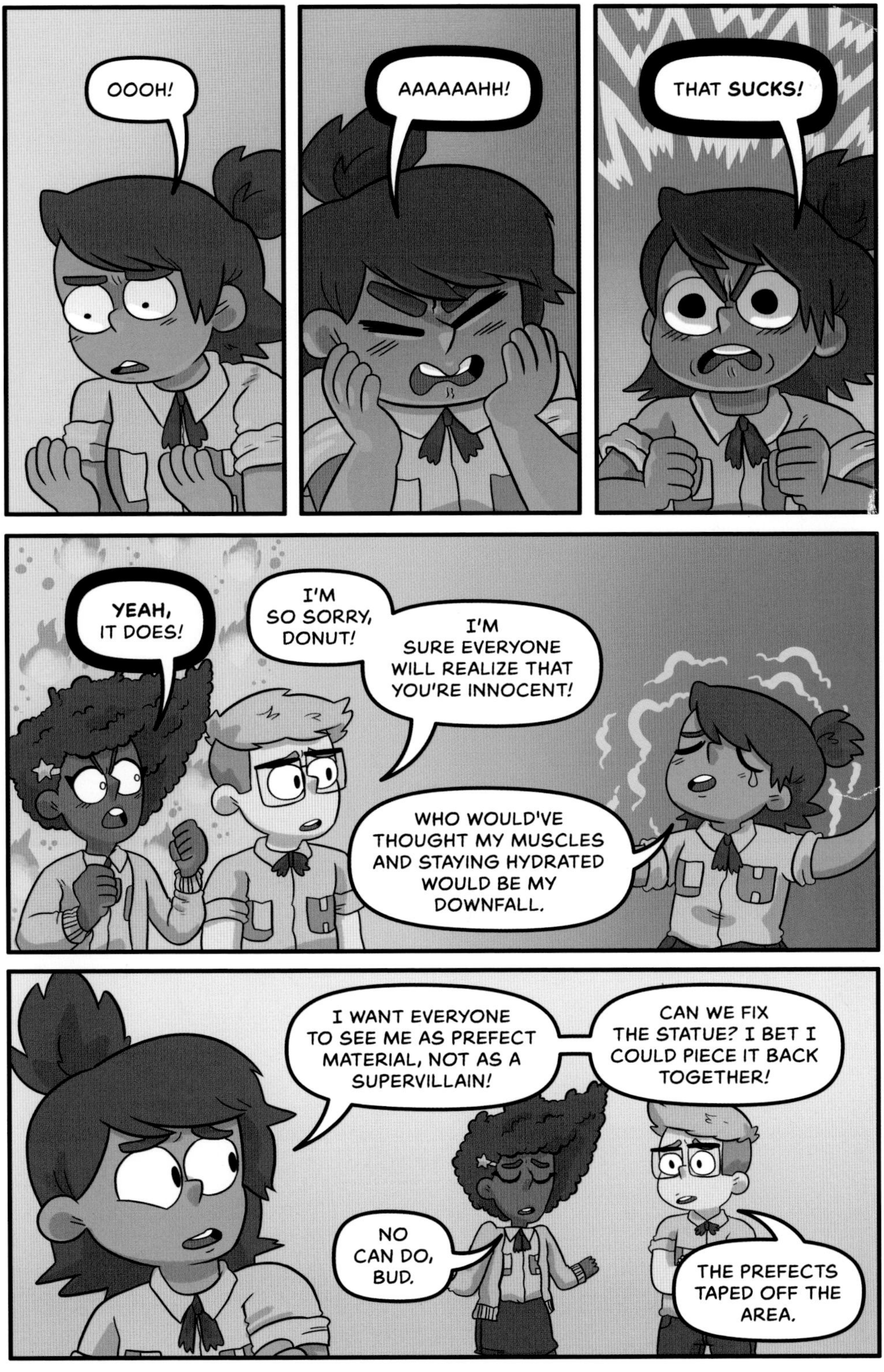
OOOH!
AAAAAAHH!
THAT SUCKS!
YEAH, IT DOES!
I'M SO SORRY, DONUT!
I'M SURE EVERYONE WILL REALIZE THAT YOU'RE INNOCENT!
WHO WOULD'VE THOUGHT MY MUSCLES AND STAYING HYDRATED WOULD BE MY DOWNFALL.
I WANT EVERYONE TO SEE ME AS PREFECT MATERIAL, NOT AS A SUPERVILLAIN!
CAN WE FIX THE STATUE? I BET I COULD PIECE IT BACK TOGETHER!
NO CAN DO, BUD.
THE PREFECTS TAPED OFF THE AREA.

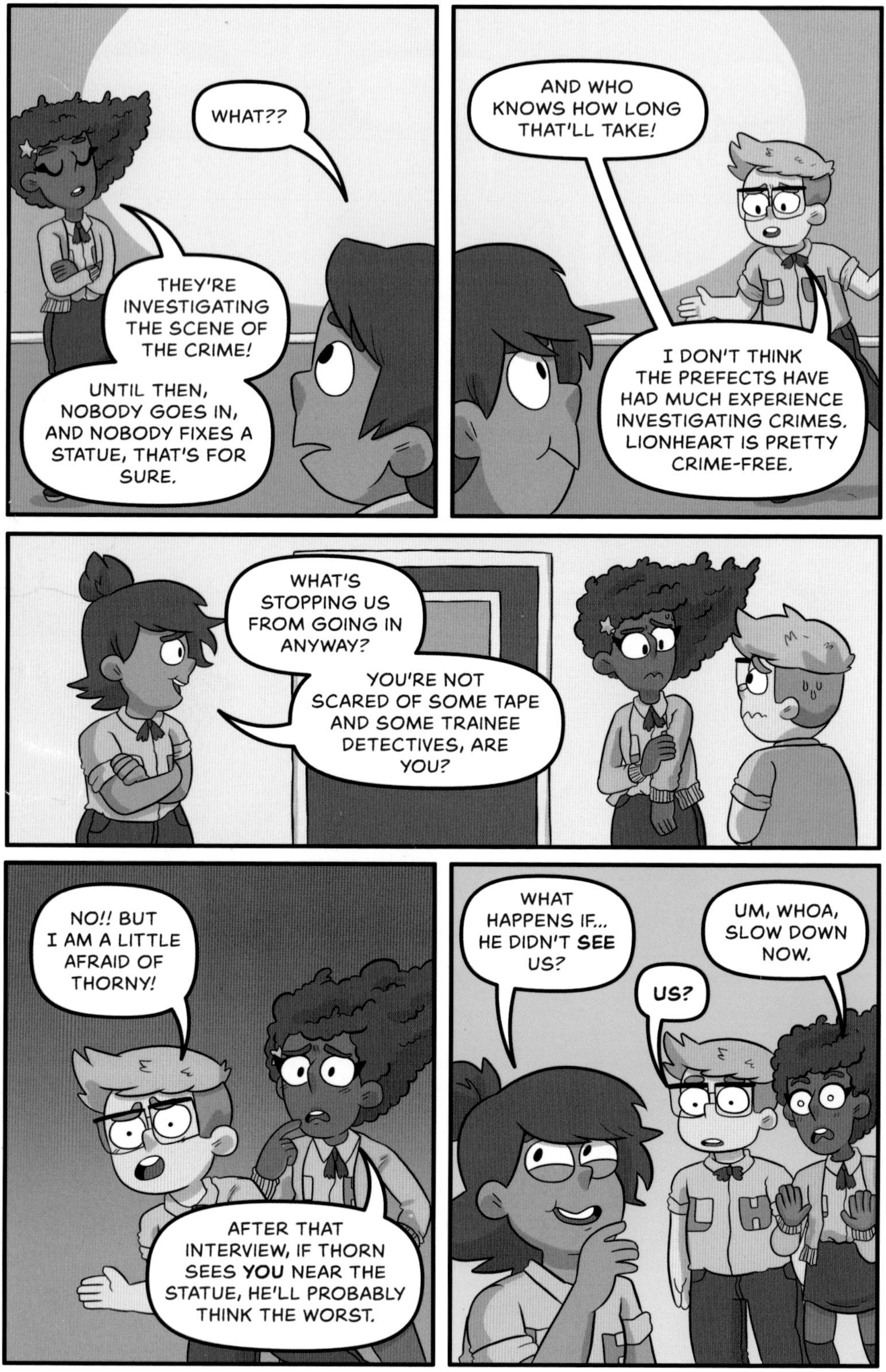
WHAT??
THEY'RE INVESTIGATING THE SCENE OF THE CRIME!
UNTIL THEN, NOBODY GOES IN, AND NOBODY FIXES A STATUE, THAT'S FOR SURE.
AND WHO KNOWS HOW LONG THAT'LL TAKE!
I DON'T THINK THE PREFECTS HAVE HAD MUCH EXPERIENCE INVESTIGATING CRIMES. LIONHEART IS PRETTY CRIME-FREE.
WHAT'S STOPPING US FROM GOING IN ANYWAY?
YOU'RE NOT SCARED OF SOME TAPE AND SOME TRAINEE DETECTIVES, ARE YOU?
NO!! BUT I AM A LITTLE AFRAID OF THORNY!
AFTER THAT INTERVIEW, IF THORN SEES **YOU** NEAR THE STATUE, HE'LL PROBABLY THINK THE WORST.
WHAT HAPPENS IF... HE DIDN'T **SEE** US?
US?
UM, WHOA, SLOW DOWN NOW.

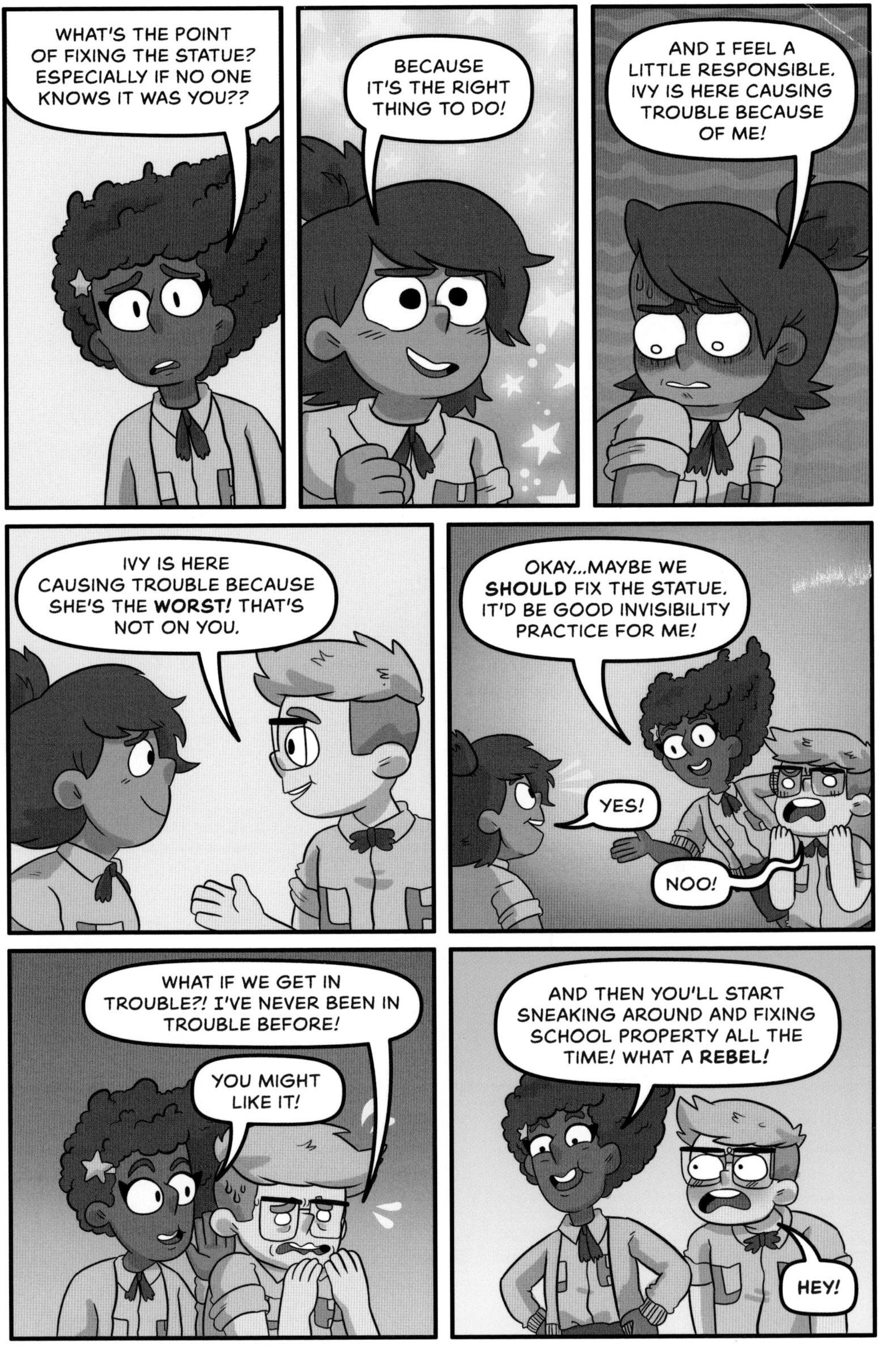
WHAT'S THE POINT OF FIXING THE STATUE? ESPECIALLY IF NO ONE KNOWS IT WAS YOU??
BECAUSE IT'S THE RIGHT THING TO DO!
AND I FEEL A LITTLE RESPONSIBLE. IVY IS HERE CAUSING TROUBLE BECAUSE OF ME!
IVY IS HERE CAUSING TROUBLE BECAUSE SHE'S THE **WORST!** THAT'S NOT ON YOU.
OKAY...MAYBE WE **SHOULD** FIX THE STATUE. IT'D BE GOOD INVISIBILITY PRACTICE FOR ME!
YES!
NOO!
WHAT IF WE GET IN TROUBLE?! I'VE NEVER BEEN IN TROUBLE BEFORE!
YOU MIGHT LIKE IT!
AND THEN YOU'LL START SNEAKING AROUND AND FIXING SCHOOL PROPERTY ALL THE TIME! WHAT A **REBEL!**
HEY!

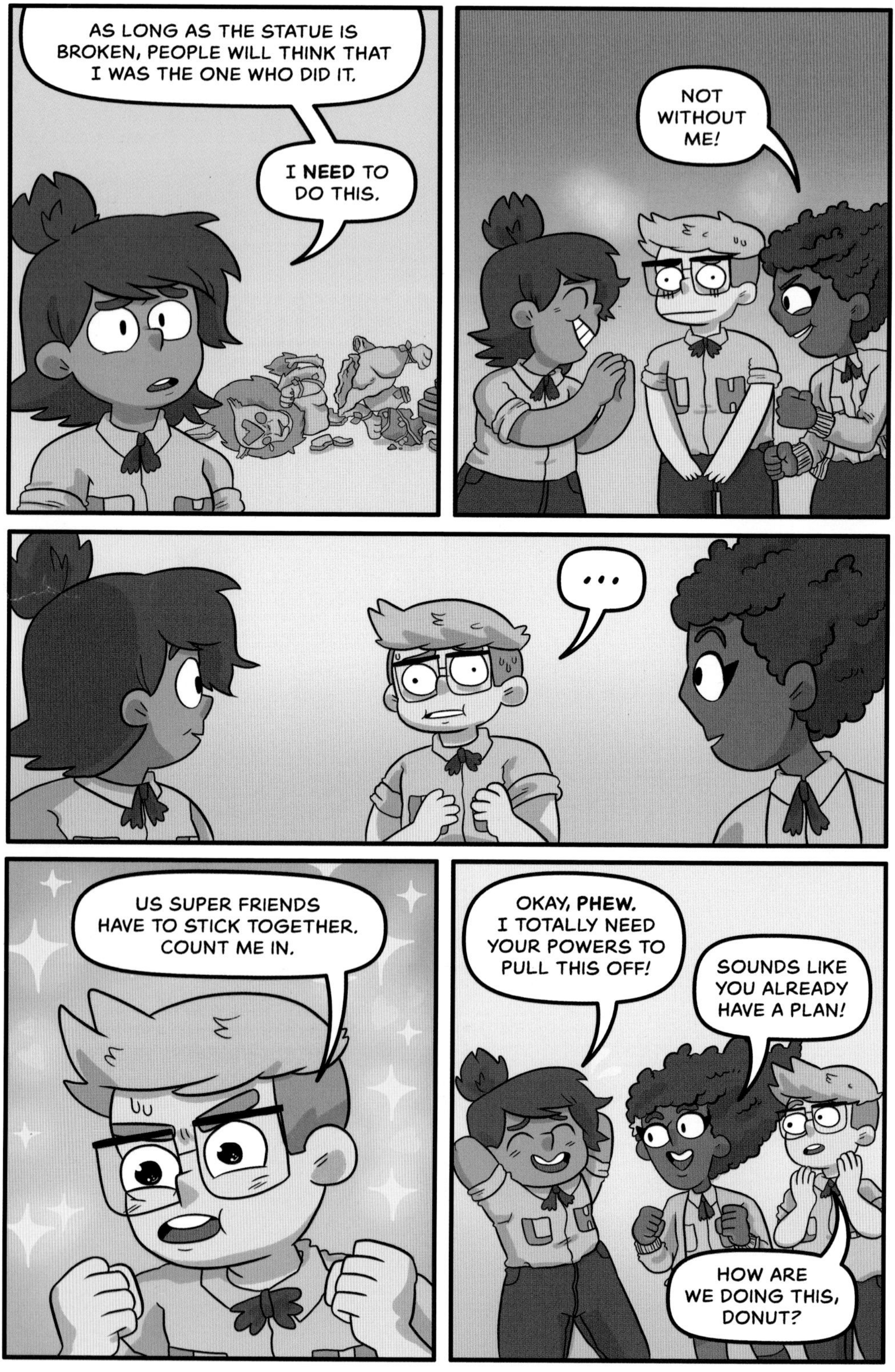
AS LONG AS THE STATUE IS BROKEN, PEOPLE WILL THINK THAT I WAS THE ONE WHO DID IT.
I **NEED** TO DO THIS.
NOT WITHOUT ME!
...
US SUPER FRIENDS HAVE TO STICK TOGETHER. COUNT ME IN.
OKAY, **PHEW.** I TOTALLY NEED YOUR POWERS TO PULL THIS OFF!
SOUNDS LIKE YOU ALREADY HAVE A PLAN!
HOW ARE WE DOING THIS, DONUT?

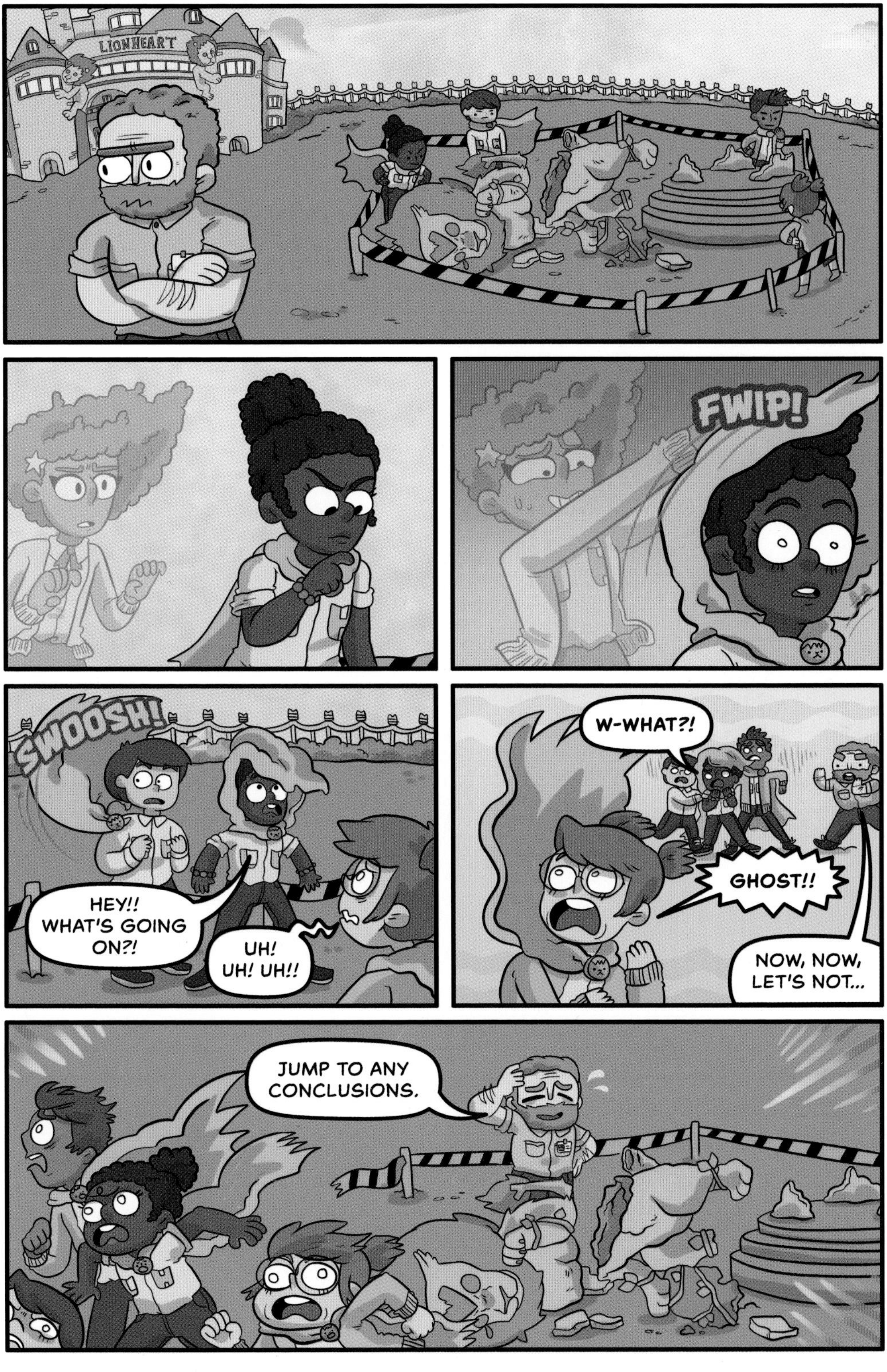
LIONHEART
FWIP!
SWOOSH!
HEY!! WHAT'S GOING ON?!
UH! UH! UH!!
W-WHAT?!
GHOST!!
NOW, NOW, LET'S NOT...
JUMP TO ANY CONCLUSIONS.

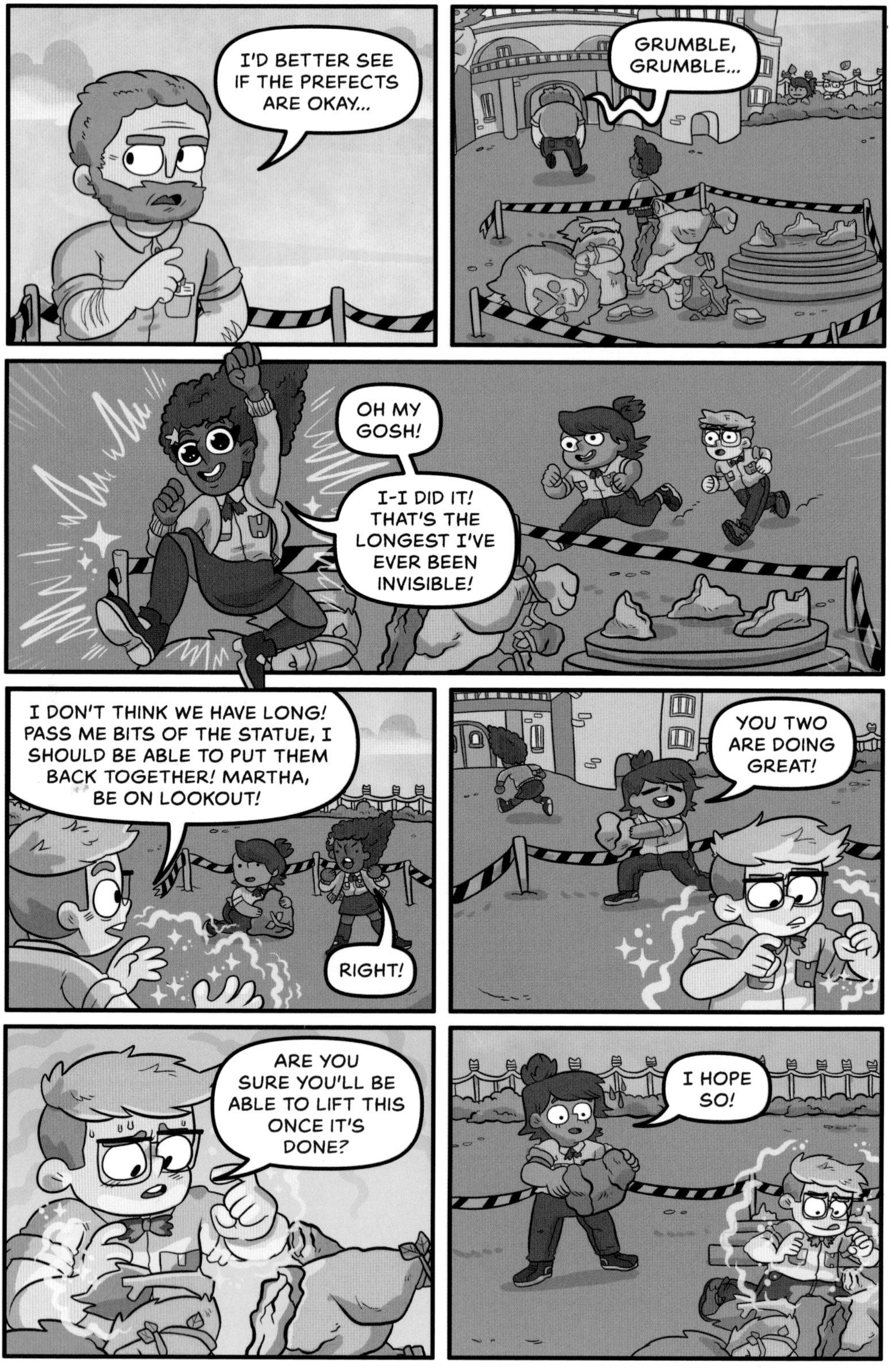
I'D BETTER SEE IF THE PREFECTS ARE OKAY...
GRUMBLE, GRUMBLE...
OH MY GOSH!
I-I DID IT! THAT'S THE LONGEST I'VE EVER BEEN INVISIBLE!
I DON'T THINK WE HAVE LONG! PASS ME BITS OF THE STATUE, I SHOULD BE ABLE TO PUT THEM BACK TOGETHER! MARTHA, BE ON LOOKOUT!
RIGHT!
YOU TWO ARE DOING GREAT!
ARE YOU SURE YOU'LL BE ABLE TO LIFT THIS ONCE IT'S DONE?
I HOPE SO!

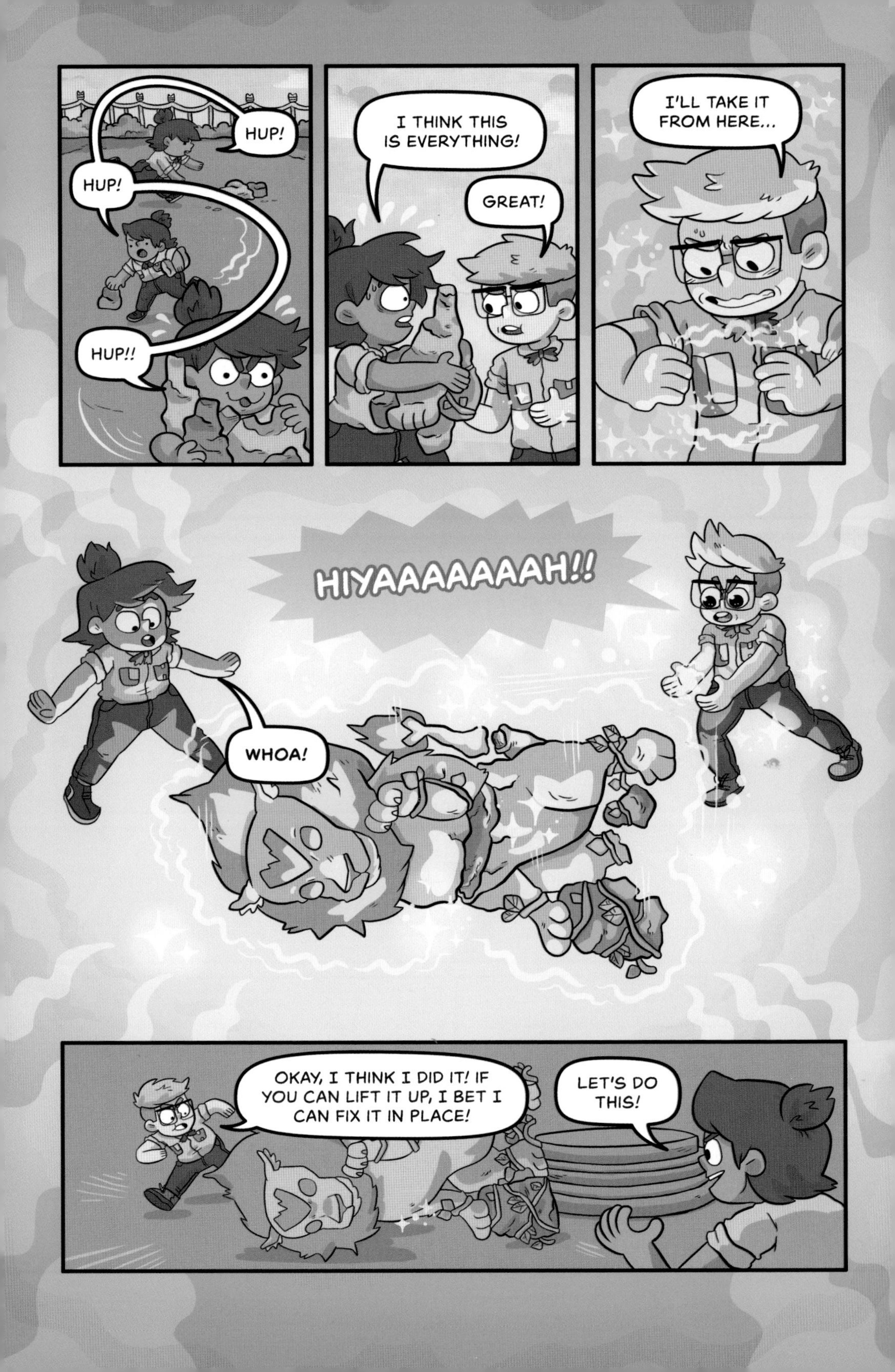
HUP!
HUP!
HUP!!
I THINK THIS IS EVERYTHING!
GREAT!
I'LL TAKE IT FROM HERE...
HIYAAAAAAAH!!
WHOA!
OKAY, I THINK I DID IT! IF YOU CAN LIFT IT UP, I BET I CAN FIX IT IN PLACE!
LET'S DO THIS!

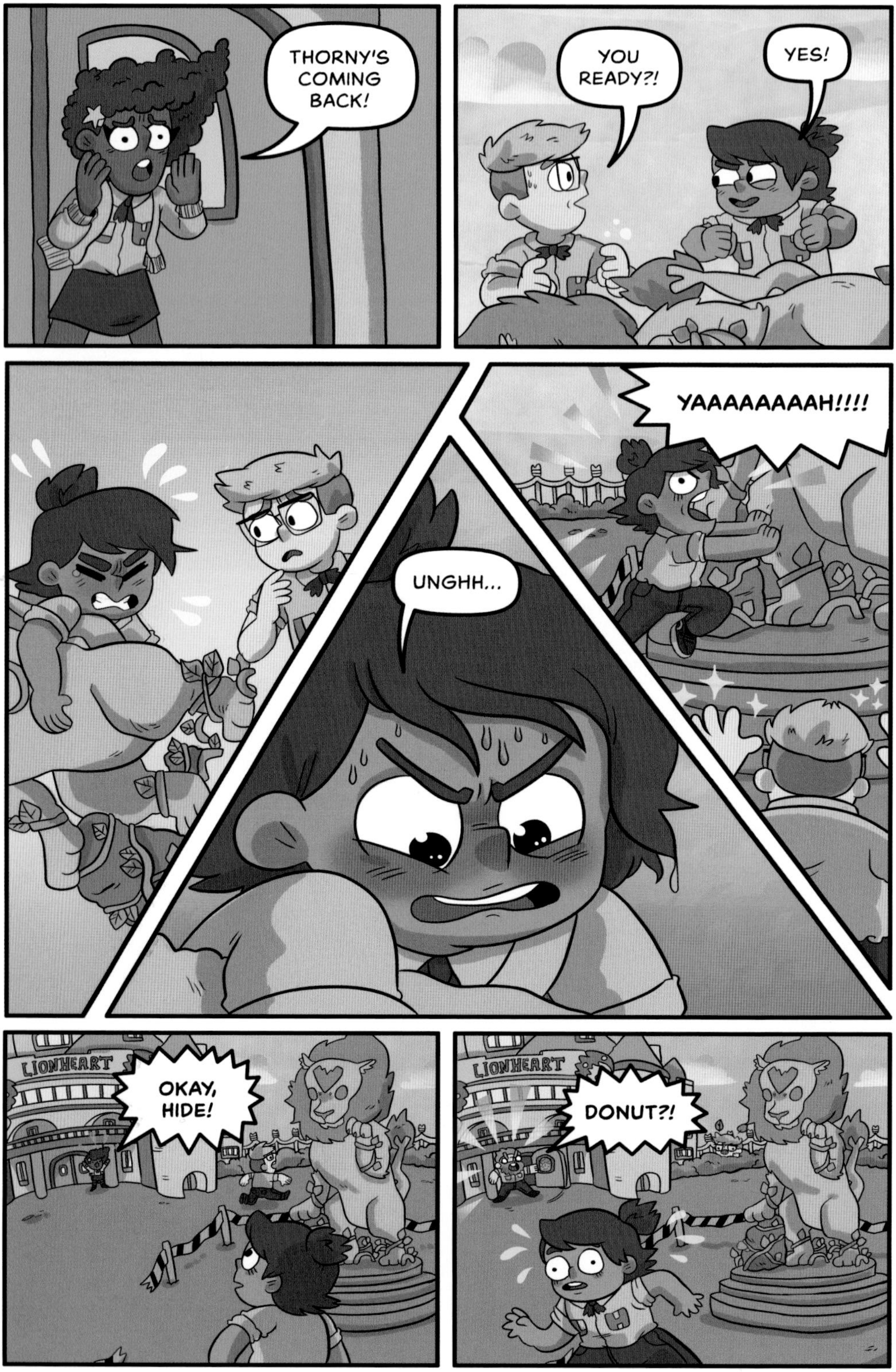
THORNY'S COMING BACK!
YOU READY?!
YES!
UNGHH...
YAAAAAAAAH!!!!
LIONHEART
OKAY, HIDE!
LIONHEART
DONUT?!

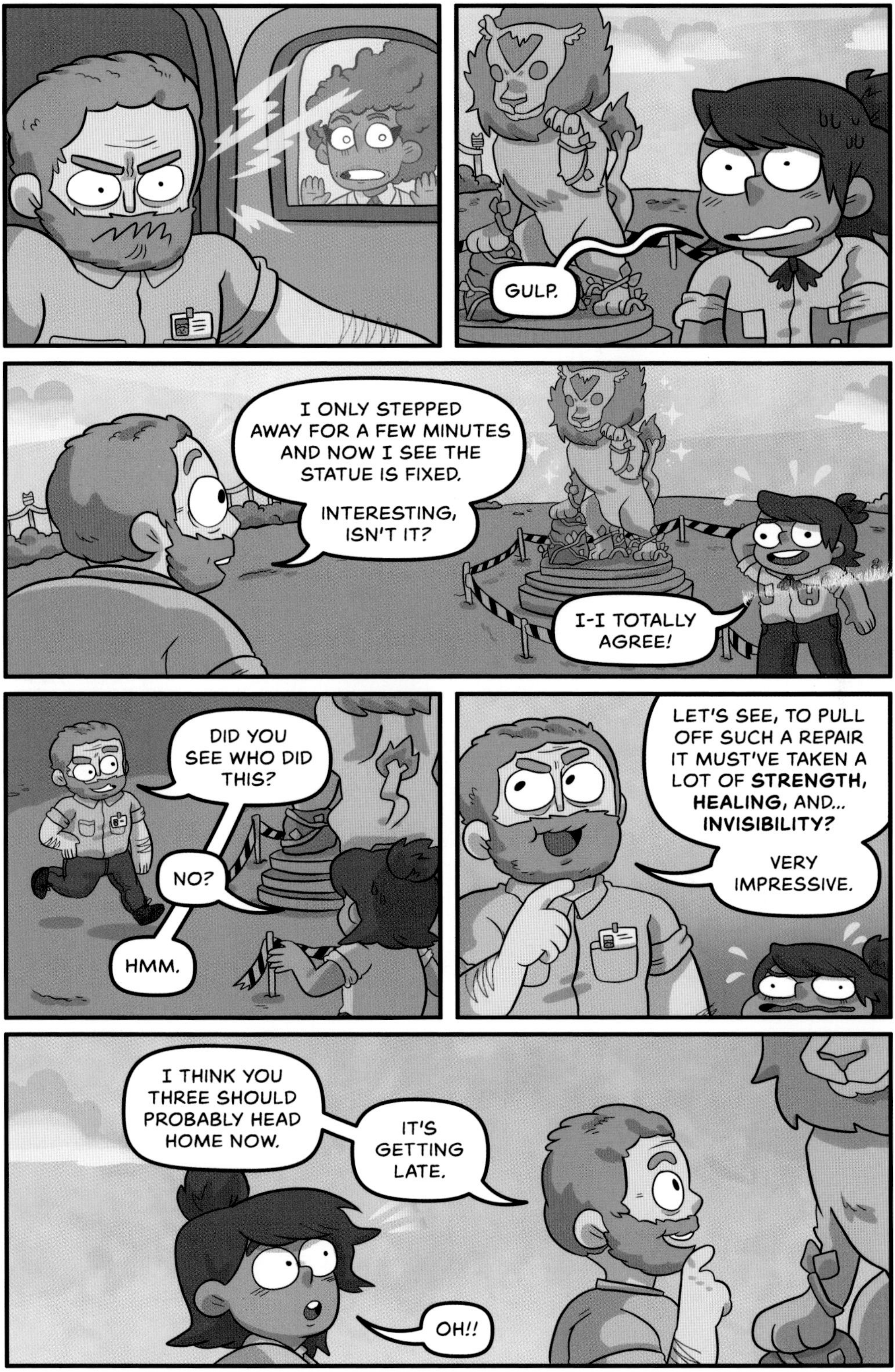
GULP.
I ONLY STEPPED AWAY FOR A FEW MINUTES AND NOW I SEE THE STATUE IS FIXED.
INTERESTING, ISN'T IT?
I-I TOTALLY AGREE!
DID YOU SEE WHO DID THIS?
NO?
HMM.
LET'S SEE, TO PULL OFF SUCH A REPAIR IT MUST'VE TAKEN A LOT OF **STRENGTH, HEALING,** AND... **INVISIBILITY?**
VERY IMPRESSIVE.
I THINK YOU THREE SHOULD PROBABLY HEAD HOME NOW.
IT'S GETTING LATE.
OH!!

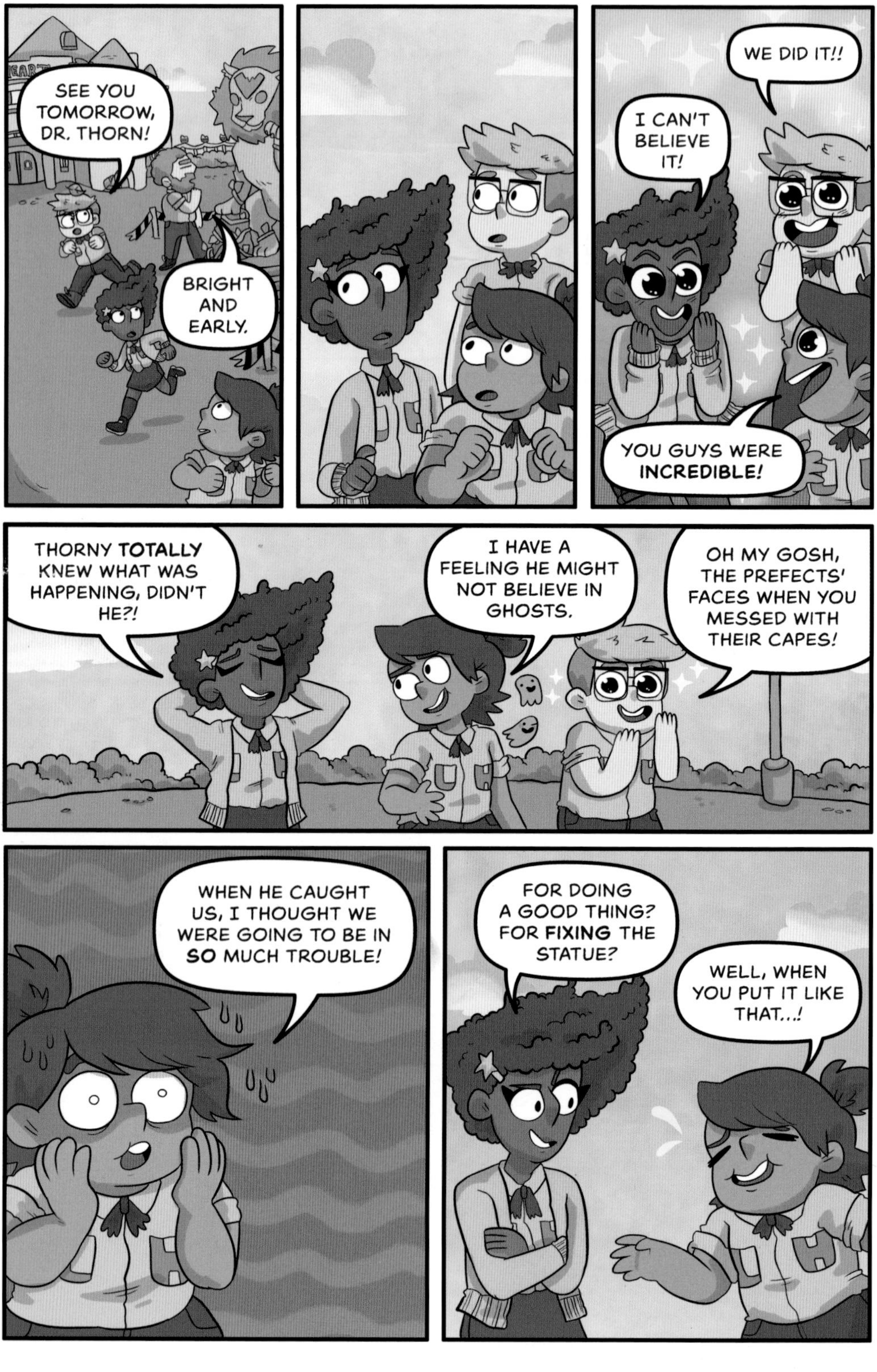
SEE YOU TOMORROW, DR. THORN!
BRIGHT AND EARLY.
I CAN'T BELIEVE IT!
WE DID IT!!
YOU GUYS WERE **INCREDIBLE!**
THORNY **TOTALLY** KNEW WHAT WAS HAPPENING, DIDN'T HE?!
I HAVE A FEELING HE MIGHT NOT BELIEVE IN GHOSTS.
OH MY GOSH, THE PREFECTS' FACES WHEN YOU MESSED WITH THEIR CAPES!
WHEN HE CAUGHT US, I THOUGHT WE WERE GOING TO BE IN **SO** MUCH TROUBLE!
FOR DOING A GOOD THING? FOR **FIXING** THE STATUE?
WELL, WHEN YOU PUT IT LIKE THAT...!

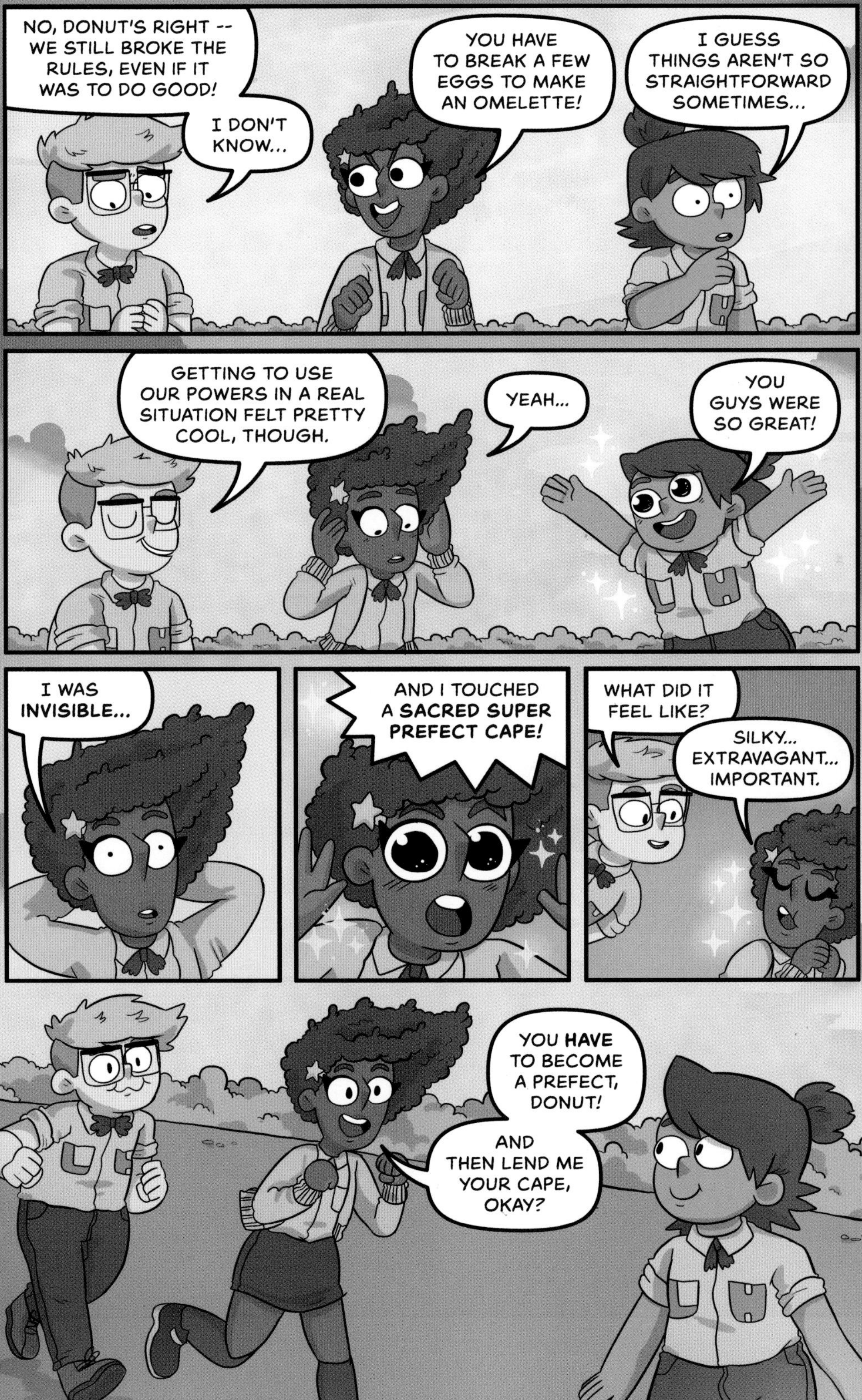
NO, DONUT'S RIGHT -- WE STILL BROKE THE RULES, EVEN IF IT WAS TO DO GOOD!
I DON'T KNOW...
YOU HAVE TO BREAK A FEW EGGS TO MAKE AN OMELETTE!
I GUESS THINGS AREN'T SO STRAIGHTFORWARD SOMETIMES...
GETTING TO USE OUR POWERS IN A REAL SITUATION FELT PRETTY COOL, THOUGH.
YEAH...
YOU GUYS WERE SO GREAT!
I WAS **INVISIBLE**...
AND I TOUCHED A **SACRED SUPER PREFECT CAPE!**
WHAT DID IT FEEL LIKE?
SILKY... EXTRAVAGANT... IMPORTANT.
YOU **HAVE** TO BECOME A PREFECT, DONUT!
AND THEN LEND ME YOUR CAPE, OKAY?

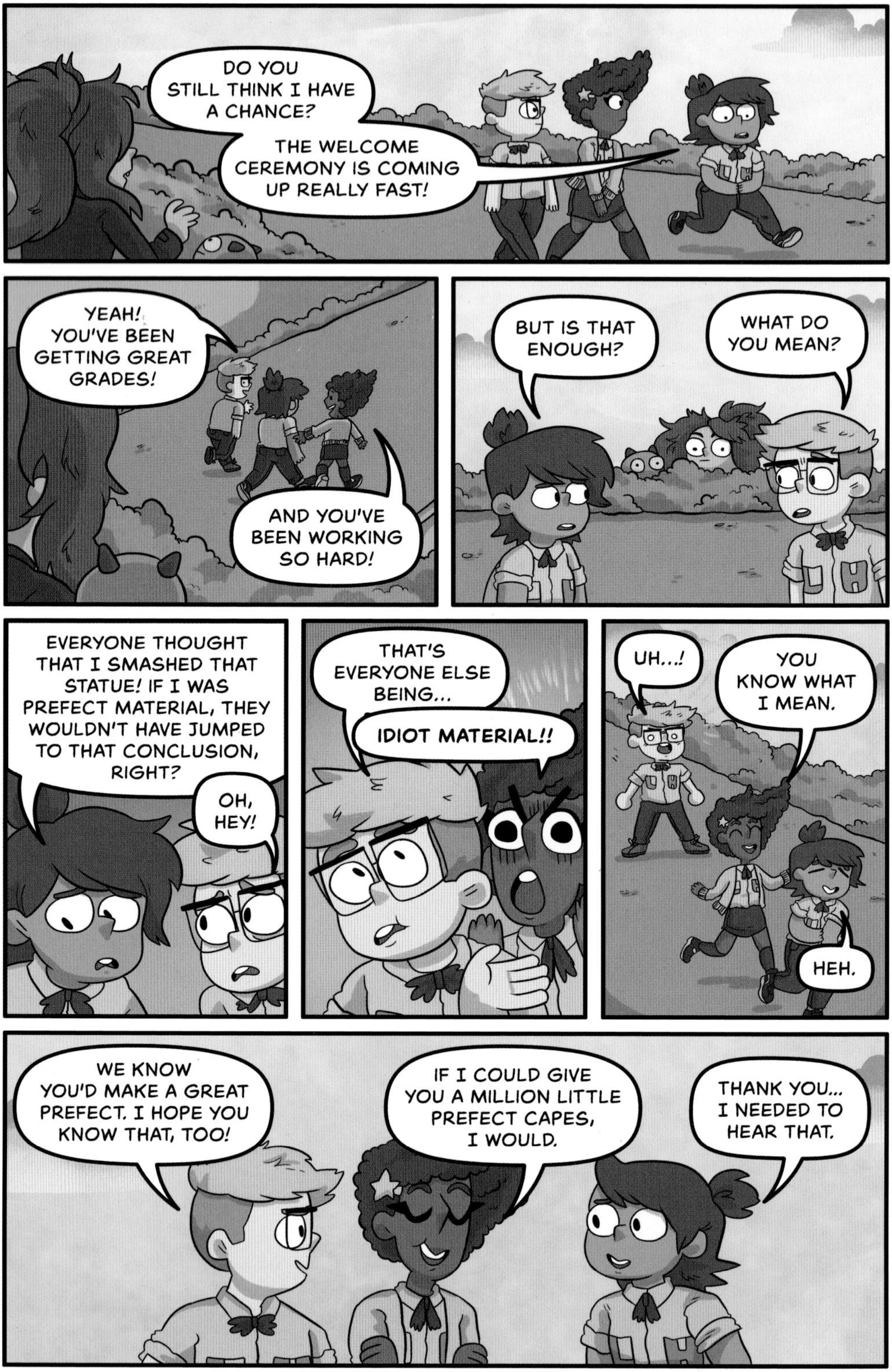
DO YOU STILL THINK I HAVE A CHANCE?
THE WELCOME CEREMONY IS COMING UP REALLY FAST!
YEAH! YOU'VE BEEN GETTING GREAT GRADES!
AND YOU'VE BEEN WORKING SO HARD!
BUT IS THAT ENOUGH?
WHAT DO YOU MEAN?
EVERYONE THOUGHT THAT I SMASHED THAT STATUE! IF I WAS PREFECT MATERIAL, THEY WOULDN'T HAVE JUMPED TO THAT CONCLUSION, RIGHT?
OH, HEY!
THAT'S EVERYONE ELSE BEING...
IDIOT MATERIAL!!
UH...!
YOU KNOW WHAT I MEAN.
HEH.
WE KNOW YOU'D MAKE A GREAT PREFECT. I HOPE YOU KNOW THAT, TOO!
IF I COULD GIVE YOU A MILLION LITTLE PREFECT CAPES, I WOULD.
THANK YOU... I NEEDED TO HEAR THAT.

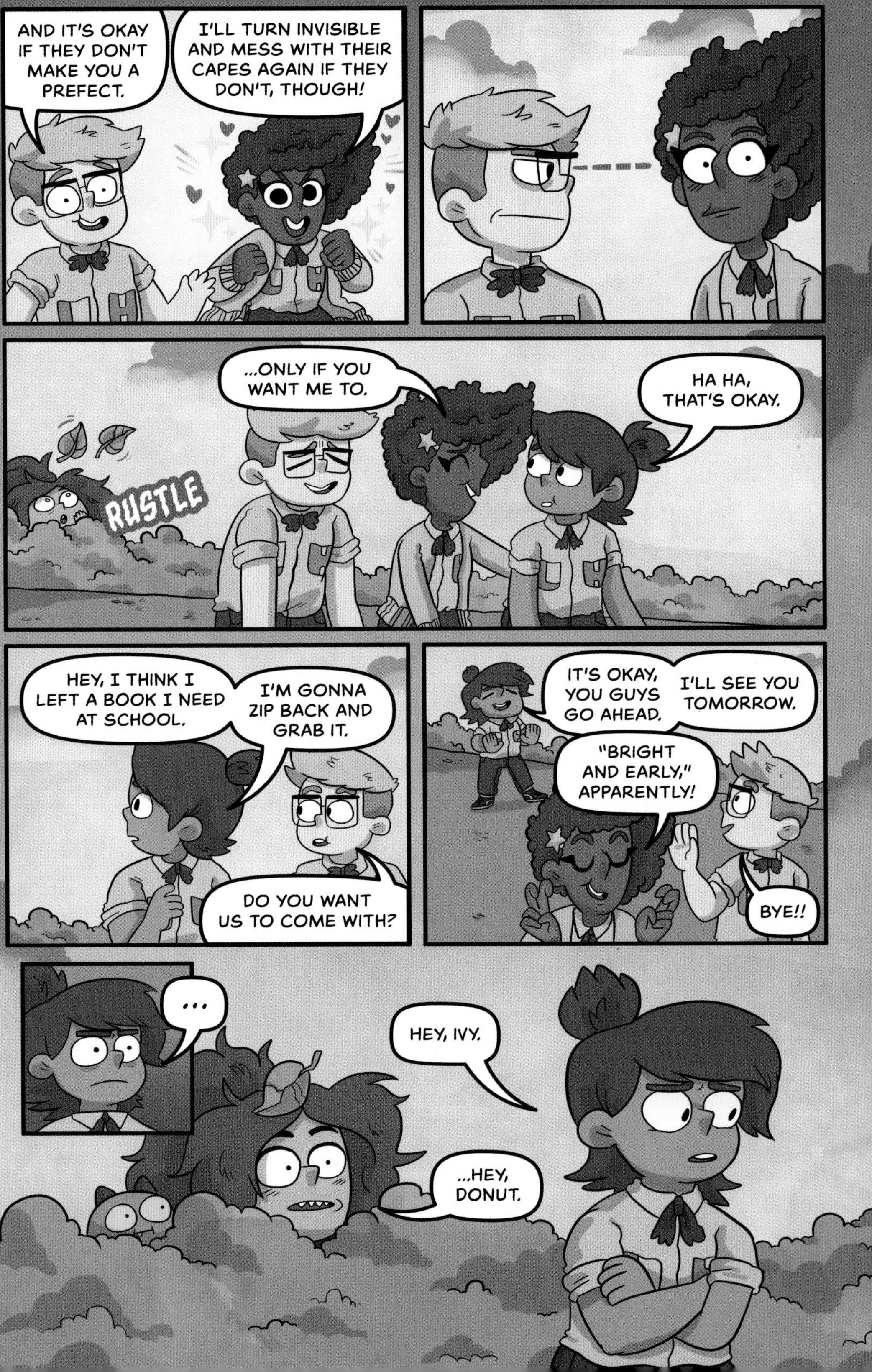
AND IT'S OKAY IF THEY DON'T MAKE YOU A PREFECT.
I'LL TURN INVISIBLE AND MESS WITH THEIR CAPES AGAIN IF THEY DON'T, THOUGH!
...ONLY IF YOU WANT ME TO.
HA HA, THAT'S OKAY.
RUSTLE
HEY, I THINK I LEFT A BOOK I NEED AT SCHOOL.
I'M GONNA ZIP BACK AND GRAB IT.
DO YOU WANT US TO COME WITH?
IT'S OKAY, YOU GUYS GO AHEAD.
I'LL SEE YOU TOMORROW.
"BRIGHT AND EARLY," APPARENTLY!
BYE!!
...
HEY, IVY.
...HEY, DONUT.

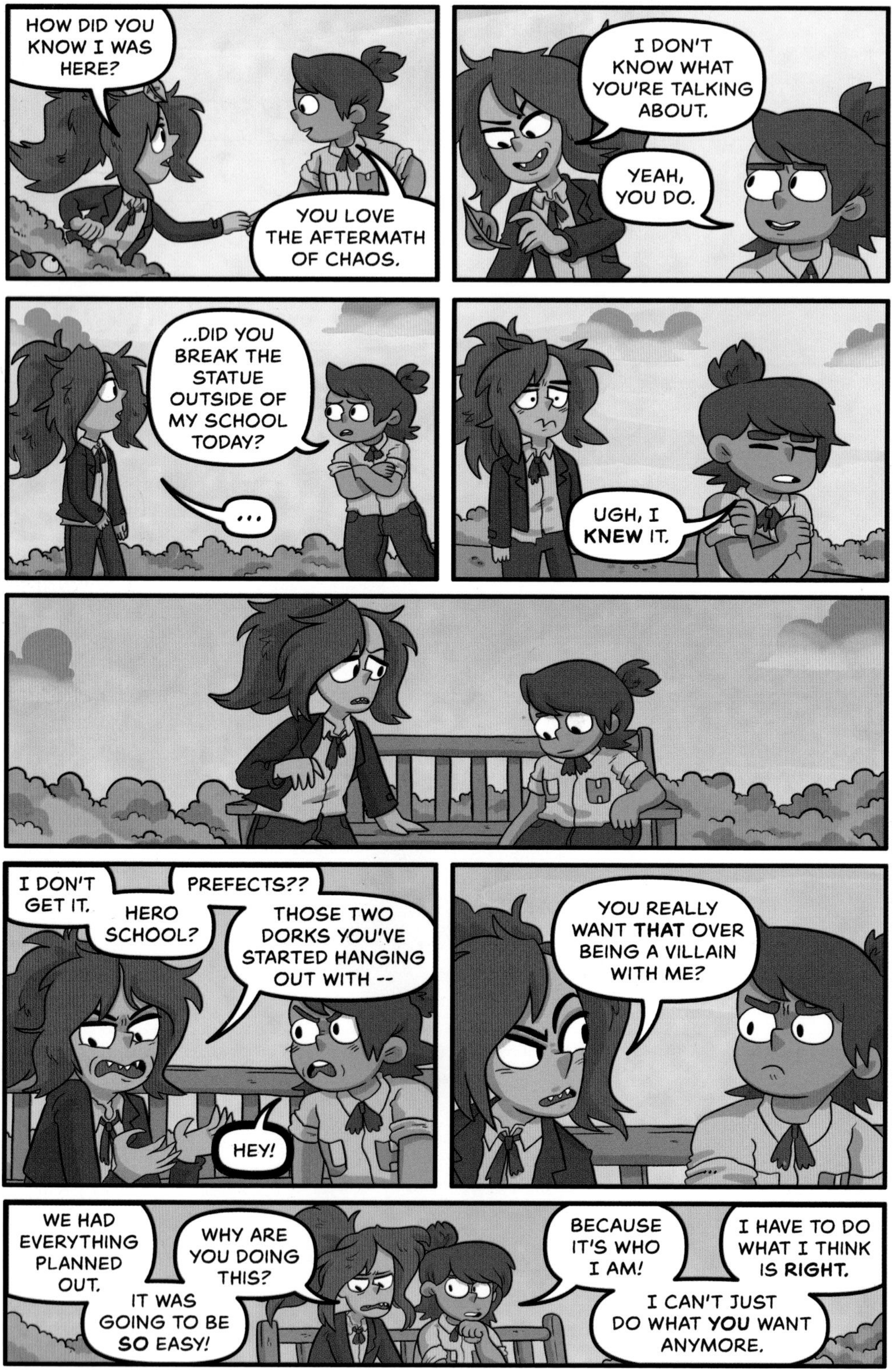
HOW DID YOU KNOW I WAS HERE?
YOU LOVE THE AFTERMATH OF CHAOS.
I DON'T KNOW WHAT YOU'RE TALKING ABOUT.
YEAH, YOU DO.
...DID YOU BREAK THE STATUE OUTSIDE OF MY SCHOOL TODAY?
...
UGH, I **KNEW** IT.
I DON'T GET IT.
HERO SCHOOL?
PREFECTS??
THOSE TWO DORKS YOU'VE STARTED HANGING OUT WITH --
HEY!
YOU REALLY WANT **THAT** OVER BEING A VILLAIN WITH ME?
WE HAD EVERYTHING PLANNED OUT.
IT WAS GOING TO BE **SO** EASY!
WHY ARE YOU DOING THIS?
BECAUSE IT'S WHO I AM!
I HAVE TO DO WHAT I THINK IS **RIGHT.**
I CAN'T JUST DO WHAT **YOU** WANT ANYMORE.

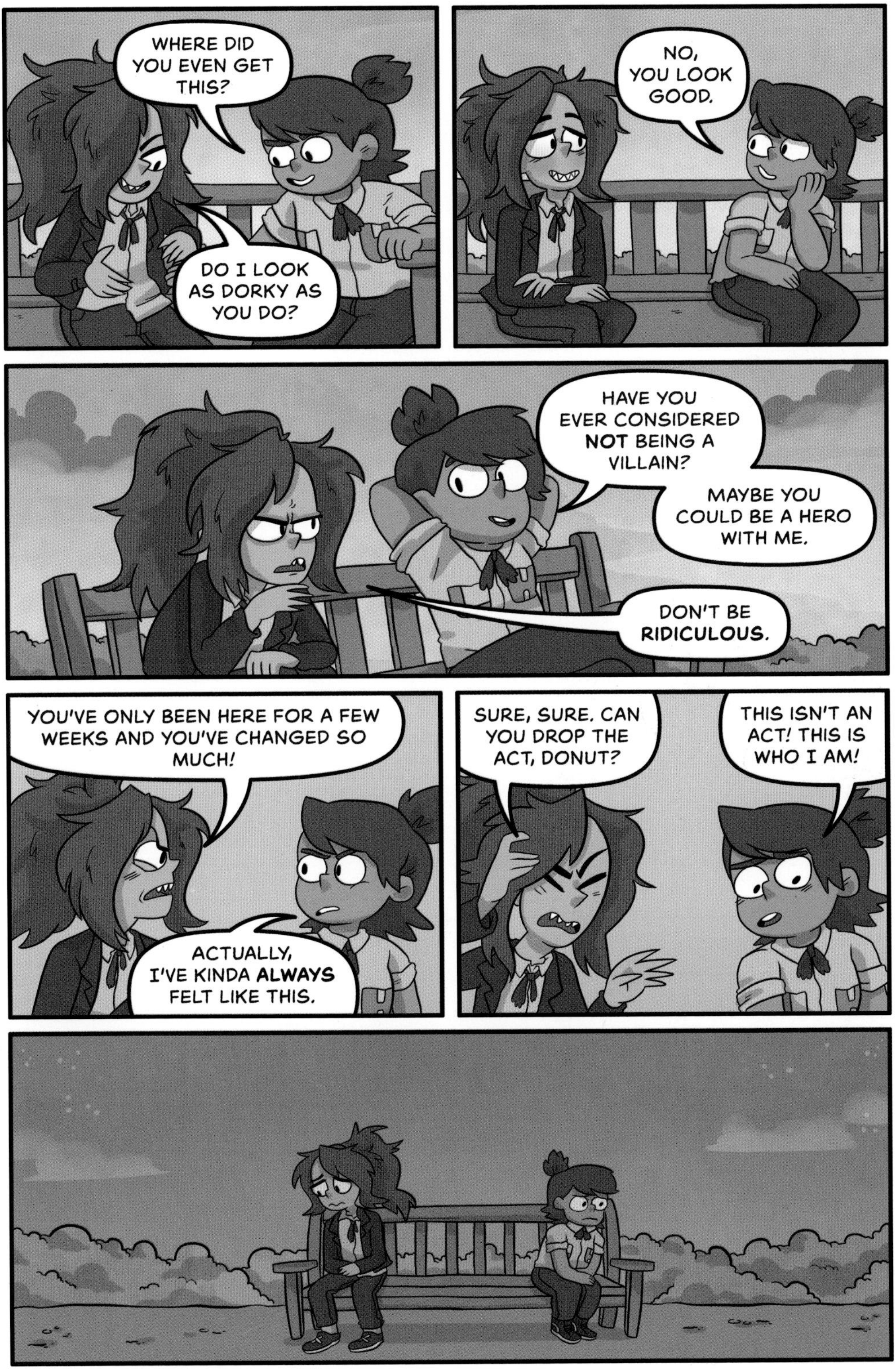
WHERE DID YOU EVEN GET THIS?
DO I LOOK AS DORKY AS YOU DO?
NO, YOU LOOK GOOD.
HAVE YOU EVER CONSIDERED **NOT** BEING A VILLAIN?
MAYBE YOU COULD BE A HERO WITH ME.
DON'T BE **RIDICULOUS**.
YOU'VE ONLY BEEN HERE FOR A FEW WEEKS AND YOU'VE CHANGED SO MUCH!
ACTUALLY, I'VE KINDA **ALWAYS** FELT LIKE THIS.
SURE, SURE. CAN YOU DROP THE ACT, DONUT?
THIS ISN'T AN ACT! THIS IS WHO I AM!

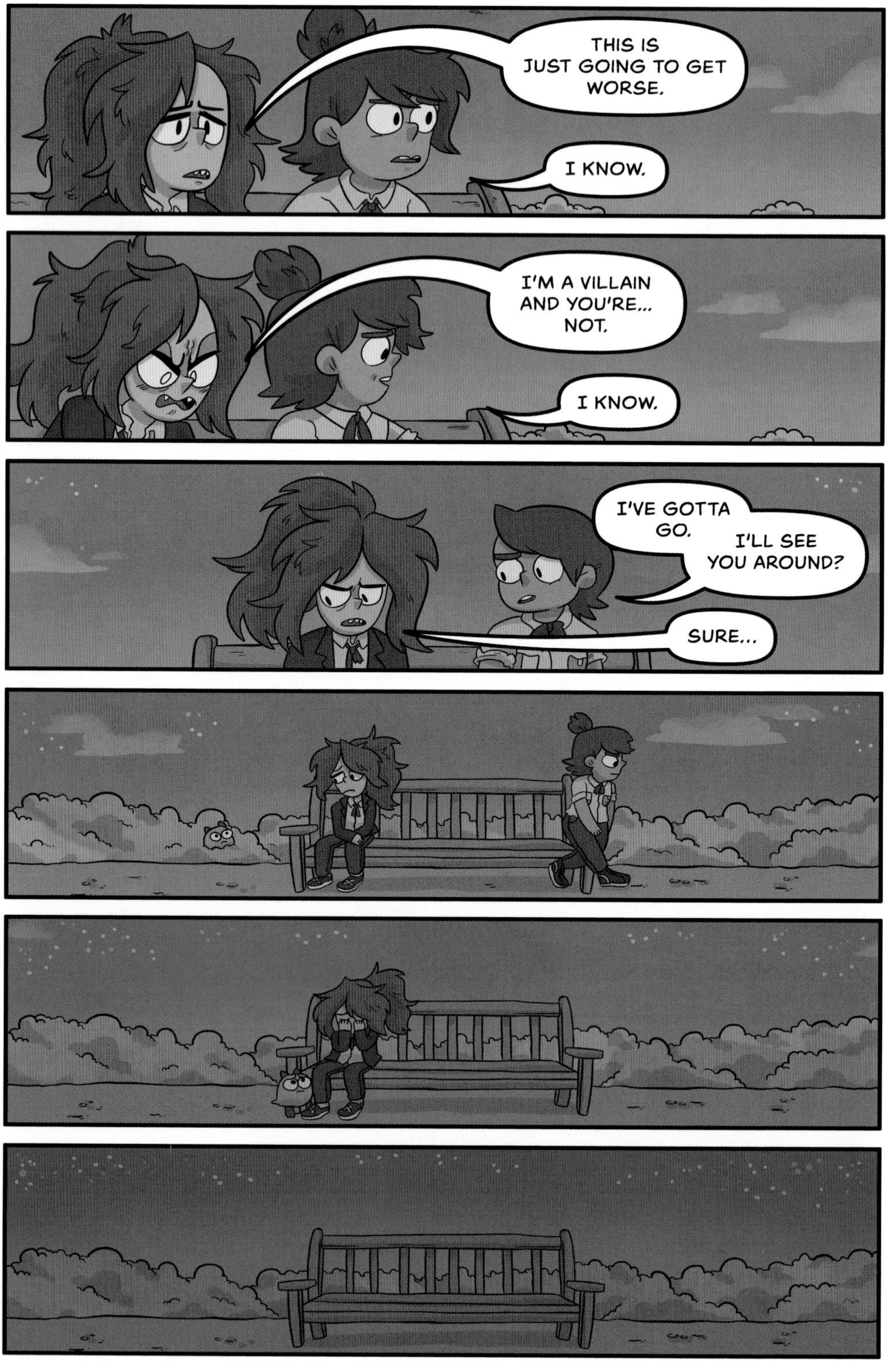
THIS IS JUST GOING TO GET WORSE.
I KNOW.
I'M A VILLAIN AND YOU'RE... NOT.
I KNOW.
I'VE GOTTA GO.
I'LL SEE YOU AROUND?
SURE...

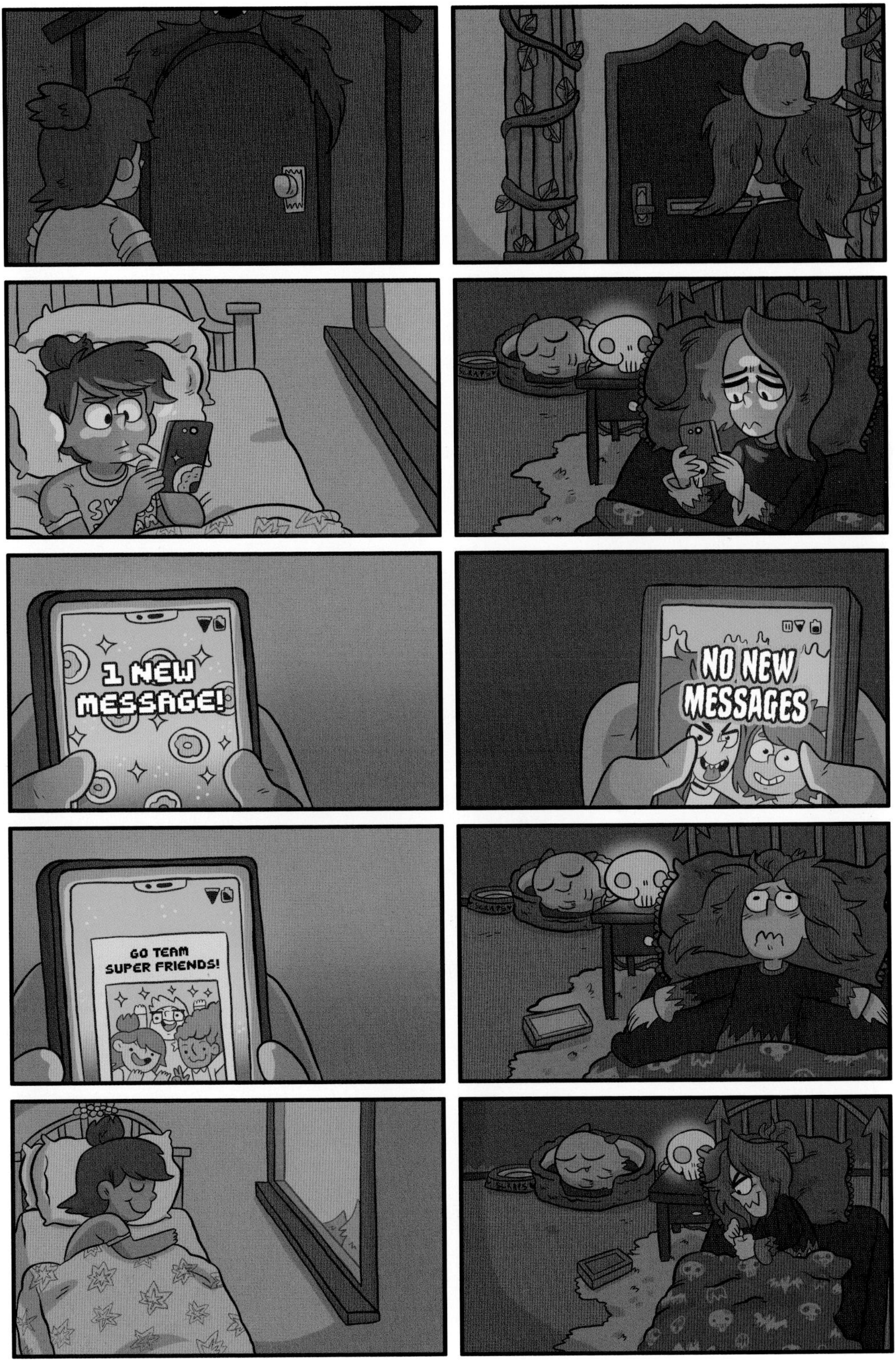
1 NEW MESSAGE!
NO NEW MESSAGES
GO TEAM SUPER FRIENDS!

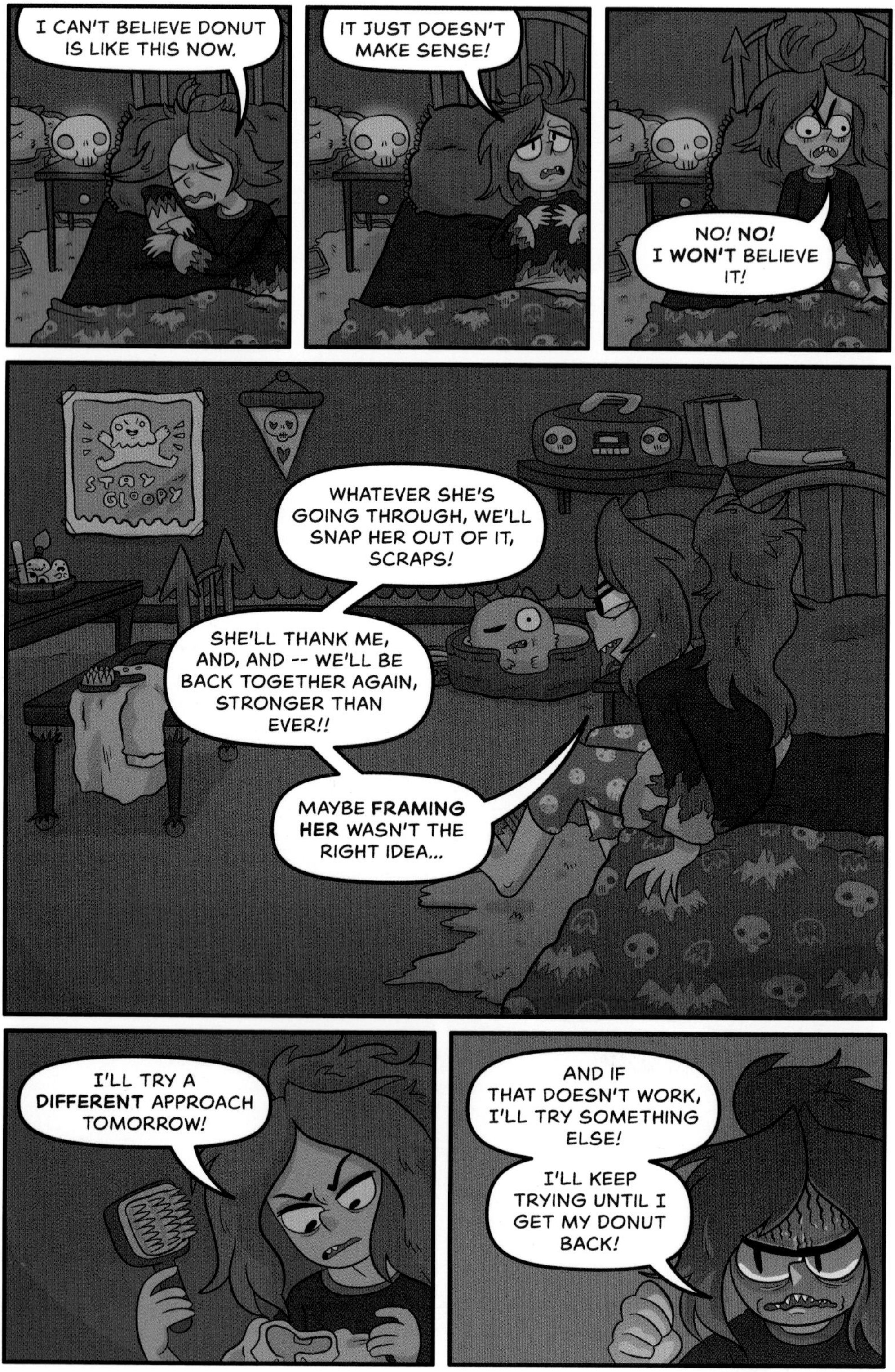
I CAN'T BELIEVE DONUT IS LIKE THIS NOW.
IT JUST DOESN'T MAKE SENSE!
NO! **NO!** I **WON'T** BELIEVE IT!
WHATEVER SHE'S GOING THROUGH, WE'LL SNAP HER OUT OF IT, SCRAPS!
SHE'LL THANK ME, AND, AND -- WE'LL BE BACK TOGETHER AGAIN, STRONGER THAN EVER!!
MAYBE **FRAMING HER** WASN'T THE RIGHT IDEA...
STAY GLOOPY
I'LL TRY A **DIFFERENT** APPROACH TOMORROW!
AND IF THAT DOESN'T WORK, I'LL TRY SOMETHING ELSE!
I'LL KEEP TRYING UNTIL I GET MY DONUT BACK!

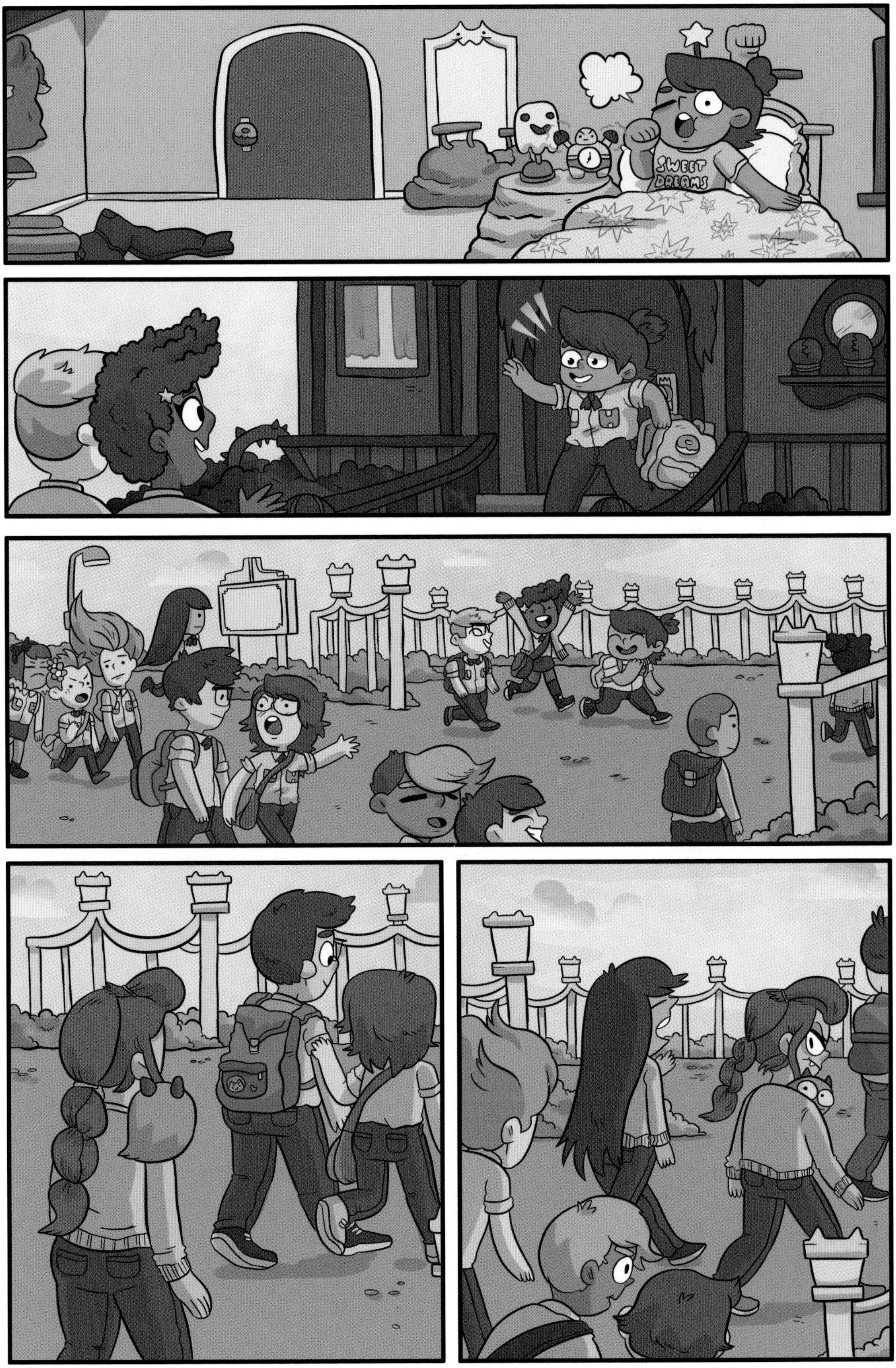
SWEET DREAMS

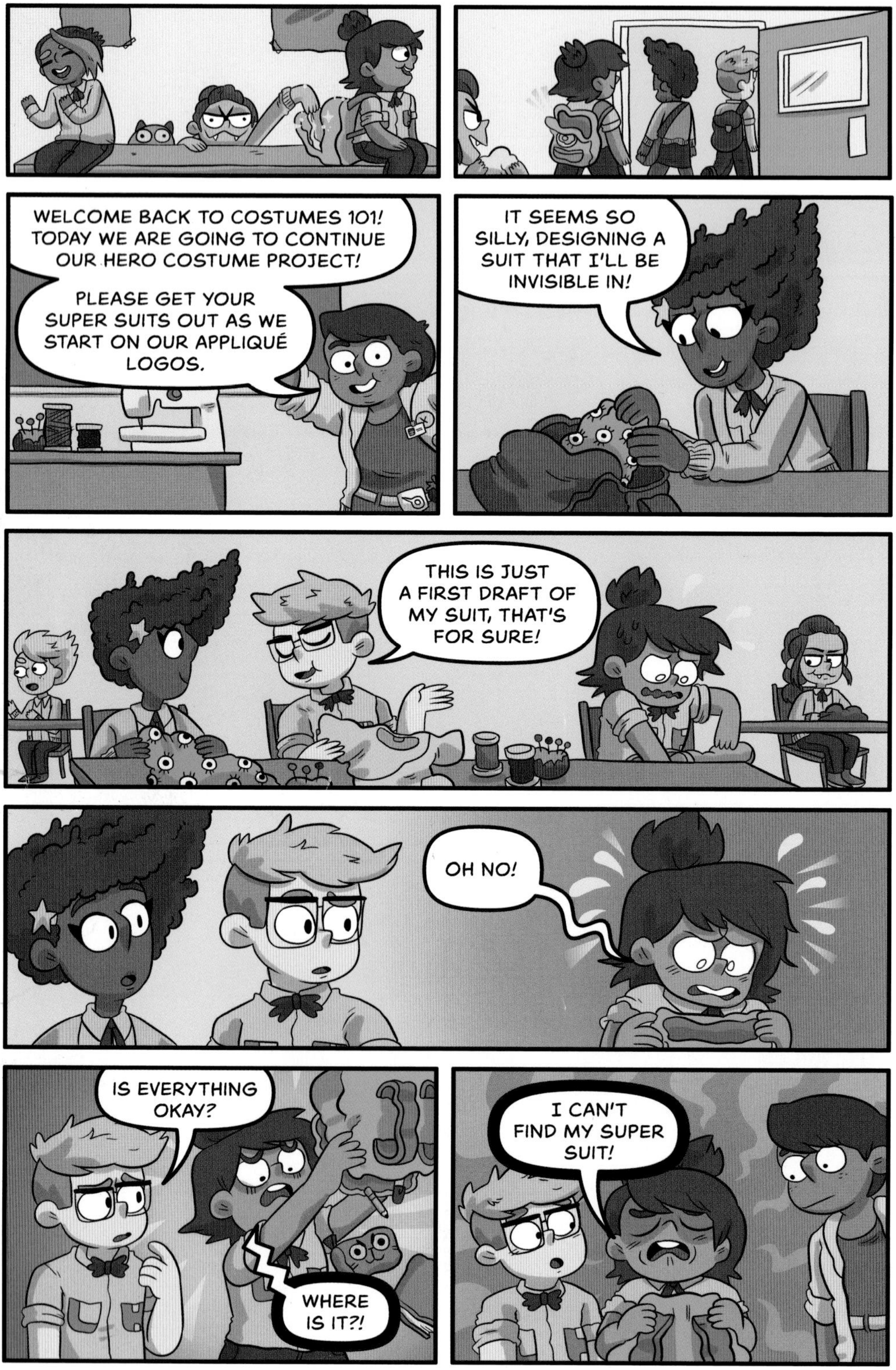
WELCOME BACK TO COSTUMES 101! TODAY WE ARE GOING TO CONTINUE OUR HERO COSTUME PROJECT!
PLEASE GET YOUR SUPER SUITS OUT AS WE START ON OUR APPLIQUÉ LOGOS.
IT SEEMS SO SILLY, DESIGNING A SUIT THAT I'LL BE INVISIBLE IN!
THIS IS JUST A FIRST DRAFT OF MY SUIT, THAT'S FOR SURE!
OH NO!
IS EVERYTHING OKAY?
WHERE IS IT?!
I CAN'T FIND MY SUPER SUIT!

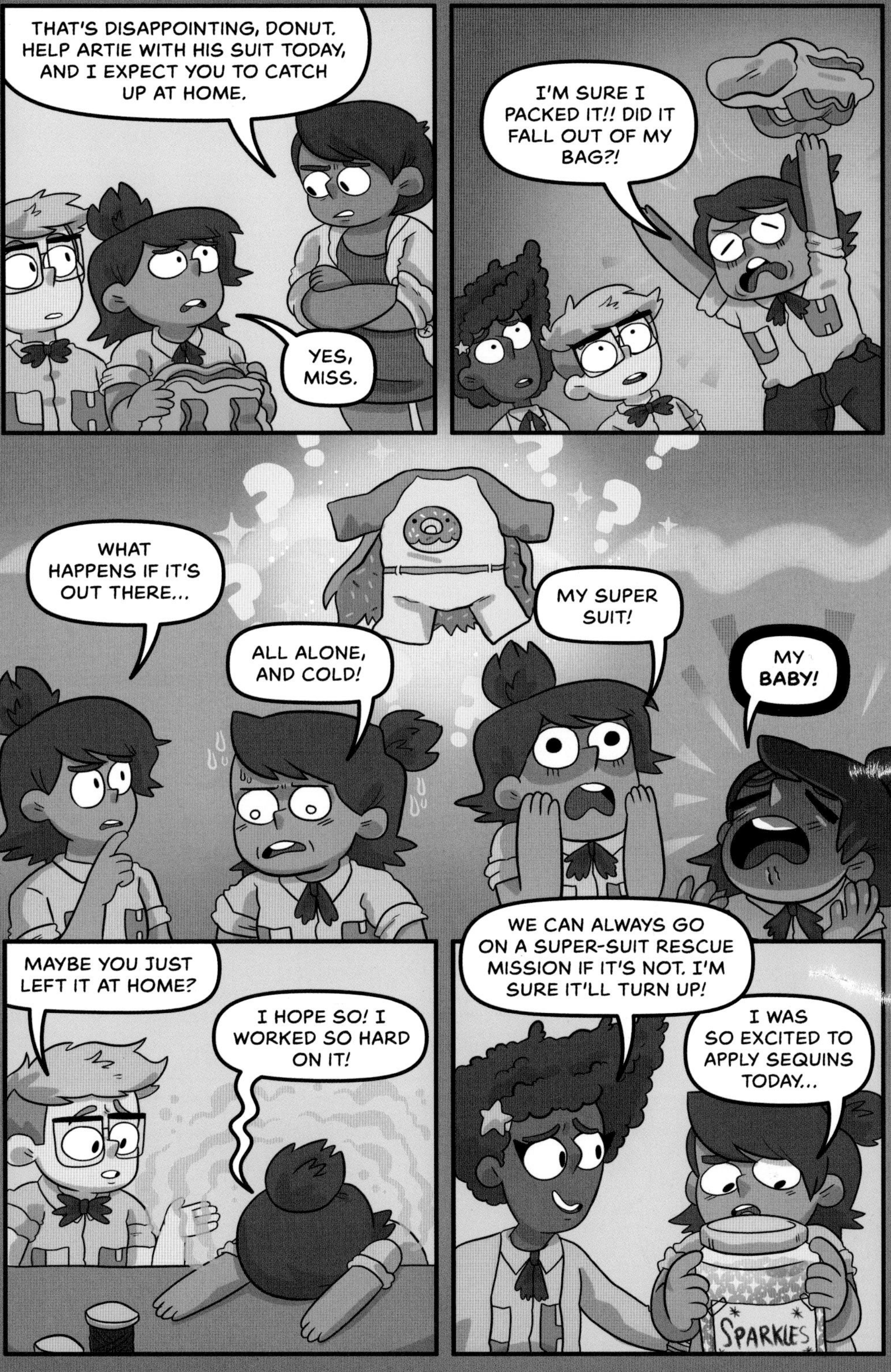
THAT'S DISAPPOINTING, DONUT. HELP ARTIE WITH HIS SUIT TODAY, AND I EXPECT YOU TO CATCH UP AT HOME.
YES, MISS.
I'M SURE I PACKED IT!! DID IT FALL OUT OF MY BAG?!
WHAT HAPPENS IF IT'S OUT THERE...
ALL ALONE, AND COLD!
MY SUPER SUIT!
MY BABY!
MAYBE YOU JUST LEFT IT AT HOME?
I HOPE SO! I WORKED SO HARD ON IT!
WE CAN ALWAYS GO ON A SUPER-SUIT RESCUE MISSION IF IT'S NOT. I'M SURE IT'LL TURN UP!
I WAS SO EXCITED TO APPLY SEQUINS TODAY...
SPARKLES

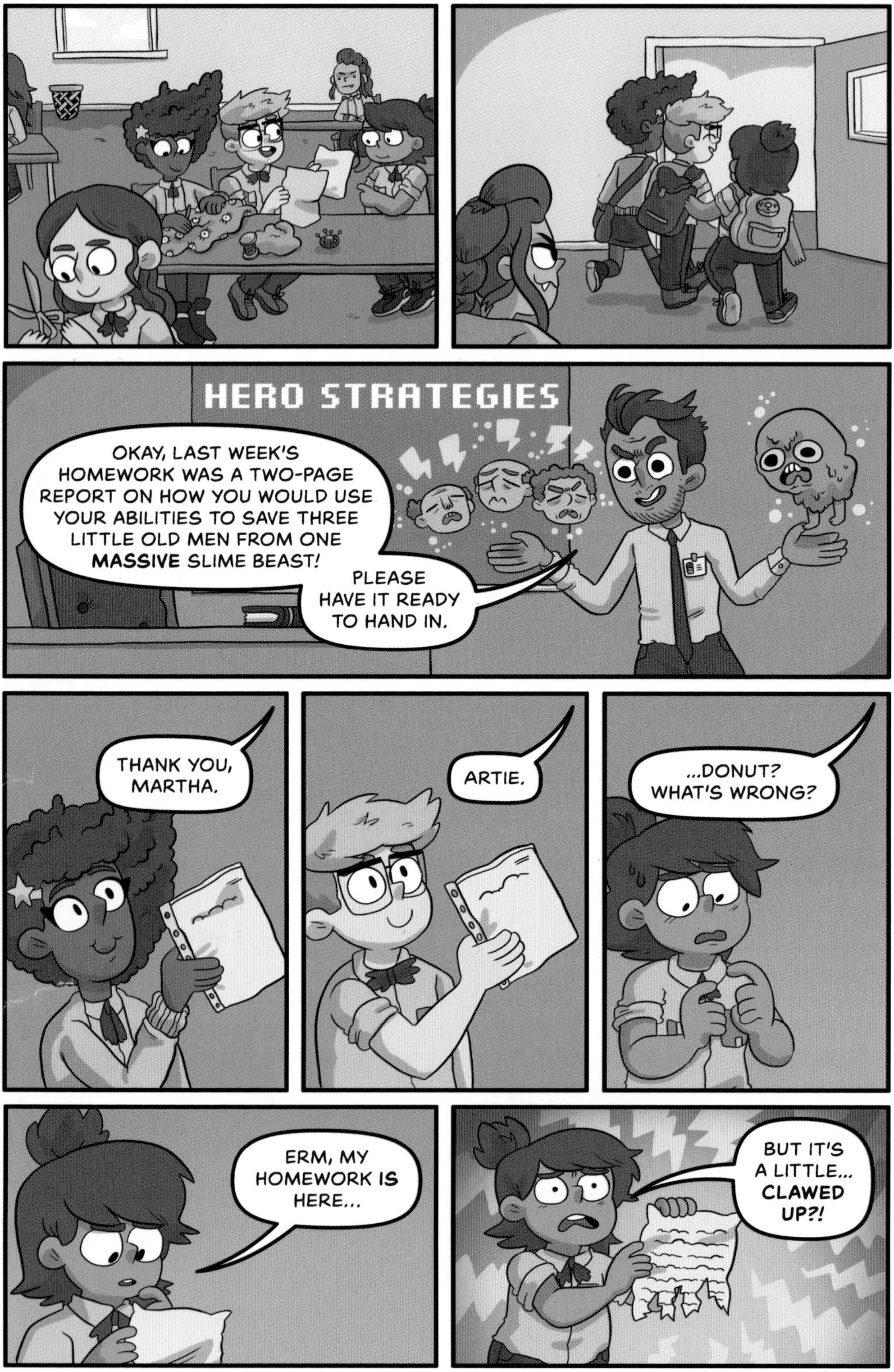
HERO STRATEGIES
OKAY, LAST WEEK'S HOMEWORK WAS A TWO-PAGE REPORT ON HOW YOU WOULD USE YOUR ABILITIES TO SAVE THREE LITTLE OLD MEN FROM ONE **MASSIVE** SLIME BEAST!
PLEASE HAVE IT READY TO HAND IN.
THANK YOU, MARTHA.
ARTIE.
...DONUT? WHAT'S WRONG?
ERM, MY HOMEWORK **IS** HERE...
BUT IT'S A LITTLE... **CLAWED UP?!**

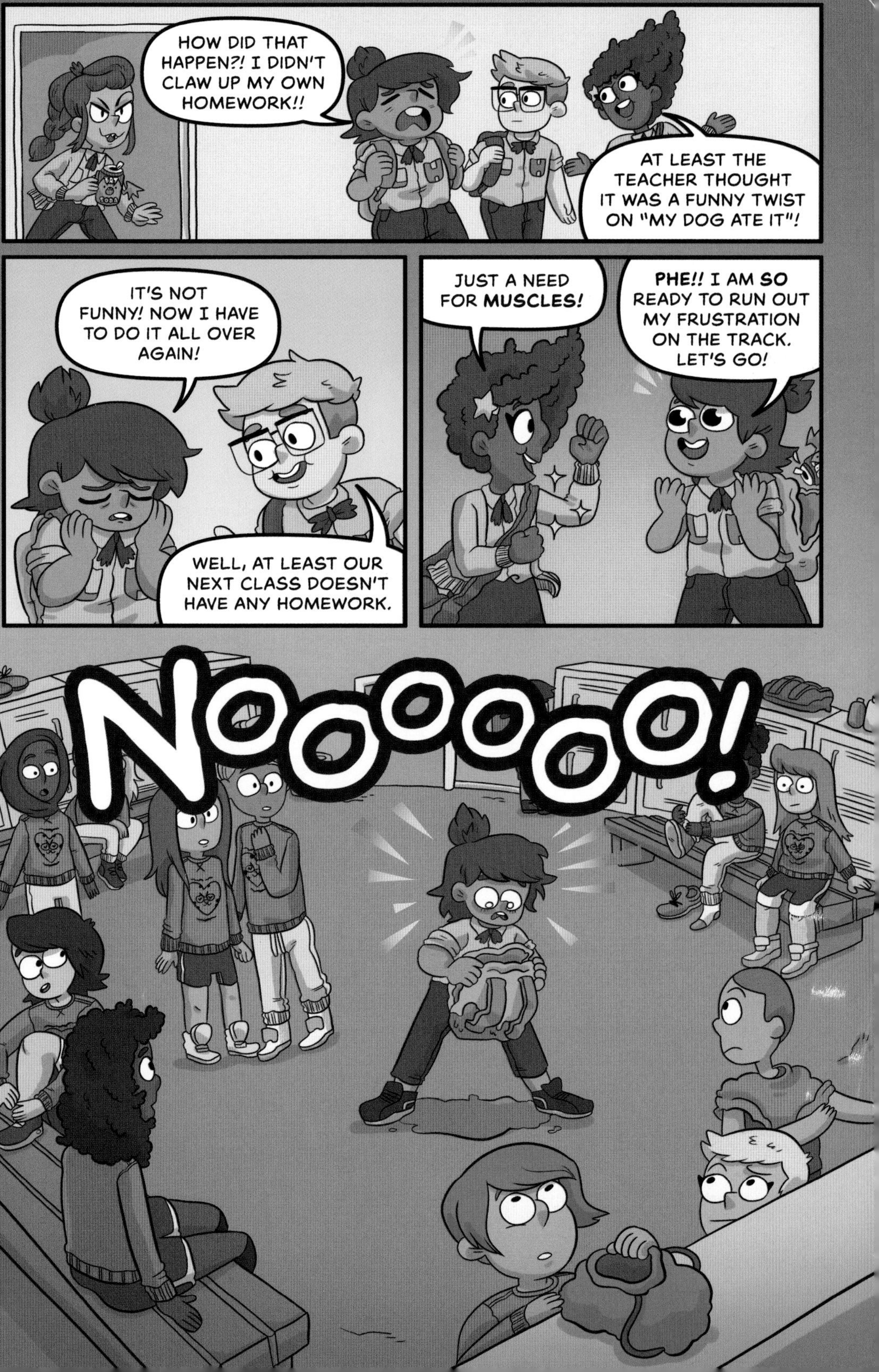
HOW DID THAT HAPPEN?! I DIDN'T CLAW UP MY OWN HOMEWORK!!
AT LEAST THE TEACHER THOUGHT IT WAS A FUNNY TWIST ON "MY DOG ATE IT"!
IT'S NOT FUNNY! NOW I HAVE TO DO IT ALL OVER AGAIN!
WELL, AT LEAST OUR NEXT CLASS DOESN'T HAVE ANY HOMEWORK.
JUST A NEED FOR MUSCLES!
PHE!! I AM SO READY TO RUN OUT MY FRUSTRATION ON THE TRACK. LET'S GO!
NOOOOOOO!

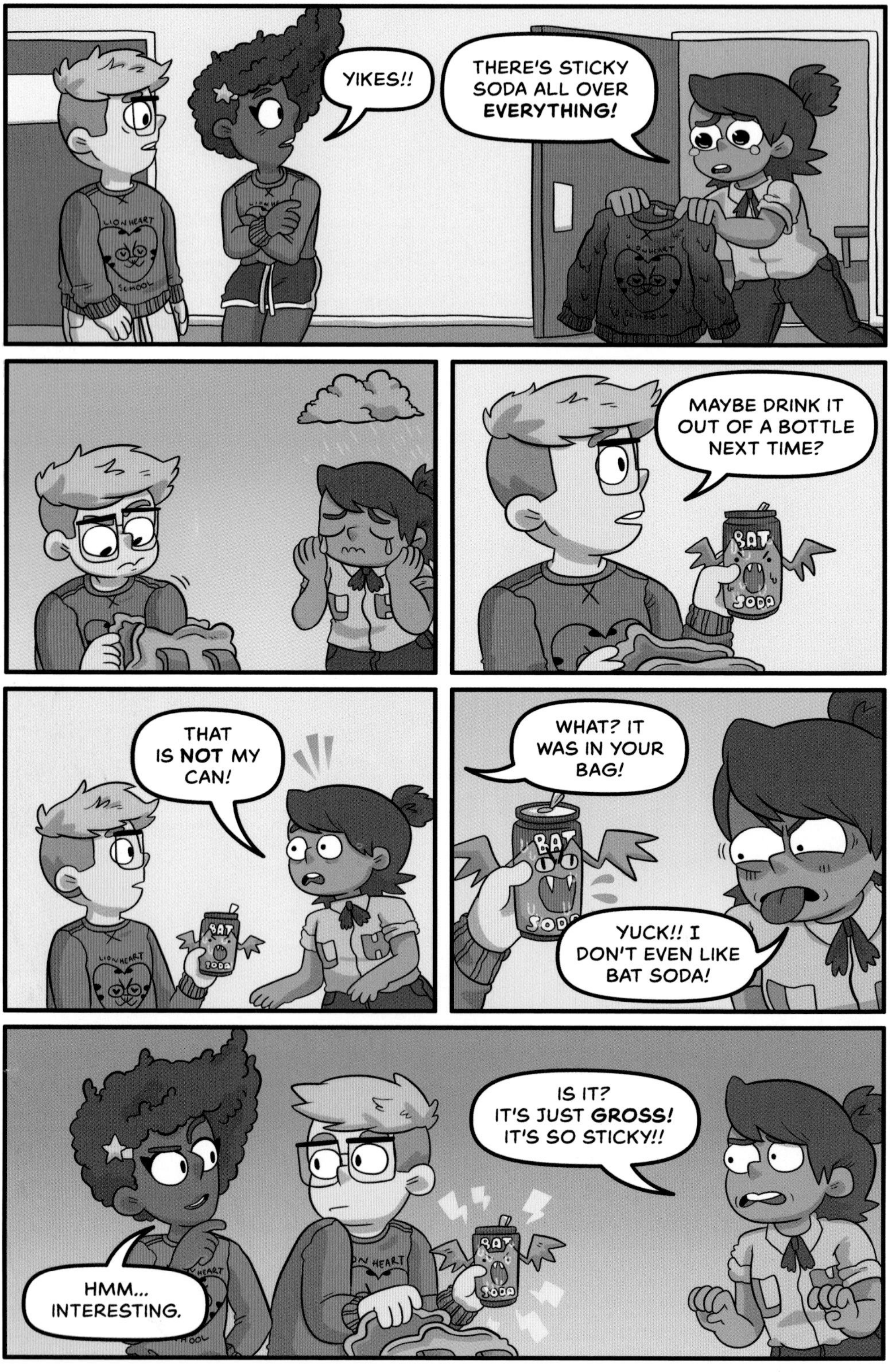
YIKES!!
THERE'S STICKY SODA ALL OVER EVERYTHING!
LIONHEART SCHOOL
MAYBE DRINK IT OUT OF A BOTTLE NEXT TIME?
BAT SODA
THAT IS NOT MY CAN!
WHAT? IT WAS IN YOUR BAG!
YUCK!! I DON'T EVEN LIKE BAT SODA!
IS IT? IT'S JUST GROSS! IT'S SO STICKY!!
HMM... INTERESTING.

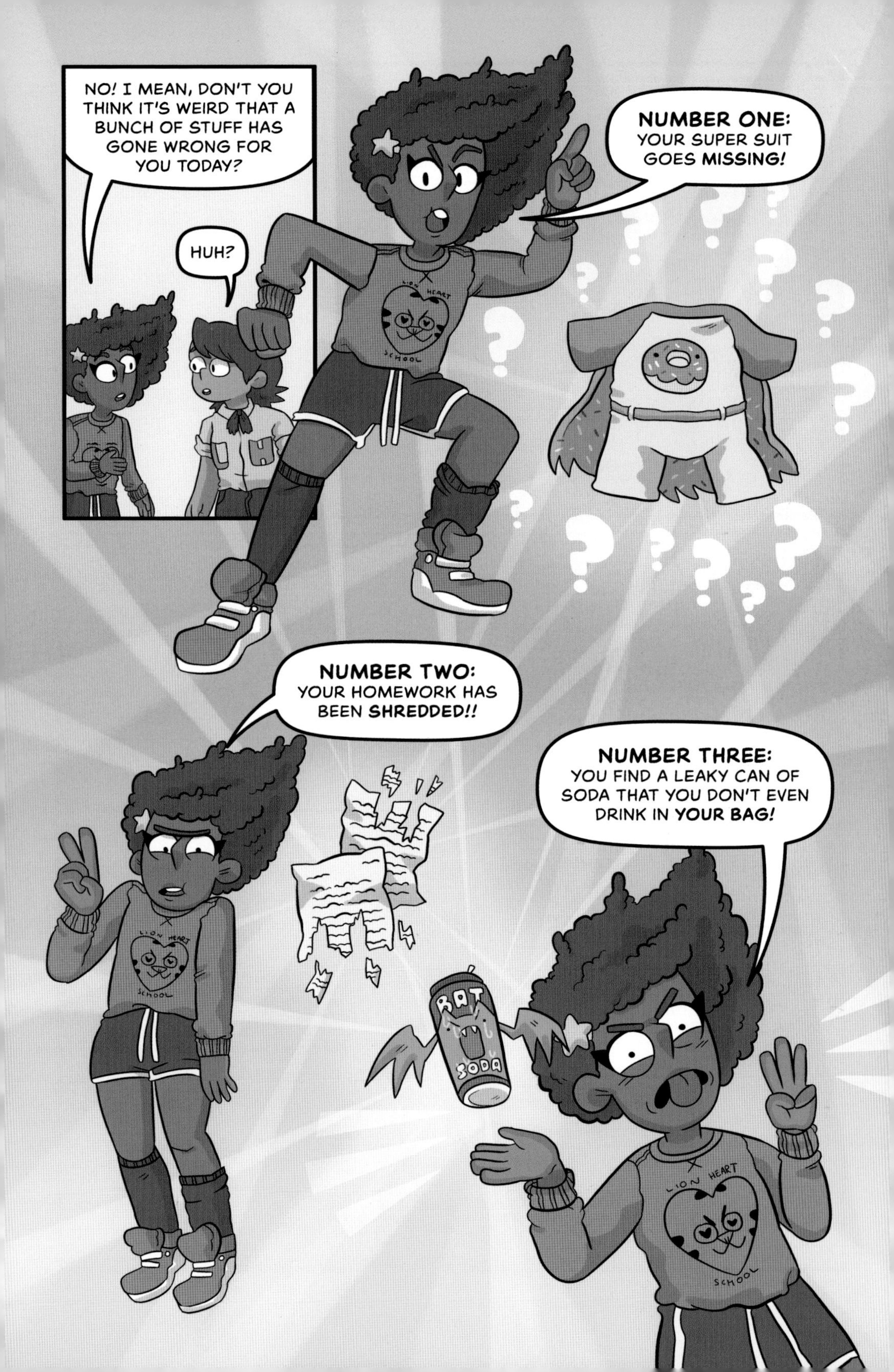
NO! I MEAN, DON'T YOU THINK IT'S WEIRD THAT A BUNCH OF STUFF HAS GONE WRONG FOR YOU TODAY?
HUH?
NUMBER ONE: YOUR SUPER SUIT GOES MISSING!
NUMBER TWO: YOUR HOMEWORK HAS BEEN SHREDDED!!
NUMBER THREE: YOU FIND A LEAKY CAN OF SODA THAT YOU DON'T EVEN DRINK IN YOUR BAG!
BAT SODA
LION HEART SCHOOL

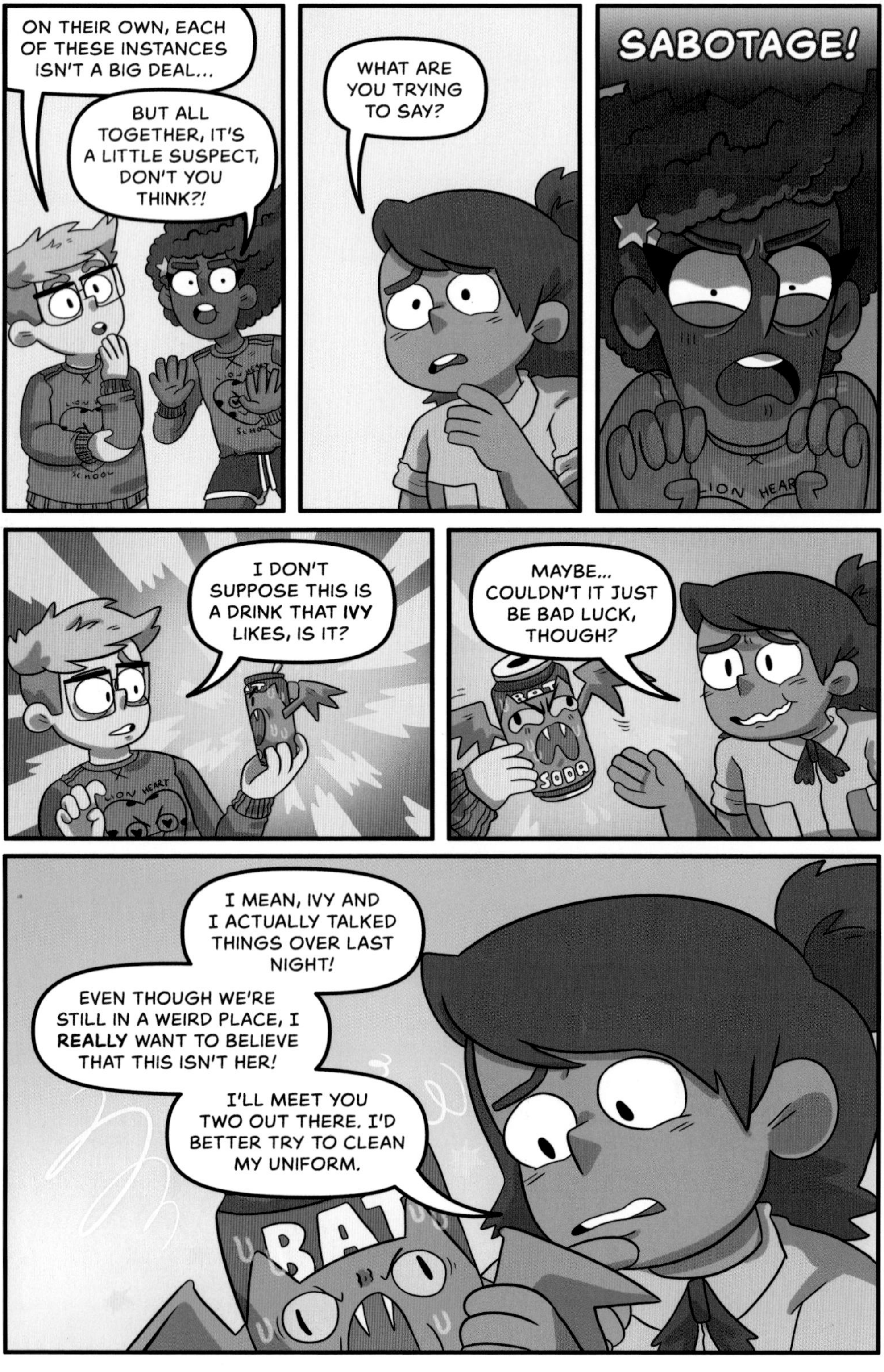
ON THEIR OWN, EACH OF THESE INSTANCES ISN'T A BIG DEAL...
BUT ALL TOGETHER, IT'S A LITTLE SUSPECT, DON'T YOU THINK?!
LION HEART
SCHOOL
WHAT ARE YOU TRYING TO SAY?
SABOTAGE!
LION HEART
I DON'T SUPPOSE THIS IS A DRINK THAT **IVY** LIKES, IS IT?
MAYBE... COULDN'T IT JUST BE BAD LUCK, THOUGH?
BAT
SODA
I MEAN, IVY AND I ACTUALLY TALKED THINGS OVER LAST NIGHT!
EVEN THOUGH WE'RE STILL IN A WEIRD PLACE, I **REALLY** WANT TO BELIEVE THAT THIS ISN'T HER!
I'LL MEET YOU TWO OUT THERE. I'D BETTER TRY TO CLEAN MY UNIFORM.
BAT

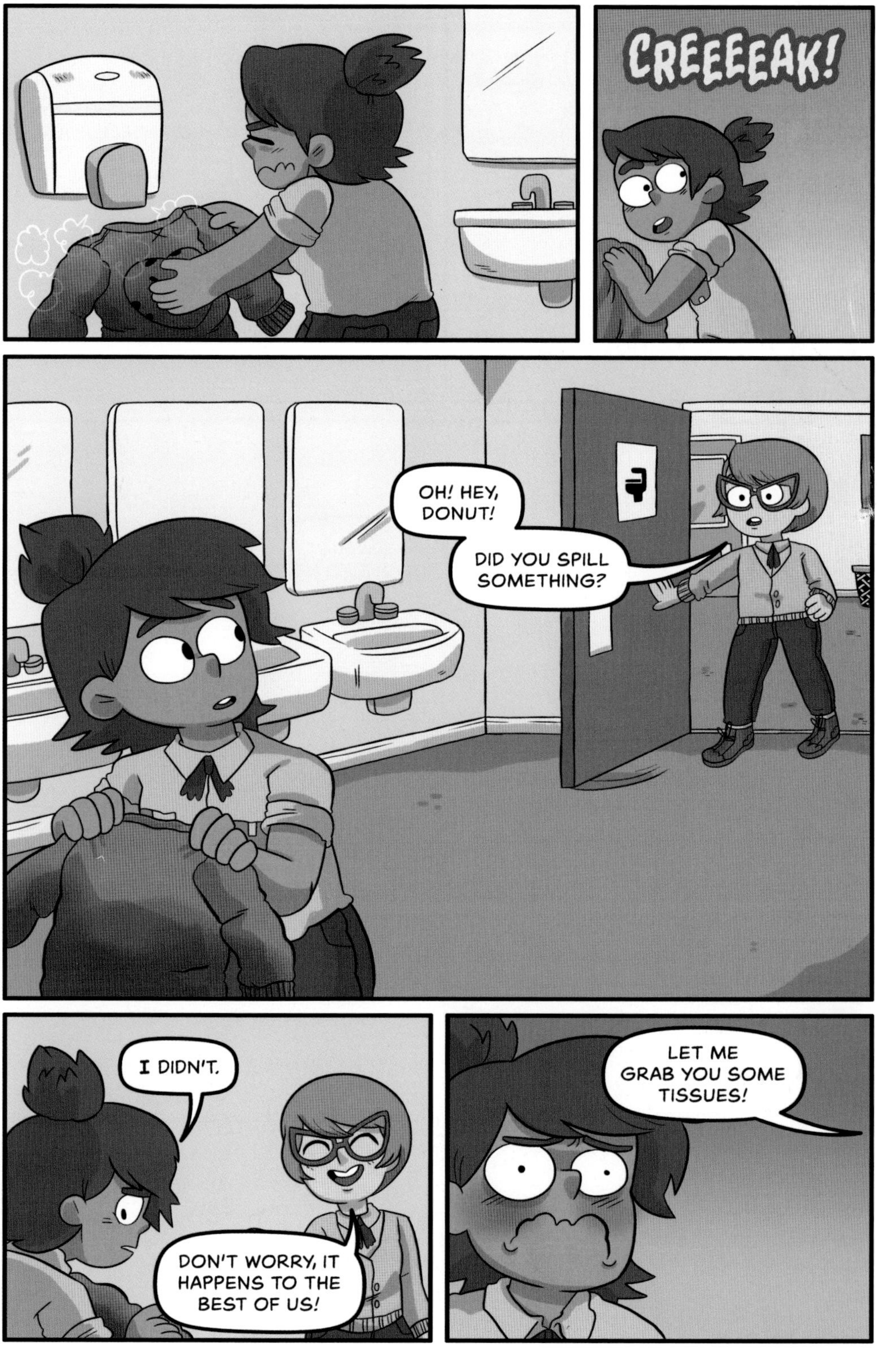
CREEEEAK!
OH! HEY, DONUT!
DID YOU SPILL SOMETHING?
I DIDN'T.
DON'T WORRY, IT HAPPENS TO THE BEST OF US!
LET ME GRAB YOU SOME TISSUES!

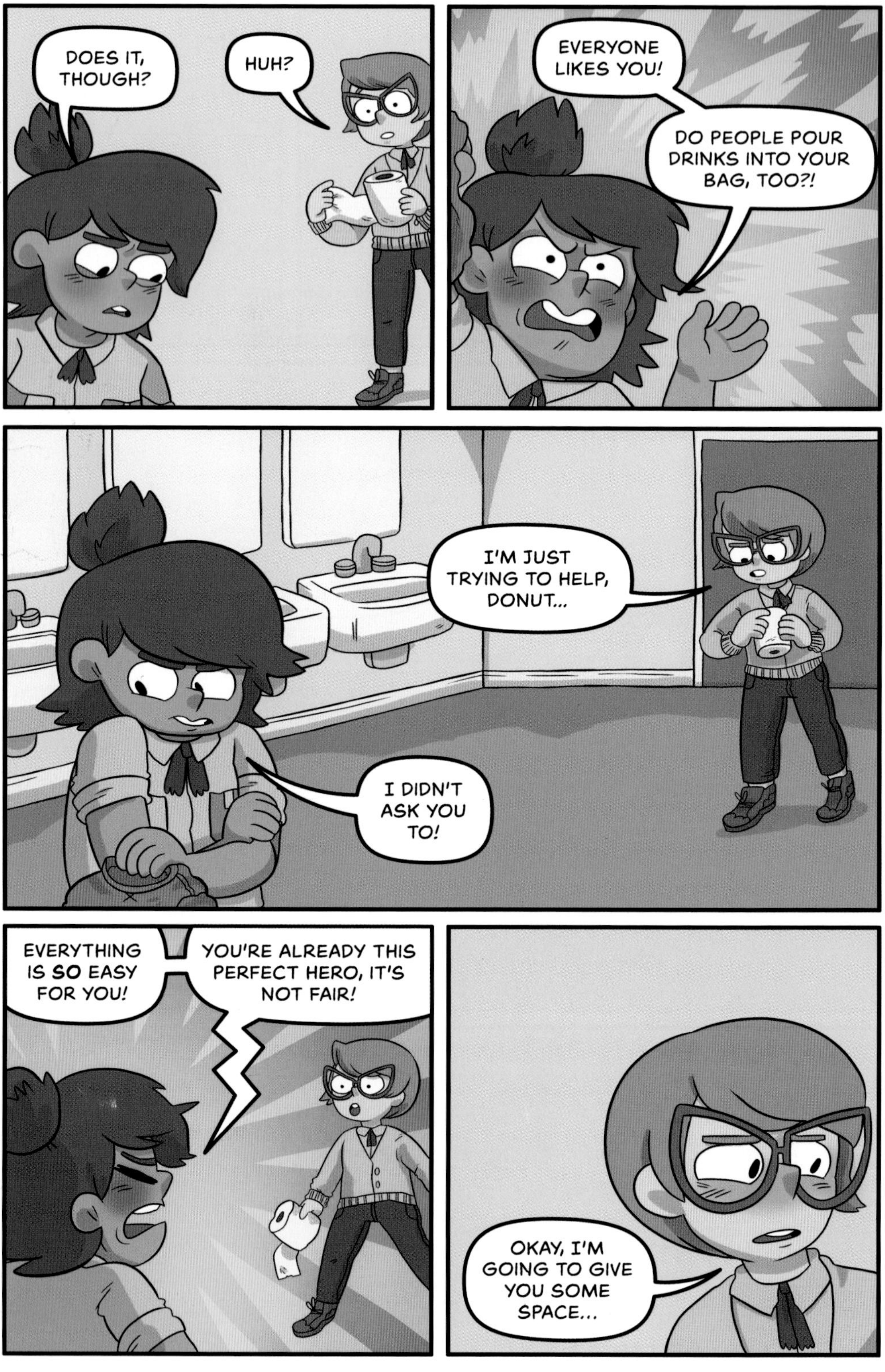
DOES IT, THOUGH?
HUH?
EVERYONE LIKES YOU!
DO PEOPLE POUR DRINKS INTO YOUR BAG, TOO?!
I'M JUST TRYING TO HELP, DONUT...
I DIDN'T ASK YOU TO!
EVERYTHING IS **SO** EASY FOR YOU!
YOU'RE ALREADY THIS PERFECT HERO, IT'S NOT FAIR!
OKAY, I'M GOING TO GIVE YOU SOME SPACE...

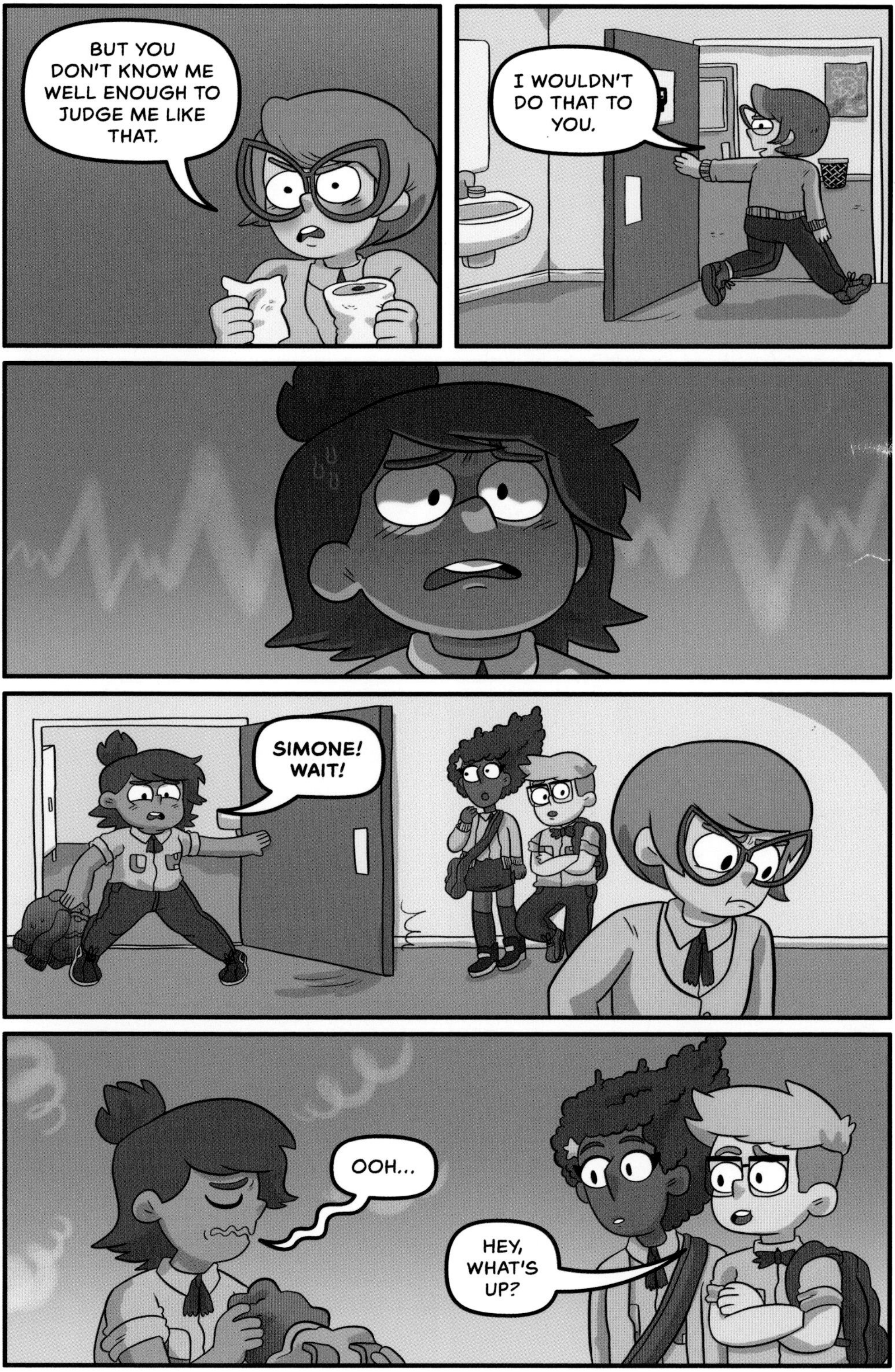

BUT YOU DON'T KNOW ME WELL ENOUGH TO JUDGE ME LIKE THAT.
I WOULDN'T DO THAT TO YOU.
SIMONE! WAIT!
OOH...
HEY, WHAT'S UP?

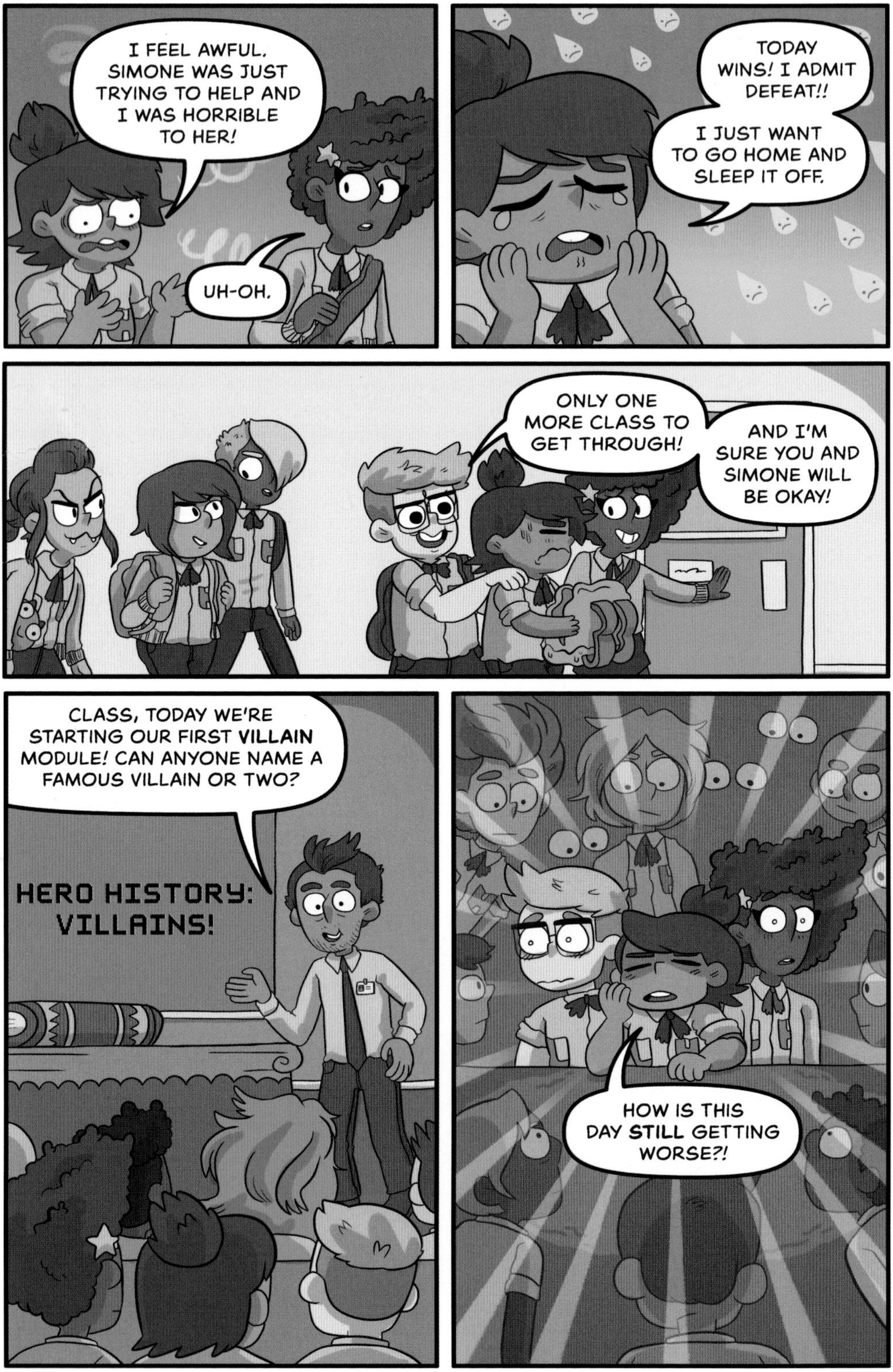
I FEEL AWFUL. SIMONE WAS JUST TRYING TO HELP AND I WAS HORRIBLE TO HER!
UH-OH.
TODAY WINS! I ADMIT DEFEAT!!
I JUST WANT TO GO HOME AND SLEEP IT OFF.
ONLY ONE MORE CLASS TO GET THROUGH!
AND I'M SURE YOU AND SIMONE WILL BE OKAY!
CLASS, TODAY WE'RE STARTING OUR FIRST **VILLAIN** MODULE! CAN ANYONE NAME A FAMOUS VILLAIN OR TWO?
HERO HISTORY: VILLAINS!
HOW IS THIS DAY **STILL** GETTING WORSE?!

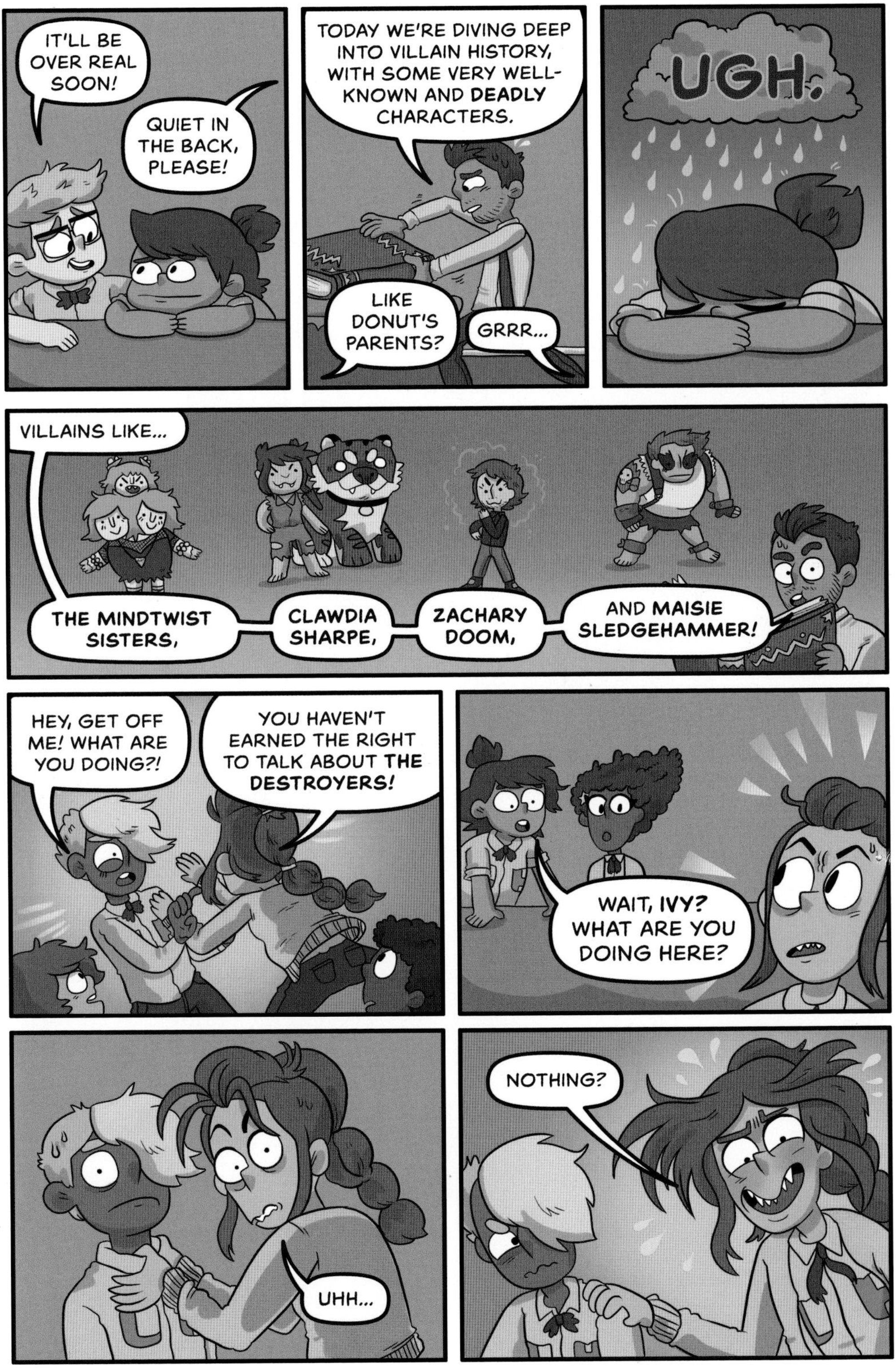
IT'LL BE OVER REAL SOON!
QUIET IN THE BACK, PLEASE!
TODAY WE'RE DIVING DEEP INTO VILLAIN HISTORY, WITH SOME VERY WELL-KNOWN AND DEADLY CHARACTERS.
LIKE DONUT'S PARENTS?
GRRR...
UGH.
VILLAINS LIKE...
THE MINDTWIST SISTERS,
CLAWDIA SHARPE,
ZACHARY DOOM,
AND MAISIE SLEDGEHAMMER!
HEY, GET OFF ME! WHAT ARE YOU DOING?!
YOU HAVEN'T EARNED THE RIGHT TO TALK ABOUT THE DESTROYERS!
WAIT, IVY? WHAT ARE YOU DOING HERE?
UHH...
NOTHING?

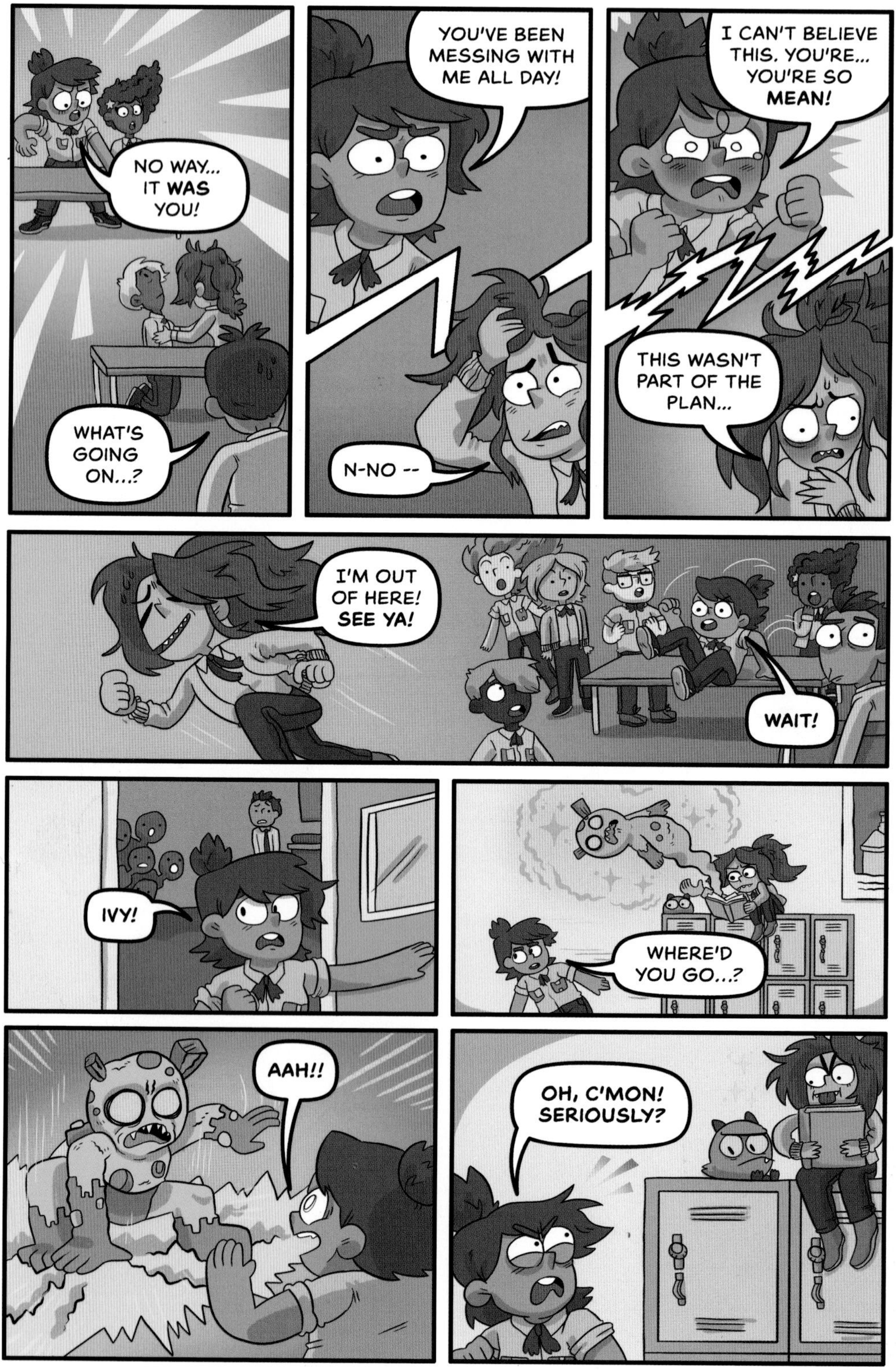
NO WAY... IT WAS YOU!
WHAT'S GOING ON...?
YOU'VE BEEN MESSING WITH ME ALL DAY!
N-NO --
I CAN'T BELIEVE THIS. YOU'RE... YOU'RE SO MEAN!
THIS WASN'T PART OF THE PLAN...
I'M OUT OF HERE! SEE YA!
WAIT!
IVY!
WHERE'D YOU GO...?
AAH!!
OH, C'MON! SERIOUSLY?

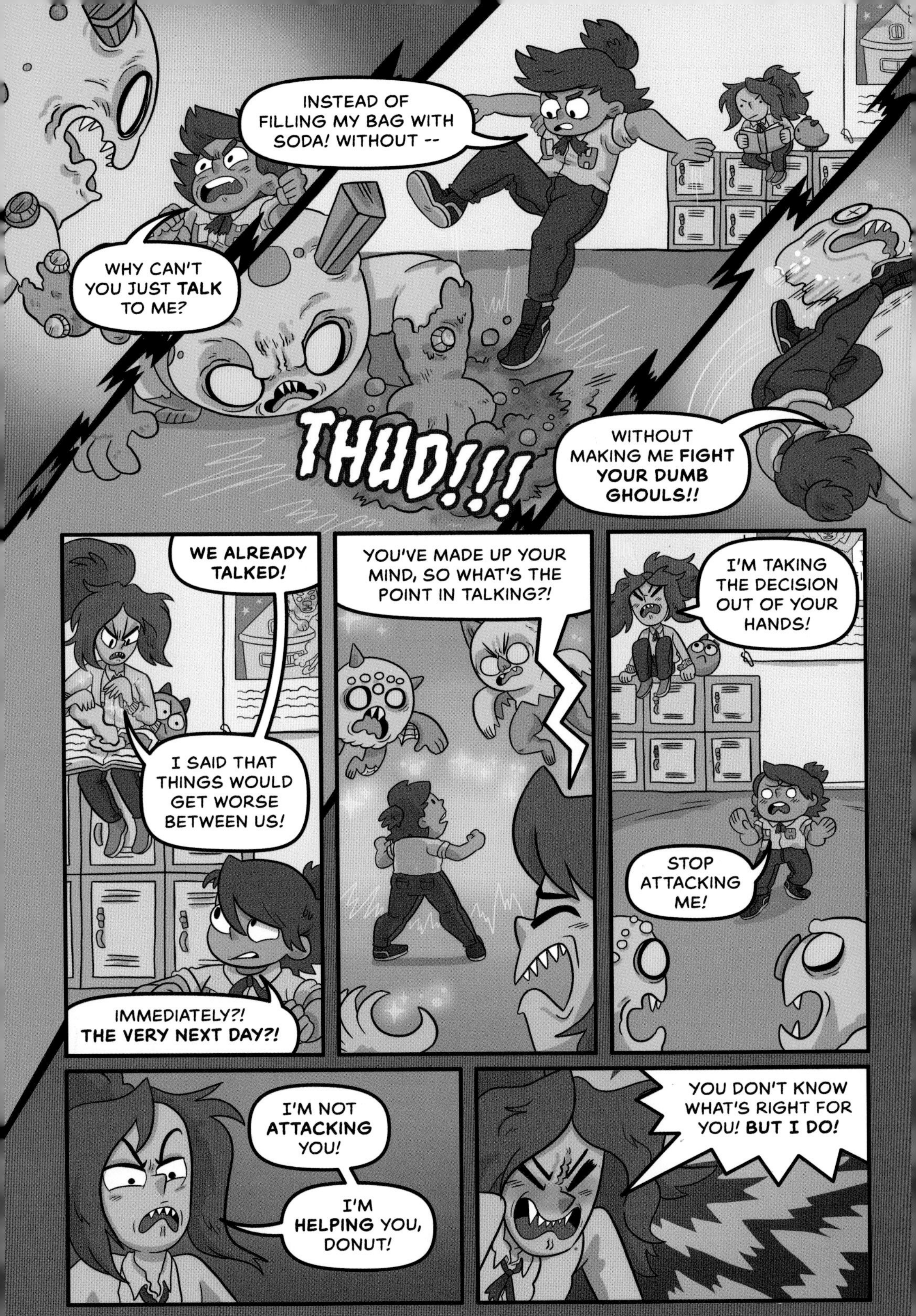
INSTEAD OF FILLING MY BAG WITH SODA! WITHOUT --
WHY CAN'T YOU JUST TALK TO ME?
THUD!!!
WITHOUT MAKING ME FIGHT YOUR DUMB GHOULS!!
WE ALREADY TALKED!
I SAID THAT THINGS WOULD GET WORSE BETWEEN US!
IMMEDIATELY?! THE VERY NEXT DAY?!
YOU'VE MADE UP YOUR MIND, SO WHAT'S THE POINT IN TALKING?!
I'M TAKING THE DECISION OUT OF YOUR HANDS!
STOP ATTACKING ME!
I'M NOT ATTACKING YOU!
I'M HELPING YOU, DONUT!
YOU DON'T KNOW WHAT'S RIGHT FOR YOU! BUT I DO!

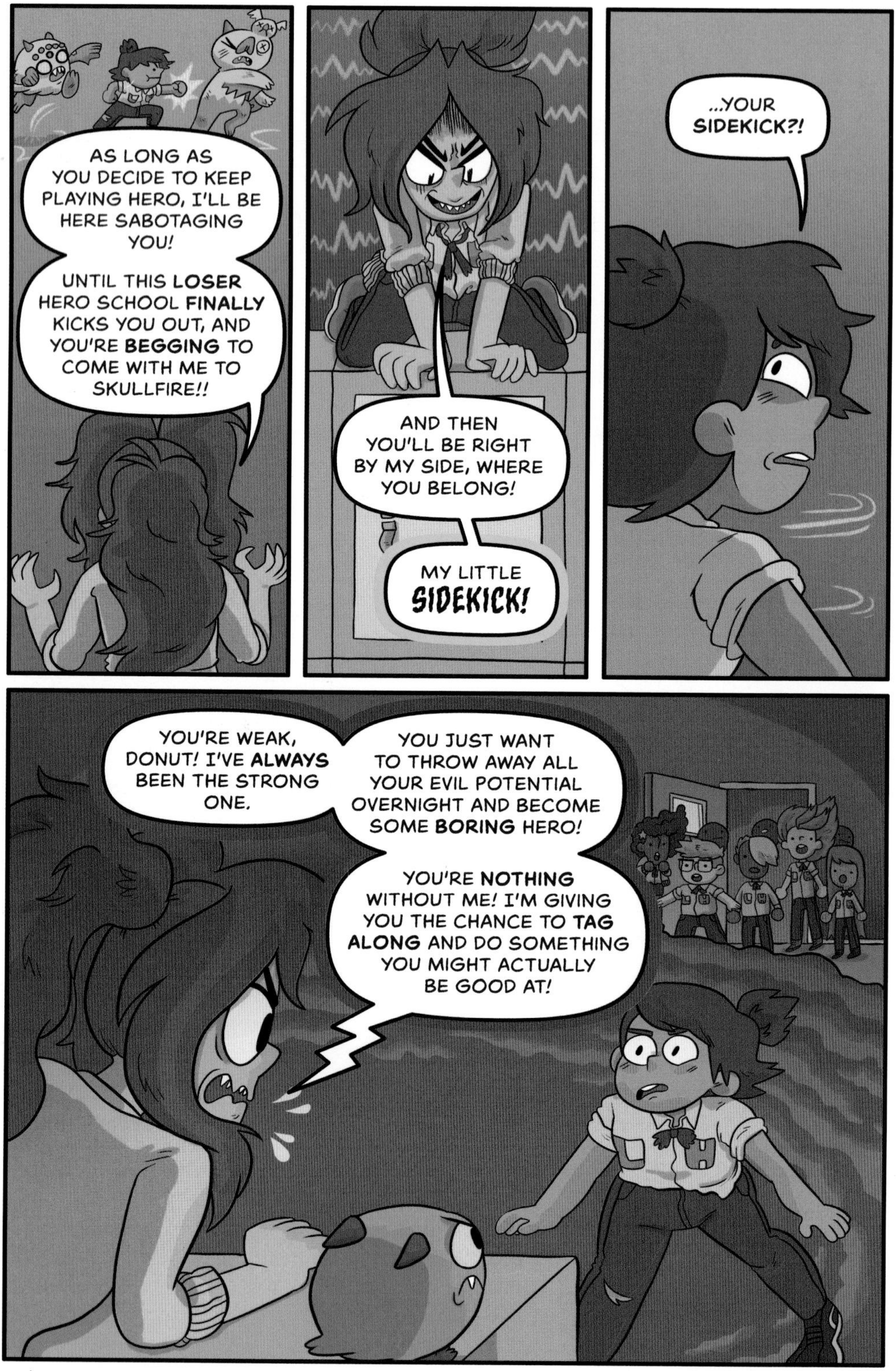
AS LONG AS YOU DECIDE TO KEEP PLAYING HERO, I'LL BE HERE SABOTAGING YOU!
UNTIL THIS LOSER HERO SCHOOL FINALLY KICKS YOU OUT, AND YOU'RE BEGGING TO COME WITH ME TO SKULLFIRE!!
AND THEN YOU'LL BE RIGHT BY MY SIDE, WHERE YOU BELONG!
MY LITTLE SIDEKICK!
...YOUR SIDEKICK?!
YOU'RE WEAK, DONUT! I'VE ALWAYS BEEN THE STRONG ONE.
YOU JUST WANT TO THROW AWAY ALL YOUR EVIL POTENTIAL OVERNIGHT AND BECOME SOME BORING HERO!
YOU'RE NOTHING WITHOUT ME! I'M GIVING YOU THE CHANCE TO TAG ALONG AND DO SOMETHING YOU MIGHT ACTUALLY BE GOOD AT!

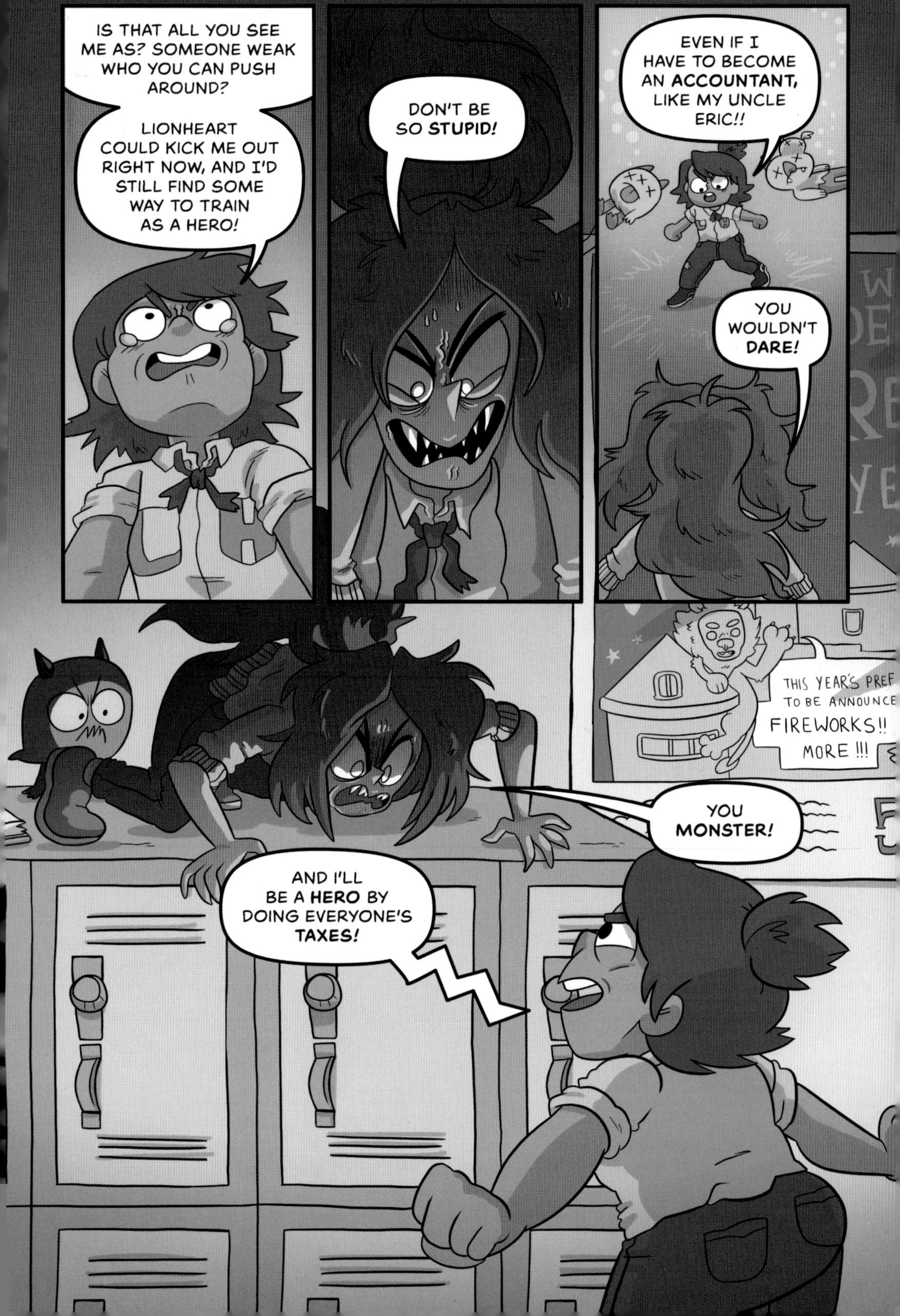
IS THAT ALL YOU SEE ME AS? SOMEONE WEAK WHO YOU CAN PUSH AROUND?
LIONHEART COULD KICK ME OUT RIGHT NOW, AND I'D STILL FIND SOME WAY TO TRAIN AS A HERO!
DON'T BE SO **STUPID!**
EVEN IF I HAVE TO BECOME AN **ACCOUNTANT,** LIKE MY UNCLE ERIC!!
YOU WOULDN'T **DARE!**
THIS YEAR'S PREF
TO BE ANNOUNCE
FIREWORKS!!
MORE !!!
YOU **MONSTER!**
AND I'LL BE A **HERO** BY DOING EVERYONE'S **TAXES!**

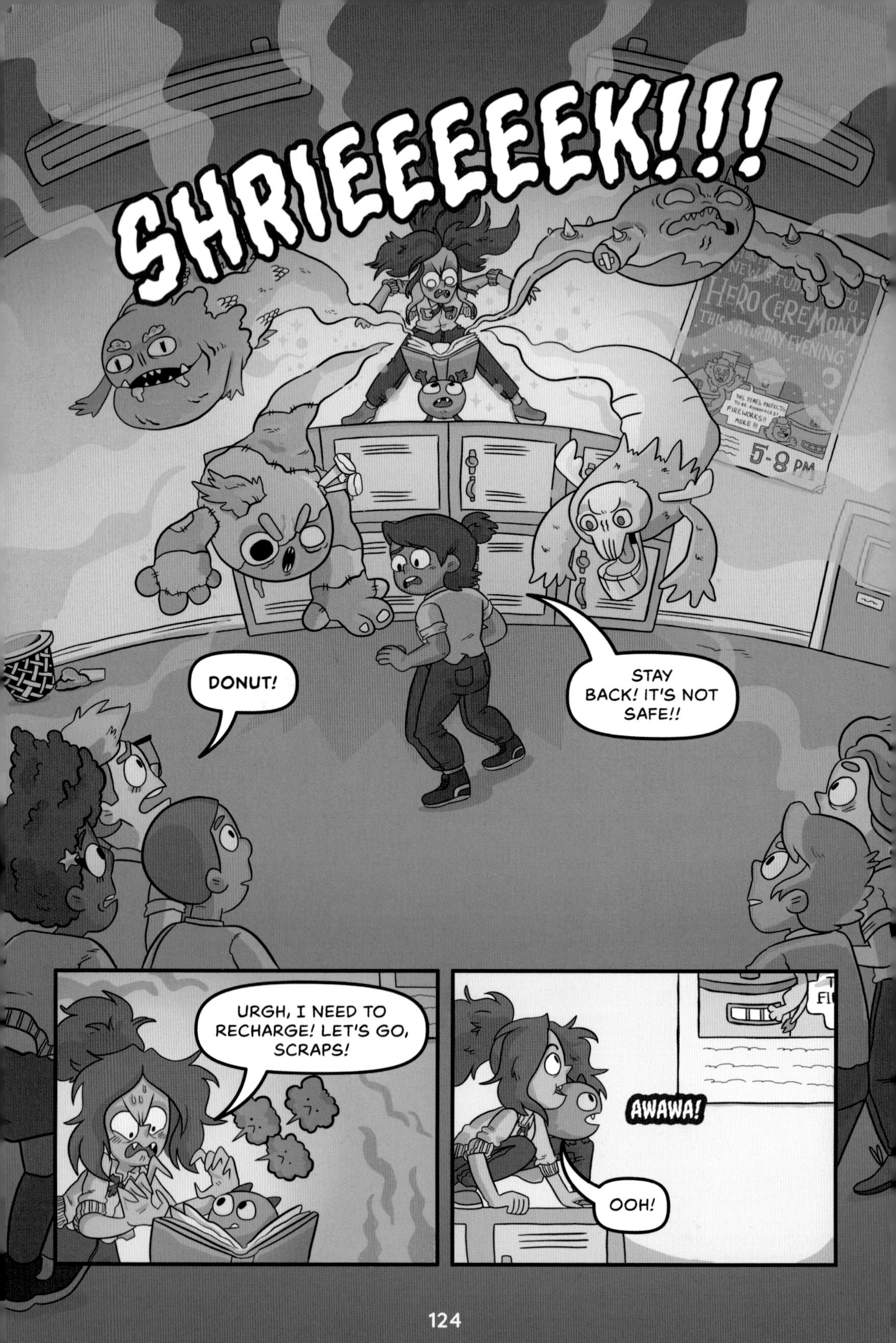
SHRIEEEEEK!!!
HERO CEREMONY
THIS SATURDAY EVENING
5-8 PM
DONUT!
STAY BACK! IT'S NOT SAFE!!
URGH, I NEED TO RECHARGE! LET'S GO, SCRAPS!
AWAWA!
OOH!

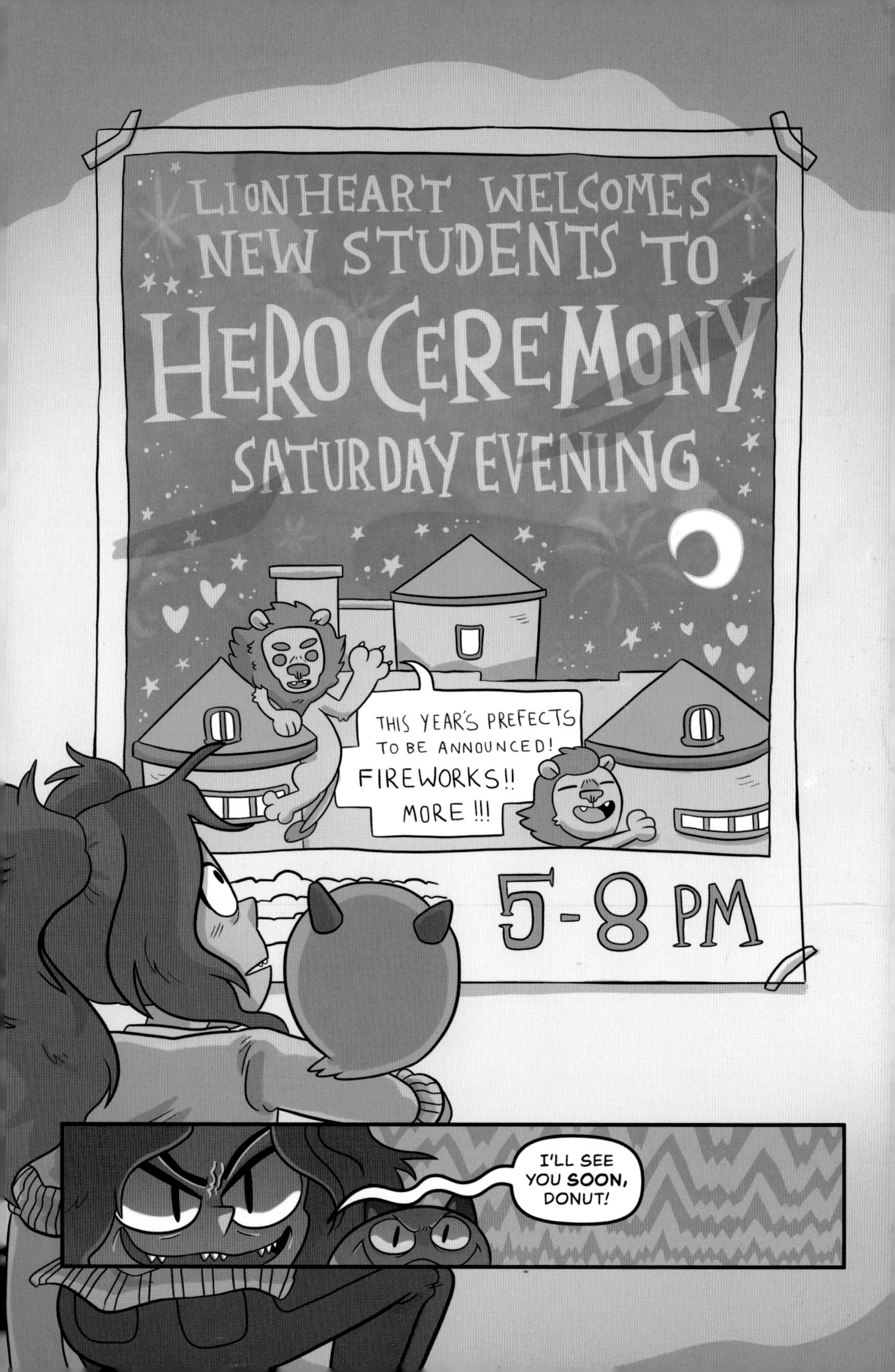
LIONHEART WELCOMES
NEW STUDENTS TO
HERO CEREMONY
SATURDAY EVENING
THIS YEAR'S PREFECTS TO BE ANNOUNCED!
FIREWORKS!!
MORE!!!
5-8 PM
I'LL SEE YOU SOON, DONUT!

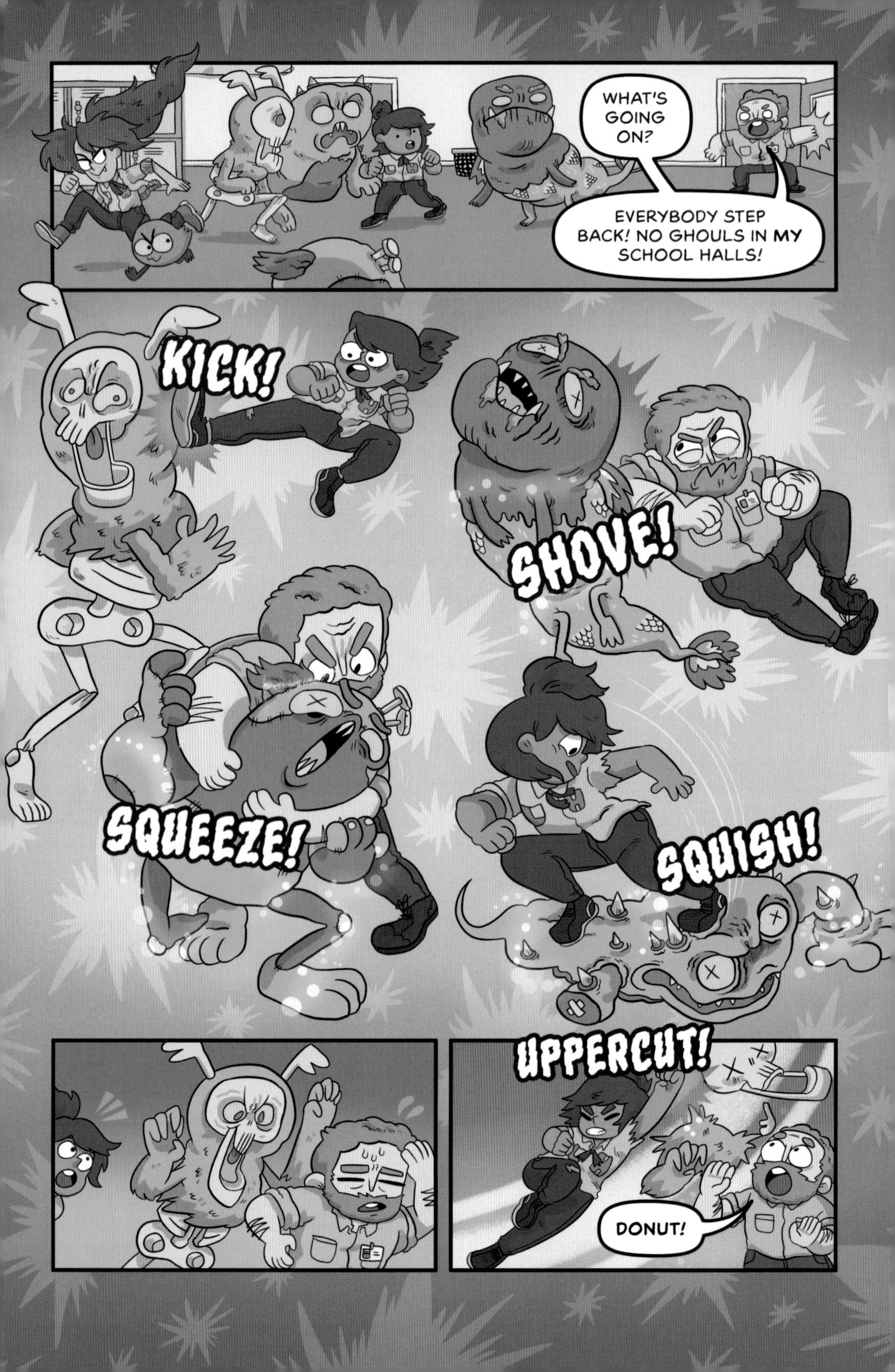
WHAT'S GOING ON?
EVERYBODY STEP BACK! NO GHOULS IN MY SCHOOL HALLS!
KICK!
SHOVE!
SQUEEZE!
SQUISH!
UPPERCUT!
DONUT!

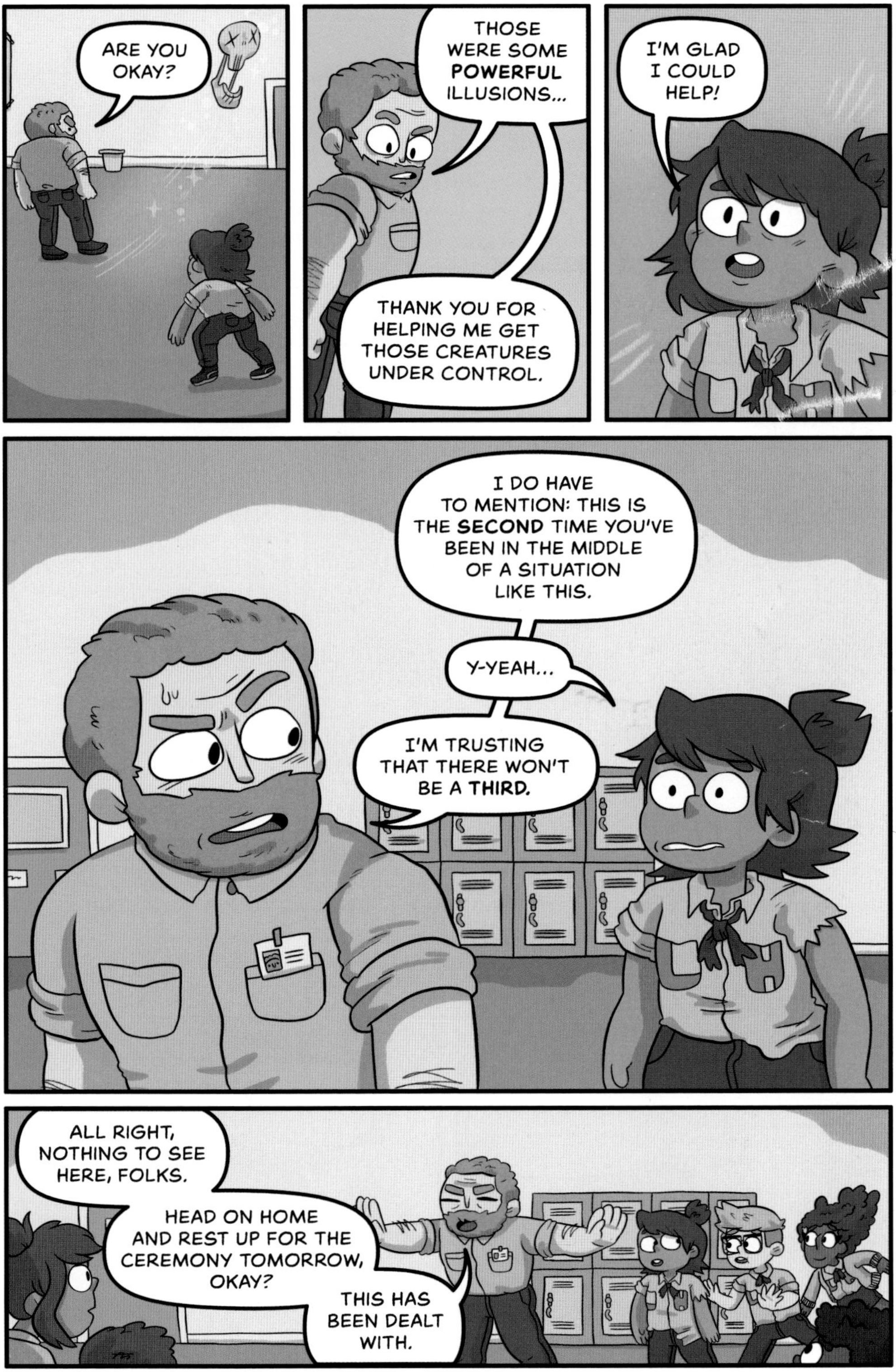
ARE YOU OKAY?
THOSE WERE SOME POWERFUL ILLUSIONS...
THANK YOU FOR HELPING ME GET THOSE CREATURES UNDER CONTROL.
I'M GLAD I COULD HELP!
I DO HAVE TO MENTION: THIS IS THE SECOND TIME YOU'VE BEEN IN THE MIDDLE OF A SITUATION LIKE THIS.
Y-YEAH...
I'M TRUSTING THAT THERE WON'T BE A THIRD.
ALL RIGHT, NOTHING TO SEE HERE, FOLKS.
HEAD ON HOME AND REST UP FOR THE CEREMONY TOMORROW, OKAY?
THIS HAS BEEN DEALT WITH.

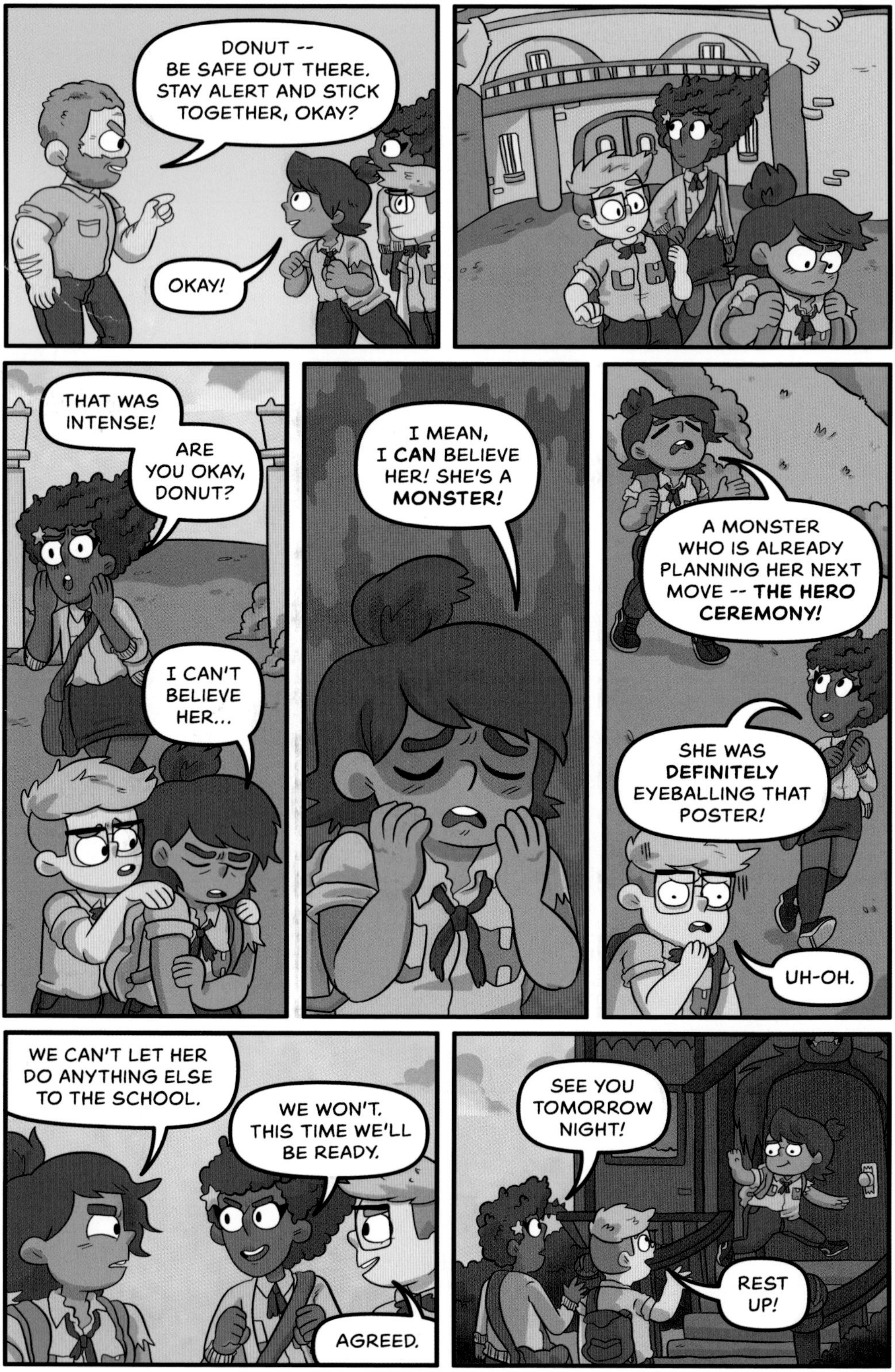
DONUT -- BE SAFE OUT THERE. STAY ALERT AND STICK TOGETHER, OKAY?
OKAY!
THAT WAS INTENSE!
ARE YOU OKAY, DONUT?
I CAN'T BELIEVE HER...
I MEAN, I **CAN** BELIEVE HER! SHE'S A **MONSTER!**
A MONSTER WHO IS ALREADY PLANNING HER NEXT MOVE -- **THE HERO CEREMONY!**
SHE WAS **DEFINITELY** EYEBALLING THAT POSTER!
UH-OH.
WE CAN'T LET HER DO ANYTHING ELSE TO THE SCHOOL.
WE WON'T. THIS TIME WE'LL BE READY.
AGREED.
SEE YOU TOMORROW NIGHT!
REST UP!

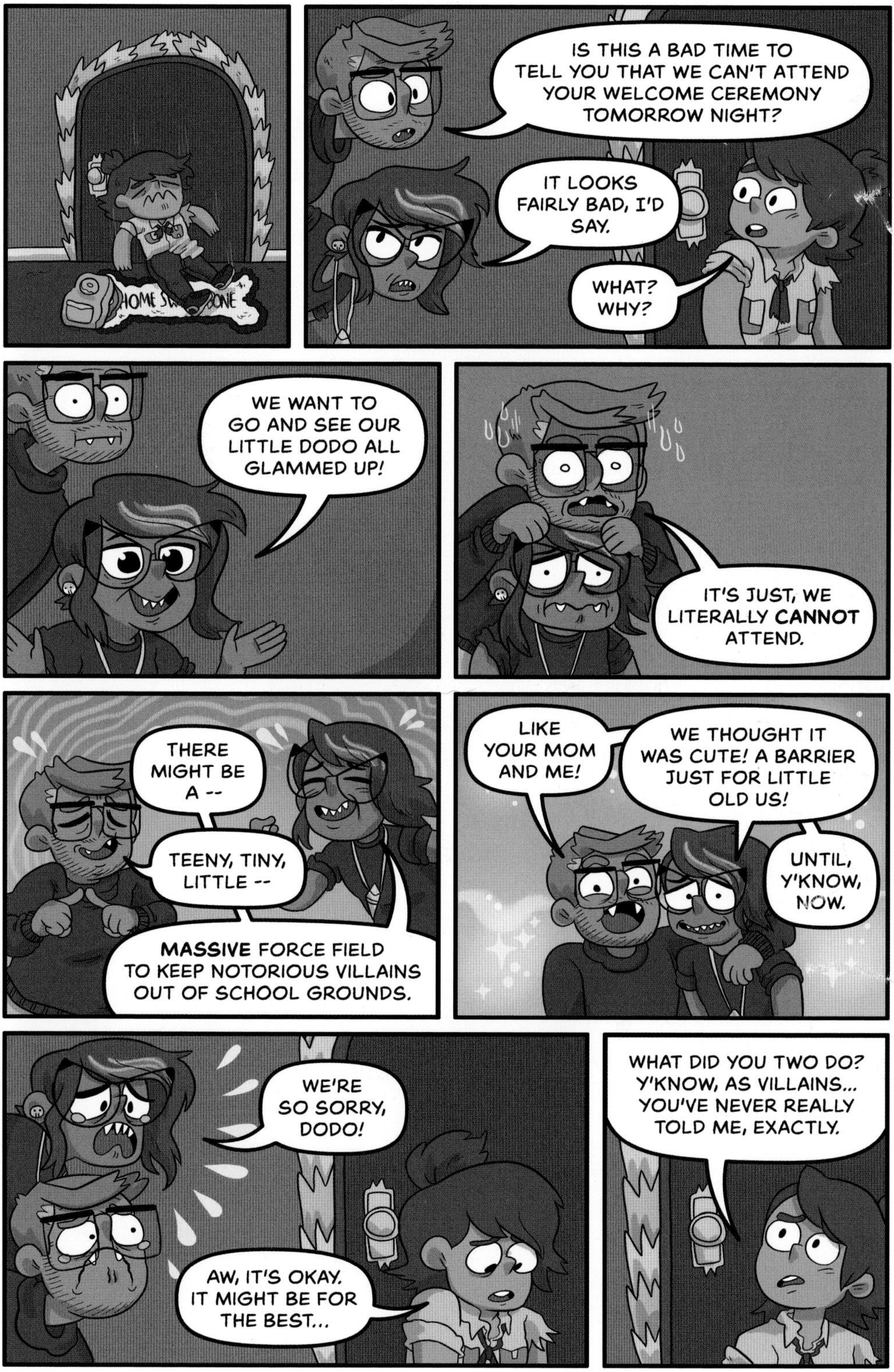
HOME SWEET BONE
IS THIS A BAD TIME TO TELL YOU THAT WE CAN'T ATTEND YOUR WELCOME CEREMONY TOMORROW NIGHT?
IT LOOKS FAIRLY BAD, I'D SAY.
WHAT? WHY?
WE WANT TO GO AND SEE OUR LITTLE DODO ALL GLAMMED UP!
IT'S JUST, WE LITERALLY **CANNOT** ATTEND.
THERE MIGHT BE A --
TEENY, TINY, LITTLE --
MASSIVE FORCE FIELD TO KEEP NOTORIOUS VILLAINS OUT OF SCHOOL GROUNDS.
LIKE YOUR MOM AND ME!
WE THOUGHT IT WAS CUTE! A BARRIER JUST FOR LITTLE OLD US!
UNTIL, Y'KNOW, NOW.
WE'RE SO SORRY, DODO!
AW, IT'S OKAY. IT MIGHT BE FOR THE BEST...
WHAT DID YOU TWO DO? Y'KNOW, AS VILLAINS... YOU'VE NEVER REALLY TOLD ME, EXACTLY.

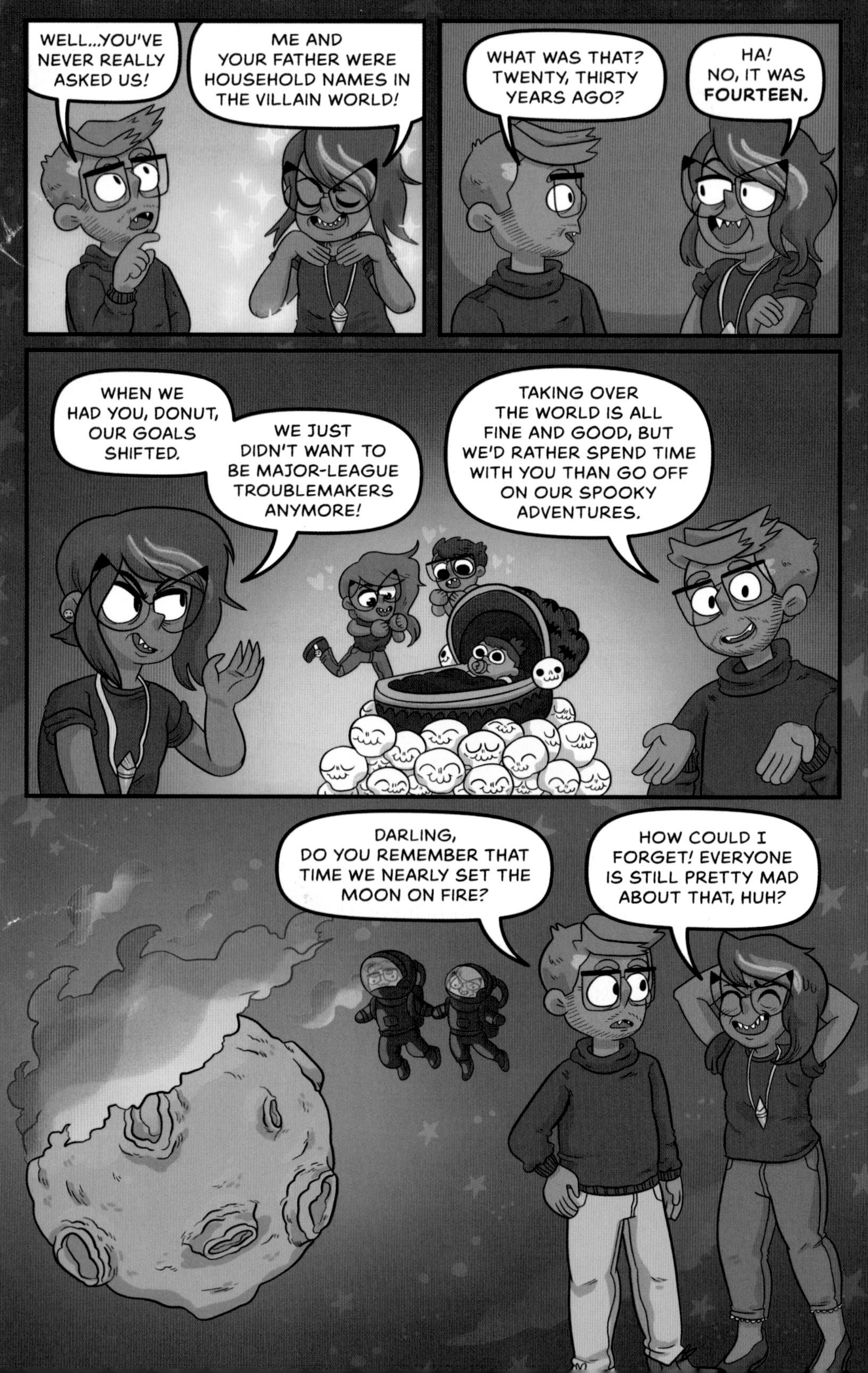
WELL...YOU'VE NEVER REALLY ASKED US!
ME AND YOUR FATHER WERE HOUSEHOLD NAMES IN THE VILLAIN WORLD!
WHAT WAS THAT? TWENTY, THIRTY YEARS AGO?
HA! NO, IT WAS **FOURTEEN.**
WHEN WE HAD YOU, DONUT, OUR GOALS SHIFTED.
WE JUST DIDN'T WANT TO BE MAJOR-LEAGUE TROUBLEMAKERS ANYMORE!
TAKING OVER THE WORLD IS ALL FINE AND GOOD, BUT WE'D RATHER SPEND TIME WITH YOU THAN GO OFF ON OUR SPOOKY ADVENTURES.
DARLING, DO YOU REMEMBER THAT TIME WE NEARLY SET THE MOON ON FIRE?
HOW COULD I FORGET! EVERYONE IS STILL PRETTY MAD ABOUT THAT, HUH?

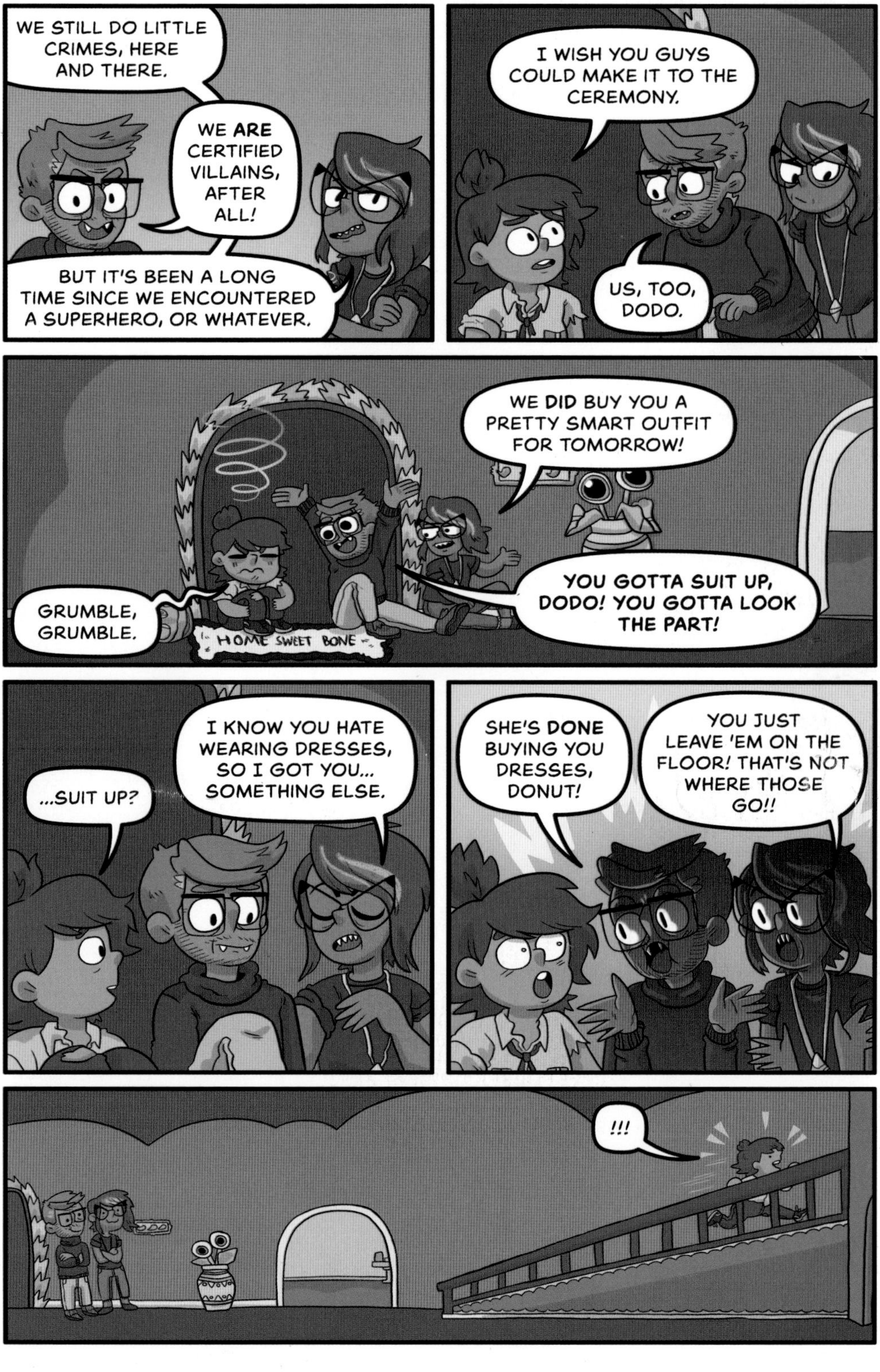
WE STILL DO LITTLE CRIMES, HERE AND THERE.
WE **ARE** CERTIFIED VILLAINS, AFTER ALL!
BUT IT'S BEEN A LONG TIME SINCE WE ENCOUNTERED A SUPERHERO, OR WHATEVER.
I WISH YOU GUYS COULD MAKE IT TO THE CEREMONY.
US, TOO, DODO.
WE **DID** BUY YOU A PRETTY SMART OUTFIT FOR TOMORROW!
GRUMBLE, GRUMBLE.
YOU GOTTA SUIT UP, DODO! YOU GOTTA LOOK THE PART!
HOME SWEET BONE
...SUIT UP?
I KNOW YOU HATE WEARING DRESSES, SO I GOT YOU... SOMETHING ELSE.
SHE'S **DONE** BUYING YOU DRESSES, DONUT!
YOU JUST LEAVE 'EM ON THE FLOOR! THAT'S NOT WHERE THOSE GO!!
!!!

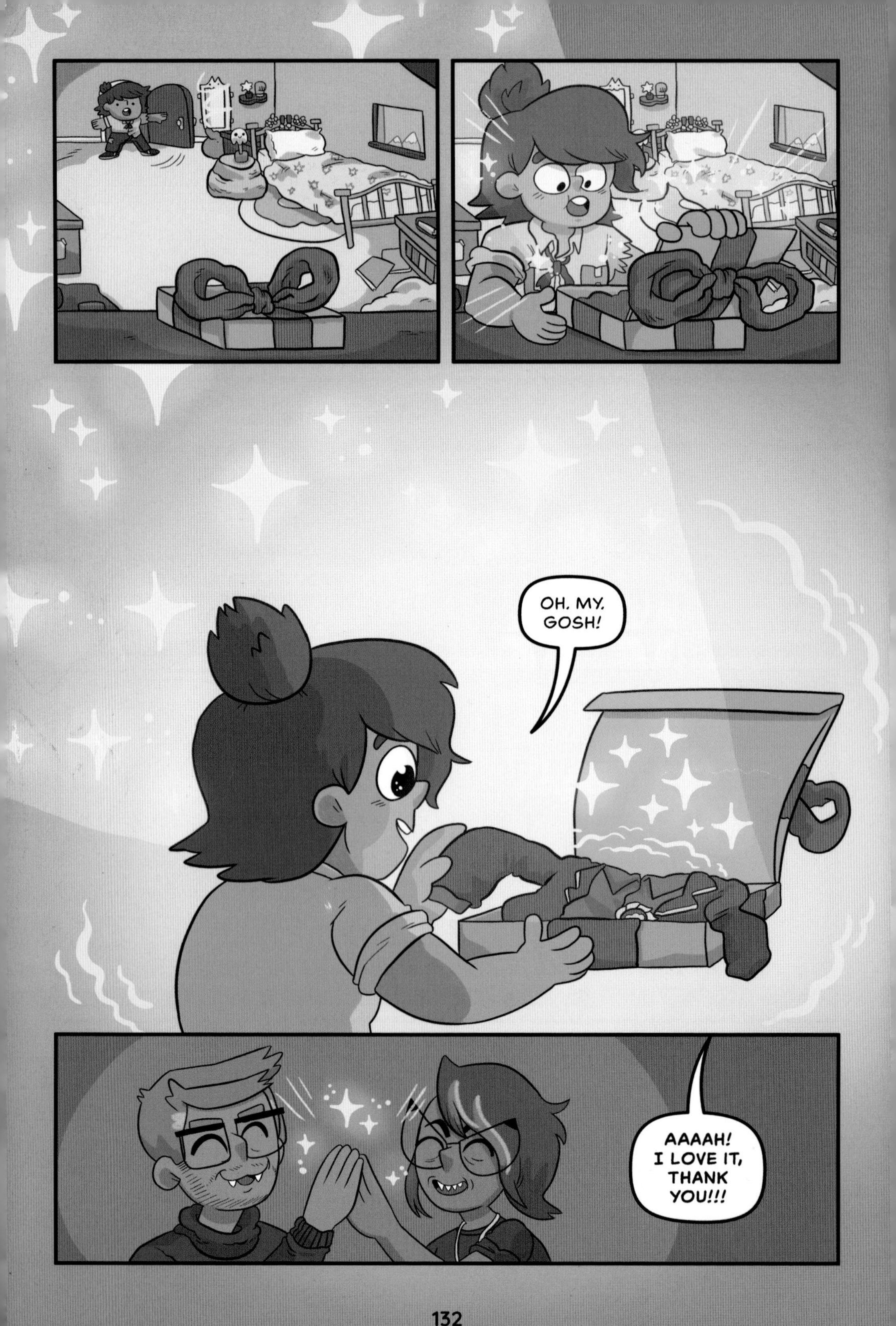
OH, MY, GOSH!
AAAAH! I LOVE IT, THANK YOU!!!

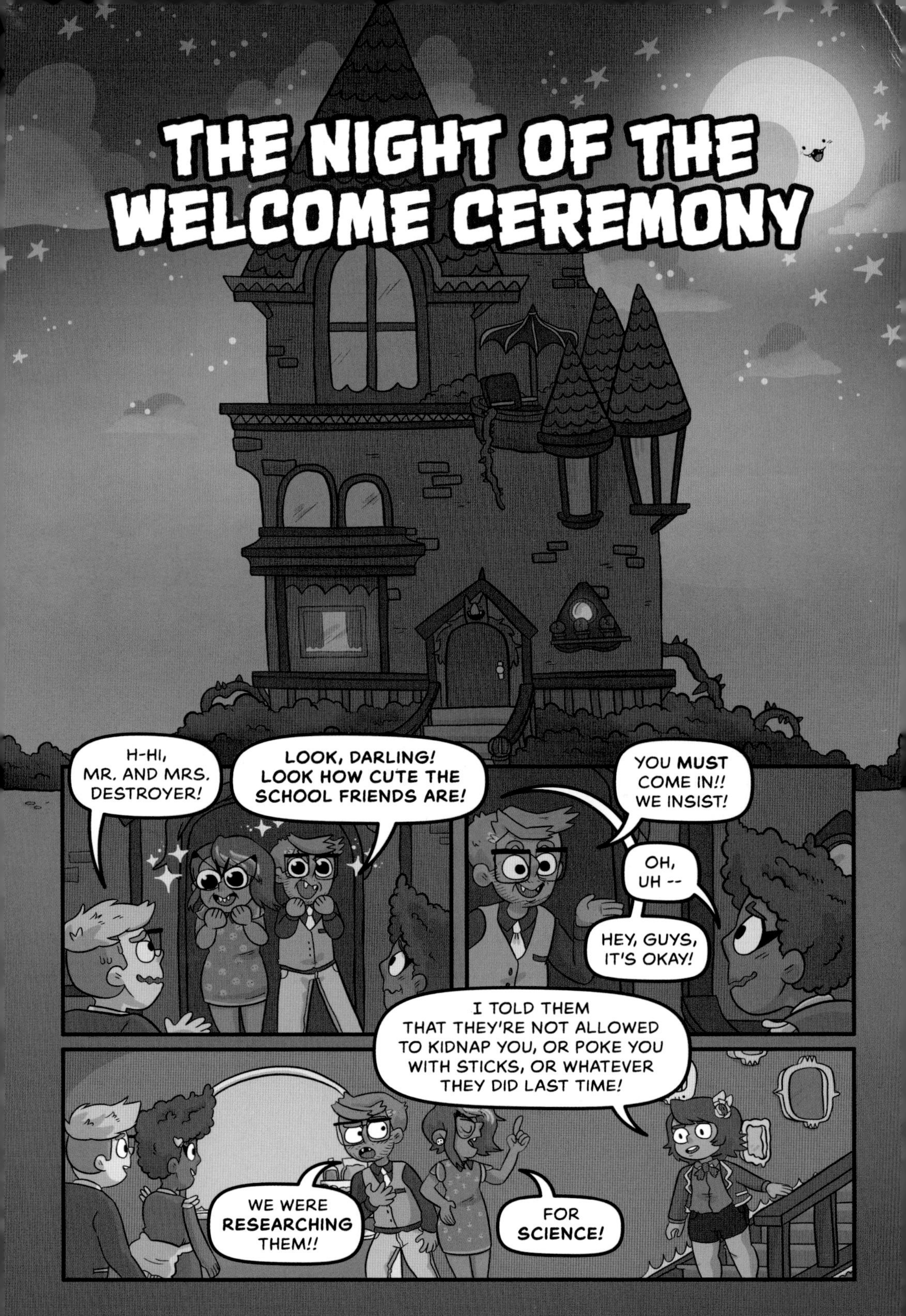
THE NIGHT OF THE WELCOME CEREMONY
H-HI, MR. AND MRS. DESTROYER!
LOOK, DARLING! LOOK HOW CUTE THE SCHOOL FRIENDS ARE!
YOU **MUST** COME IN!! WE INSIST!
OH, UH --
HEY, GUYS, IT'S OKAY!
I TOLD THEM THAT THEY'RE NOT ALLOWED TO KIDNAP YOU, OR POKE YOU WITH STICKS, OR WHATEVER THEY DID LAST TIME!
WE WERE **RESEARCHING** THEM!!
FOR **SCIENCE!**

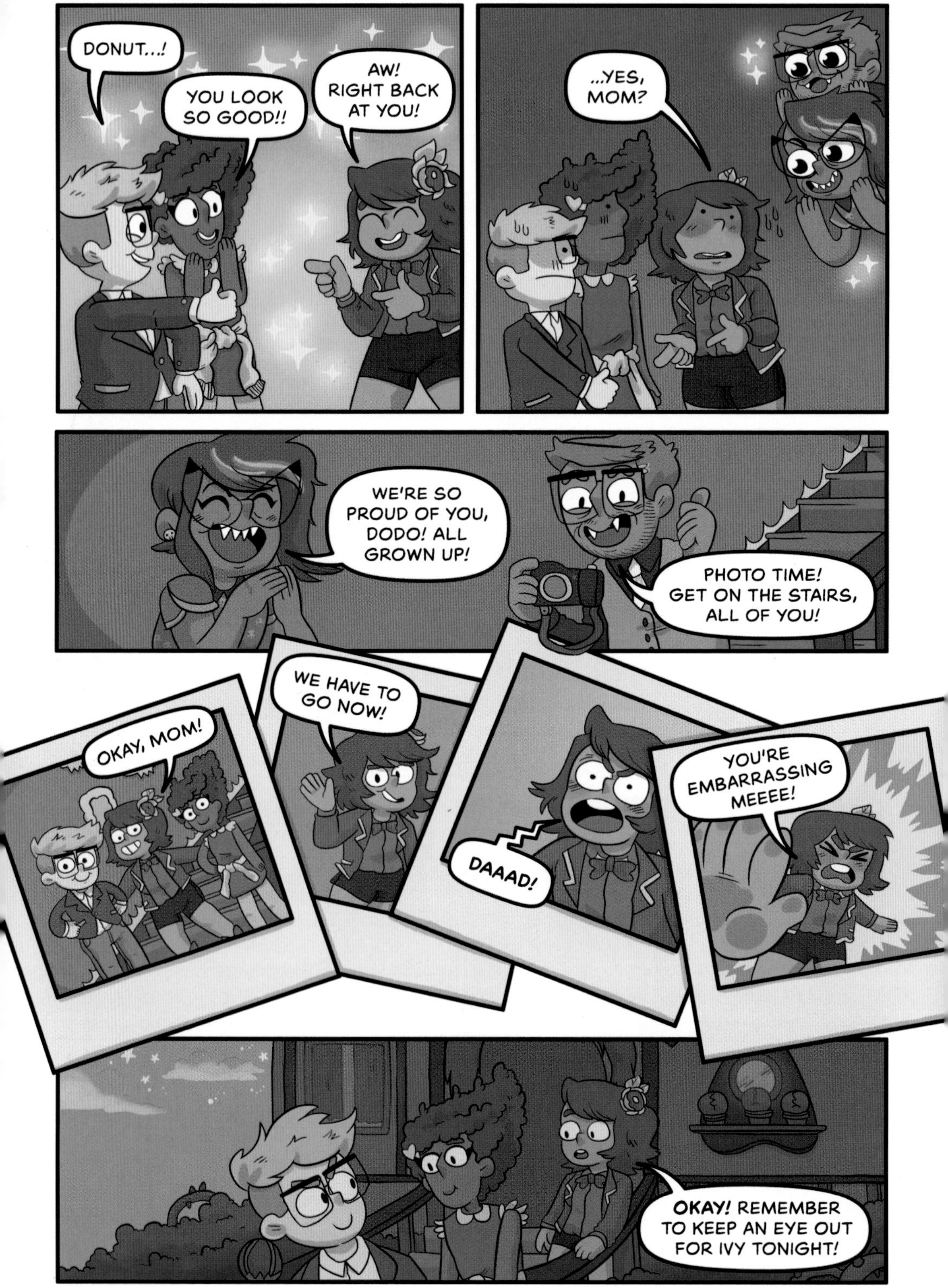
DONUT...!
YOU LOOK SO GOOD!!
AW! RIGHT BACK AT YOU!
...YES, MOM?
WE'RE SO PROUD OF YOU, DODO! ALL GROWN UP!
PHOTO TIME! GET ON THE STAIRS, ALL OF YOU!
OKAY, MOM!
WE HAVE TO GO NOW!
DAAAD!
YOU'RE EMBARRASSING MEEEE!
OKAY! REMEMBER TO KEEP AN EYE OUT FOR IVY TONIGHT!

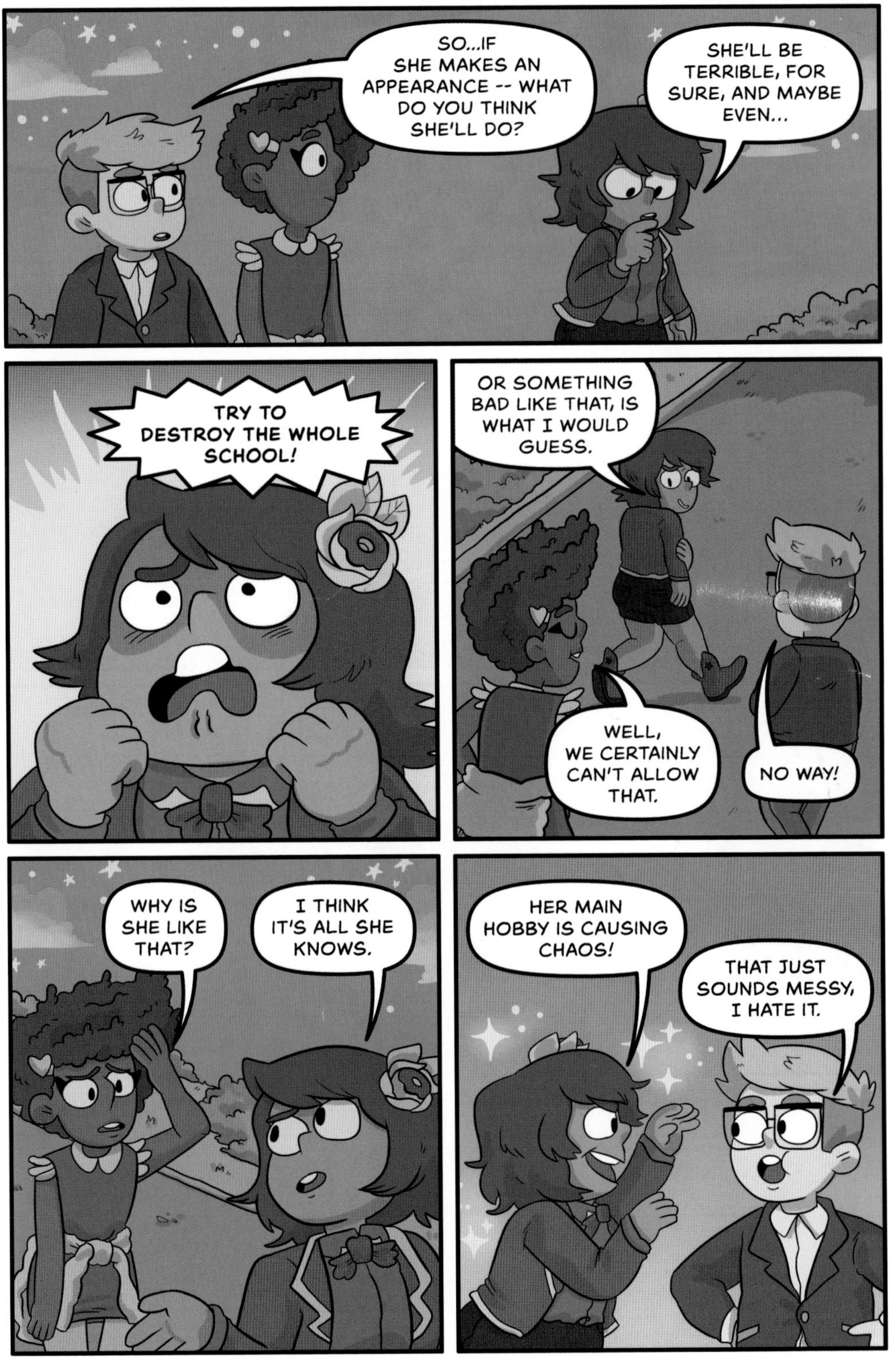
SO...IF SHE MAKES AN APPEARANCE -- WHAT DO YOU THINK SHE'LL DO?
SHE'LL BE TERRIBLE, FOR SURE, AND MAYBE EVEN...
TRY TO DESTROY THE WHOLE SCHOOL!
OR SOMETHING BAD LIKE THAT, IS WHAT I WOULD GUESS.
WELL, WE CERTAINLY CAN'T ALLOW THAT.
NO WAY!
WHY IS SHE LIKE THAT?
I THINK IT'S ALL SHE KNOWS.
HER MAIN HOBBY IS CAUSING CHAOS!
THAT JUST SOUNDS MESSY, I HATE IT.

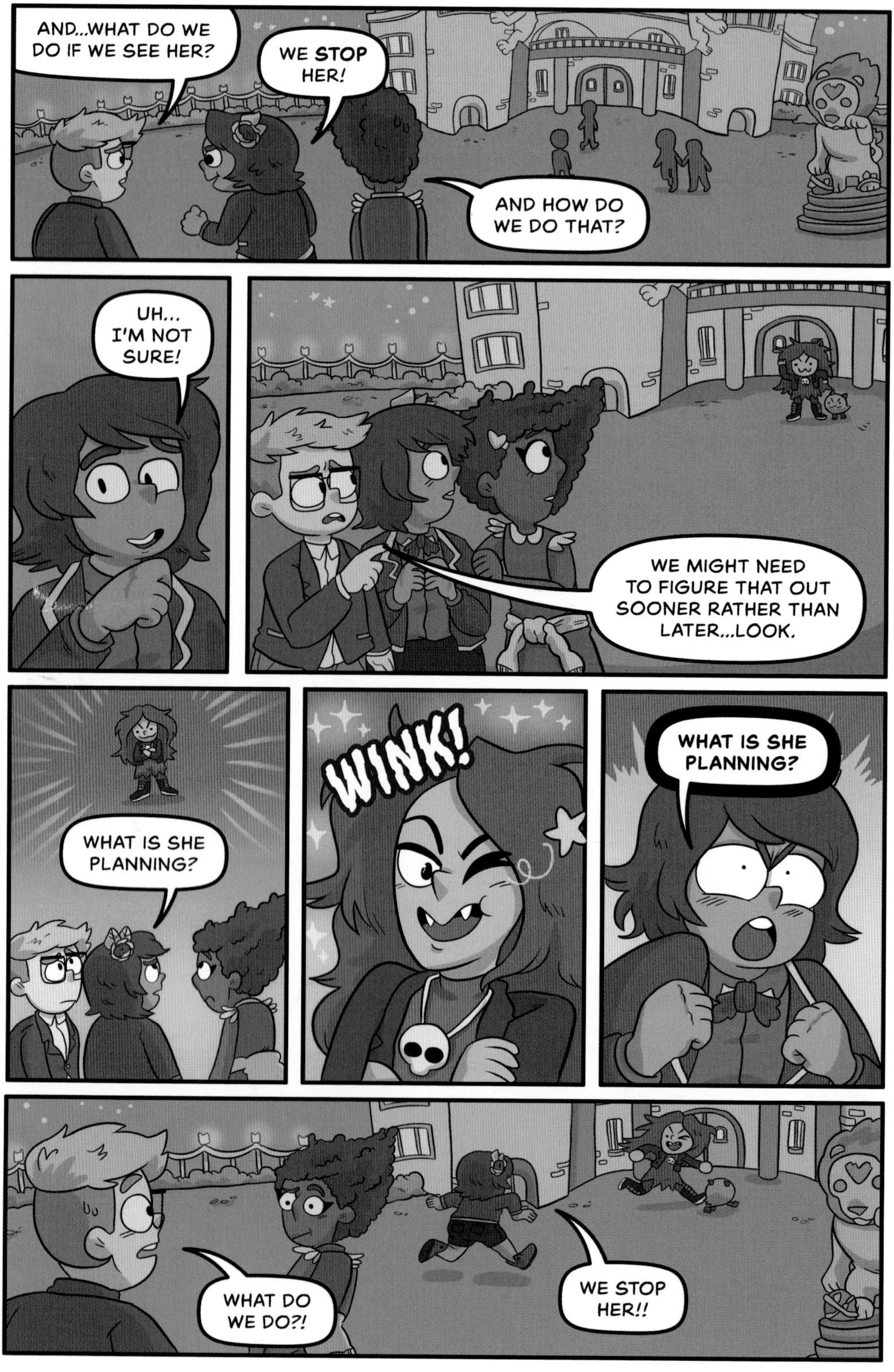
AND...WHAT DO WE DO IF WE SEE HER?
WE STOP HER!
AND HOW DO WE DO THAT?
UH... I'M NOT SURE!
WE MIGHT NEED TO FIGURE THAT OUT SOONER RATHER THAN LATER...LOOK.
WHAT IS SHE PLANNING?
WINK!
WHAT IS SHE PLANNING?
WHAT DO WE DO?!
WE STOP HER!!

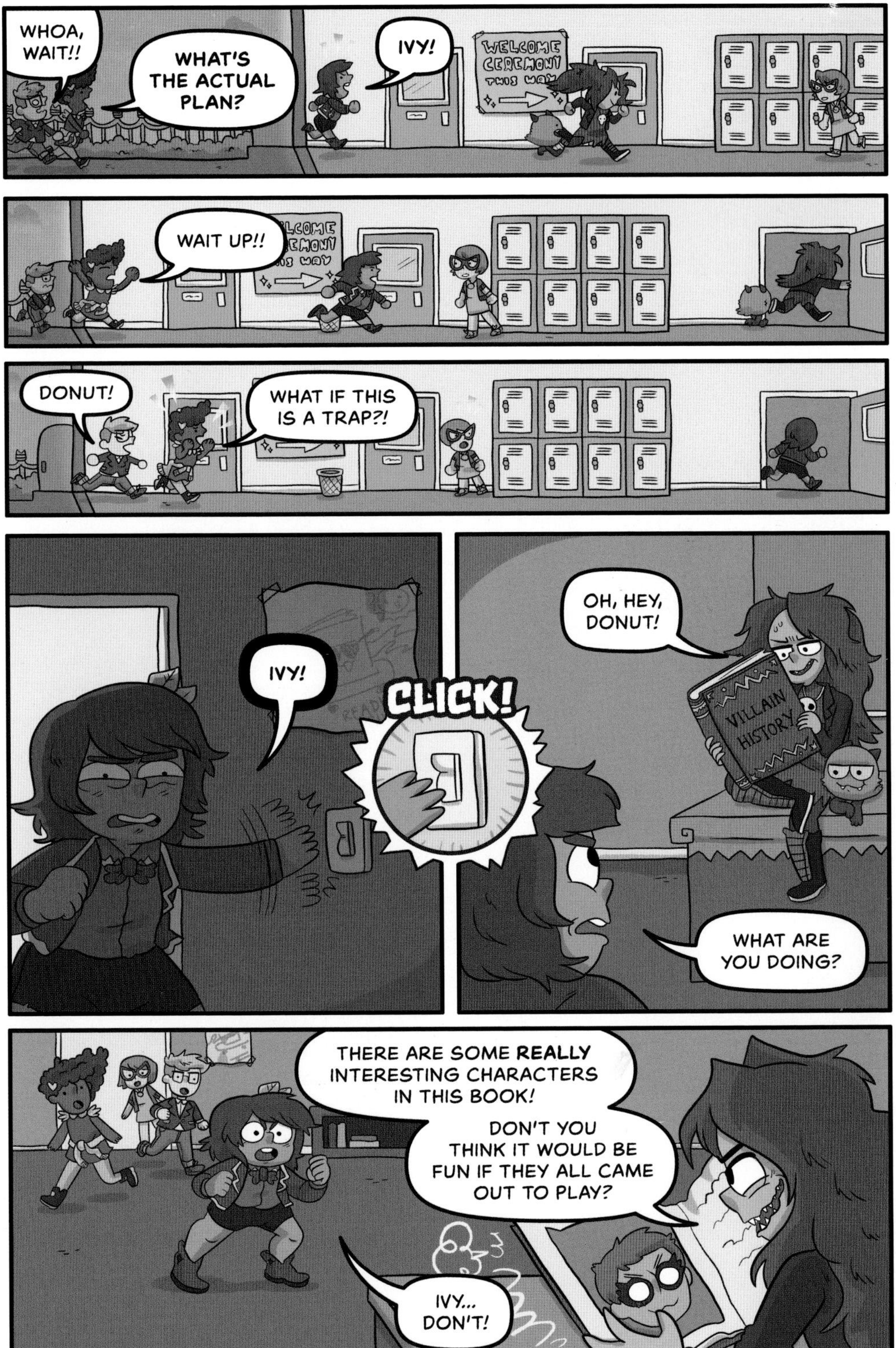
WHOA, WAIT!!
WHAT'S THE ACTUAL PLAN?
IVY!
WELCOME CEREMONY THIS WAY
WAIT UP!!
DONUT!
WHAT IF THIS IS A TRAP?!
IVY!
CLICK!
OH, HEY, DONUT!
VILLAIN HISTORY
WHAT ARE YOU DOING?
THERE ARE SOME **REALLY** INTERESTING CHARACTERS IN THIS BOOK!
DON'T YOU THINK IT WOULD BE FUN IF THEY ALL CAME OUT TO PLAY?
IVY... DON'T!

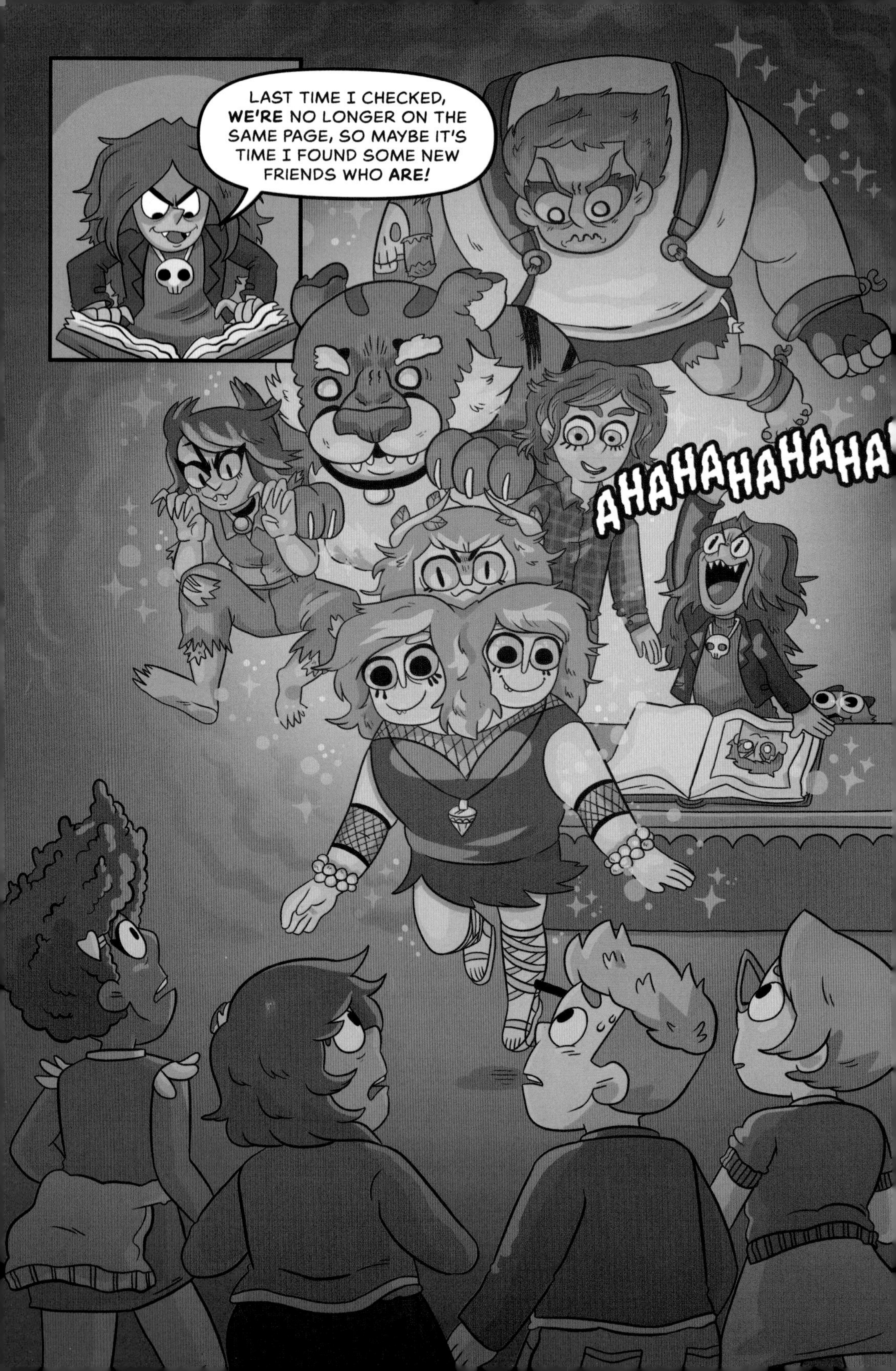
LAST TIME I CHECKED, **WE'RE** NO LONGER ON THE SAME PAGE, SO MAYBE IT'S TIME I FOUND SOME NEW FRIENDS WHO **ARE!**
AHAHAHAHAHA

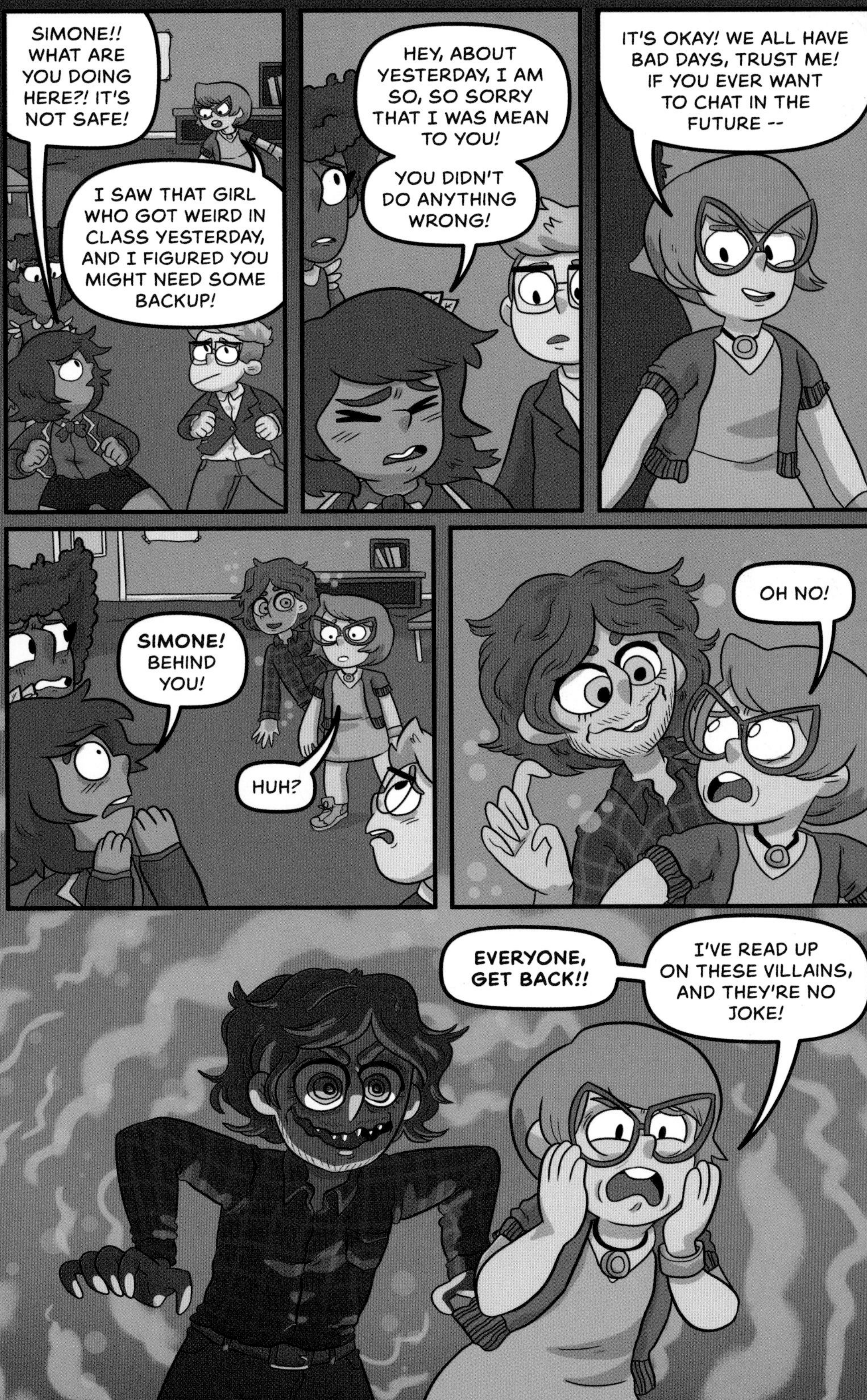
SIMONE!! WHAT ARE YOU DOING HERE?! IT'S NOT SAFE!
I SAW THAT GIRL WHO GOT WEIRD IN CLASS YESTERDAY, AND I FIGURED YOU MIGHT NEED SOME BACKUP!
HEY, ABOUT YESTERDAY, I AM SO, SO SORRY THAT I WAS MEAN TO YOU!
YOU DIDN'T DO ANYTHING WRONG!
IT'S OKAY! WE ALL HAVE BAD DAYS, TRUST ME! IF YOU EVER WANT TO CHAT IN THE FUTURE --
SIMONE! BEHIND YOU!
HUH?
OH NO!
EVERYONE, GET BACK!!
I'VE READ UP ON THESE VILLAINS, AND THEY'RE NO JOKE!

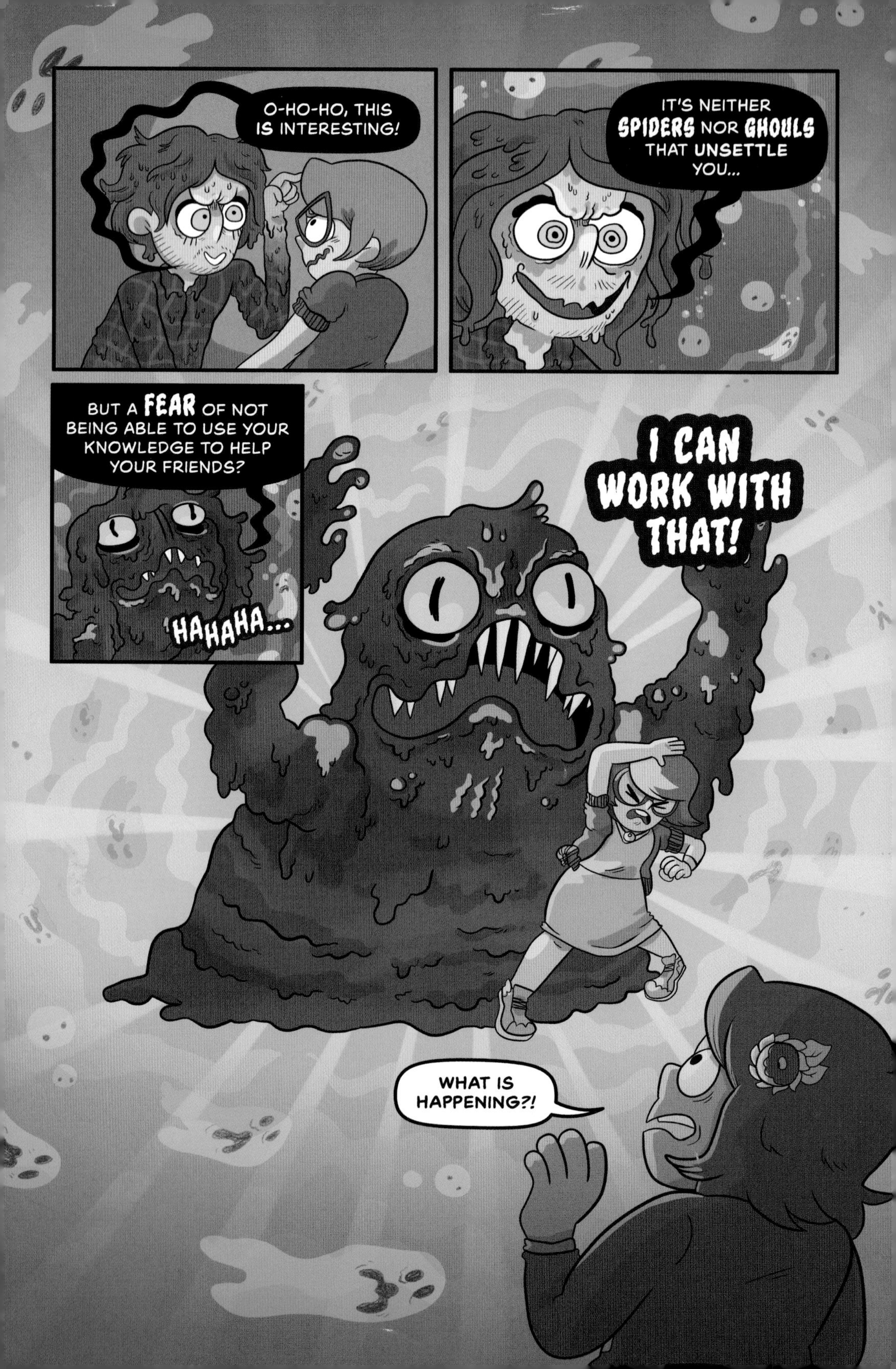
O-HO-HO, THIS IS INTERESTING!
IT'S NEITHER SPIDERS NOR GHOULS THAT UNSETTLE YOU...
BUT A FEAR OF NOT BEING ABLE TO USE YOUR KNOWLEDGE TO HELP YOUR FRIENDS?
HAHAHA...
I CAN WORK WITH THAT!
WHAT IS HAPPENING?!

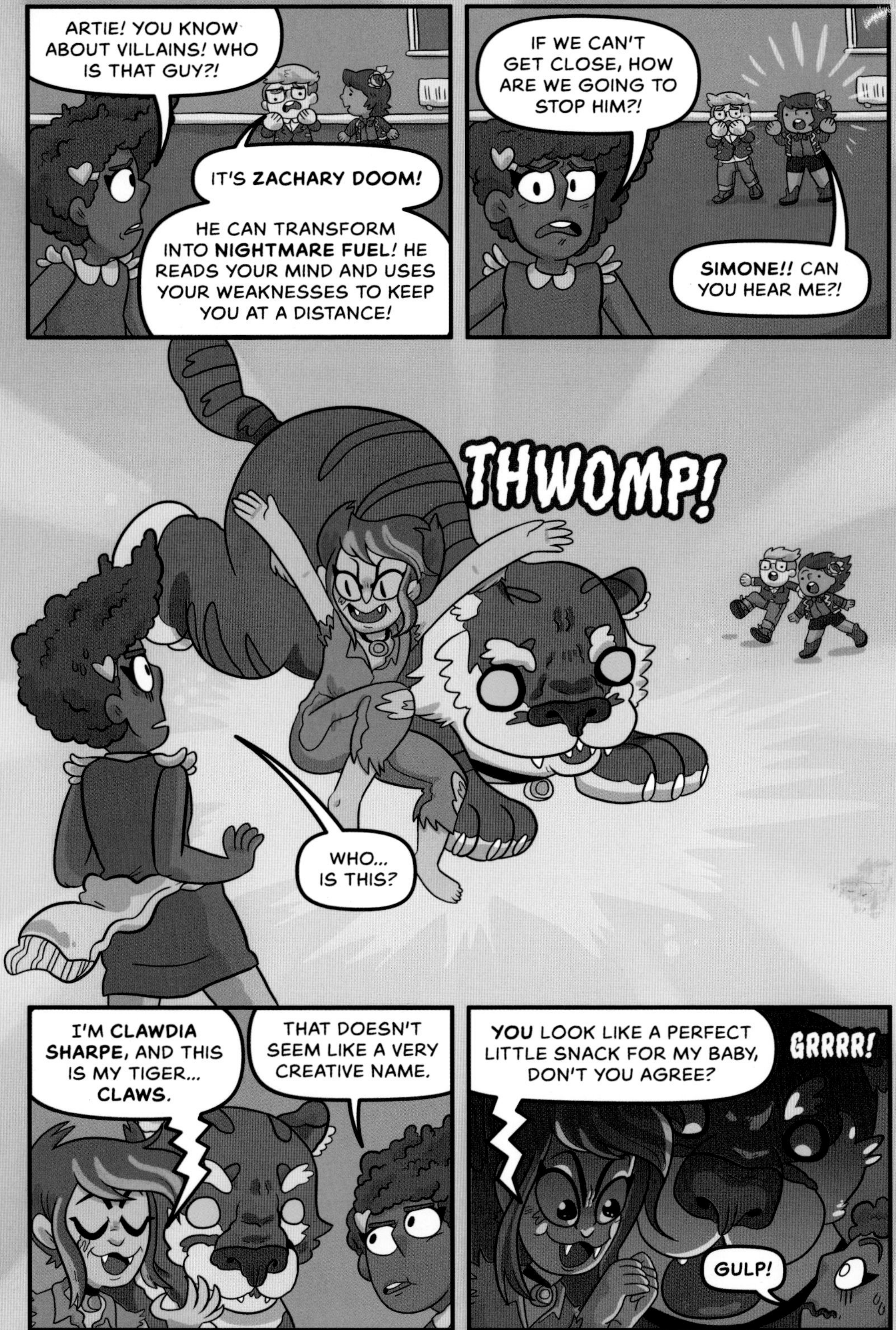
ARTIE! YOU KNOW ABOUT VILLAINS! WHO IS THAT GUY?!
IT'S **ZACHARY DOOM!**
HE CAN TRANSFORM INTO **NIGHTMARE FUEL!** HE READS YOUR MIND AND USES YOUR WEAKNESSES TO KEEP YOU AT A DISTANCE!
IF WE CAN'T GET CLOSE, HOW ARE WE GOING TO STOP HIM?!
SIMONE!! CAN YOU HEAR ME?!
THWOMP!
WHO... IS THIS?
I'M **CLAWDIA SHARPE,** AND THIS IS MY TIGER... **CLAWS.**
THAT DOESN'T SEEM LIKE A VERY CREATIVE NAME.
YOU LOOK LIKE A PERFECT LITTLE SNACK FOR MY BABY, DON'T YOU AGREE?
GRRRR!
GULP!

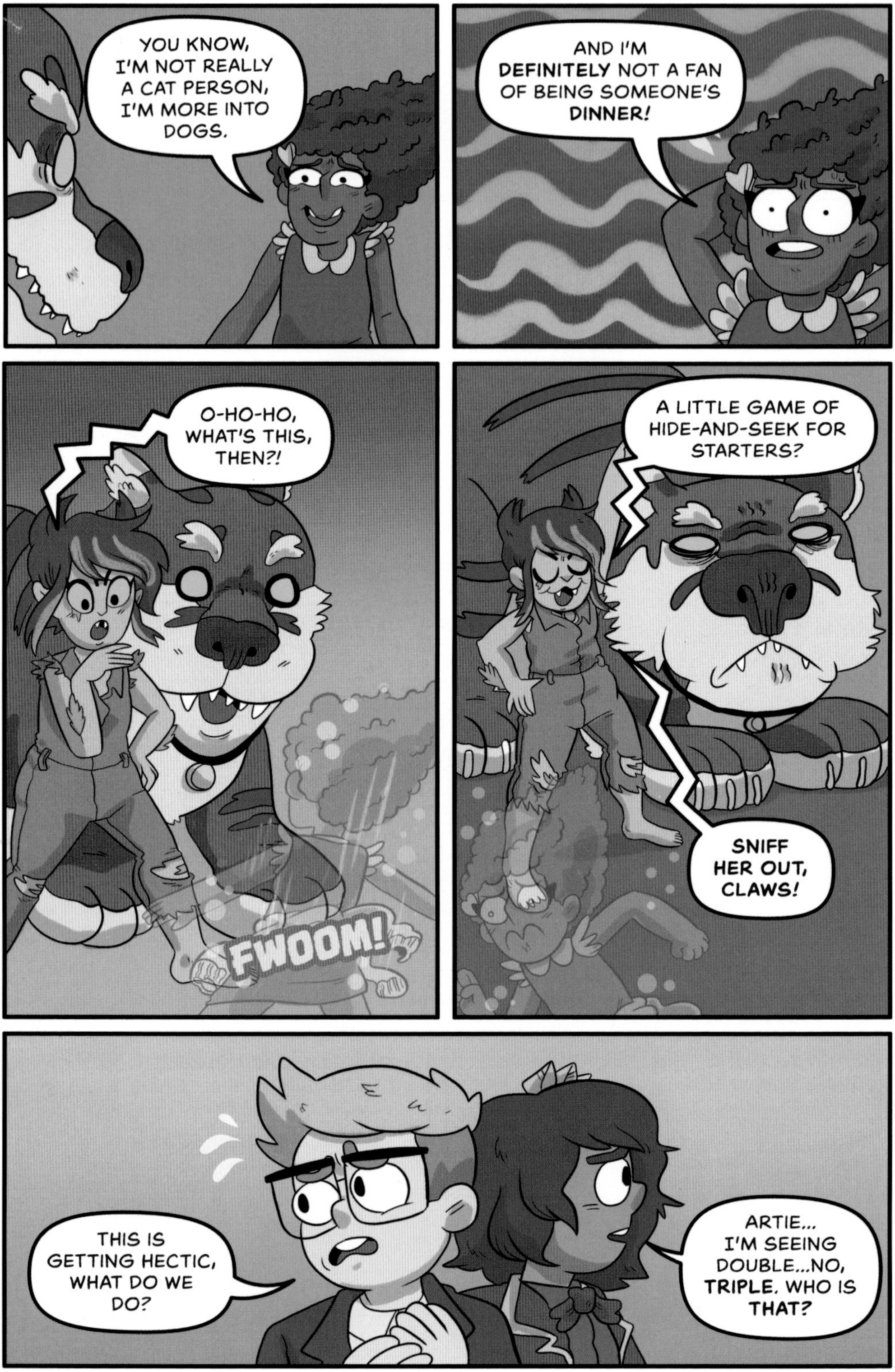
YOU KNOW, I'M NOT REALLY A CAT PERSON, I'M MORE INTO DOGS.
AND I'M DEFINITELY NOT A FAN OF BEING SOMEONE'S DINNER!
O-HO-HO, WHAT'S THIS, THEN?!
FWOOM!
A LITTLE GAME OF HIDE-AND-SEEK FOR STARTERS?
SNIFF HER OUT, CLAWS!
THIS IS GETTING HECTIC, WHAT DO WE DO?
ARTIE... I'M SEEING DOUBLE...NO, TRIPLE. WHO IS THAT?

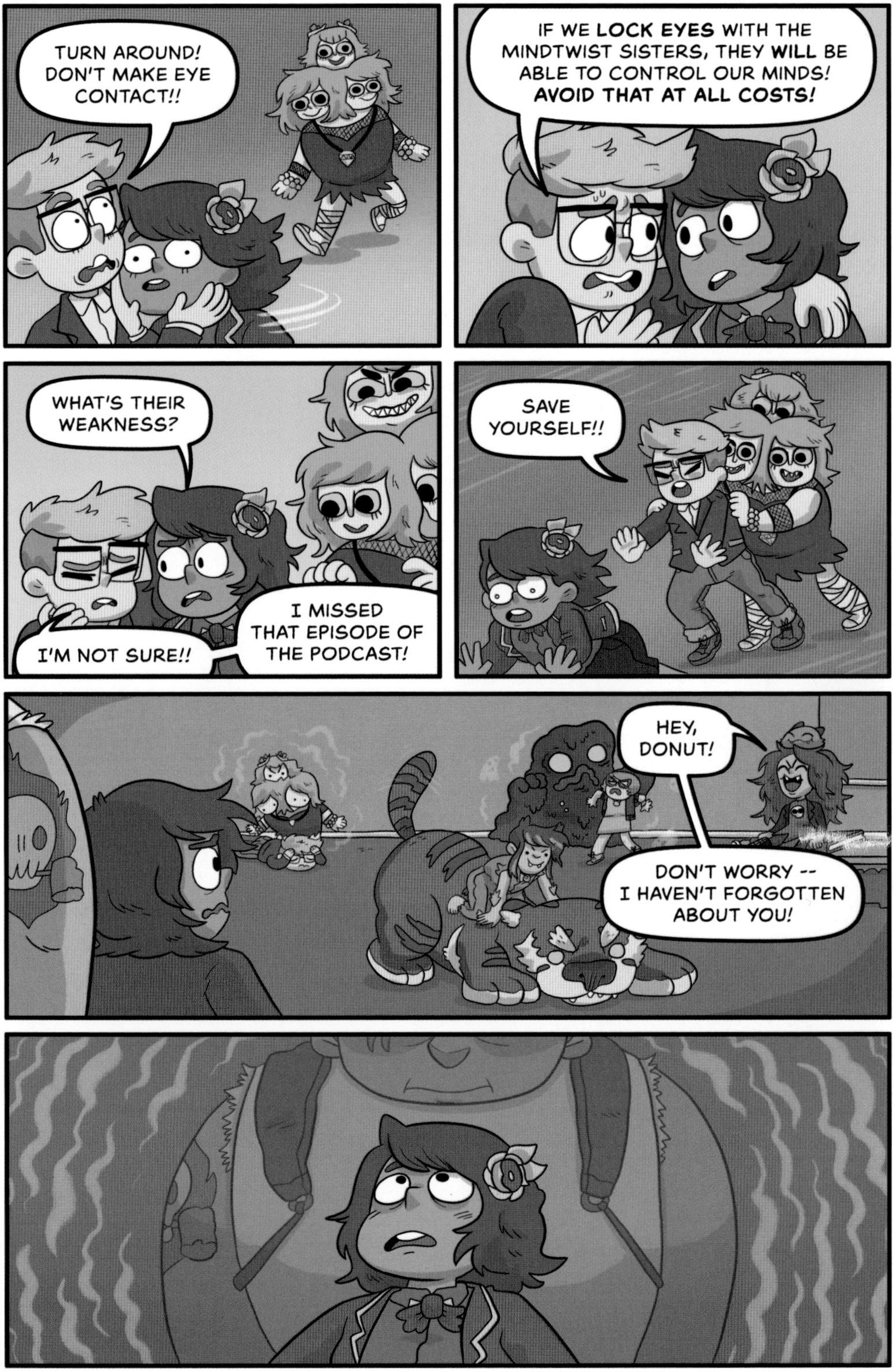
TURN AROUND! DON'T MAKE EYE CONTACT!!
IF WE **LOCK EYES** WITH THE MINDTWIST SISTERS, THEY **WILL** BE ABLE TO CONTROL OUR MINDS! **AVOID THAT AT ALL COSTS!**
WHAT'S THEIR WEAKNESS?
I'M NOT SURE!!
I MISSED THAT EPISODE OF THE PODCAST!
SAVE YOURSELF!!
HEY, DONUT!
DON'T WORRY -- I HAVEN'T FORGOTTEN ABOUT YOU!

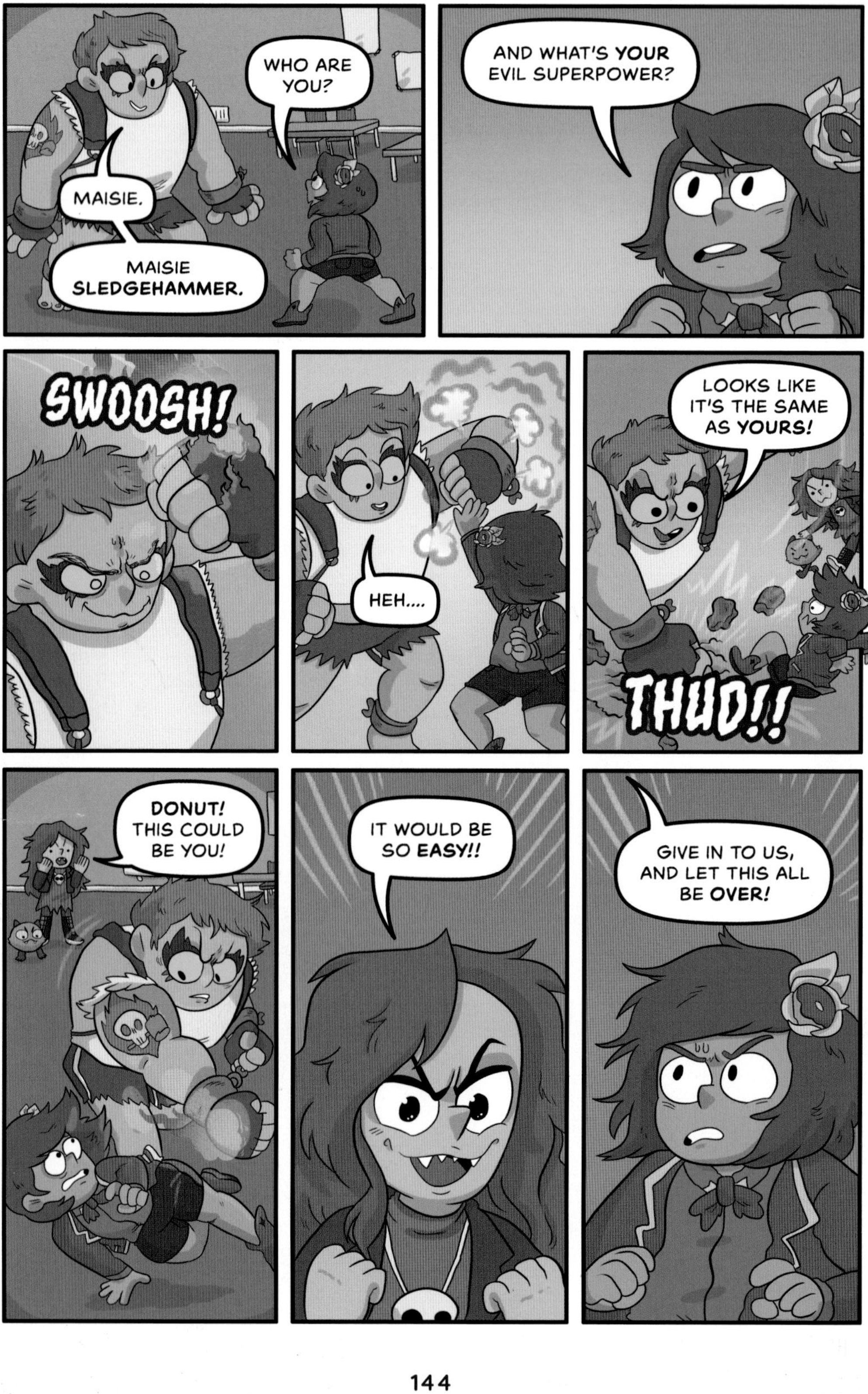
WHO ARE YOU?
MAISIE.
MAISIE SLEDGEHAMMER.
AND WHAT'S YOUR EVIL SUPERPOWER?
SWOOSH!
HEH....
LOOKS LIKE IT'S THE SAME AS YOURS!
THUD!!
DONUT! THIS COULD BE YOU!
IT WOULD BE SO EASY!!
GIVE IN TO US, AND LET THIS ALL BE OVER!

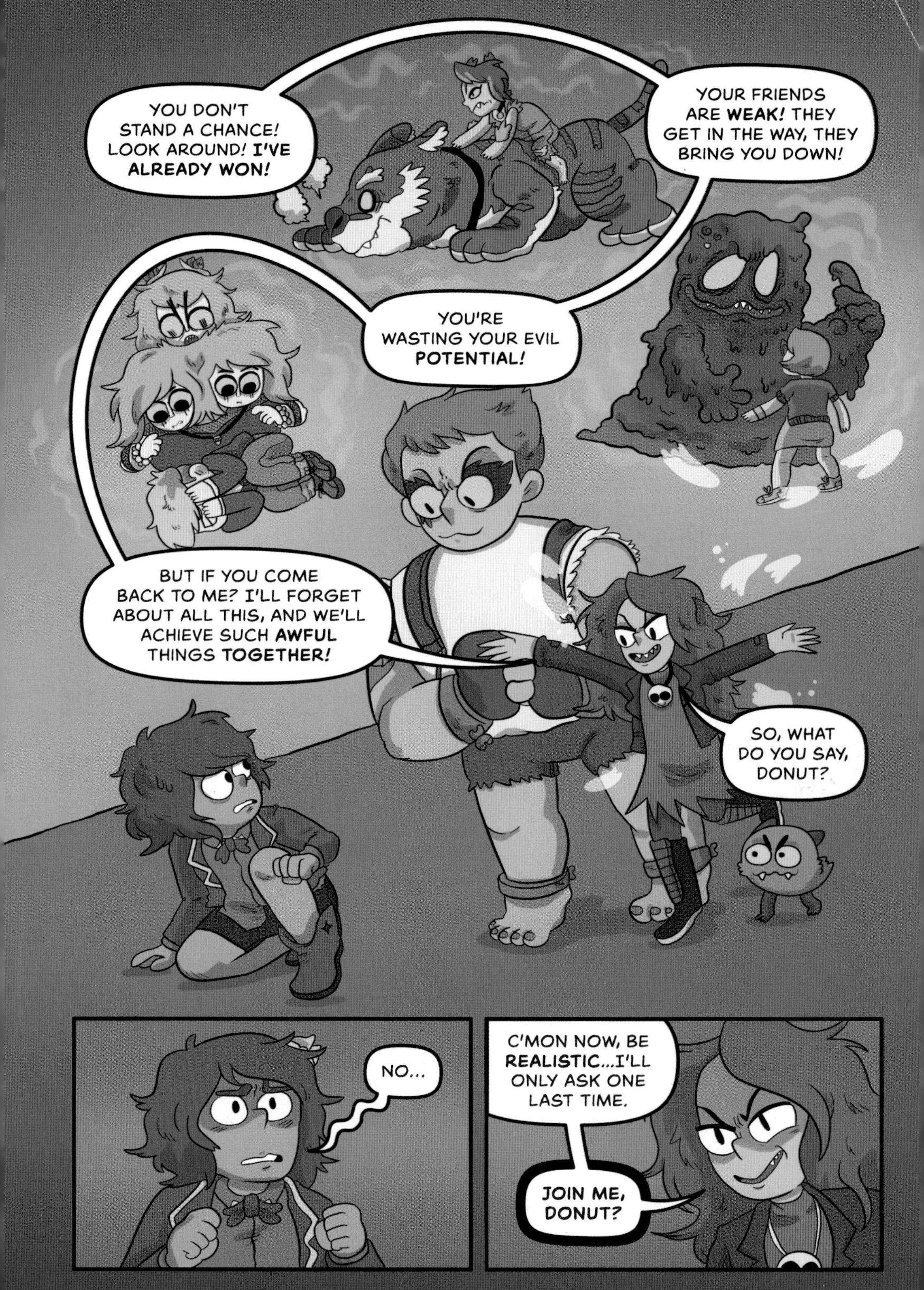

YOU DON'T STAND A CHANCE! LOOK AROUND! I'VE ALREADY WON!
YOUR FRIENDS ARE WEAK! THEY GET IN THE WAY, THEY BRING YOU DOWN!
YOU'RE WASTING YOUR EVIL POTENTIAL!
BUT IF YOU COME BACK TO ME? I'LL FORGET ABOUT ALL THIS, AND WE'LL ACHIEVE SUCH AWFUL THINGS TOGETHER!
SO, WHAT DO YOU SAY, DONUT?
NO...
C'MON NOW, BE REALISTIC...I'LL ONLY ASK ONE LAST TIME.
JOIN ME, DONUT?

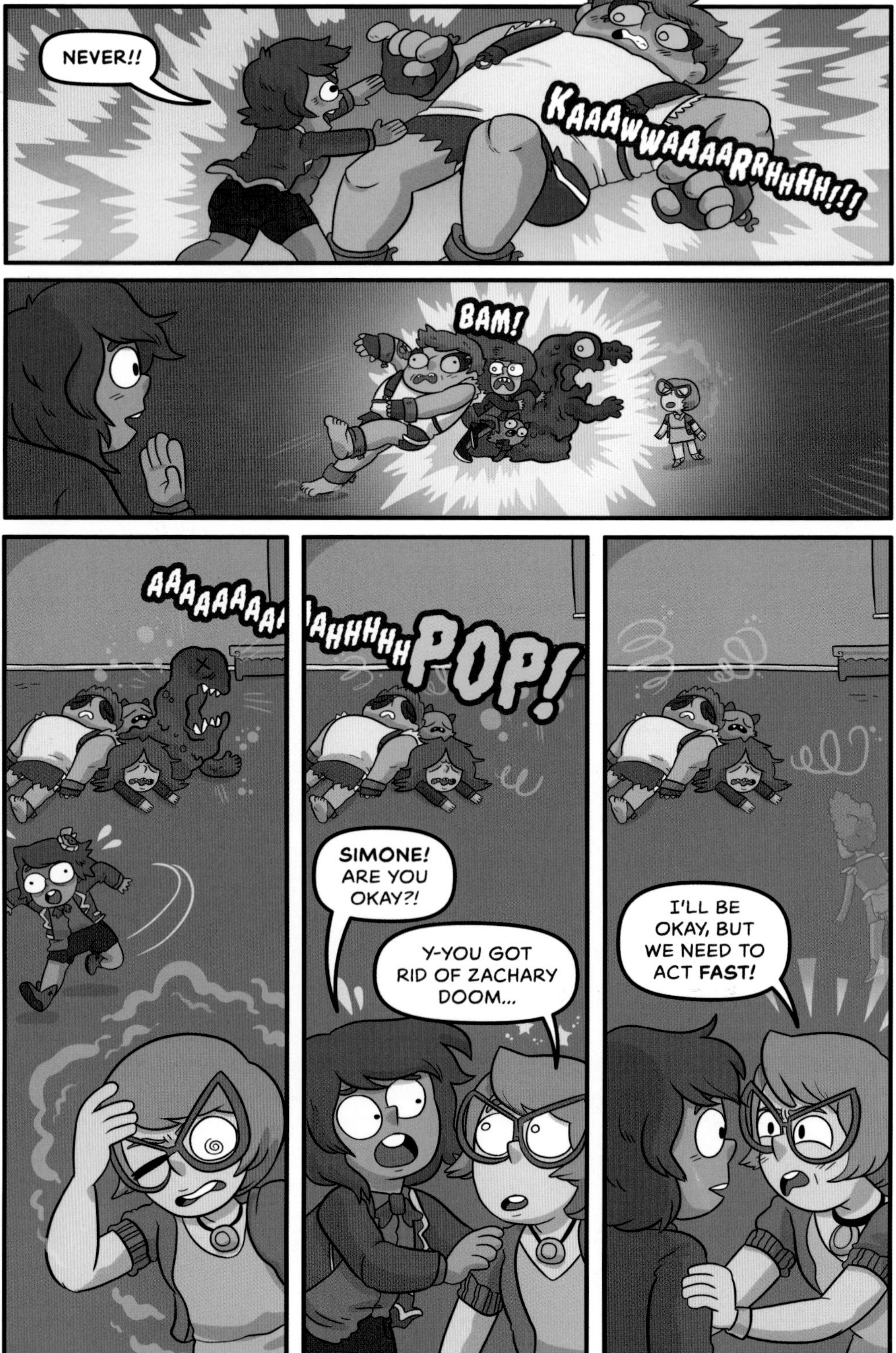
NEVER!!
KAAAWWAAAARRHHHH!!!
BAM!
AAAAAAAAAAAHHHHHPOP!
SIMONE! ARE YOU OKAY?!
Y-YOU GOT RID OF ZACHARY DOOM...
I'LL BE OKAY, BUT WE NEED TO ACT **FAST!**

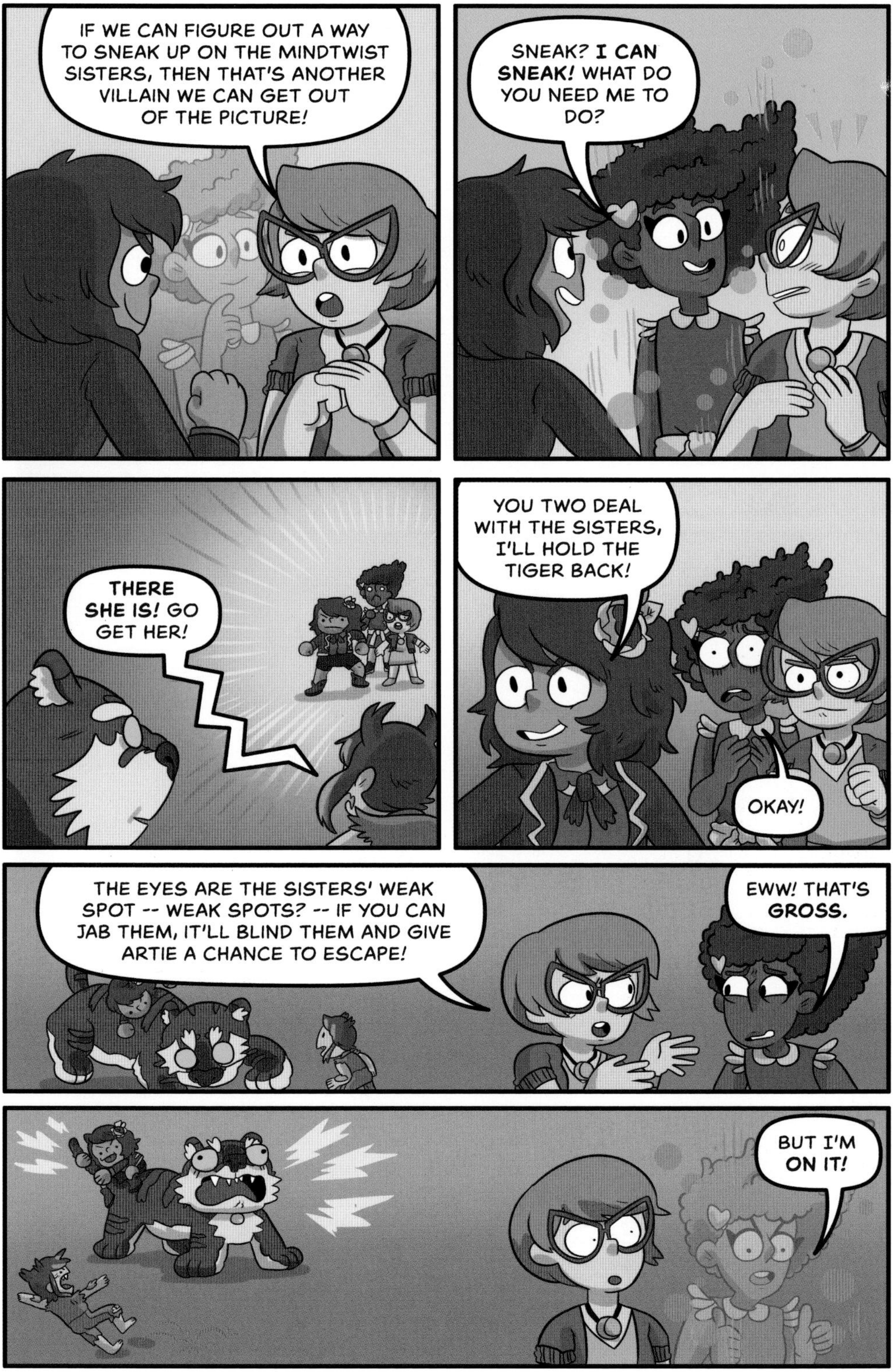
IF WE CAN FIGURE OUT A WAY TO SNEAK UP ON THE MINDTWIST SISTERS, THEN THAT'S ANOTHER VILLAIN WE CAN GET OUT OF THE PICTURE!
SNEAK? I CAN SNEAK! WHAT DO YOU NEED ME TO DO?
THERE SHE IS! GO GET HER!
YOU TWO DEAL WITH THE SISTERS, I'LL HOLD THE TIGER BACK!
OKAY!
THE EYES ARE THE SISTERS' WEAK SPOT -- WEAK SPOTS? -- IF YOU CAN JAB THEM, IT'LL BLIND THEM AND GIVE ARTIE A CHANCE TO ESCAPE!
EWW! THAT'S GROSS.
BUT I'M ON IT!

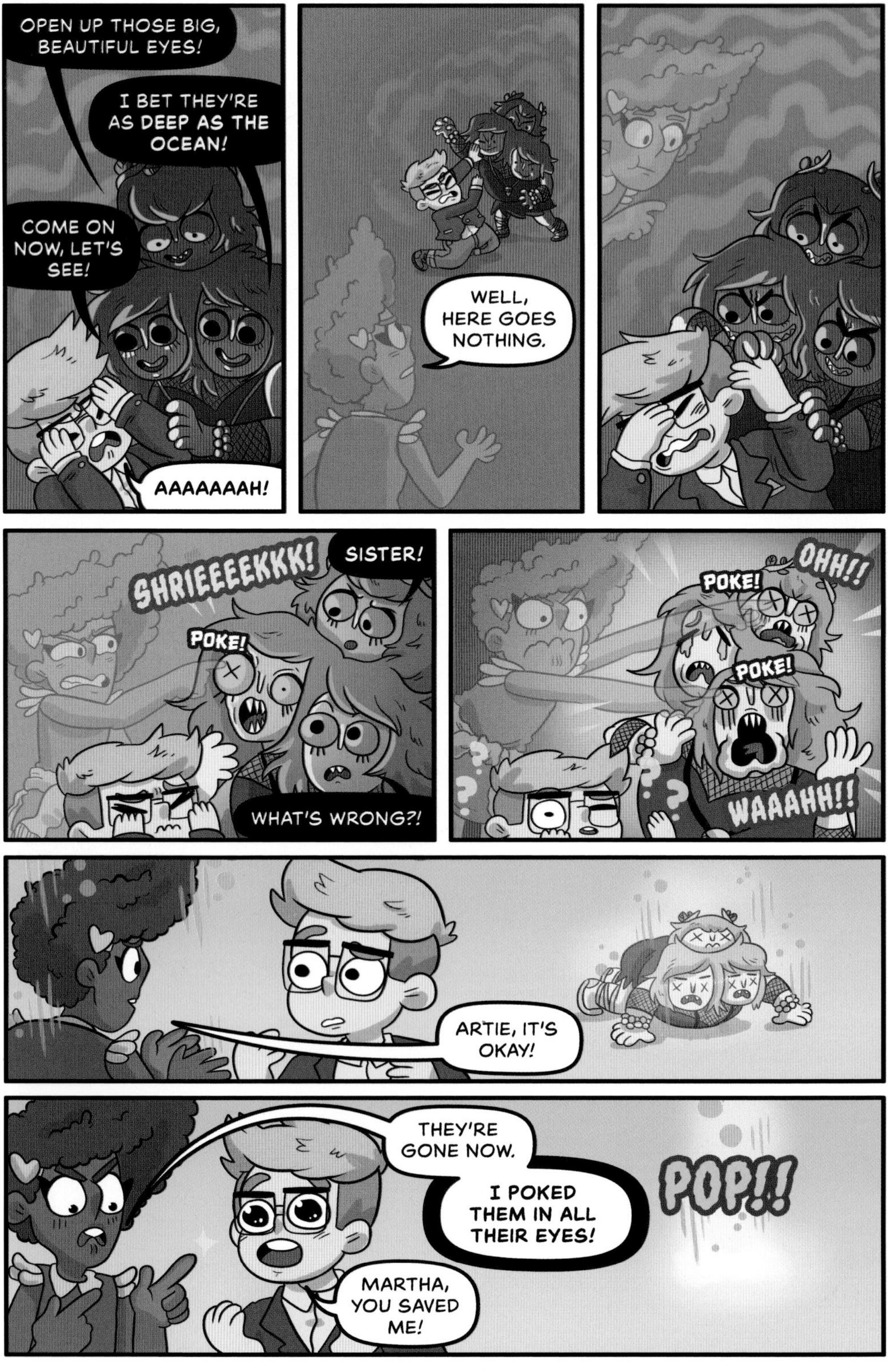
OPEN UP THOSE BIG, BEAUTIFUL EYES!
I BET THEY'RE AS DEEP AS THE OCEAN!
COME ON NOW, LET'S SEE!
AAAAAAAH!
WELL, HERE GOES NOTHING.
SHRIEEEEKKK!
SISTER!
POKE!
WHAT'S WRONG?!
POKE!
OHH!!
POKE!
WAAAHH!!
ARTIE, IT'S OKAY!
THEY'RE GONE NOW.
I POKED THEM IN ALL THEIR EYES!
POP!!
MARTHA, YOU SAVED ME!

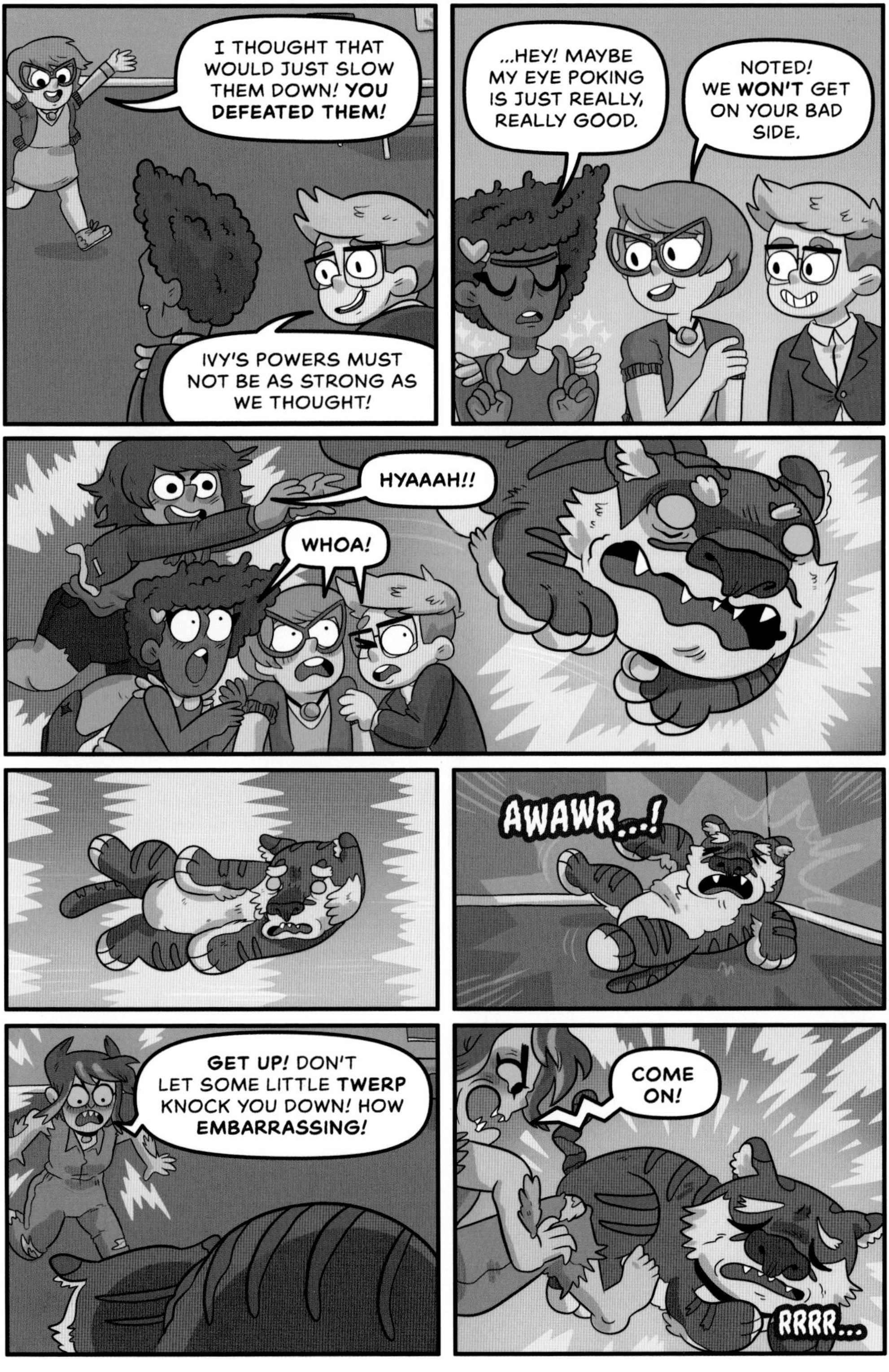
I THOUGHT THAT WOULD JUST SLOW THEM DOWN! YOU DEFEATED THEM!
IVY'S POWERS MUST NOT BE AS STRONG AS WE THOUGHT!
...HEY! MAYBE MY EYE POKING IS JUST REALLY, REALLY GOOD.
NOTED! WE WON'T GET ON YOUR BAD SIDE.
HYAAAH!!
WHOA!
AWAWR...!
GET UP! DON'T LET SOME LITTLE TWERP KNOCK YOU DOWN! HOW EMBARRASSING!
COME ON!
RRRR...

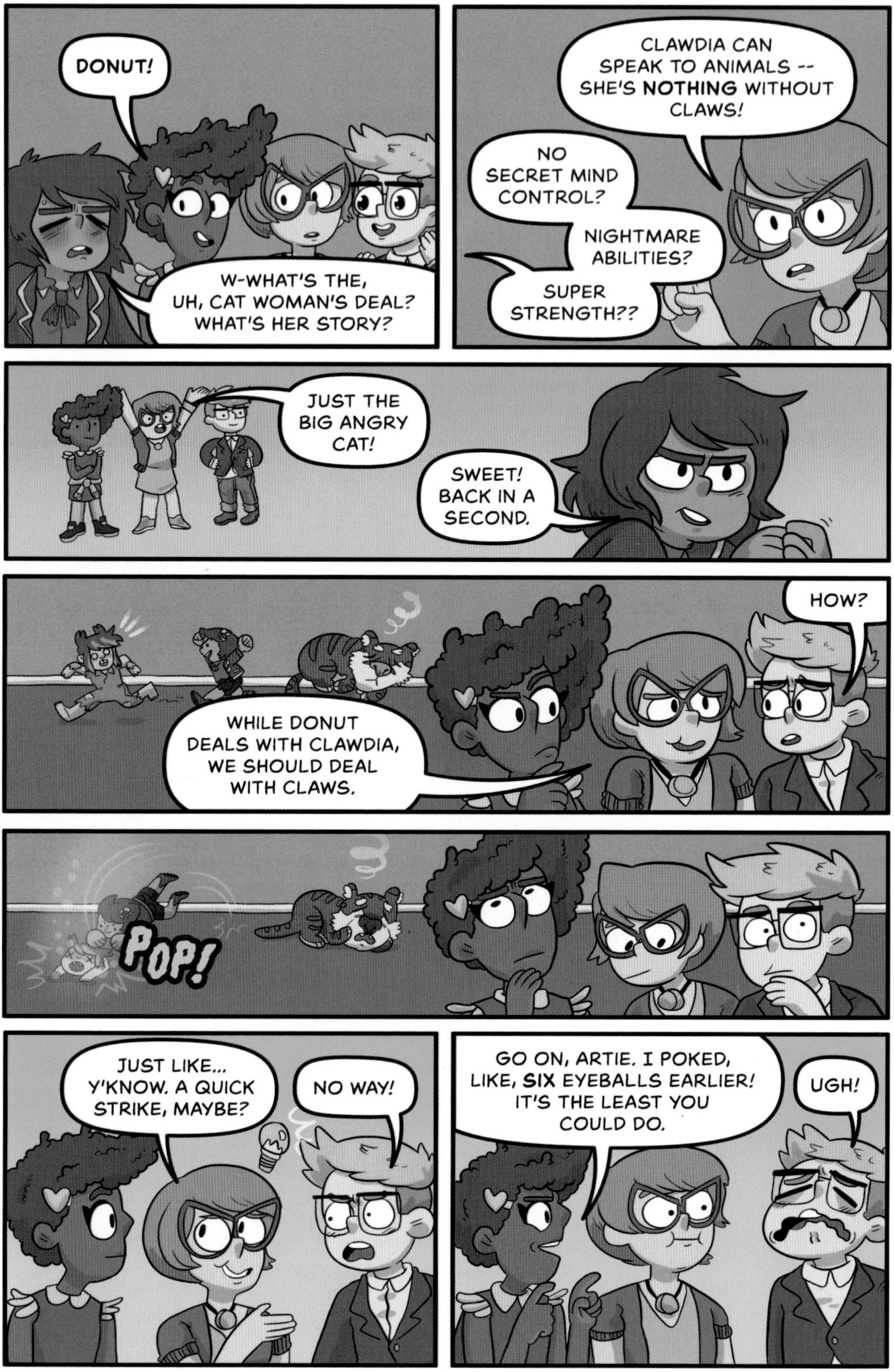
DONUT!
W-WHAT'S THE, UH, CAT WOMAN'S DEAL? WHAT'S HER STORY?
CLAWDIA CAN SPEAK TO ANIMALS -- SHE'S **NOTHING** WITHOUT CLAWS!
NO SECRET MIND CONTROL?
NIGHTMARE ABILITIES?
SUPER STRENGTH??
JUST THE BIG ANGRY CAT!
SWEET! BACK IN A SECOND.
HOW?
WHILE DONUT DEALS WITH CLAWDIA, WE SHOULD DEAL WITH CLAWS.
POP!
JUST LIKE... Y'KNOW. A QUICK STRIKE, MAYBE?
NO WAY!
GO ON, ARTIE. I POKED, LIKE, **SIX** EYEBALLS EARLIER! IT'S THE LEAST YOU COULD DO.
UGH!

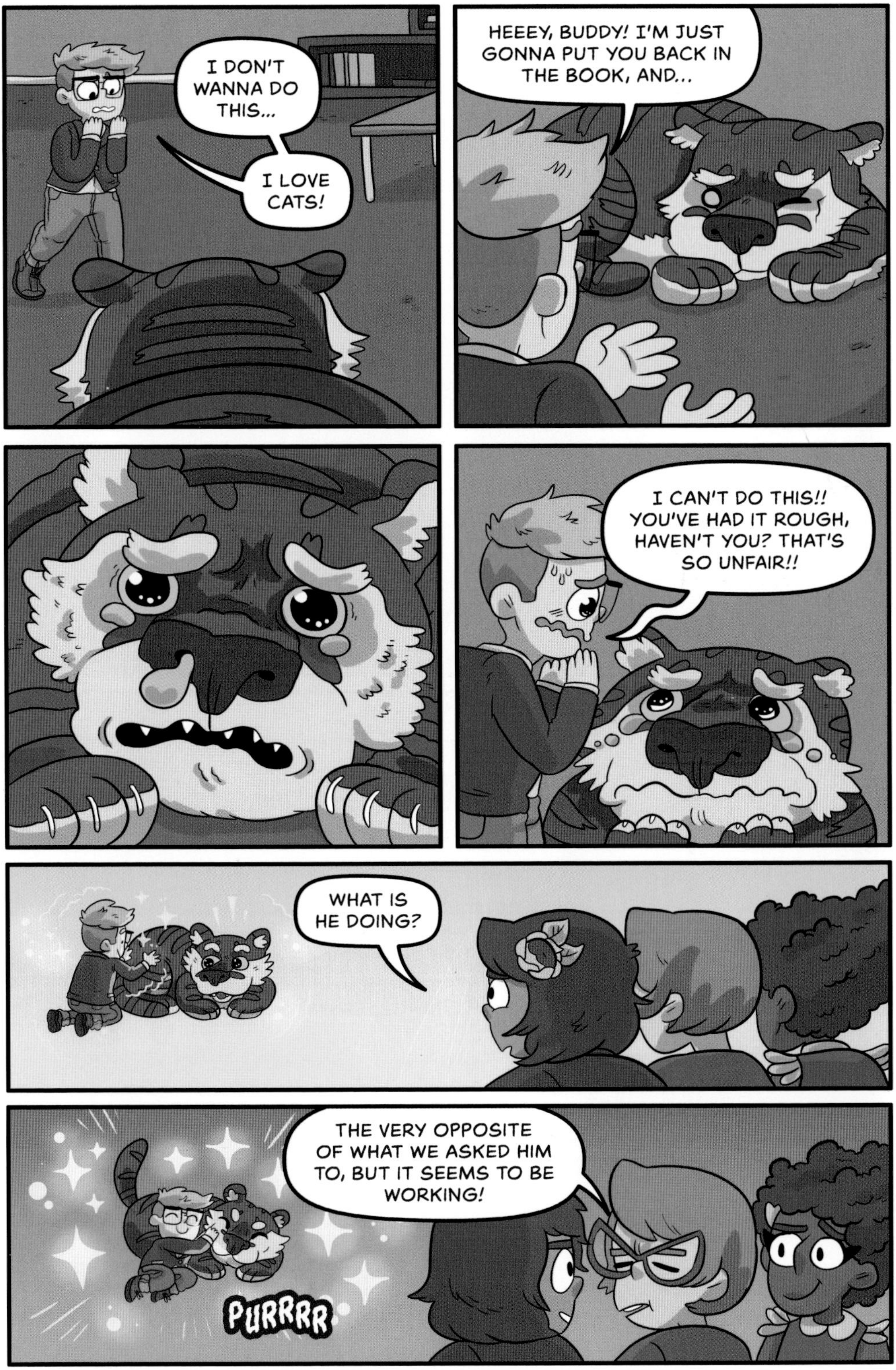
I DON'T WANNA DO THIS...
I LOVE CATS!
HEEEY, BUDDY! I'M JUST GONNA PUT YOU BACK IN THE BOOK, AND...
I CAN'T DO THIS!! YOU'VE HAD IT ROUGH, HAVEN'T YOU? THAT'S SO UNFAIR!!
WHAT IS HE DOING?
THE VERY OPPOSITE OF WHAT WE ASKED HIM TO, BUT IT SEEMS TO BE WORKING!
PURRRR

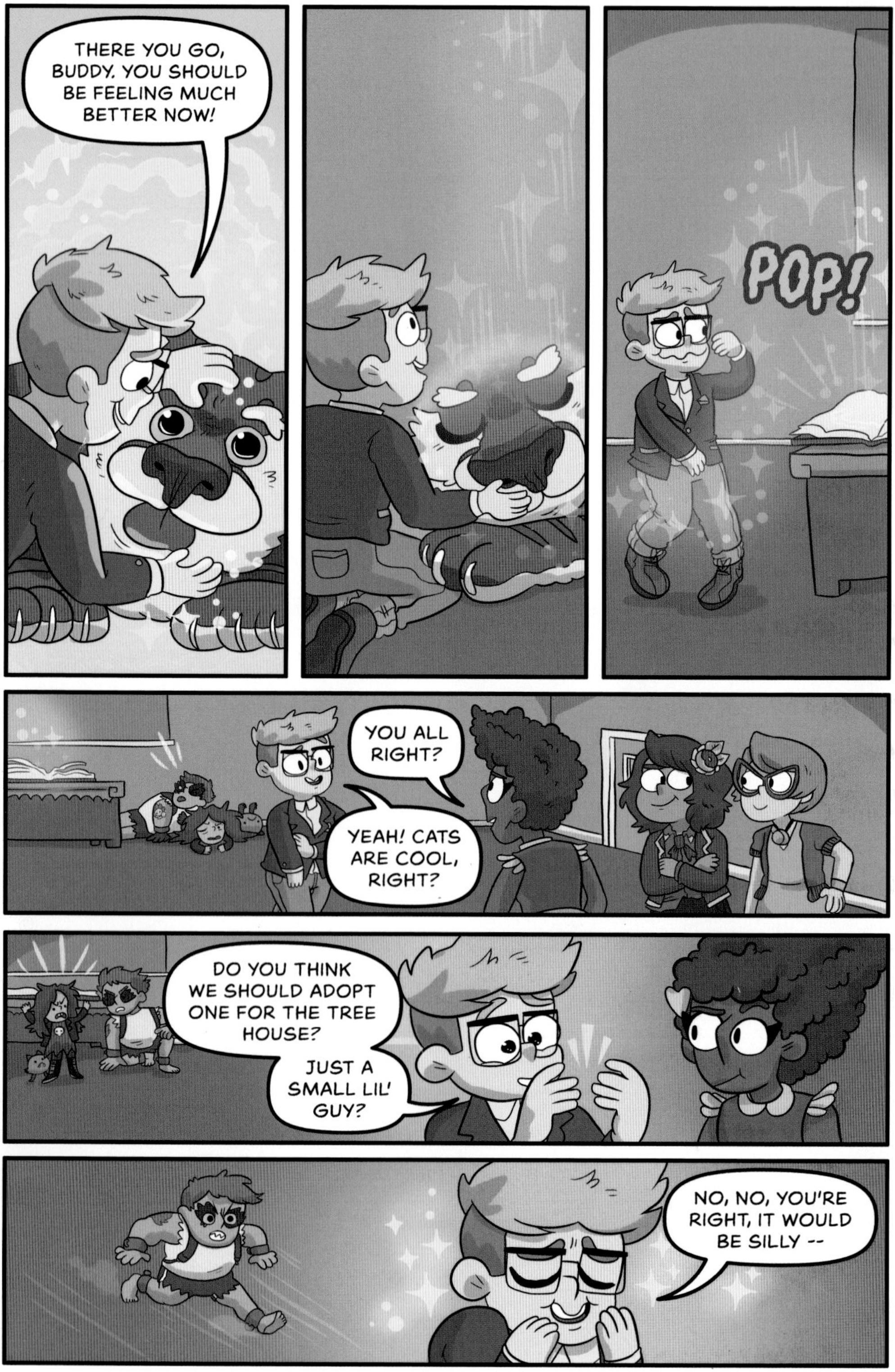
THERE YOU GO, BUDDY. YOU SHOULD BE FEELING MUCH BETTER NOW!
POP!
YOU ALL RIGHT?
YEAH! CATS ARE COOL, RIGHT?
DO YOU THINK WE SHOULD ADOPT ONE FOR THE TREE HOUSE?
JUST A SMALL LIL' GUY?
NO, NO, YOU'RE RIGHT, IT WOULD BE SILLY --

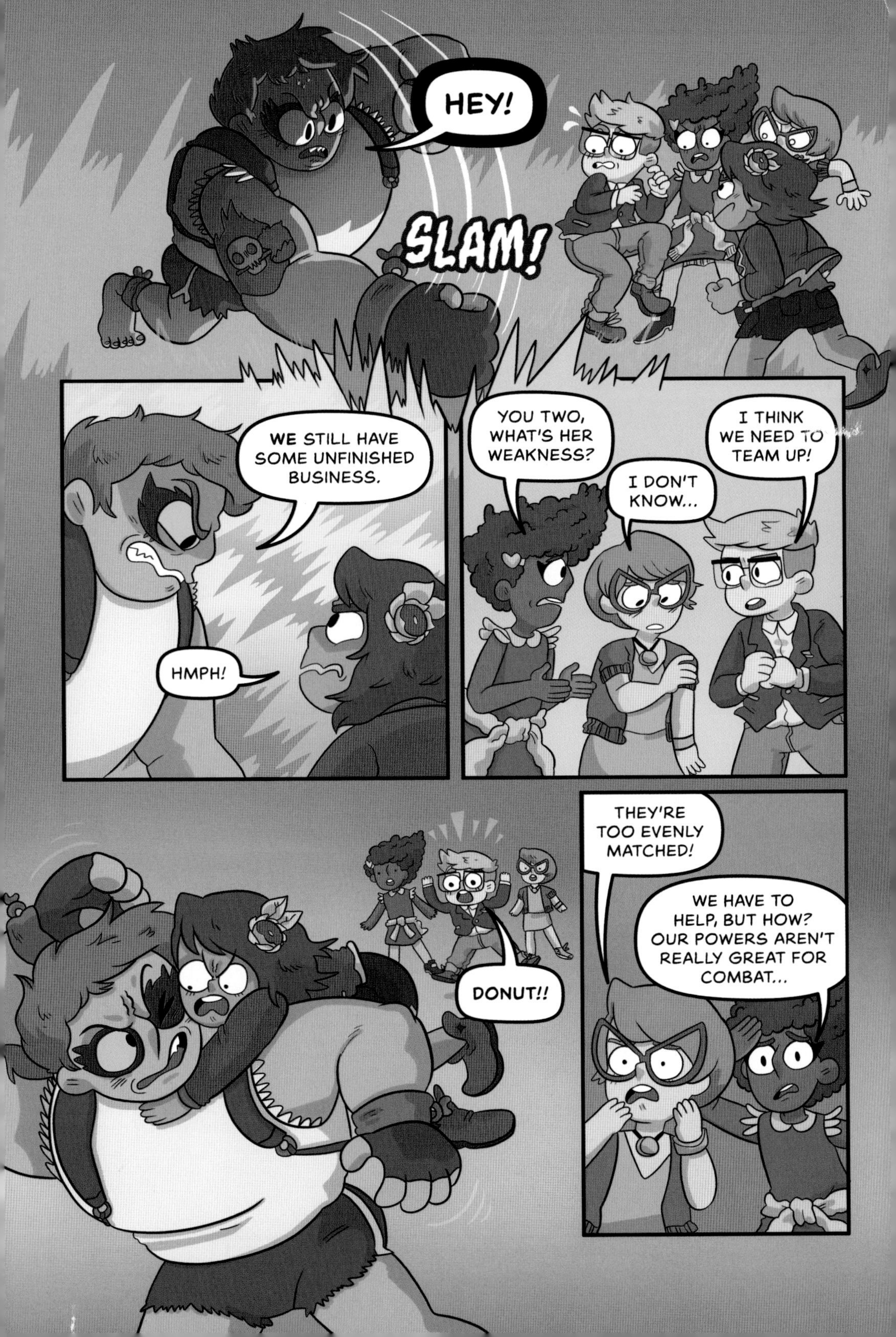
HEY!
SLAM!
WE STILL HAVE SOME UNFINISHED BUSINESS.
HMPH!
YOU TWO, WHAT'S HER WEAKNESS?
I DON'T KNOW...
I THINK WE NEED TO TEAM UP!
DONUT!!
THEY'RE TOO EVENLY MATCHED!
WE HAVE TO HELP, BUT HOW? OUR POWERS AREN'T REALLY GREAT FOR COMBAT...

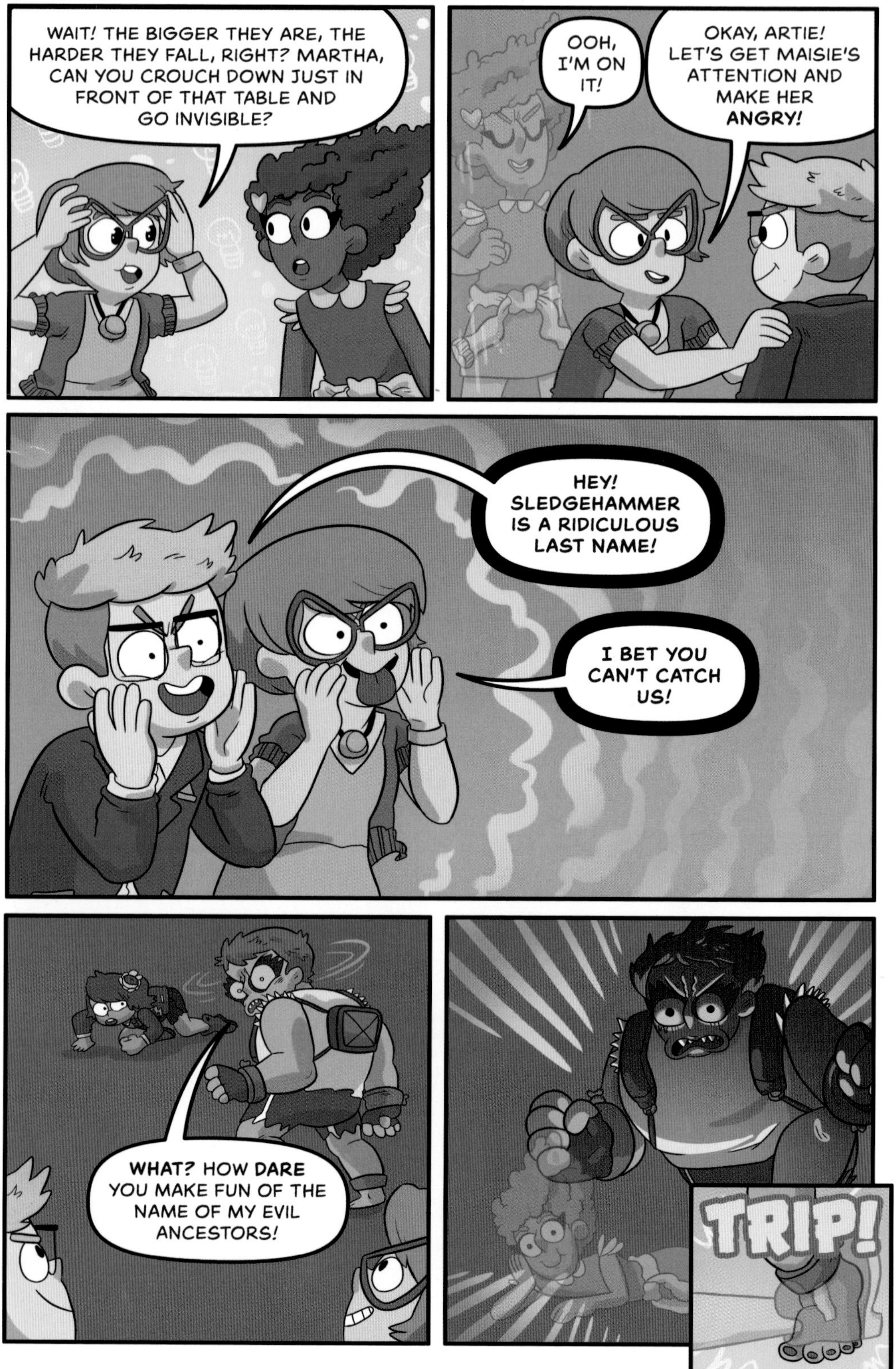
WAIT! THE BIGGER THEY ARE, THE HARDER THEY FALL, RIGHT? MARTHA, CAN YOU CROUCH DOWN JUST IN FRONT OF THAT TABLE AND GO INVISIBLE?
OOH, I'M ON IT!
OKAY, ARTIE! LET'S GET MAISIE'S ATTENTION AND MAKE HER ANGRY!
HEY! SLEDGEHAMMER IS A RIDICULOUS LAST NAME!
I BET YOU CAN'T CATCH US!
WHAT? HOW DARE YOU MAKE FUN OF THE NAME OF MY EVIL ANCESTORS!
TRIP!

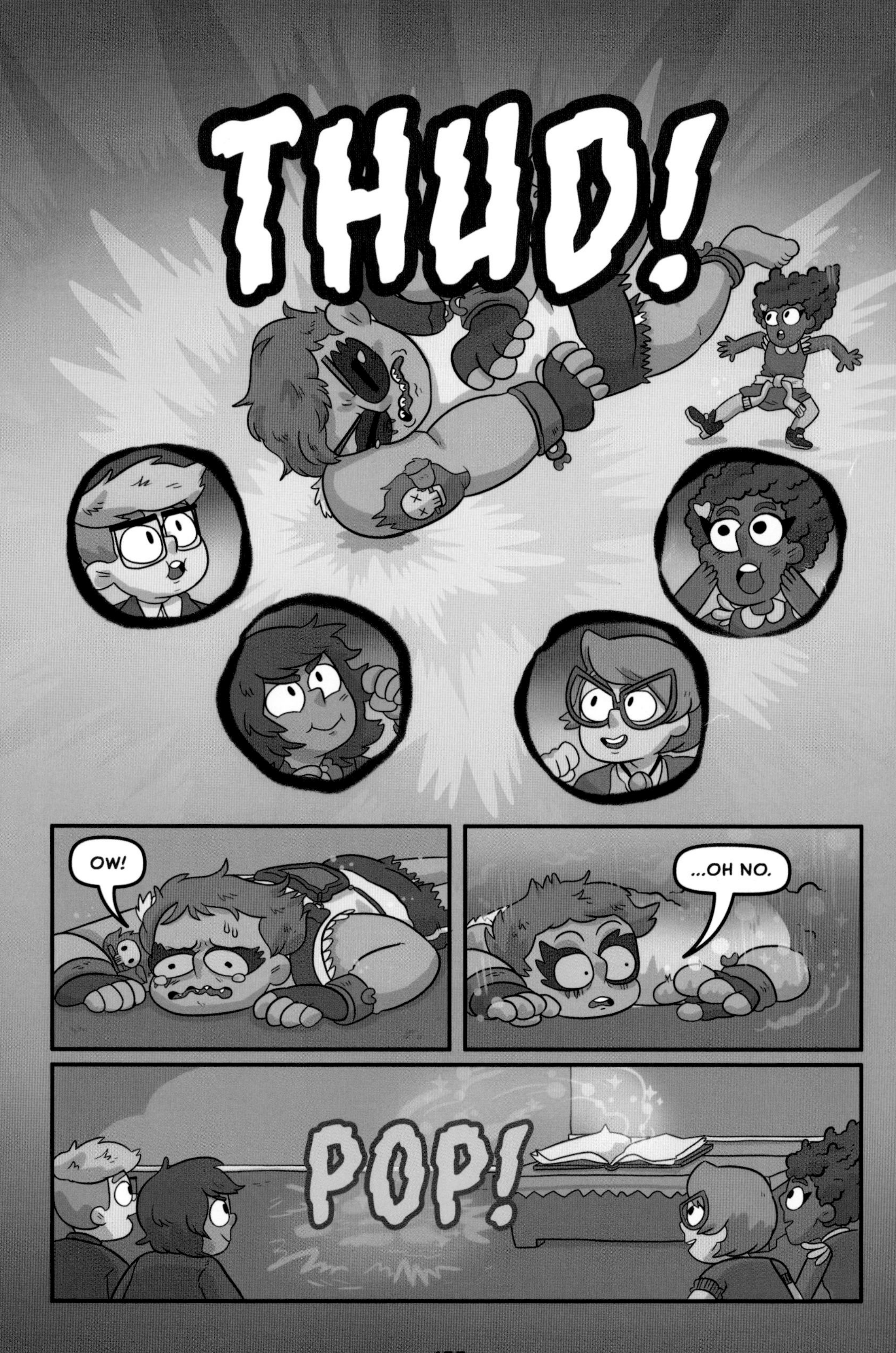
THUD!
OW!
...OH NO.
POP!

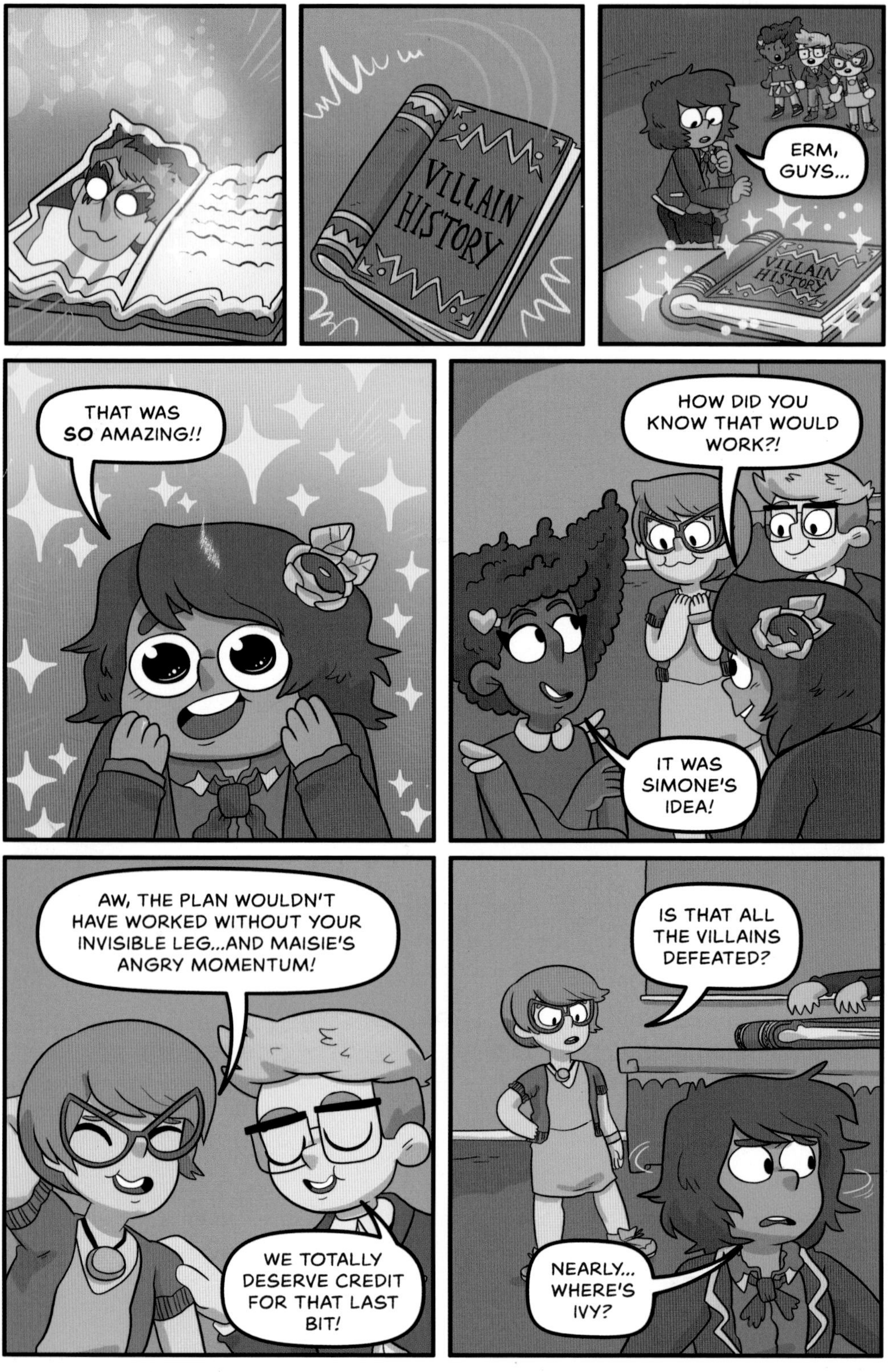

VILLAIN HISTORY
VILLAIN HISTORY
ERM, GUYS...
THAT WAS SO AMAZING!!
HOW DID YOU KNOW THAT WOULD WORK?!
IT WAS SIMONE'S IDEA!
AW, THE PLAN WOULDN'T HAVE WORKED WITHOUT YOUR INVISIBLE LEG...AND MAISIE'S ANGRY MOMENTUM!
WE TOTALLY DESERVE CREDIT FOR THAT LAST BIT!
IS THAT ALL THE VILLAINS DEFEATED?
NEARLY... WHERE'S IVY?

OVER THERE!

SHE'S SNEAKING OUT WITH THE VILLAIN HISTORY BOOK!

N-NO! AS LONG AS YOU'RE A HERO, I CAN'T!

IVY! PUT IT DOWN!

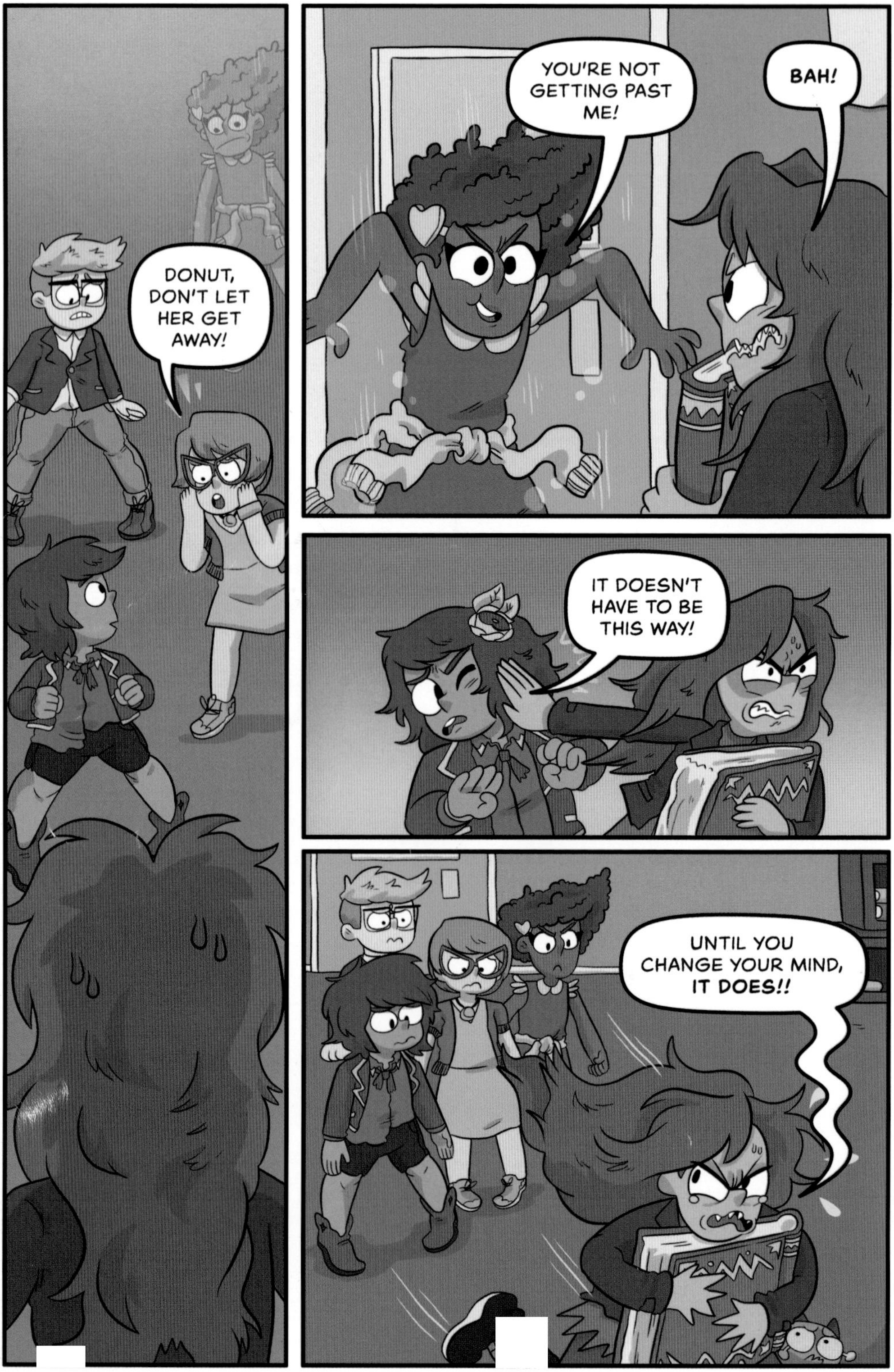

DONUT, DON'T LET HER GET AWAY!
YOU'RE NOT GETTING PAST ME!
BAH!
IT DOESN'T HAVE TO BE THIS WAY!
UNTIL YOU CHANGE YOUR MIND, IT DOES!!

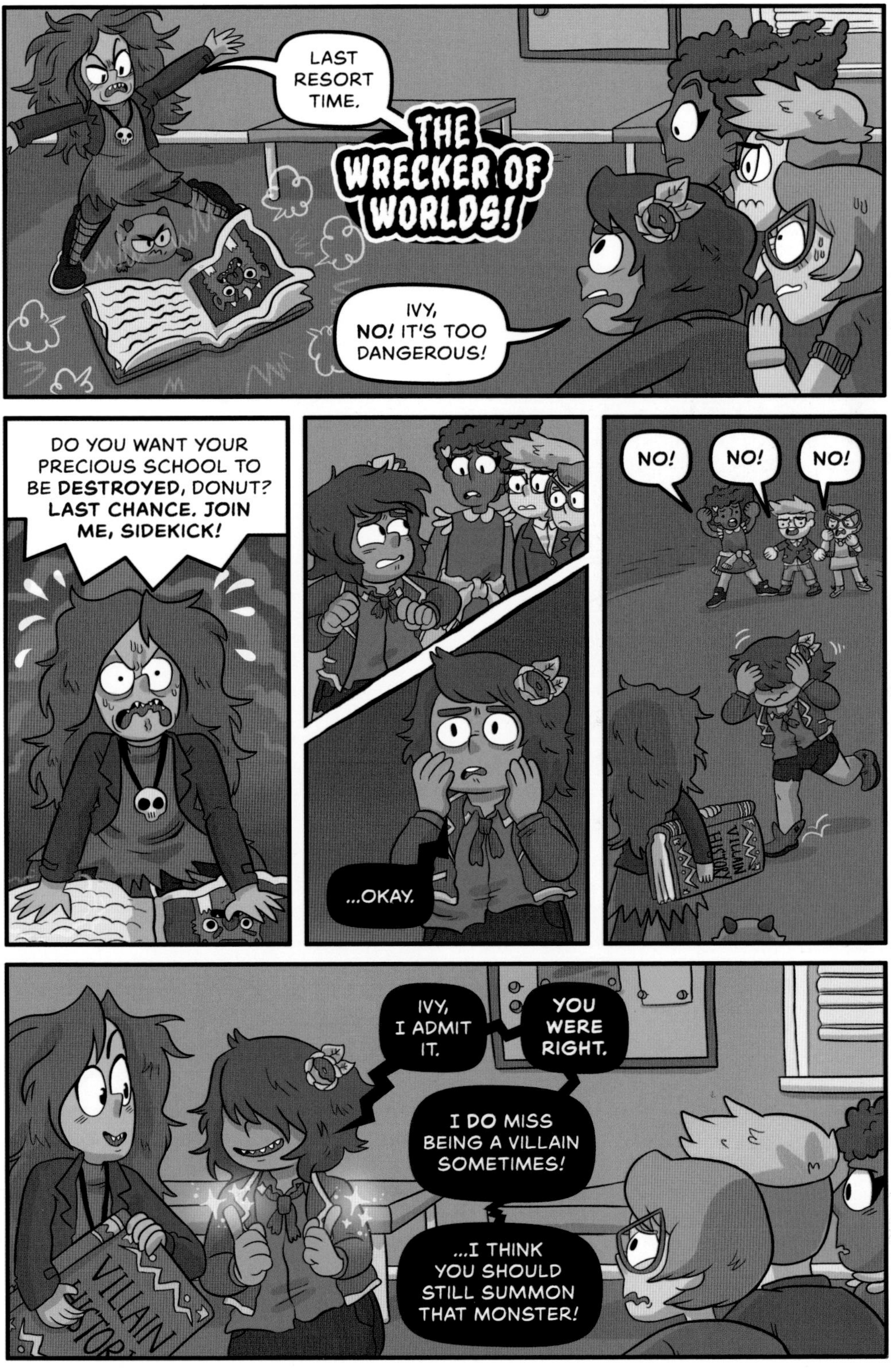
LAST RESORT TIME.
THE WRECKER OF WORLDS!
IVY, NO! IT'S TOO DANGEROUS!
DO YOU WANT YOUR PRECIOUS SCHOOL TO BE DESTROYED, DONUT? LAST CHANCE. JOIN ME, SIDEKICK!
...OKAY.
NO!
NO!
NO!
VILLAIN HISTORY
IVY, I ADMIT IT.
YOU WERE RIGHT.
I DO MISS BEING A VILLAIN SOMETIMES!
...I THINK YOU SHOULD STILL SUMMON THAT MONSTER!

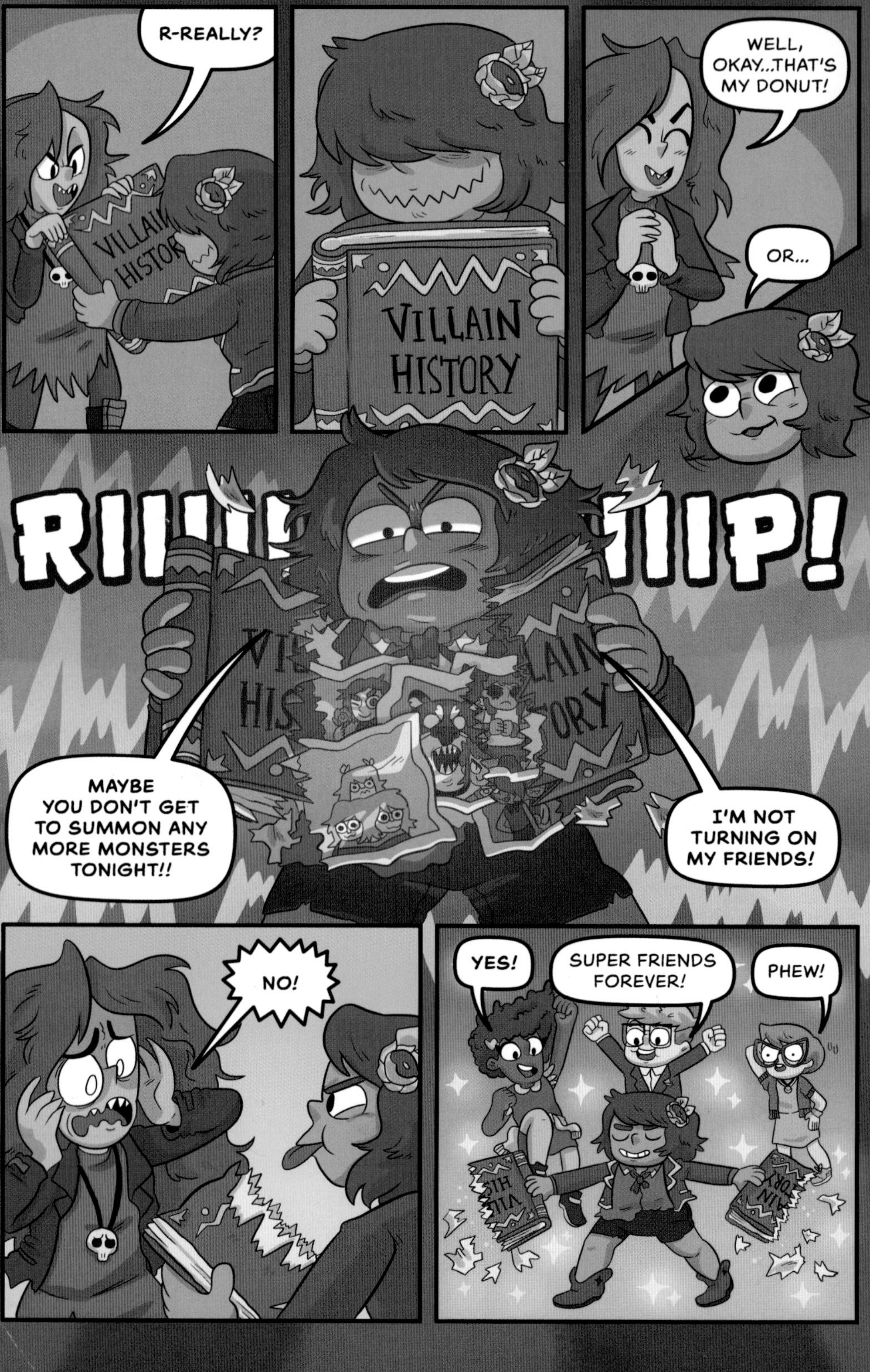
R-REALLY?
VILLAIN HISTORY
VILLAIN HISTORY
WELL, OKAY...THAT'S MY DONUT!
OR...
RIIIIP!
MAYBE YOU DON'T GET TO SUMMON ANY MORE MONSTERS TONIGHT!!
I'M NOT TURNING ON MY FRIENDS!
NO!
YES!
SUPER FRIENDS FOREVER!
PHEW!

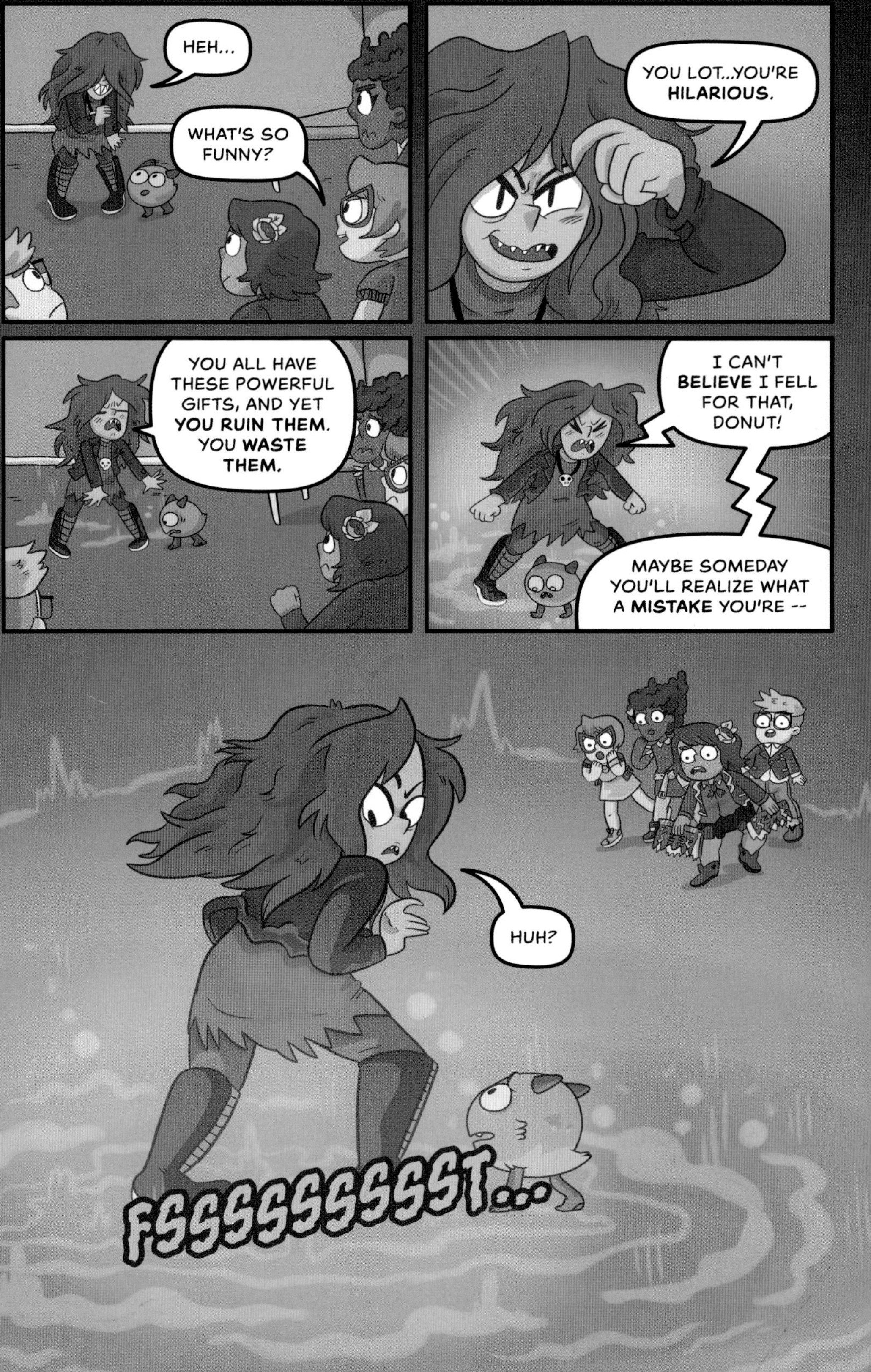
HEH...
WHAT'S SO FUNNY?
YOU LOT...YOU'RE **HILARIOUS.**
YOU ALL HAVE THESE POWERFUL GIFTS, AND YET **YOU RUIN THEM.** YOU **WASTE THEM.**
I CAN'T **BELIEVE** I FELL FOR THAT, DONUT!
MAYBE SOMEDAY YOU'LL REALIZE WHAT A **MISTAKE** YOU'RE --
HUH?
FSSSSSSSSSST...

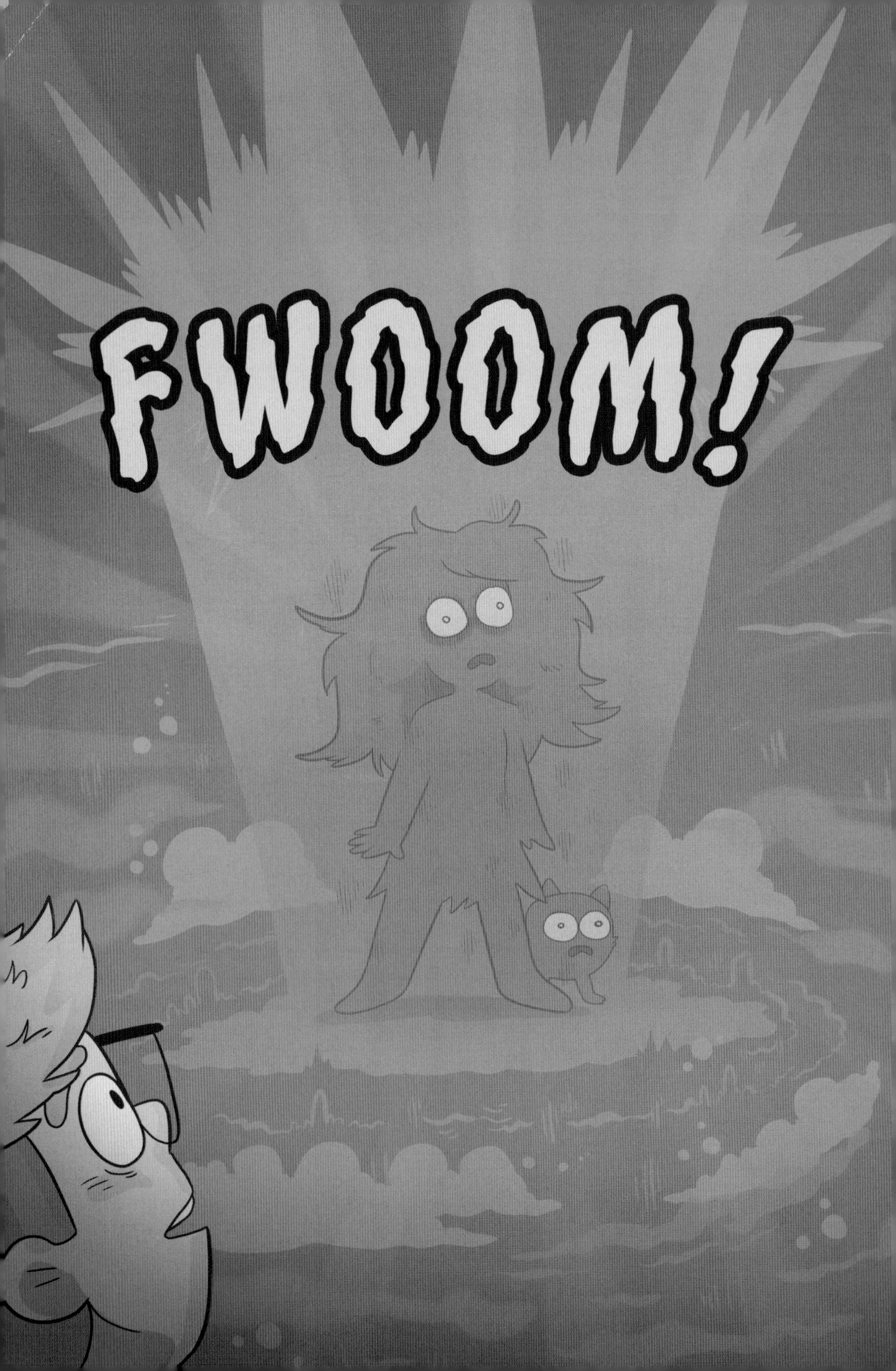
FWOOM!

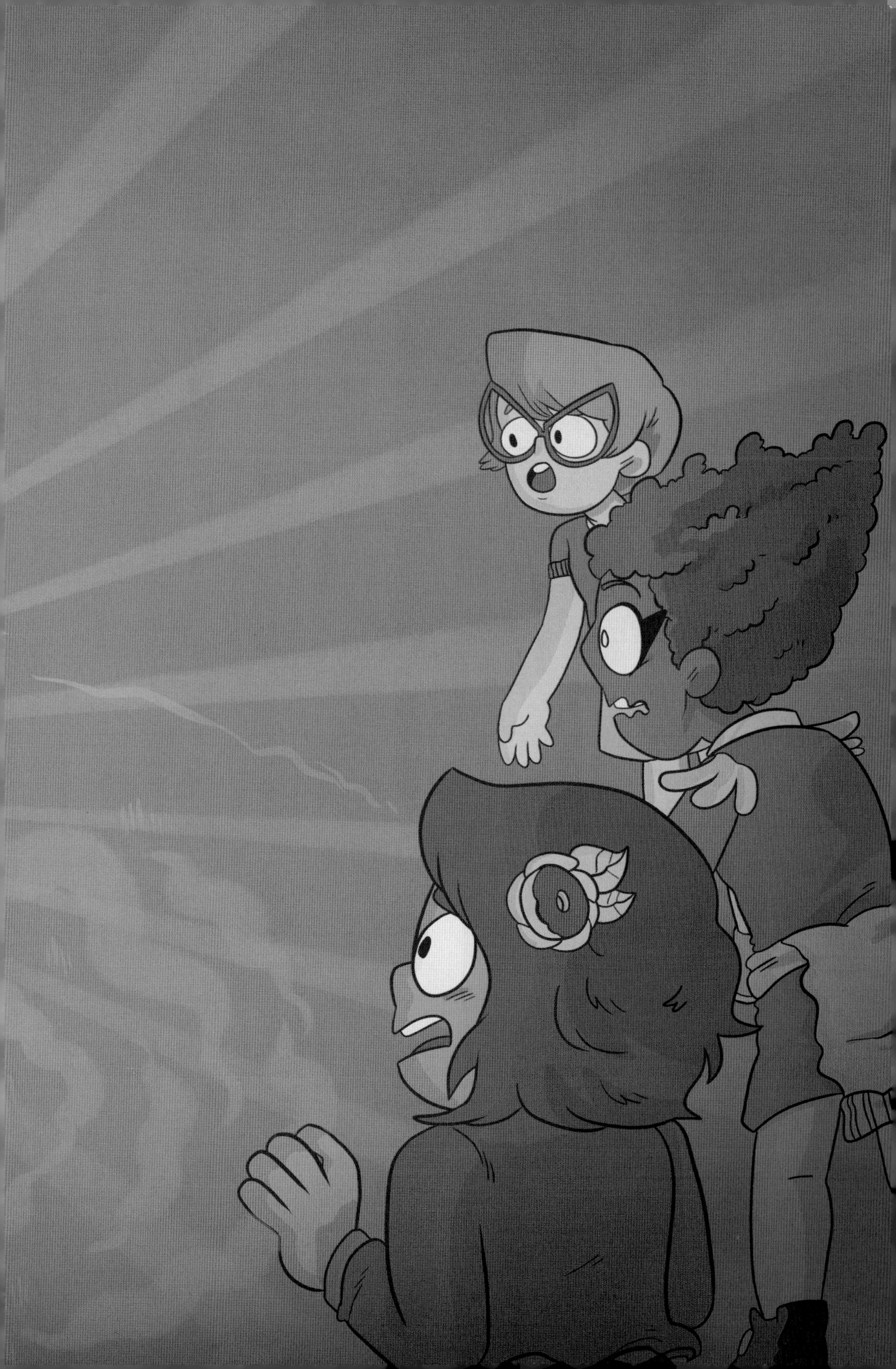

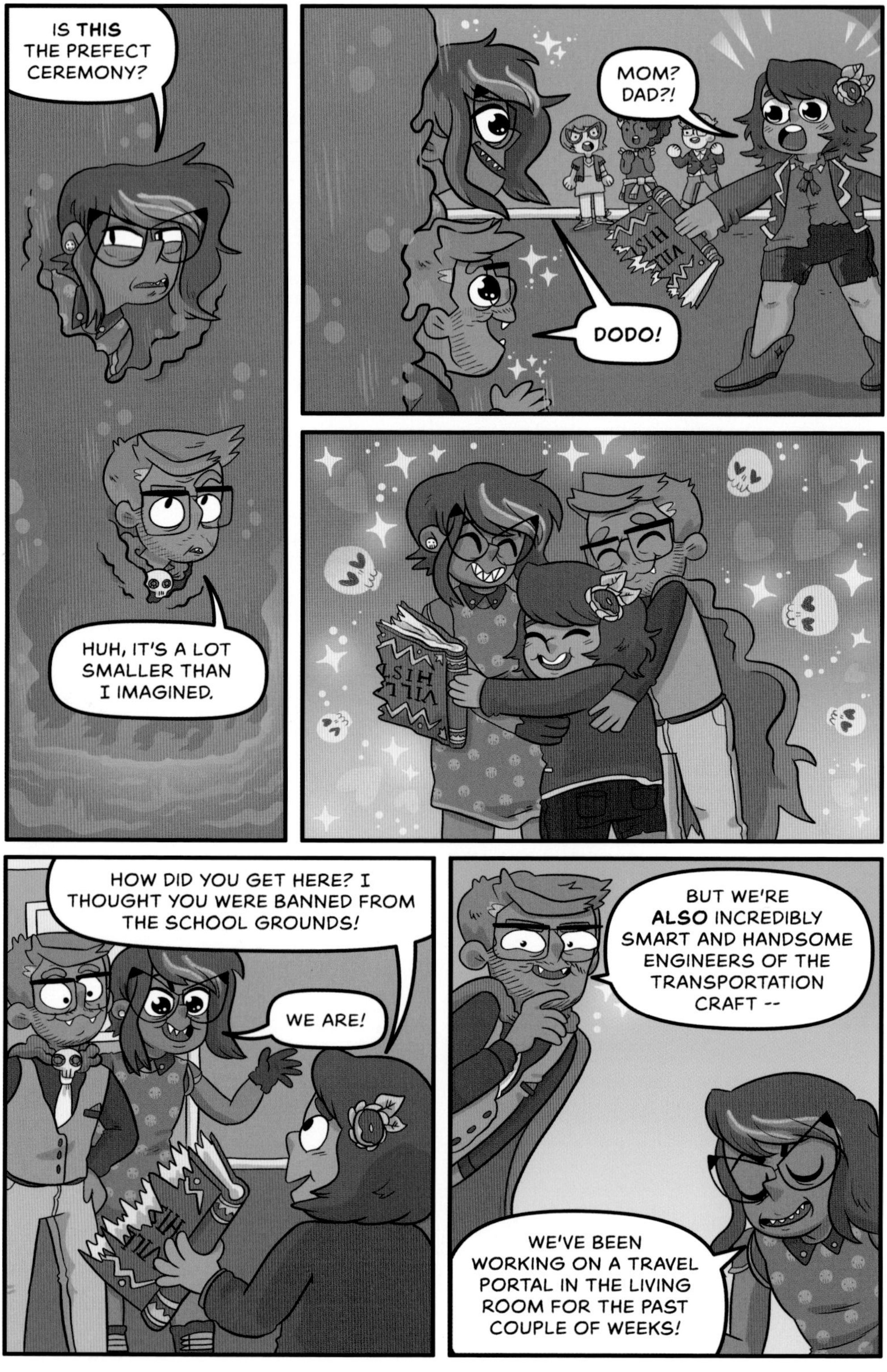
IS THIS THE PREFECT CEREMONY?
HUH, IT'S A LOT SMALLER THAN I IMAGINED.
MOM? DAD?!
DODO!
HOW DID YOU GET HERE? I THOUGHT YOU WERE BANNED FROM THE SCHOOL GROUNDS!
WE ARE!
BUT WE'RE ALSO INCREDIBLY SMART AND HANDSOME ENGINEERS OF THE TRANSPORTATION CRAFT --
WE'VE BEEN WORKING ON A TRAVEL PORTAL IN THE LIVING ROOM FOR THE PAST COUPLE OF WEEKS!

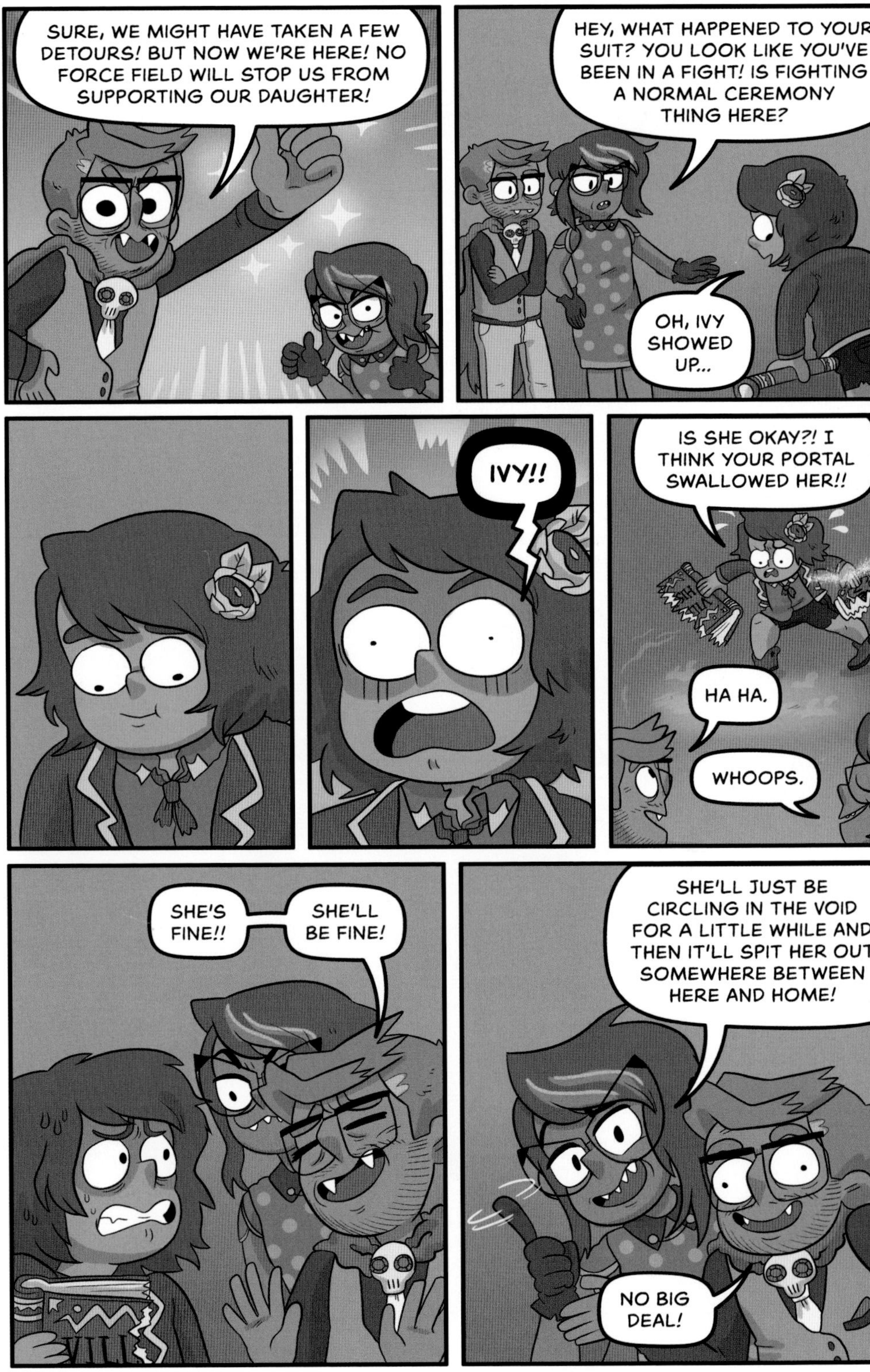
SURE, WE MIGHT HAVE TAKEN A FEW DETOURS! BUT NOW WE'RE HERE! NO FORCE FIELD WILL STOP US FROM SUPPORTING OUR DAUGHTER!
HEY, WHAT HAPPENED TO YOUR SUIT? YOU LOOK LIKE YOU'VE BEEN IN A FIGHT! IS FIGHTING A NORMAL CEREMONY THING HERE?
OH, IVY SHOWED UP...
IVY!!
IS SHE OKAY?! I THINK YOUR PORTAL SWALLOWED HER!!
HA HA.
WHOOPS.
SHE'S FINE!!
SHE'LL BE FINE!
SHE'LL JUST BE CIRCLING IN THE VOID FOR A LITTLE WHILE AND THEN IT'LL SPIT HER OUT SOMEWHERE BETWEEN HERE AND HOME!
NO BIG DEAL!

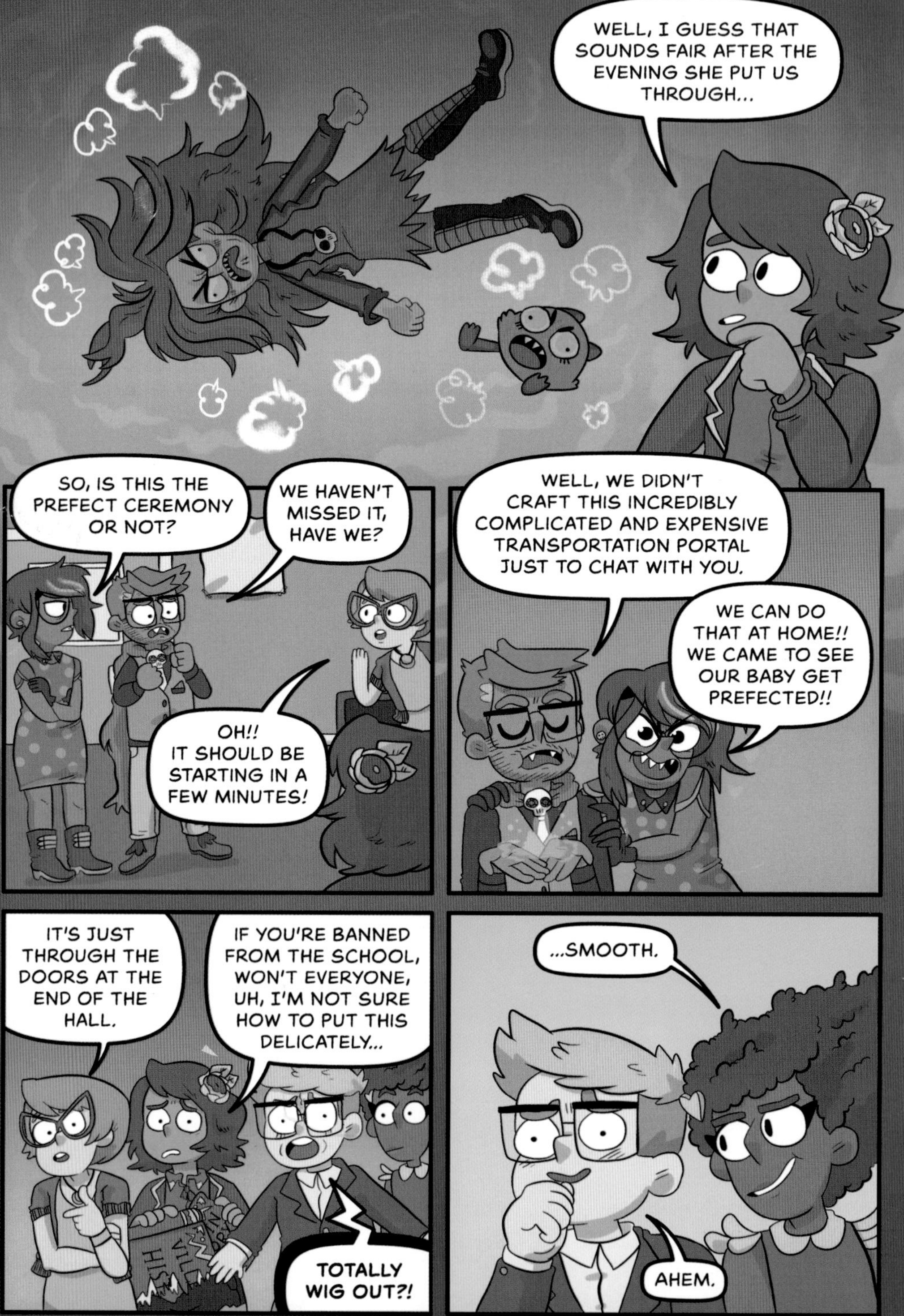
WELL, I GUESS THAT SOUNDS FAIR AFTER THE EVENING SHE PUT US THROUGH...
SO, IS THIS THE PREFECT CEREMONY OR NOT?
WE HAVEN'T MISSED IT, HAVE WE?
OH!! IT SHOULD BE STARTING IN A FEW MINUTES!
WELL, WE DIDN'T CRAFT THIS INCREDIBLY COMPLICATED AND EXPENSIVE TRANSPORTATION PORTAL JUST TO CHAT WITH YOU.
WE CAN DO THAT AT HOME!! WE CAME TO SEE OUR BABY GET PREFECTED!!
IT'S JUST THROUGH THE DOORS AT THE END OF THE HALL.
IF YOU'RE BANNED FROM THE SCHOOL, WON'T EVERYONE, UH, I'M NOT SURE HOW TO PUT THIS DELICATELY...
TOTALLY WIG OUT?!
...SMOOTH.
AHEM.

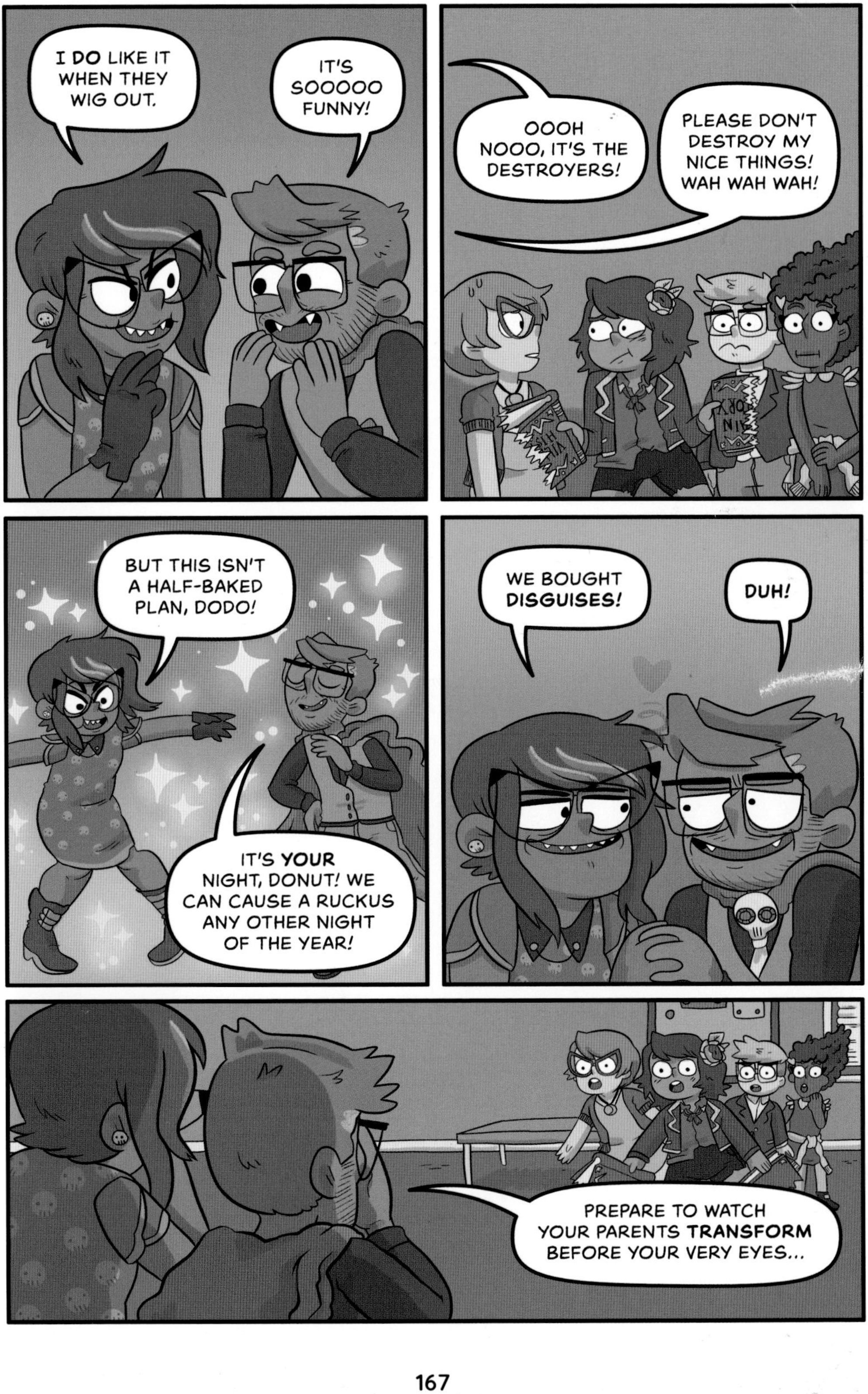
I DO LIKE IT WHEN THEY WIG OUT.
IT'S SOOOOO FUNNY!
OOOH NOOO, IT'S THE DESTROYERS!
PLEASE DON'T DESTROY MY NICE THINGS! WAH WAH WAH!
BUT THIS ISN'T A HALF-BAKED PLAN, DODO!
IT'S YOUR NIGHT, DONUT! WE CAN CAUSE A RUCKUS ANY OTHER NIGHT OF THE YEAR!
WE BOUGHT DISGUISES!
DUH!
PREPARE TO WATCH YOUR PARENTS TRANSFORM BEFORE YOUR VERY EYES...

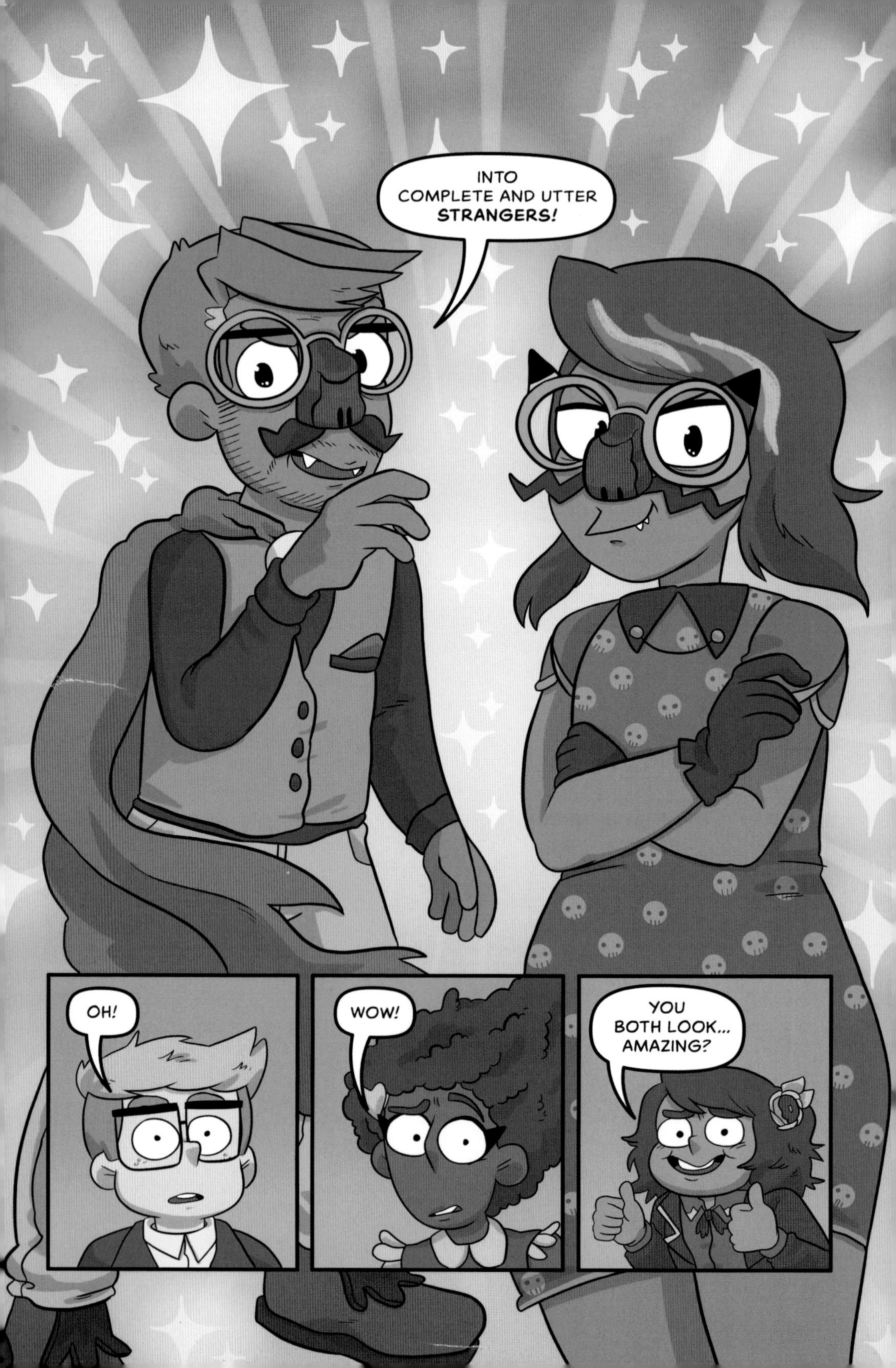
INTO COMPLETE AND UTTER STRANGERS!
OH!
WOW!
YOU BOTH LOOK... AMAZING?

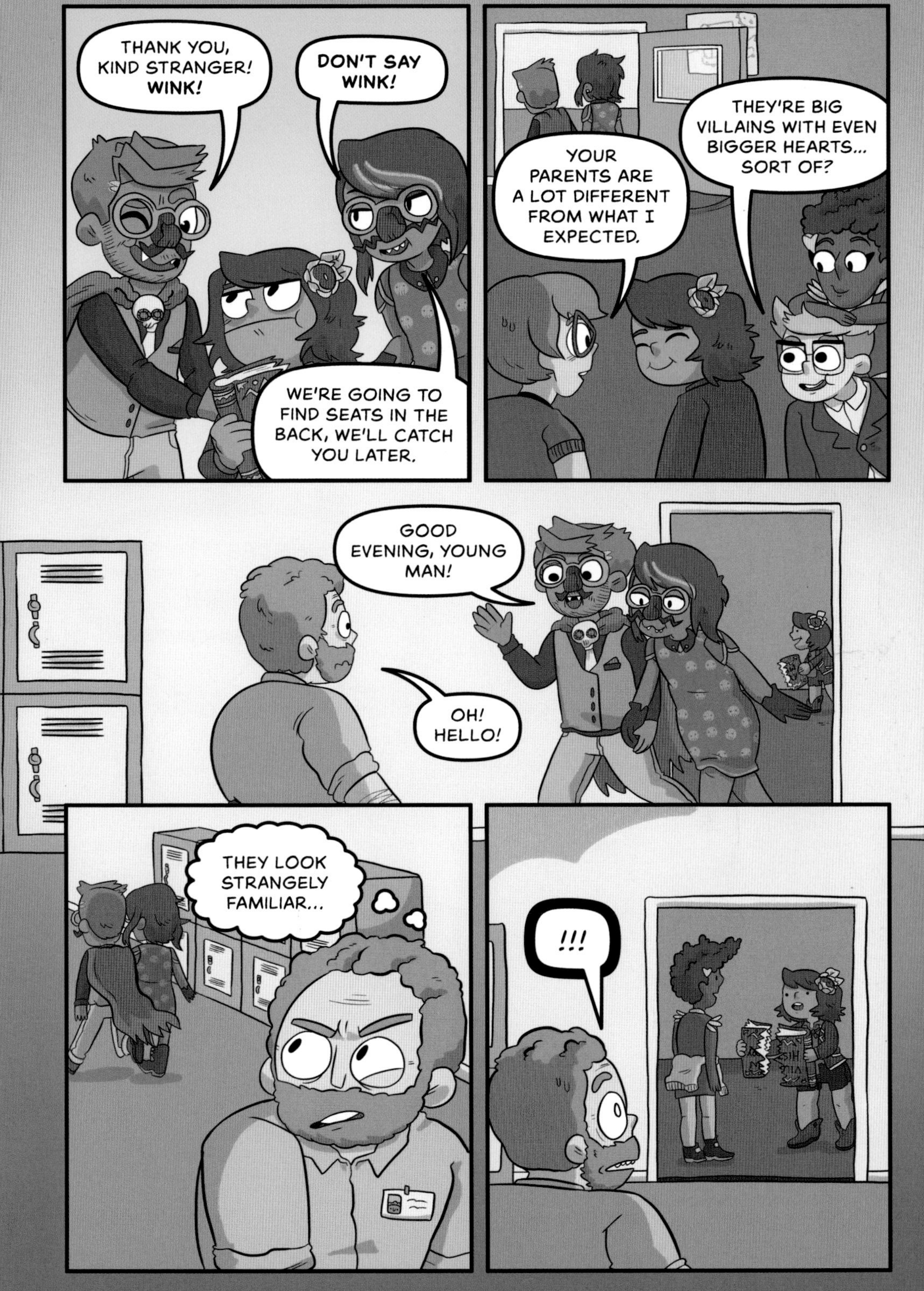
THANK YOU, KIND STRANGER! WINK!
DON'T SAY WINK!
WE'RE GOING TO FIND SEATS IN THE BACK, WE'LL CATCH YOU LATER.
YOUR PARENTS ARE A LOT DIFFERENT FROM WHAT I EXPECTED.
THEY'RE BIG VILLAINS WITH EVEN BIGGER HEARTS... SORT OF?
GOOD EVENING, YOUNG MAN!
OH! HELLO!
THEY LOOK STRANGELY FAMILIAR...
!!!

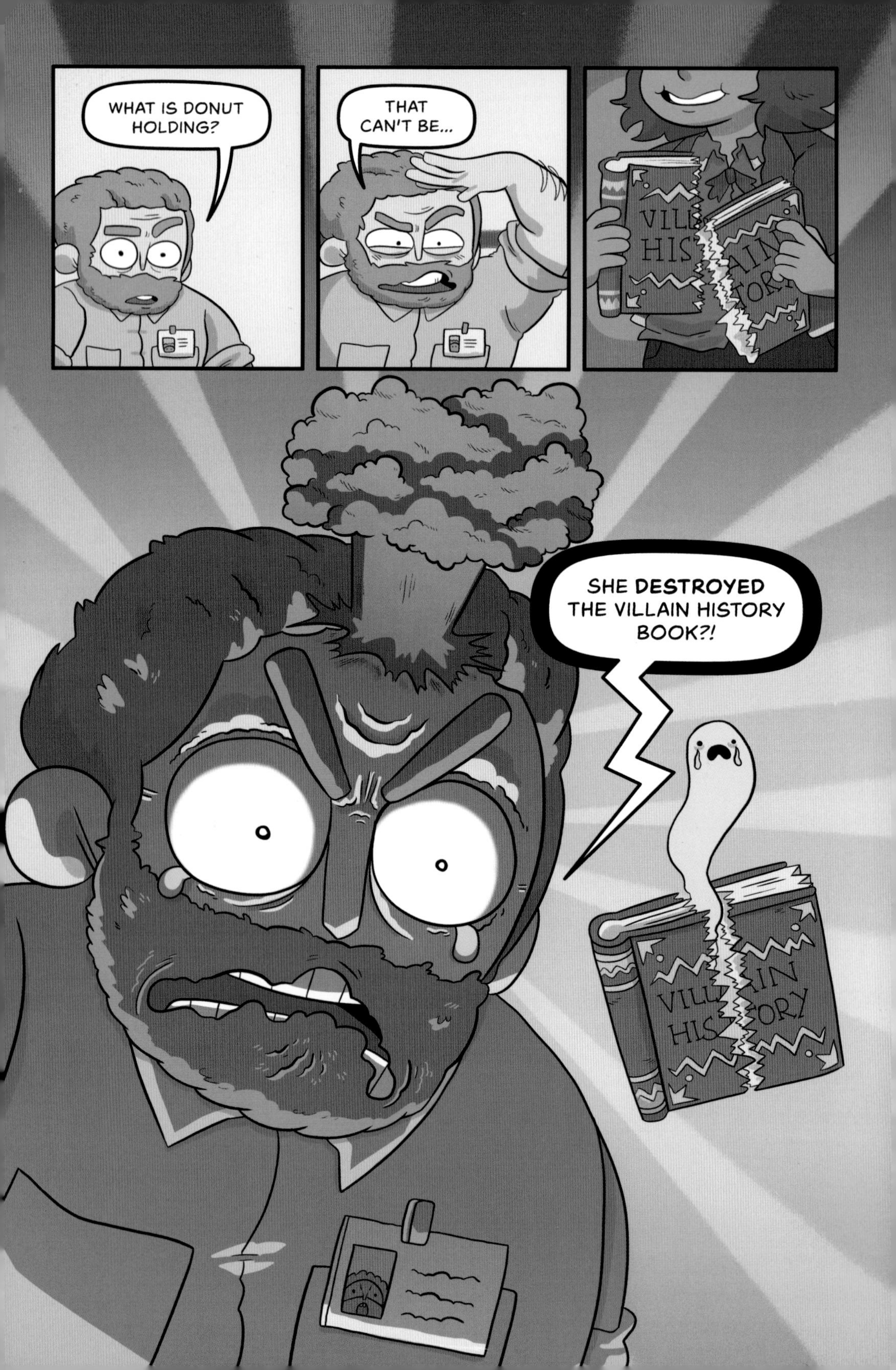
WHAT IS DONUT HOLDING?
THAT CAN'T BE...
VILLAIN HISTORY
SHE **DESTROYED** THE VILLAIN HISTORY BOOK?!
VILLAIN HISTORY

DONUT!

UH-OH.

WHAT HAPPENED IN HERE?! THIS ROOM IS A MESS!

AND WHY HAVE YOU TORN UP THAT BOOK?

IT'S UNIQUE TO THE SCHOOL AND ONE OF OUR MOST IMPORTANT AND PRICELESS TOMES!

DONUT THE **DESTROYER**, INDEED!

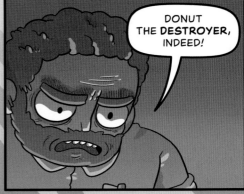

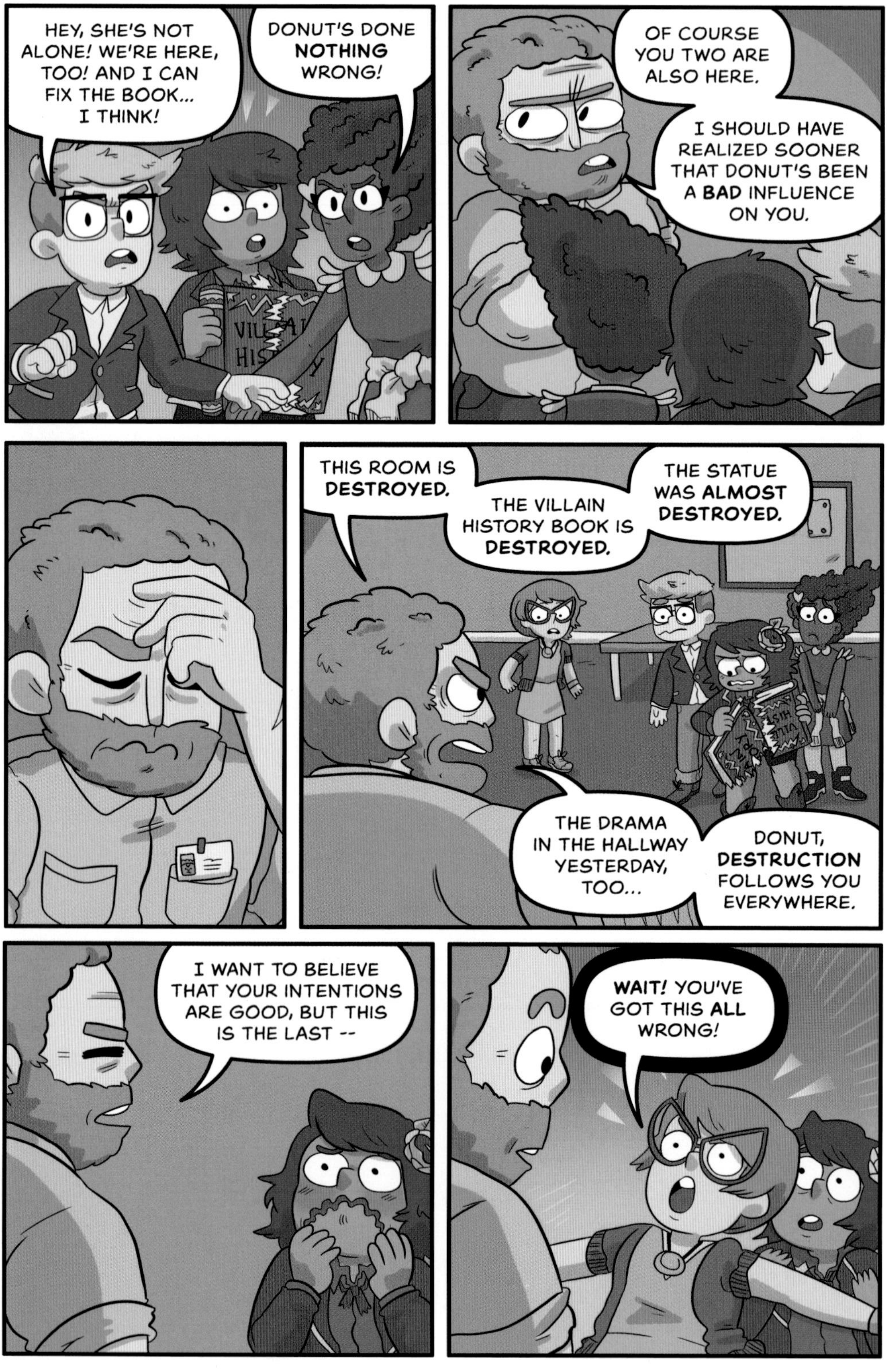
HEY, SHE'S NOT ALONE! WE'RE HERE, TOO! AND I CAN FIX THE BOOK... I THINK!
DONUT'S DONE **NOTHING** WRONG!
OF COURSE YOU TWO ARE ALSO HERE.
I SHOULD HAVE REALIZED SOONER THAT DONUT'S BEEN A **BAD** INFLUENCE ON YOU.
THIS ROOM IS **DESTROYED.**
THE VILLAIN HISTORY BOOK IS **DESTROYED.**
THE STATUE WAS **ALMOST DESTROYED.**
THE DRAMA IN THE HALLWAY YESTERDAY, TOO...
DONUT, **DESTRUCTION** FOLLOWS YOU EVERYWHERE.
I WANT TO BELIEVE THAT YOUR INTENTIONS ARE GOOD, BUT THIS IS THE LAST --
WAIT! YOU'VE GOT THIS **ALL** WRONG!

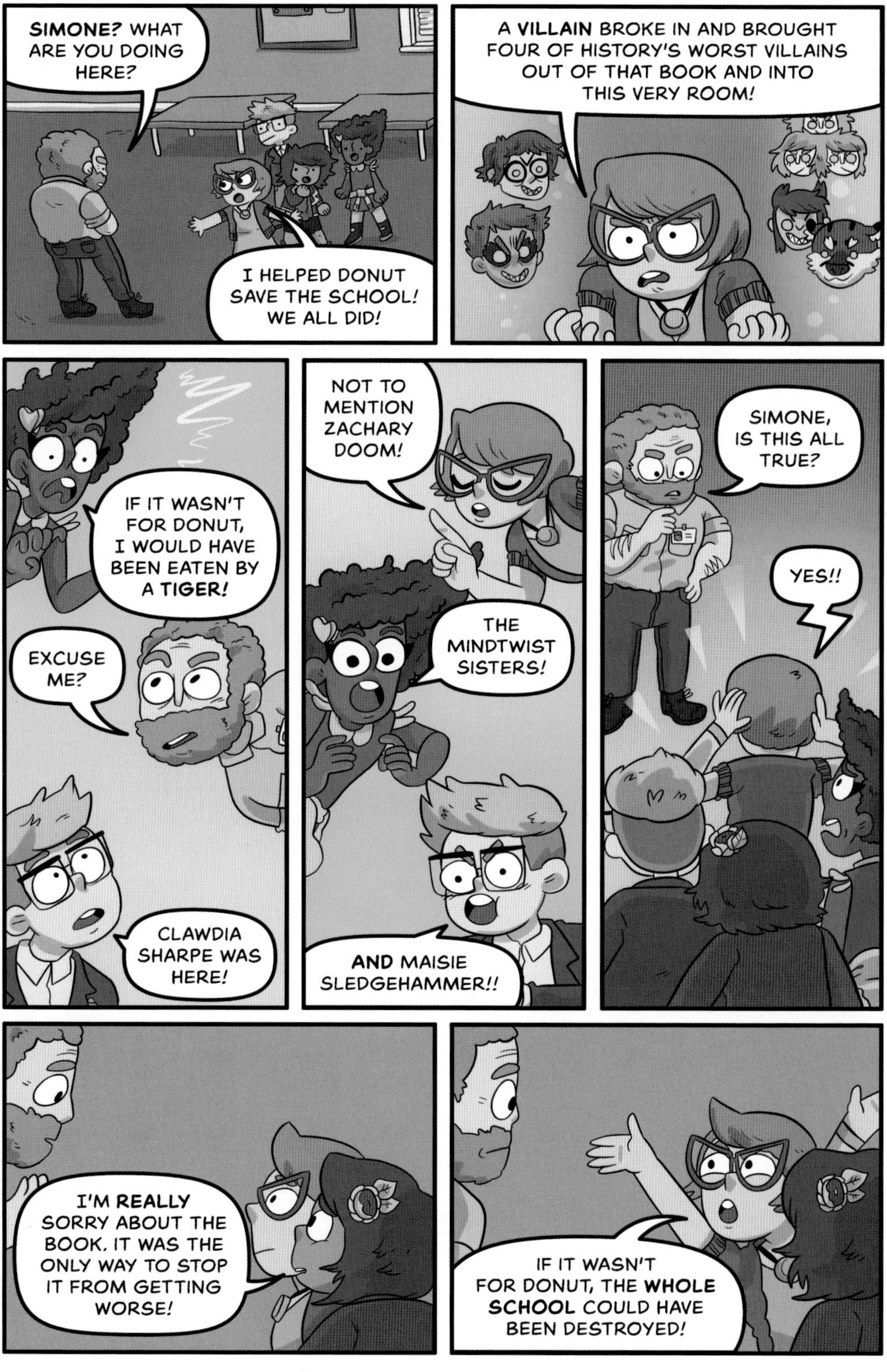
SIMONE? WHAT ARE YOU DOING HERE?
I HELPED DONUT SAVE THE SCHOOL! WE ALL DID!
A VILLAIN BROKE IN AND BROUGHT FOUR OF HISTORY'S WORST VILLAINS OUT OF THAT BOOK AND INTO THIS VERY ROOM!
IF IT WASN'T FOR DONUT, I WOULD HAVE BEEN EATEN BY A TIGER!
EXCUSE ME?
CLAWDIA SHARPE WAS HERE!
NOT TO MENTION ZACHARY DOOM!
THE MINDTWIST SISTERS!
AND MAISIE SLEDGEHAMMER!!
SIMONE, IS THIS ALL TRUE?
YES!!
I'M REALLY SORRY ABOUT THE BOOK. IT WAS THE ONLY WAY TO STOP IT FROM GETTING WORSE!
IF IT WASN'T FOR DONUT, THE WHOLE SCHOOL COULD HAVE BEEN DESTROYED!

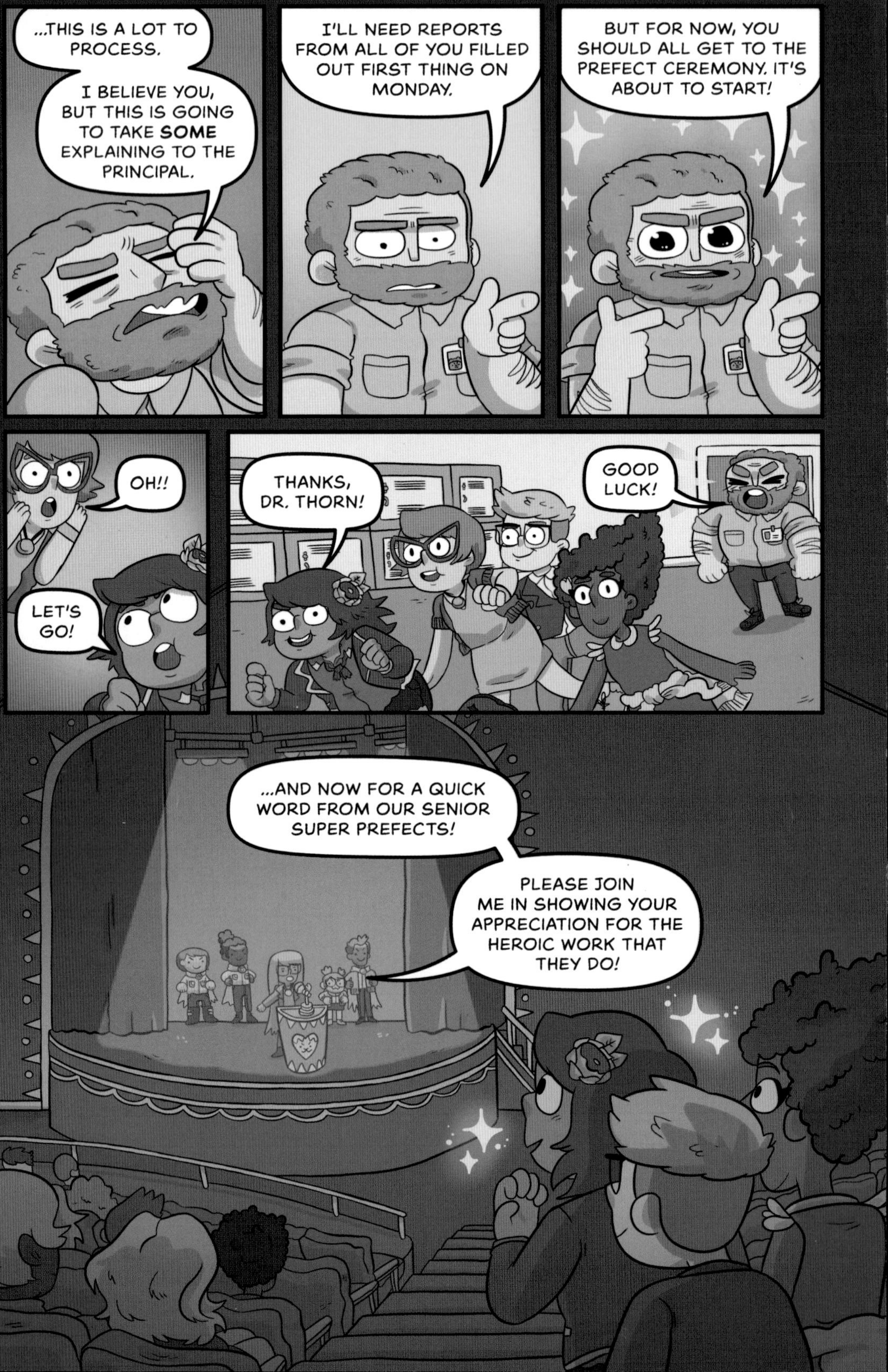
...THIS IS A LOT TO PROCESS.
I BELIEVE YOU, BUT THIS IS GOING TO TAKE **SOME** EXPLAINING TO THE PRINCIPAL.
I'LL NEED REPORTS FROM ALL OF YOU FILLED OUT FIRST THING ON MONDAY.
BUT FOR NOW, YOU SHOULD ALL GET TO THE PREFECT CEREMONY. IT'S ABOUT TO START!
OH!!
LET'S GO!
THANKS, DR. THORN!
GOOD LUCK!
...AND NOW FOR A QUICK WORD FROM OUR SENIOR SUPER PREFECTS!
PLEASE JOIN ME IN SHOWING YOUR APPRECIATION FOR THE HEROIC WORK THAT THEY DO!

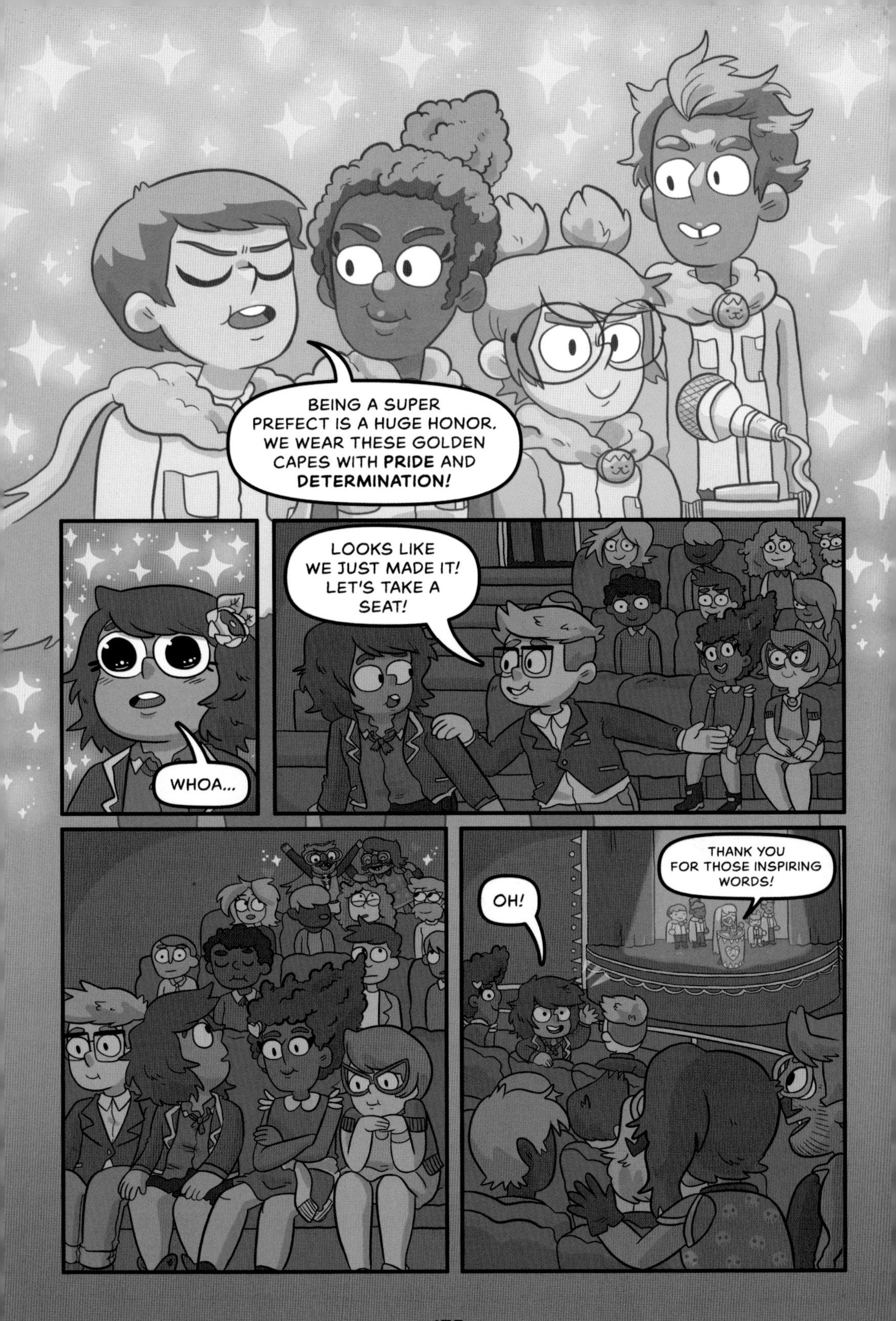
BEING A SUPER PREFECT IS A HUGE HONOR. WE WEAR THESE GOLDEN CAPES WITH **PRIDE** AND **DETERMINATION!**
WHOA...
LOOKS LIKE WE JUST MADE IT! LET'S TAKE A SEAT!
OH!
THANK YOU FOR THOSE INSPIRING WORDS!

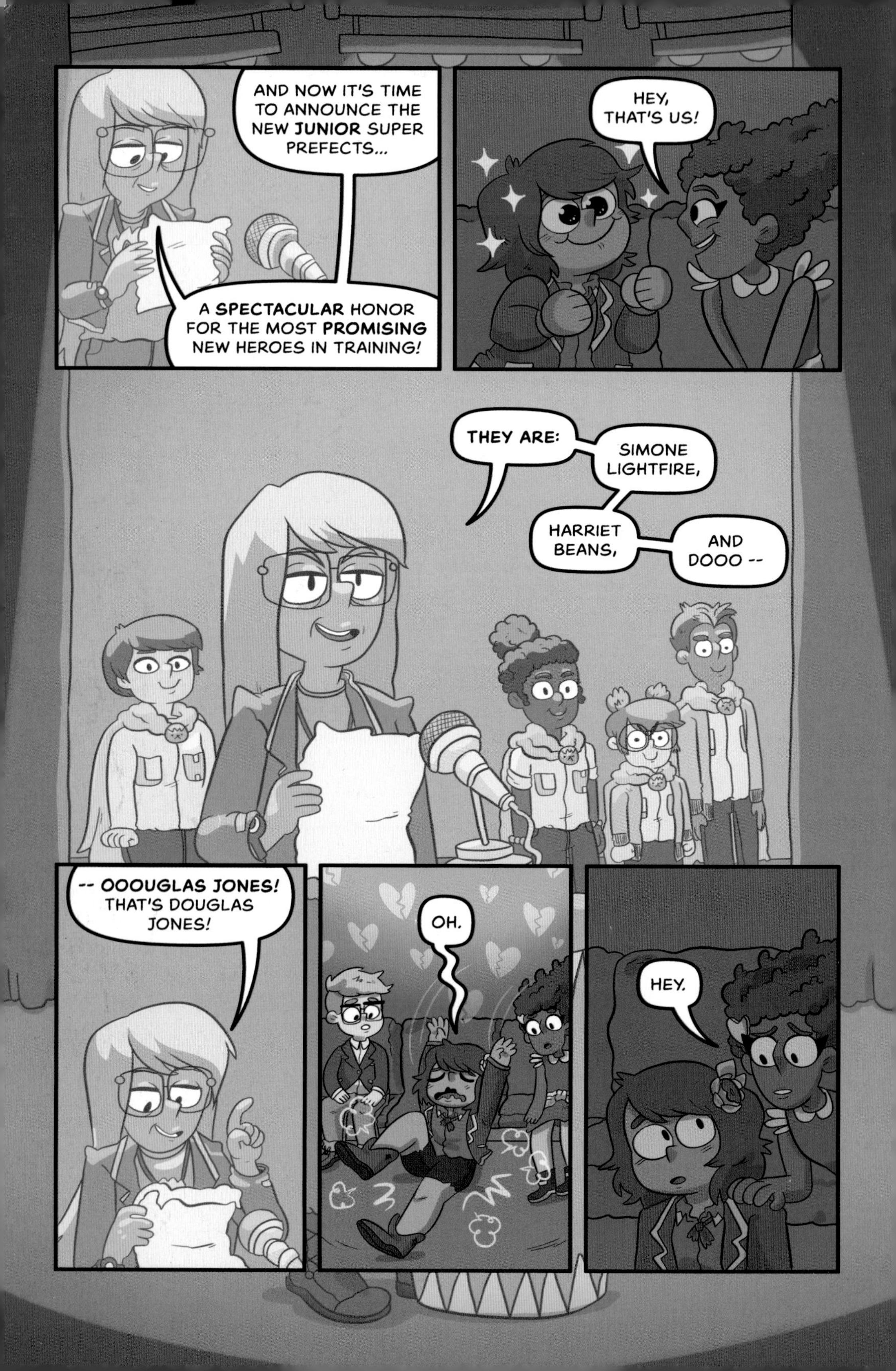
AND NOW IT'S TIME TO ANNOUNCE THE NEW JUNIOR SUPER PREFECTS...
A SPECTACULAR HONOR FOR THE MOST PROMISING NEW HEROES IN TRAINING!
HEY, THAT'S US!
THEY ARE:
SIMONE LIGHTFIRE,
HARRIET BEANS,
AND DOOO --
-- OOOUGLAS JONES! THAT'S DOUGLAS JONES!
OH.
HEY.

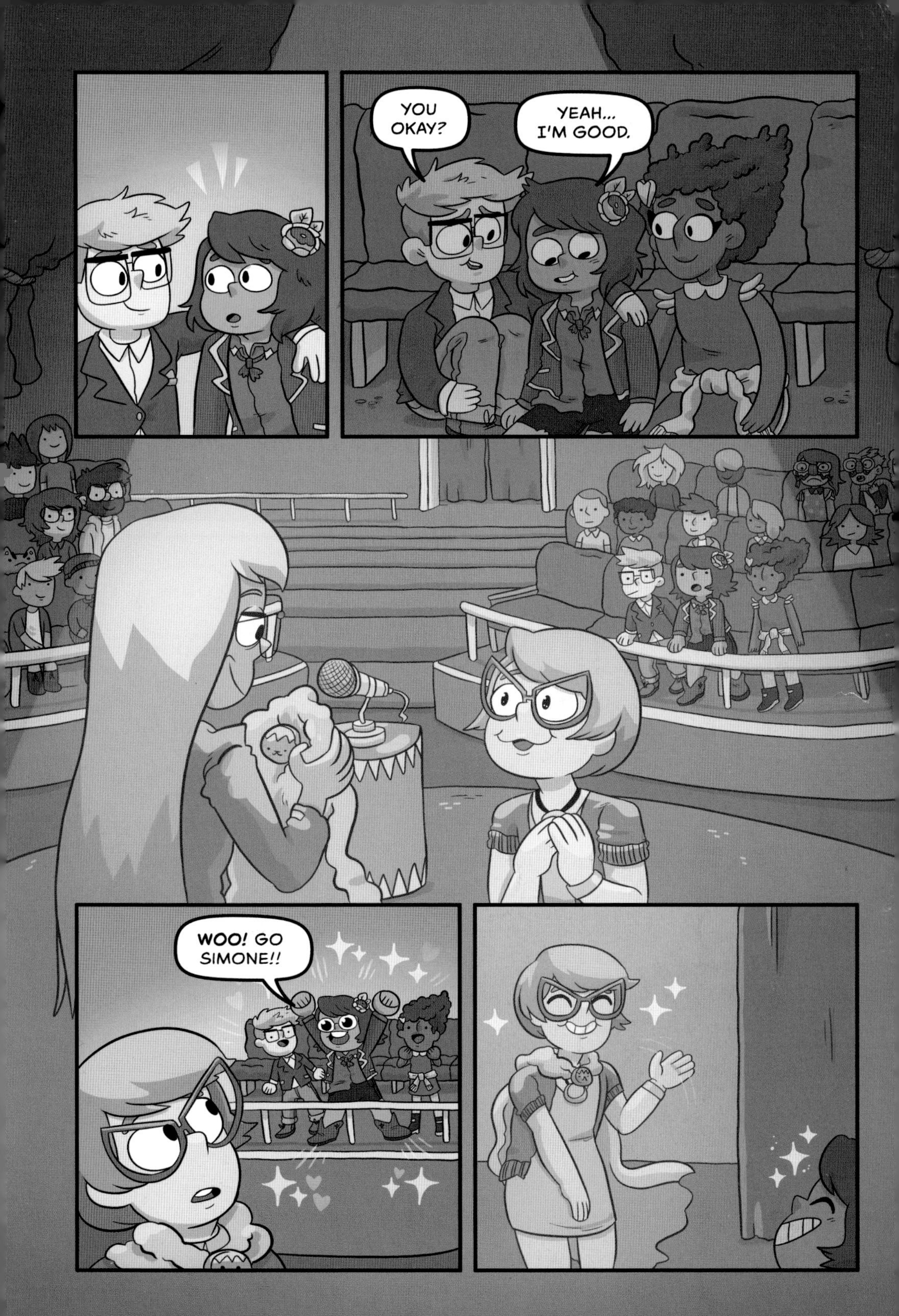
YOU OKAY?
YEAH... I'M GOOD.
WOO! GO SIMONE!!

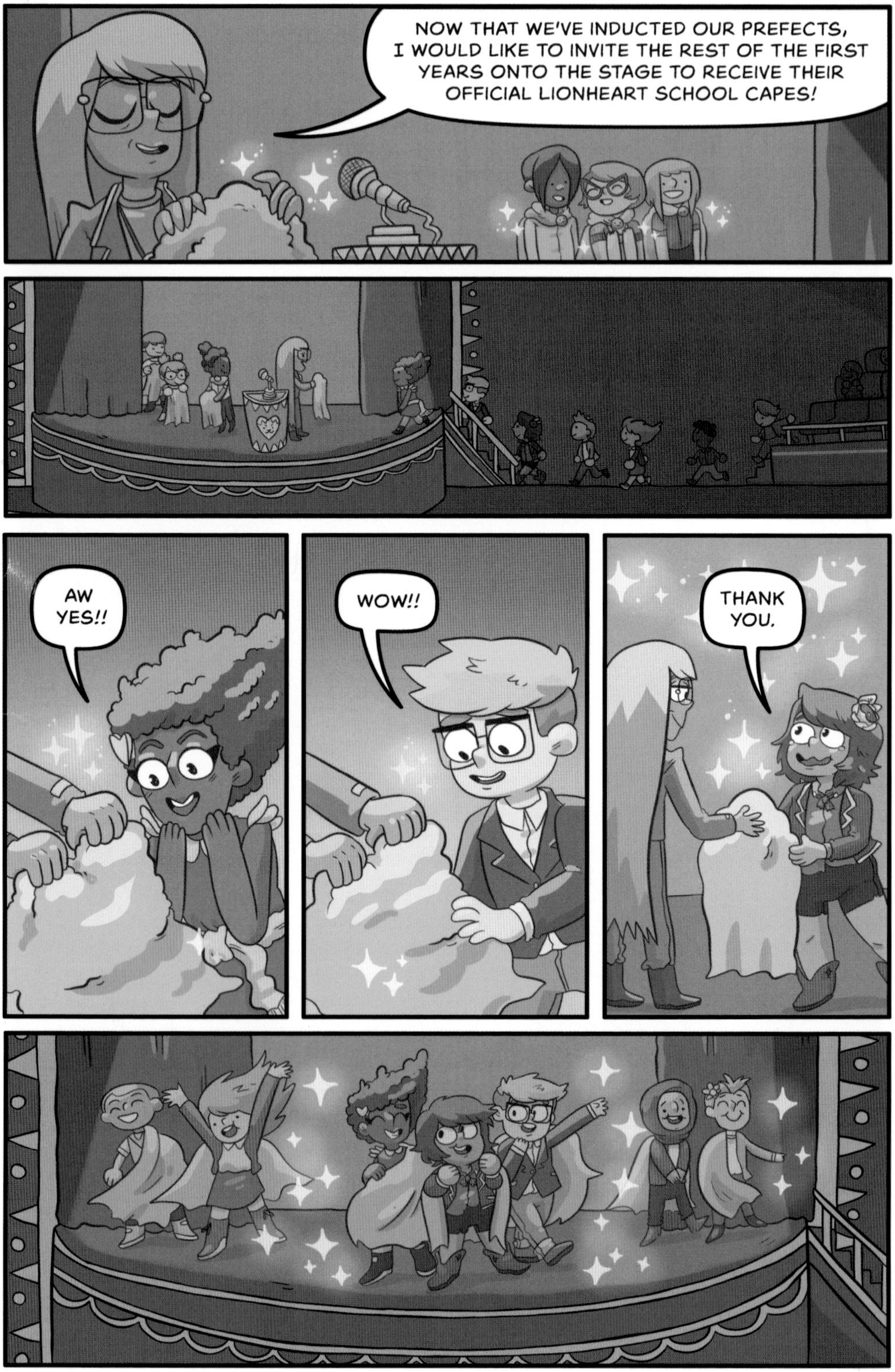
NOW THAT WE'VE INDUCTED OUR PREFECTS, I WOULD LIKE TO INVITE THE REST OF THE FIRST YEARS ONTO THE STAGE TO RECEIVE THEIR OFFICIAL LIONHEART SCHOOL CAPES!
AW YES!!
WOW!!
THANK YOU.

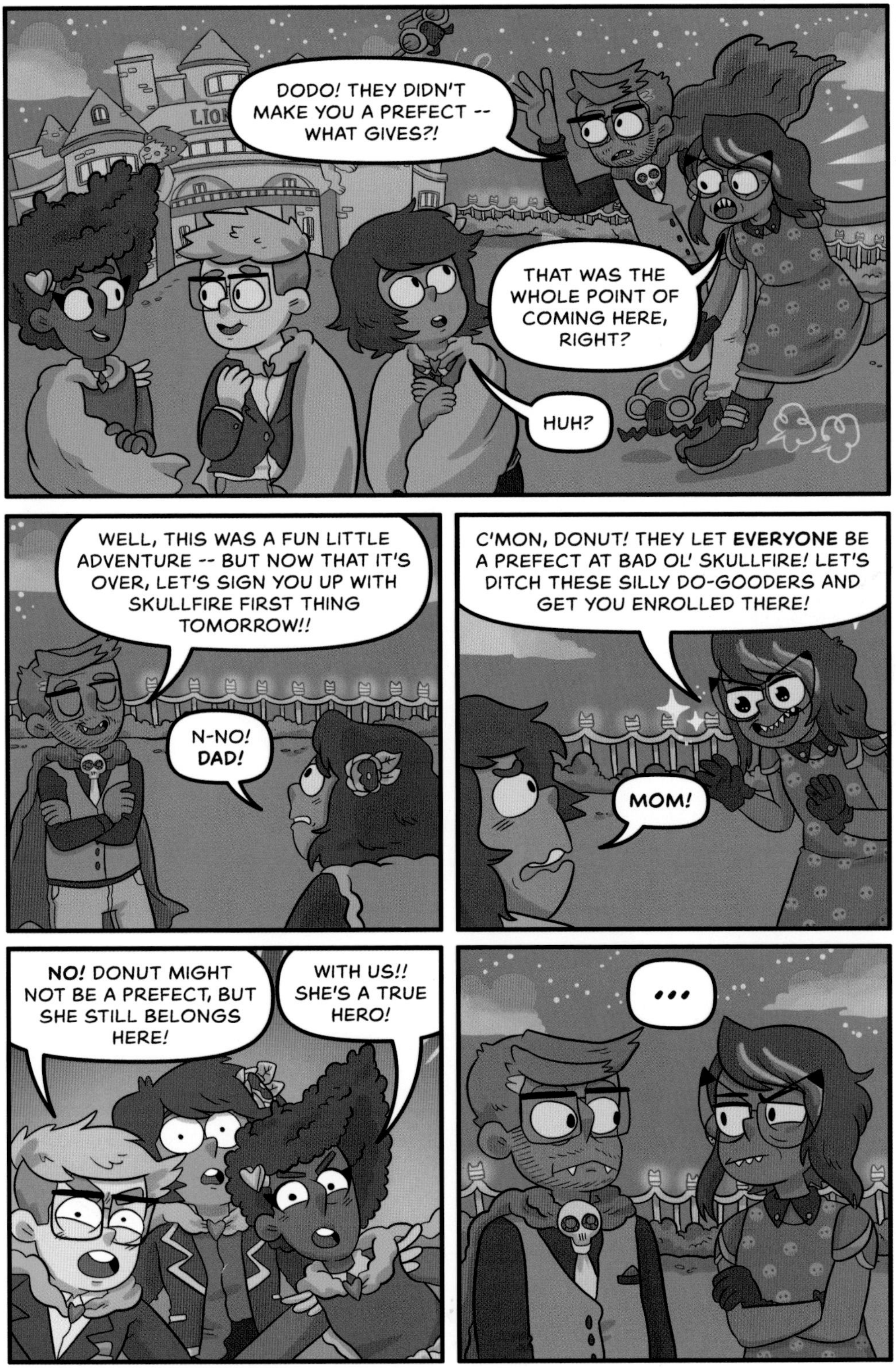
DODO! THEY DIDN'T MAKE YOU A PREFECT -- WHAT GIVES?!
THAT WAS THE WHOLE POINT OF COMING HERE, RIGHT?
HUH?
WELL, THIS WAS A FUN LITTLE ADVENTURE -- BUT NOW THAT IT'S OVER, LET'S SIGN YOU UP WITH SKULLFIRE FIRST THING TOMORROW!!
N-NO! **DAD!**
C'MON, DONUT! THEY LET **EVERYONE** BE A PREFECT AT BAD OL' SKULLFIRE! LET'S DITCH THESE SILLY DO-GOODERS AND GET YOU ENROLLED THERE!
MOM!
NO! DONUT MIGHT NOT BE A PREFECT, BUT SHE STILL BELONGS HERE!
WITH US!! SHE'S A TRUE HERO!
...

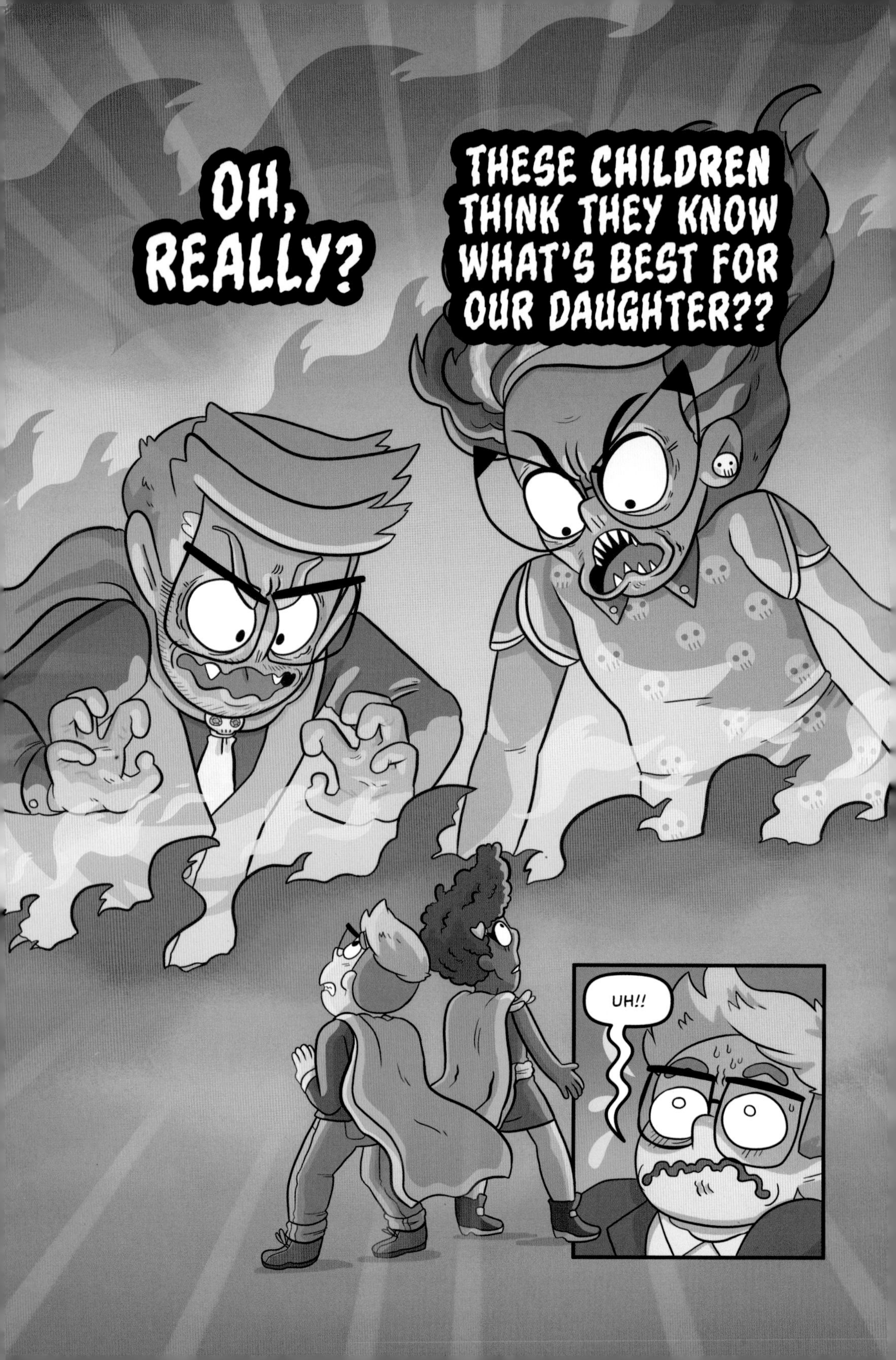
OH, REALLY?
THESE CHILDREN THINK THEY KNOW WHAT'S BEST FOR OUR DAUGHTER??
UH!!

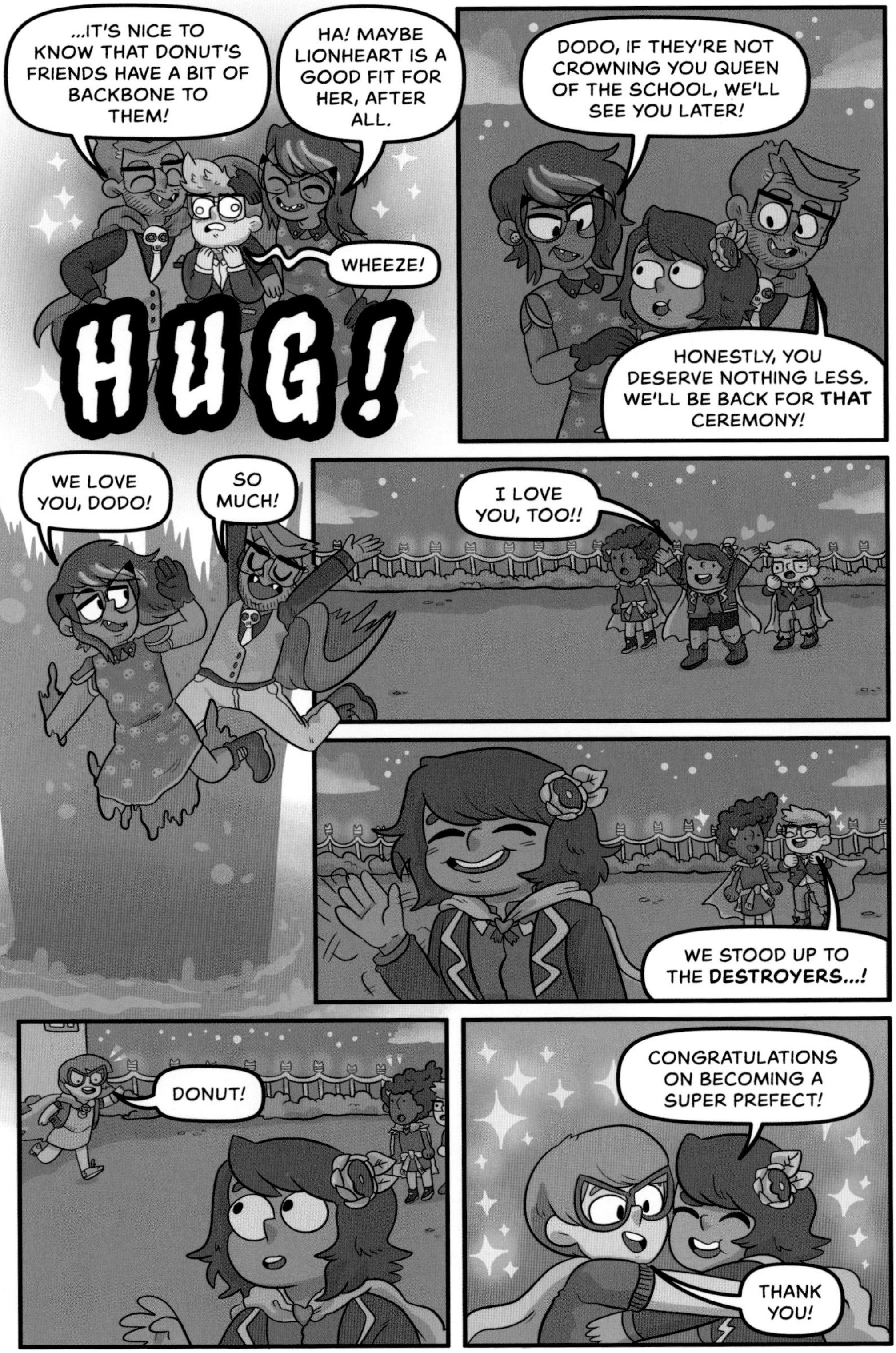
...IT'S NICE TO KNOW THAT DONUT'S FRIENDS HAVE A BIT OF BACKBONE TO THEM!
HA! MAYBE LIONHEART IS A GOOD FIT FOR HER, AFTER ALL.
WHEEZE!
HUG!
DODO, IF THEY'RE NOT CROWNING YOU QUEEN OF THE SCHOOL, WE'LL SEE YOU LATER!
HONESTLY, YOU DESERVE NOTHING LESS. WE'LL BE BACK FOR **THAT** CEREMONY!
WE LOVE YOU, DODO!
SO MUCH!
I LOVE YOU, TOO!!
WE STOOD UP TO THE **DESTROYERS**...!
DONUT!
CONGRATULATIONS ON BECOMING A SUPER PREFECT!
THANK YOU!

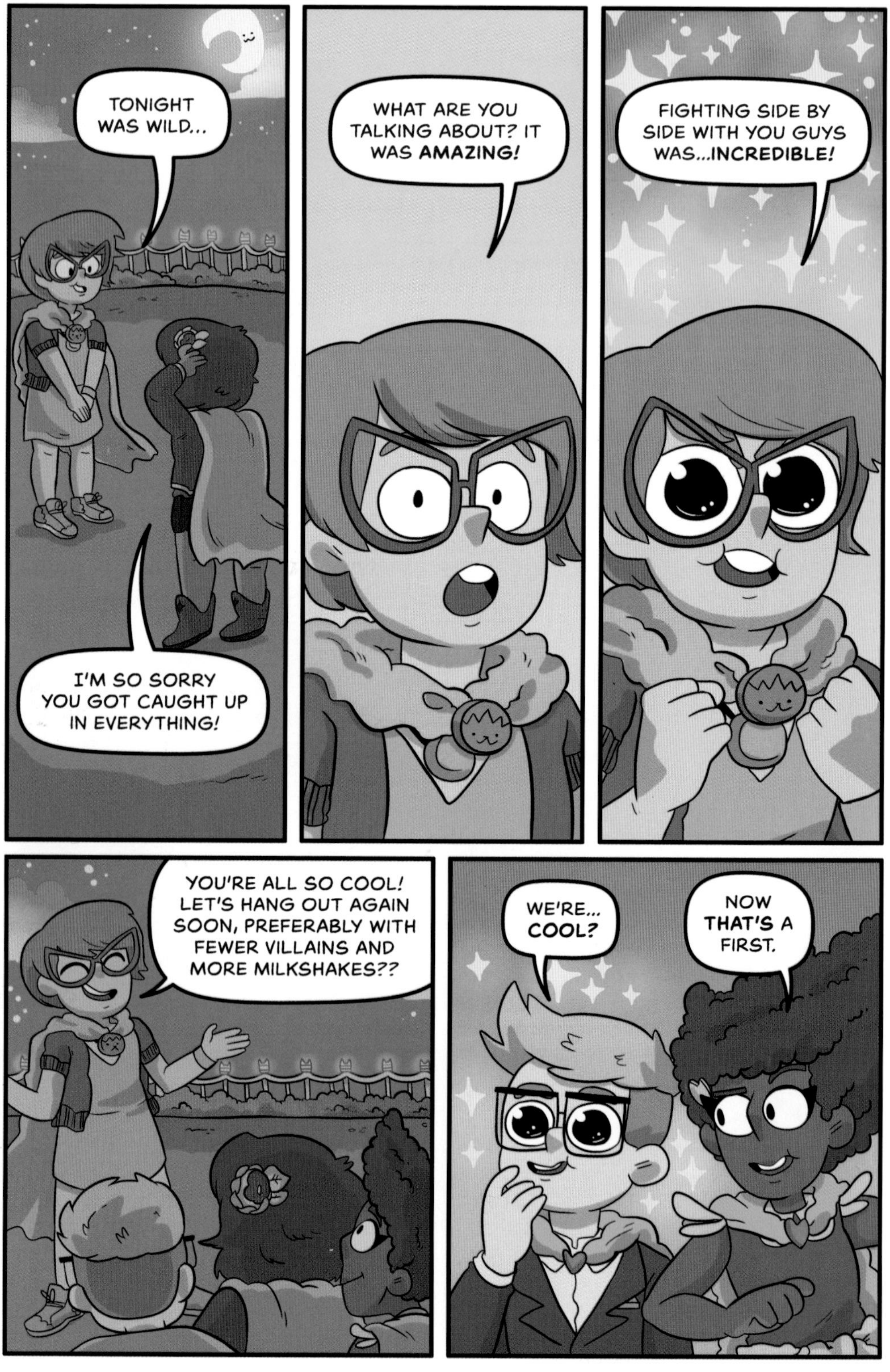
TONIGHT WAS WILD...
I'M SO SORRY YOU GOT CAUGHT UP IN EVERYTHING!
WHAT ARE YOU TALKING ABOUT? IT WAS **AMAZING!**
FIGHTING SIDE BY SIDE WITH YOU GUYS WAS...**INCREDIBLE!**
YOU'RE ALL SO COOL! LET'S HANG OUT AGAIN SOON, PREFERABLY WITH FEWER VILLAINS AND MORE MILKSHAKES??
WE'RE... **COOL?**
NOW **THAT'S** A FIRST.

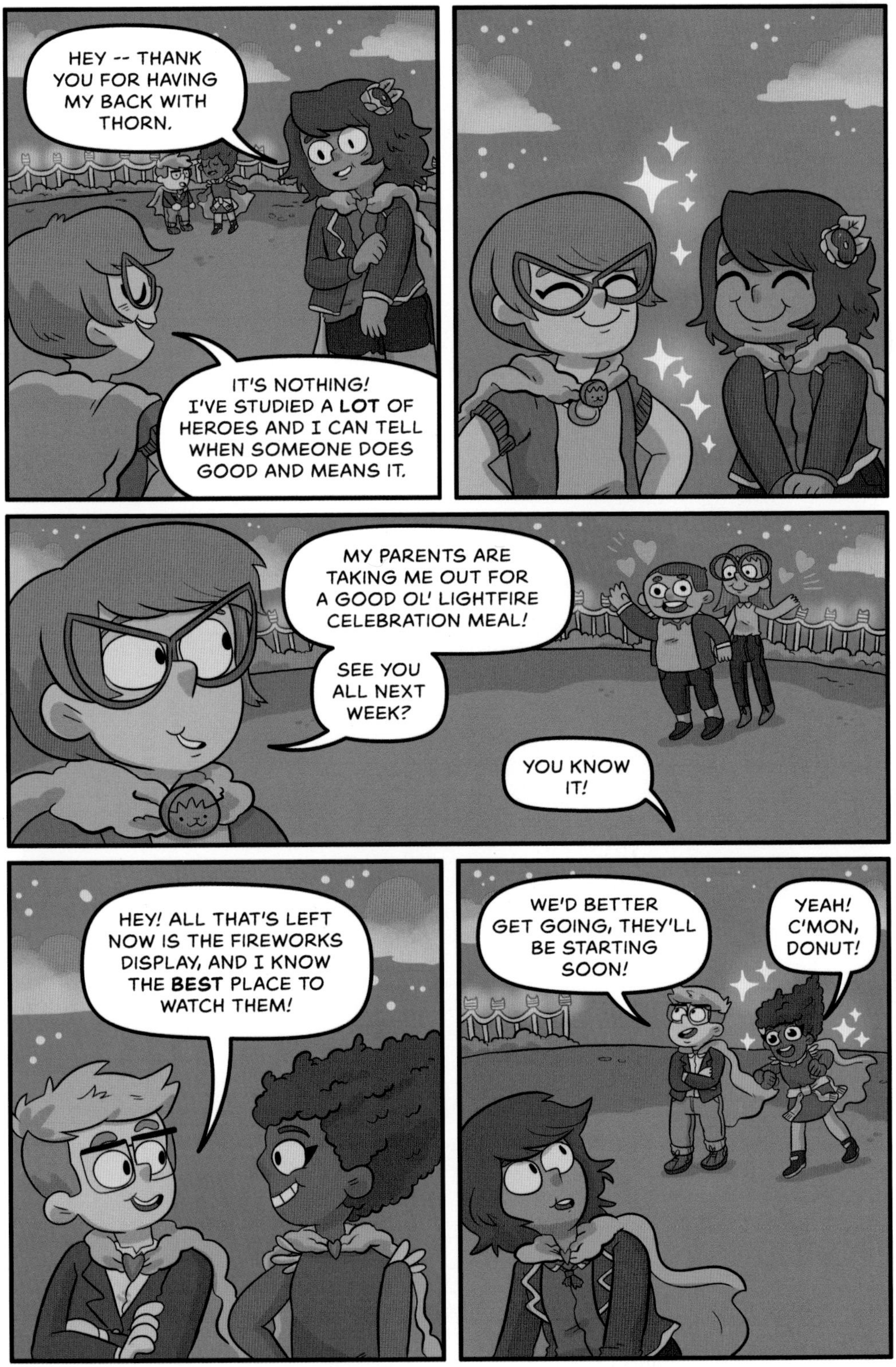
HEY -- THANK YOU FOR HAVING MY BACK WITH THORN.
IT'S NOTHING! I'VE STUDIED A **LOT** OF HEROES AND I CAN TELL WHEN SOMEONE DOES GOOD AND MEANS IT.
MY PARENTS ARE TAKING ME OUT FOR A GOOD OL' LIGHTFIRE CELEBRATION MEAL!
SEE YOU ALL NEXT WEEK?
YOU KNOW IT!
HEY! ALL THAT'S LEFT NOW IS THE FIREWORKS DISPLAY, AND I KNOW THE **BEST** PLACE TO WATCH THEM!
WE'D BETTER GET GOING, THEY'LL BE STARTING SOON!
YEAH! C'MON, DONUT!

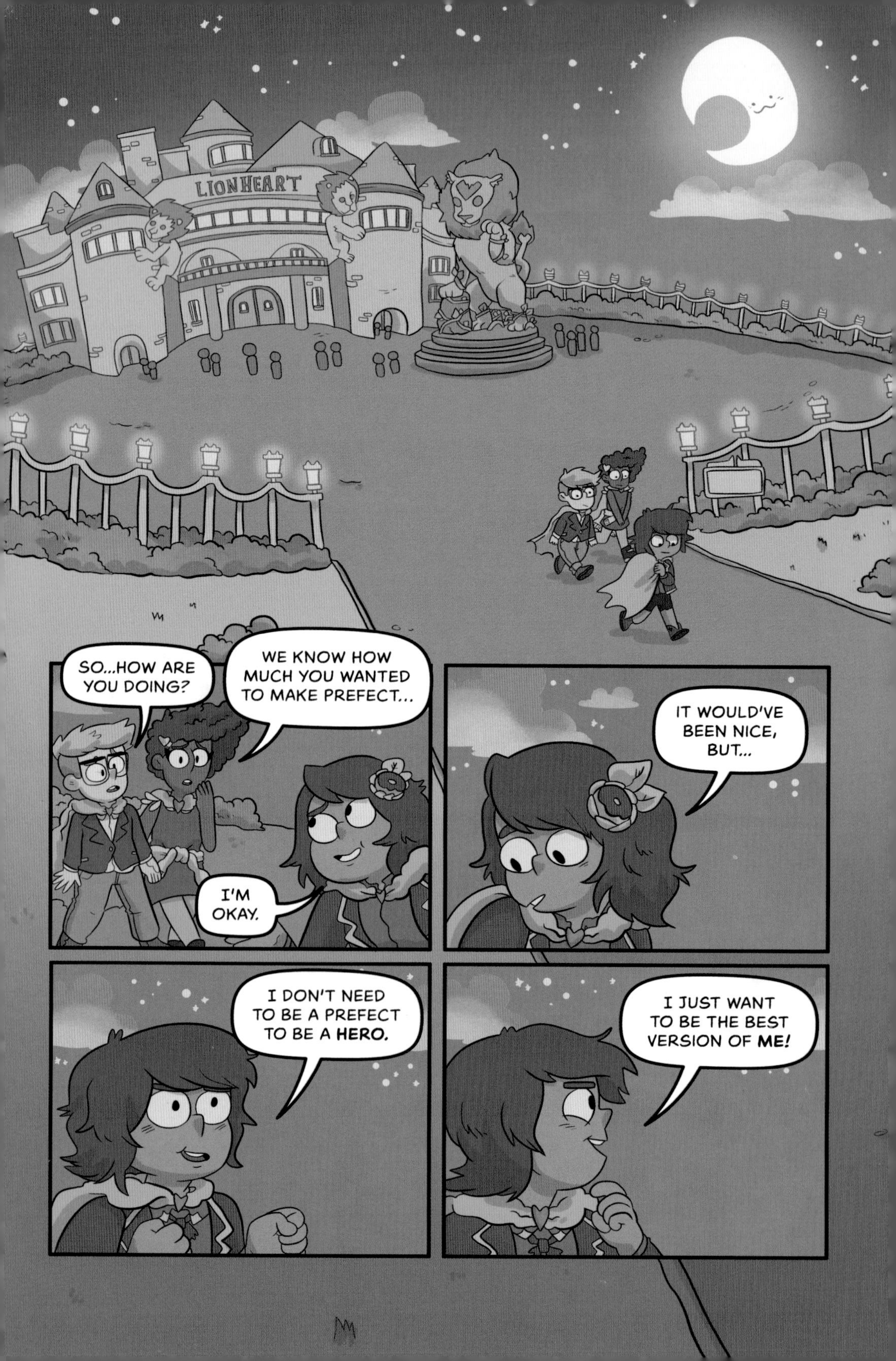
LIONHEART
SO...HOW ARE YOU DOING?
WE KNOW HOW MUCH YOU WANTED TO MAKE PREFECT...
I'M OKAY.
IT WOULD'VE BEEN NICE, BUT...
I DON'T NEED TO BE A PREFECT TO BE A **HERO.**
I JUST WANT TO BE THE BEST VERSION OF **ME!**

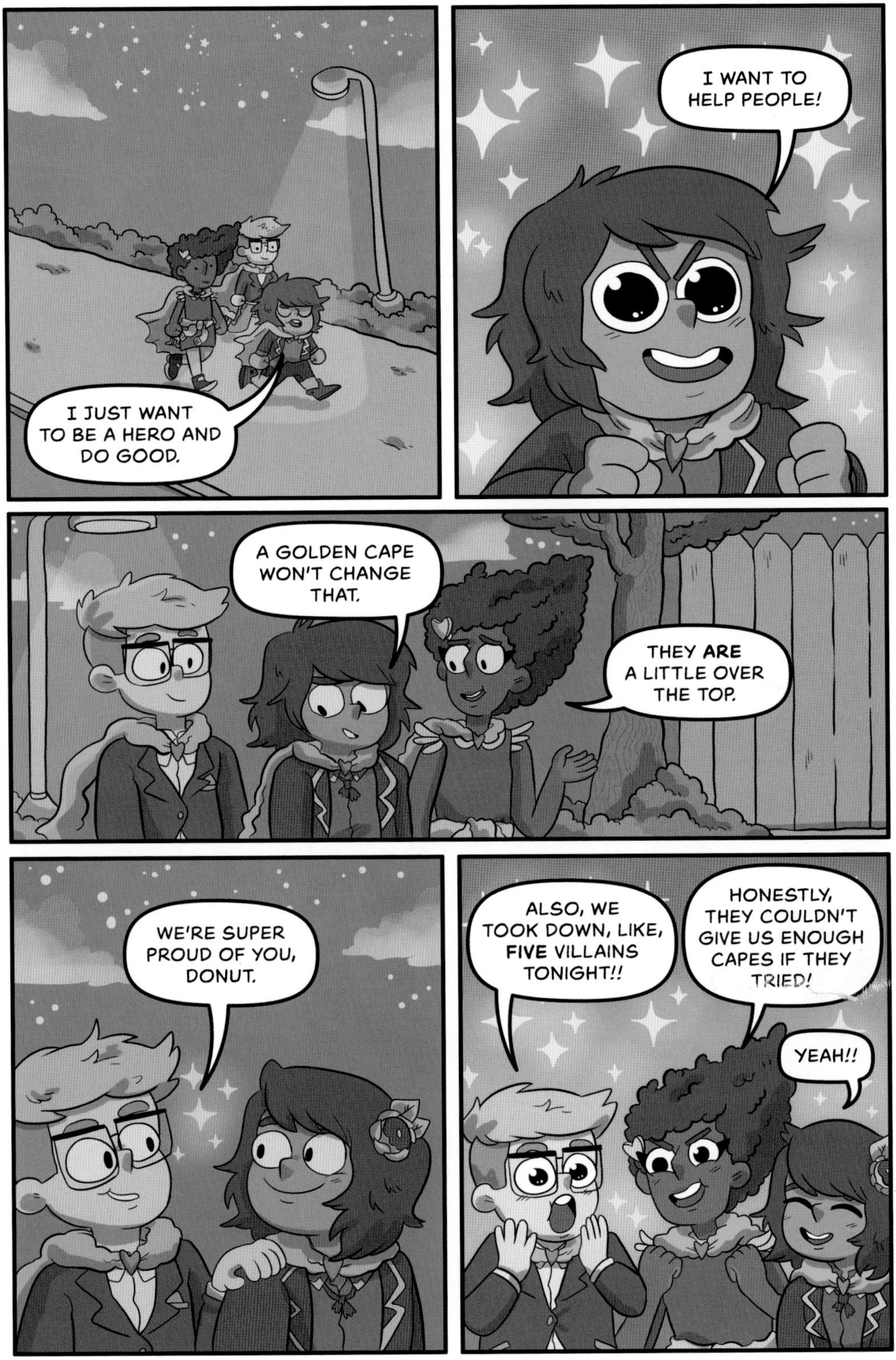
I JUST WANT TO BE A HERO AND DO GOOD.
I WANT TO HELP PEOPLE!
A GOLDEN CAPE WON'T CHANGE THAT.
THEY **ARE** A LITTLE OVER THE TOP.
WE'RE SUPER PROUD OF YOU, DONUT.
ALSO, WE TOOK DOWN, LIKE, **FIVE** VILLAINS TONIGHT!!
HONESTLY, THEY COULDN'T GIVE US ENOUGH CAPES IF THEY TRIED!
YEAH!!

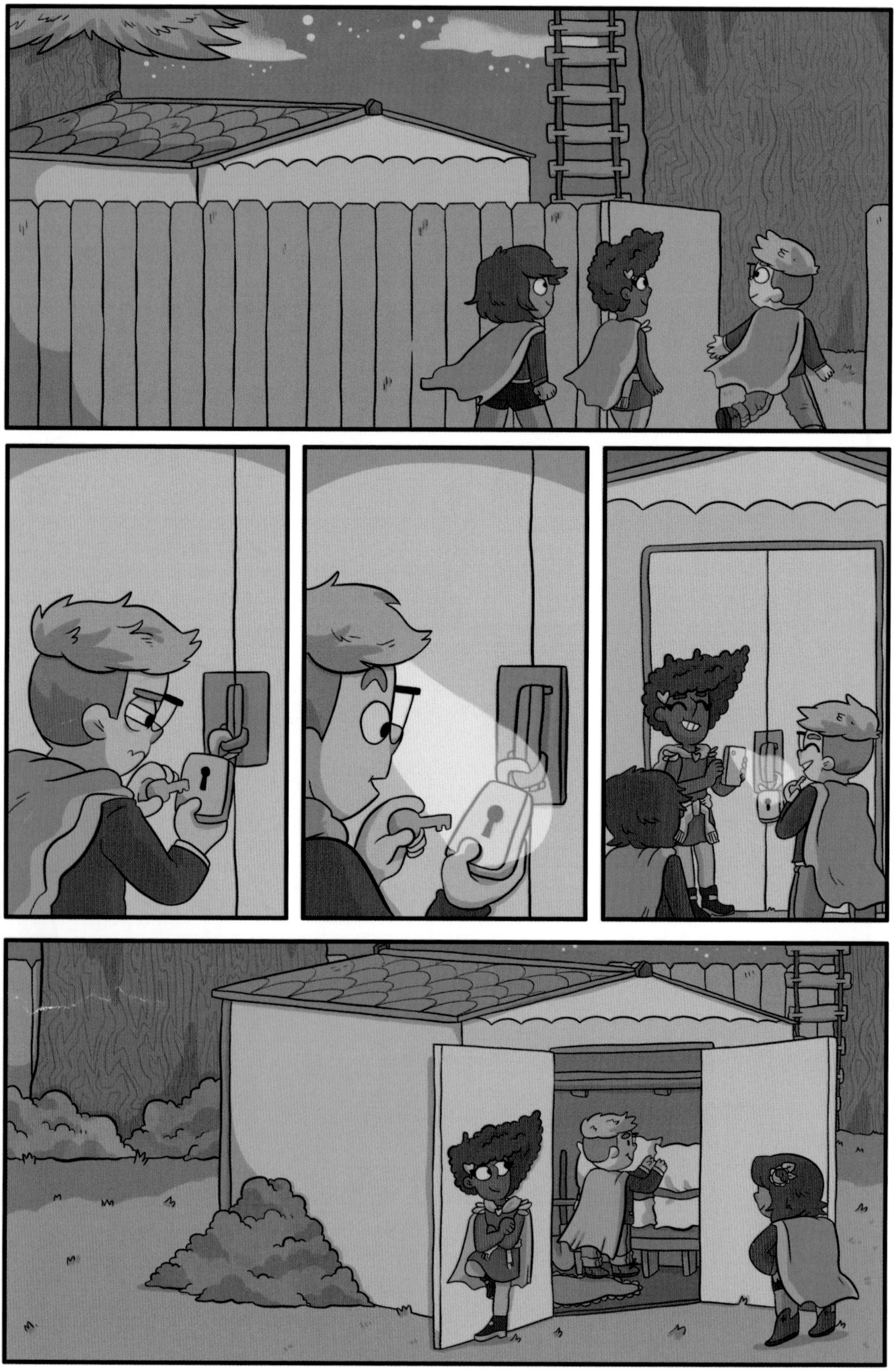

THE FIREWORKS ARE GOING TO START ANY MINUTE NOW. **LET'S GO!**

EVERYBODY COMFORTABLE?

YES! C'MON, SIT DOWN!

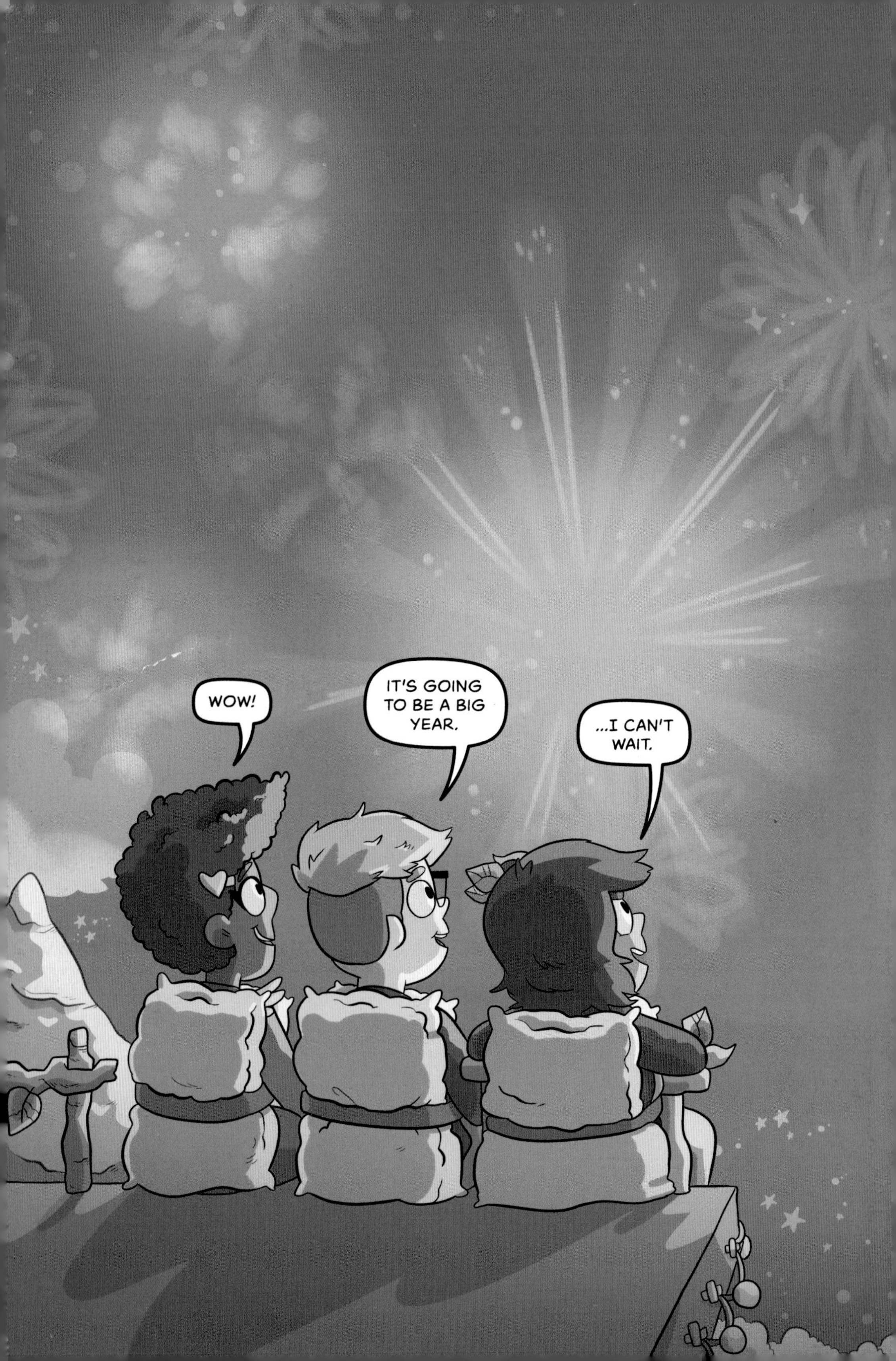
WOW!
IT'S GOING TO BE A BIG YEAR.
...I CAN'T WAIT.

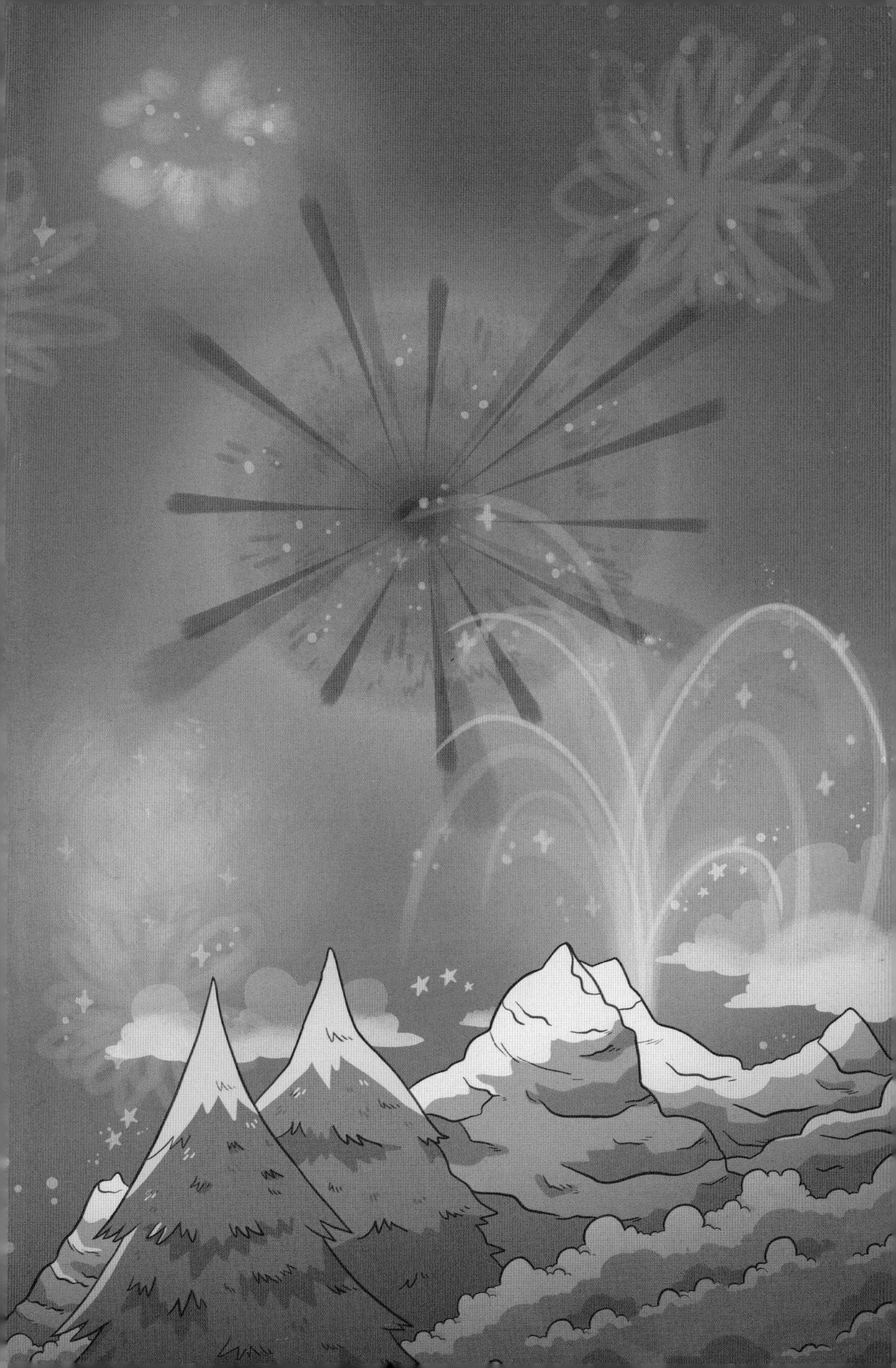

ACKNOWLEDGMENTS

We would like to thank our parents and families for always being supportive!

A huge thanks to our agent, Steven Salpeter, who is always so helpful and full of advice, and the hardworking and wonderful team at Curtis Brown!

A massive thank-you to Cassandra Pelham Fulton, David Saylor, Phil Falco, Shivana Sookdeo, and everyone else at Scholastic who has helped take this story from its early stages to its final finished form!

Thank you to all our friends who also create wonderful art! We are incredibly lucky to know so many talented people, and seeing their work always helps inspire us to make the best comics that we can!

A tiny shout-out to our four wonderful cats: Pesto, Toby, Wilson, and Pixel! They bring us so much joy and happiness while we're hard at work making comics!

Finally, an incredibly big thank-you to all the readers out there — it means a lot that you read the books we create! Whether you picked this book up from a shop, ordered it online, or got it from your local library or book fair — we are so appreciative and we think you're the best!